To hell with the training exercise.

The SEAL divers needed help. Now.

Aleesha kicked into trauma surgeon mode instantly. Possible crushed ribs. Punctured lungs. Contused heart. Inability to breathe. And blood. *Oh, God. Blood.* There were sharks in these waters.

"His heart's failing on me." She reached for the carotid artery in the patient's neck. Yup. Pulse uneven and fading fast. "Here's the thing," she told the other diver. "His sternum may be fractured. If we do CPR on him, we run a risk of puncturing his heart. If we don't do CPR, we risk brain damage and possibly not getting his heart going again once I get access to a defibrillator."

"You're the doctor. You make the call," the SEAL replied.

She wasn't a top-notch emergency physician for nothing. She could only pray her current patient didn't have a lacerated aorta on top of his other injuries.

Well, she'd wanted adventure....

Dear Reader,

What is a Bombshell? Sometimes it's a femme fatale. Sometimes it's unexpected news that changes everything. Sometimes it's a book you just can't put down! And that's what we're bringing to you—four fascinating stories about women you'll cheer for!

Such as Angel Baker, star of *USA TODAY* bestselling author Julie Beard's *Touch of the White Tiger.* This twenty-second-century gal doesn't know who is killing her colleagues, but she's not about to let an aggravating homicide cop stop her from finding out. Too bad tracking the killer is *exactly* what someone wants her to do....

Enter an exclusive world as we kick off a new continuity series featuring society's secret weapons—a group of heiresses recruited to bring down the world's most powerful criminals! THE IT GIRLS have it going on, and you'll love Erica Orloff's *The Golden Girl* as she tracks a corporate spy in her spiked Jimmy Choos!

Ever feel like pushing the boundaries? So does Kimmer Reed, heroine of *Beyond the Rules* by Doranna Durgin. When her brother sics his enemies on her, Kimmer's ready to take them out. But the rules change when she learns her nieces are pawns in the deadly game....

And don't miss the Special Forces women of the Medusa Project as they track down a hijacked cruise ship, in *Medusa Rising* by Cindy Dees! Medusa surgeon Aleesha Gautier doesn't trust the hijacker who claims he's on their side, but joining forces will allow her to keep her enemy closer....

Enjoy! And please send your comments to me, c/o Silhouette Books, 233 Broadway Ste. 1001, New York, NY 10279.

Sincerely,

Natashya Wilson

Natashya Wilson
Associate Senior Editor, Silhouette Bombshell

Please address questions and book requests to:
Silhouette Reader Service
U.S.: 3010 Walden Ave., P.O. Box 1325, Buffalo, NY 14269
Canadian: P.O. Box 609, Fort Erie, Ont. L2A 5X3

CINDY DEES

MEDUSA RISING

Published by Silhouette Books

America's Publisher of Contemporary Romance

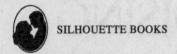

SILHOUETTE BOOKS

ISBN 0-373-51374-7

MEDUSA RISING

Copyright © 2005 by Cynthia Dees

www.SilhouetteBombshell.com

Printed in U.S.A.

CINDY DEES

started flying airplanes while sitting in her dad's lap at the age of three and got a pilot's license before she got a driver's license. At age fifteen, she dropped out of high school and left the horse farm in Michigan where she grew up to attend the University of Michigan. She was one of the youngest students in her class.

After earning a degree in Russian and East European Studies, she joined the U.S. Air Force and became the youngest female pilot in its history. She flew supersonic jets, VIP airlift and the C-5 Galaxy, the world's largest airplane. She also worked part-time gathering intelligence. During her military career, she traveled to forty countries on five continents, was detained by the KGB and East German secret police, got shot at, flew in the first Gulf War, met her husband and amassed a lifetime's worth of war stories.

Her hobbies include professional Middle Eastern dancing, Japanese gardening and medieval reenacting. She started writing on a one-dollar bet with her mother and was thrilled to win that bet with the publication of her first book in 2001. She loves to hear from readers and can be contacted at www.cindydees.com.

For Sterling,
without whom this book would never have happened.
And I'll go on a cruise with you anytime!

Chapter 1

The sun glittered like a diamond through the surface of the water overhead, sending glowing, three-dimensional shafts of light downward in shimmering pillars of gold. From below, the cool, blue depths reached up, embracing her like a silent lover. Only the rasping of her inhalations and bubbling of her exhalations disturbed the utter peace of the ocean. Even the insidious cold seeping through her wet suit couldn't ruin the moment. Nothing and no one in her life gave Aleesha Gautier as much pleasure as diving.

In fact, she'd joined the U.S. Navy on the assumption that she'd be able to do a lot of it all over the world. Plus, a military career was a way to escape the life she would've had if she'd stayed in Jamaica. She'd always wanted to see more, to *be* more, than she could if she'd stayed on the shabby little street in the run-down neighborhood where she'd grown up.

Ironic then that she had spent years cooped up in classrooms and hospital wards on a Navy scholarship, pursuing her dream of becoming a doctor. Then, in the six years after med school, every last assignment had been landlocked. Her grandmama called it bad *juju*. She said the angry spirits were getting even with Aleesha for leaving her native land and never looking back. Oh, how wrong Grandmama was. She'd looked back all right. And kept right on running in the other direction.

It had taken a cross transfer to the Medusa Project, an Army unit of all things, to get her back into the water like this. And now Uncle Sam was paying her to do the one thing she'd empty her bank account for the privilege of doing.

A stingray sailed beneath her feet, its silent, rippling passage a ballet in grace. Aleesha's mind snapped back to business. Something had disturbed that stingray, and it was her job to find out what. She popped to the surface for a quick look around and rode the waves like a cork, scanning the horizon when the swells carried her high. She spied a white boat maybe a half mile away, a private sport fishing vessel. What was it doing way out here on this isolated piece of water? Its passengers weren't going to have a lick of luck catching supper. They were sitting on top of a commercial shipping lane, for crying out loud. Her father piloted a fishing boat for tourists back home, and staying away from the big ships was Sport Fishing 101. They fouled the water and scared off the good fish.

She made out a couple of guys on deck examining the water with binoculars. Landlubbers. Using binoculars to fish was like using a bowling ball to stir a pot of soup. Completely useless. She shrugged. It was their time to waste. She swam easily against the current, which flowed from the fishing boat toward her. If that boat wasn't anchored and was drift fishing, in a few minutes she'd have to be careful not to get tangled in its lines and hooks.

She took one more look around. The "hostiles" she was on patrol to catch had either been dropped off already or their boat wasn't here yet. They would no doubt come in on an RIB—a rigid inflatable boat that was little more than a lightweight hull and a really big engine. It would be low and fast, a dark smudge on the surface of the ocean. It would take a real stroke of luck for her to spot it. Better to rely on disturbances underwater, like that stingray, to signal the arrival of the simulated terrorists she was out here to neutralize.

This might be an exercise, but the Navy SEALs who'd be posing as the bad guys weren't known for playing nice. If they caught her, they'd make sure she regretted it. Big time. A surge of adrenaline rippled through her, not fear but excitement at being out here working with these dangerous men. Never in her wildest dreams had she imagined she'd get a chance to train with the Navy's elite underwater Special Forces unit. But her own unit, the Medusas—a highly classified, all-female Special Forces team that had been formed a few months ago—needed to learn how to work with its fellow special-ops units from the other branches of the military. The Medusas weren't anywhere near fully operational yet. Most top operators took several years of training to reach peak form. Hence, the training with the SEALs.

Her instinct said the SEAL "hostiles" were already in the area, and she'd learned long ago to trust her gut feelings. The locals back home said the women in her family had The Sight, and who was she to argue with them?

The SEALs were capable of swimming insane distances and frequently did so just for the hell of it. She'd bet they'd been dropped off a couple miles from here and were swimming in to the target—a stretch of shipping lane running from behind her straight over toward that fishing boat.

She'd scoped out the underwater terrain on diving maps and sonar during a quick surface pass of the area by her drop-off boat. She figured the SEALs would head for the cave complex a couple of hundred feet from her current position and make their "terrorist" hit out of it. It was what she'd do if she were a Tango.

She turned her back on the fishing boat and swam in the direction the stingray had come from. The sandy shelf of the Gulf of Mexico's coast ended without warning beneath her, turning abruptly into a stone cliff that plunged into the murky depths. On a previous dive, the Medusas had explored a few of the caves that peppered the cliff face. Perfect place for hostiles to hide until an unwary ship came along in the deep channel beside them.

Kat was supposed to be down here with her today, but Aleesha'd gotten one of those voodoo intuitions of hers and had run one last equipment check right before they jumped in the water. Following the sneaking suspicion nagging at her, she'd checked the unlikeliest spot—the back of Kat's air hose where it joined her air tank. Sure enough, she found a neat slit in a fold of the hose, maybe a quarter-inch long. Not big enough to be noticeable but big enough to cause a slow leak that would erase half of Kat's dive time.

It smacked of a SEAL training scenario. Send the Medusas on a deep dive and set them up to run out of air about a half hour in—at the exact time when they wouldn't be able to surface quickly. Jerks.

Fortunately, Aleesha's intuition had led her to the sabotage. Although, if she'd been thinking ahead, common sense would've told her not to trust the SEALs to set up Kat's gear. As it was, when she got back to base, the SEALs were going to ream her out for not bringing an adequate repair kit to fix the hose, not to mention for proceeding with this mission by diving alone. But she hated to fail. She'd argued fiercely with Vanessa Blake, the Medusa's commanding officer, and finally talked her boss into reluctantly letting her do this dive.

She sighed. It would be painstaking work to clear every last nook and cranny below. But nobody ever said being on an elite Special Forces team would be all fun and games. In her limited experience, actual missions broke down to about seventy-five percent sheer boredom in the form of tense inaction, twenty percent sheer thrill ride and five percent sheer terror. Time for some of that seventy-five-percent stuff. She swam down to the shelf and headed for the nearest cave.

Two men stood on the deck of the sport fishing boat, scanning the water with binoculars. In reality they were scanning the horizon for incoming vessels that might jeopardize their clandestine operation currently underway beneath the boat, out of sight of any casual observer. Four divers were hard at work chaining a magnetically activated explosive mine to a concrete block they'd sunk here several weeks before. The trick was to float the device far enough below the surface so mine hunting planes couldn't spot it from the air, but shallow enough that a ship's steel hull would set it off. For now, the devices would be left inactive, ready for the time when they might be needed as an emergency measure. Terrorists couldn't be too careful these days.

A tug on one of the fishing poles indicated that the mine was set. Time to move to the next location. There were sixteen sunken concrete anchor points in all, and each one would receive its payload of death in preparation for Operation Defiance, by far the most ambitious project ever conceived or attempted by the *Alliance de la Liberté*. If all went well, in a few days' time the group would burst onto the international scene and, good Lord willing, they would win independence for their home, the tiny Basque region straddling France and Spain.

Their captain had picked up a blip on the radar a half hour before, but it disappeared nearly as quickly as it appeared. It was either a ghost image or—highly unlikely out here in the middle of an isolated shipping lane—some sort of very low radar profile boat like the U.S. Navy used. But they were well into international waters, in a little-used stretch of the Caribbean that no self-respecting naval unit would give a damn about. Now one of the men wielding binoculars glanced up at the pilothouse and got a thumb's-up from the captain. No recurrence of that one fleeting radar image. It was safe to bring up the divers. Two tugs on the fishing pole, and the four wet-suited men surfaced, slipping quickly aboard the vessel and inside where they wouldn't be seen.

The captain raised anchor in a leisurely fashion and moved north, against the current, to the next position, pretending to trawl for fish. He navigated via Global Positioning System to a precise position over another cluster of concrete blocks. Only a few more to go and the field would be complete. And then Operation Defiance could begin.

Aleesha drifted along the cliff face. It was dark down here, and she paused to equalize the pressure on her eardrums. Being careful not to disturb any silt from the jagged ledge beside her, she eased forward.

Then she saw it. A movement not of this world. Like the swim fins of a diver kicking slowly to hold position against the current. Adrenaline kicked in, shooting her pulse and respiration into overdrive. Not good. Hyperventilating while diving was a big no-no.

She counted down from ten to one, forcibly relaxing her body and slowing her respiration. It was an old voodoo trick she'd known since she was a child. High voodoo priests were said to be able to nearly stop their hearts on command, but her formal medical training made her skeptical of that claim.

She switched to her bubble-free air regulator and eased forward, plastering herself to the rugged rock face. Being careful not to snag her gear on a stray outcropping, she glided forward a few more feet.

Definitely a diver. And then another shadowy shape moved. And another! Three men, working intently on something. All of them looked exceptionally fit in their wet suits. Distinctly like SEALs. She squinted, trying to make out what they were doing. It looked like they were installing a radio receiver on a big, oblong device of some kind. She made out harpoons slung across their backs and knives strapped to ankles and thighs. No casual diver in the Caribbean swam around armed like that. Oh, yeah, mon. Definitely the SEALs. And that was a torpedo they were wiring for sound.

She eased forward a few more inches and started as an eel lurched violently, shooting out of a slit in the rocks inches from her face. Damn. Please God, don't let them investigate what had startled the eel!

One of the divers pulled out his harpoon. She braced to turn and swim for her simulated life. But the guy didn't come after her. Instead, he used the spear's sharp tip to poke at the cliff face. She was safe. The SEALs looked to be having trouble stabilizing the torpedo on a ledge where it would apparently perch until its target sailed past. The diver with the harpoon broke off a soccer-ball-size piece of rock and swam under the long, steel cylinder of the weapon to wedge it more firmly in place.

Then, without warning, the torpedo slipped, tipping downward sharply. The two divers above it tried to hold the tail down, but the weapon weighed more than a ton. It slid off the ledge, sinking quickly, and struck the bottom diver squarely in the chest, shoving him downward. Fast. He slammed into an outcropping maybe fifteen feet below the ledge, the torpedo pinning him down. He spasmed once and then lay still, crushed between the rocks and the enormous weight of the weapon.

She kicked into trauma-surgeon mode instantly. Possible crushed ribs. Punctured lungs. Contused heart. Inability to breathe. And blood. *Oh, God. Blood.* There were sharks in these waters.

The other divers pulled at the torpedo's tail, trying to lift it off their comrade. It wasn't budging. They needed help. Now. That victim wouldn't be able to breathe until the torpedo was off his chest. Seconds counted. She took a quick time hack on her dive watch and then kicked for all she was worth. To hell with the training exercise. Her flippers and a sharp dose of adrenaline propelled her forward like a rocket.

The two remaining divers started as she streaked out of nowhere, but they didn't pause in their efforts to lift the torpedo. They'd never pick that thing up with nothing but the water for leverage. They had to get beside it and push off from the cliff wall. It would roll the weapon across their man, maybe break an arm or a leg, but if the alternative was the guy suffocating in the next few moments, a busted limb or two was an acceptable sacrifice.

She positioned herself next to the wall and planted her shoul-

der against the torpedo's curving hull. The other divers caught
on immediately and moved to help her. She and the two SEALs
shoved as one, and the weapon rolled across the downed man and
onto his right arm and leg. One more push and it rolled completely
off the ledge, disappearing quickly into the darkness below.

One of the other men reached for the injured diver, and she
lifted his well-meaning hands out of the way. Fortunately, these
guys had recognized her by now and knew she was a Harvard-
educated trauma surgeon. The first order of business was to re-
establish breathing, not to surface. She inhaled a mouthful of
oxygen from her own regulator, holding it in her cheeks. She put
her mouth on the injured man's and blew into it forcefully to clear
the water. Quickly, she placed the victim's oxygen regulator
back in his mouth. She grabbed one of the other SEALs' hands
and put it over the regulator to hold it in place. He nodded his
understanding. Thankfully, all SEALs had extensive first-aid
training and were the equivalent of EMTs.

Next, she slid around to the top of the hurt diver's head. They
had to immobilize his chest cavity as best they could while they
surfaced. She slid her hands behind him, grabbing his armpits
from underneath. Bracing her elbows on either side of his head,
she used her forearms as a makeshift backboard and then
nodded to the other men. *Now* it was time to go.

They were deep enough that a rapid ascent put them all at risk
of getting the bends, that bane of divers where nitrogen bubbles
formed in the blood causing great pain and possible death. She
controlled her breathing carefully so as not to rupture a lung of
her own as they swam toward the light above.

She watched the victim's chest. No movement. The guy wasn't
breathing. Apparently, the SEAL with his hand on his buddy's
oxygen regulator figured that out, too, because partway up, he
pressed the button on the regulator that released a stream of air
into the victim's mouth. If they were lucky, the air was under
enough pressure to drive at least some of it into the guy's lungs.

She spared a glance downward and saw an ominous smudge

of brown trailing in the water behind them. Dammit. Sharks could smell a few drops of blood at distances of a mile or more. That long, swirling trail was more than enough to attract any sharks in the vicinity.

She fished around with her fingers, looking for a pulse in the guy's armpit. It was faint and thready, but she felt a throb of circulation beneath her finger. Thank God. Maybe this guy stood a chance of pulling through, even though every second without air was costly.

It seemed to take forever, but in less than a minute they burst onto the surface of the ocean. Aleesha tore off her mask and immediately put her mouth on the injured man's. In-the-water resuscitation was Diving 101. She felt a distinctive gurgle in the exhaled air against her lips. Bloody hell. Collapsed lung. Nothing she could do about that at the moment.

"Take over this mouth-to-mouth," she ordered one of the other divers. He nodded and glided into her place, treading water and breathing into his comrade's mouth.

The second diver commented dryly, "Glad you could join us, Doc."

She glanced up as she traced the victim's rib cage with her fingers and slipped into a heavy Jamaican accent. "Din' wan' no jammin' fun slidin' me by, mon."

"Save him, eh?"

She dropped the Rasta rap and replied in all seriousness, "I'll do my best. Wrap a couple buoyancy belts around his hips, will you? It's damn hard to stabilize a patient who keeps trying to sink." Not only did the injured SEAL have practically no body fat to help him float, but that collapsed lung had cost him a lot of flotation capacity.

The second SEAL complied rapidly. Meanwhile, the first SEAL lifted his head and announced, "He's breathing again."

"Glory, mon," she muttered. She glanced at her watch. One minute and forty seconds after the torpedo landed on his chest. Not bad. In fact, it was amazing given the situation. If he lived, the guy probably wouldn't suffer any brain damage. Big *if*, though.

She glanced around to see if that fishing boat was still close. Nada. The horizon was an uninterrupted line of blue on blue. "I'm going underneath him to see where he's bleeding. Either of you got a med kit on you?"

The resuscitator shook his head in the negative. "Got a crash kit on the Zodiac, but that's it."

"Speaking of which, get one of those out here stat." Zodiac was the kind of rubber dinghy the SEALs tooled around in much of the time.

"I already hit the panic button. Boat should be here in ten to fifteen minutes."

Ten to fifteen? Hellfire and damnation, that was a long time to keep this guy alive until she could render proper medical treatment. She nodded grimly and pulled her mask over her face. Quickly she submerged beneath her patient. A long, ragged tear in the back of his wet suit marked the source of the blood. She reached for her thigh and pulled out her field knife, slashing the rubber away from the wound. It was a deep flesh tear, and, as she feared, a pulsing flow of red came from the wound. Arterial bleeding. Not good. Swishing bloody water away from the wound, she slapped her finger on top of the lacerated artery and pressed as hard as she could. Using her fin, she kicked one of the guys above in the leg to get his attention. Quickly he submerged beside her. She gestured for him to take over the pressure. His finger pressed hard against hers for a moment as she slipped out of the way.

She did a quick inspection of the rest of the victim's underside. Some scrapes and cuts, but nothing else life threatening. Something hard smacked her in the side of the head. She lurched and saw a swim fin headed directly at her face. She dodged out of the way, popping back up to the surface.

The guy didn't need to explain why he'd kicked her. The rattling, rasping gasps from her patient were self-explanatory. He was in huge respiratory distress, and as she repositioned herself to have another look at his chest, he went into a seizure. His back arched and his face dipped below the water. Any buoyancy he'd had was completely lost and he began to go under. She and the other topside diver grabbed him and muscled his rigid body higher. She kicked for all she was worth, her legs burning like fire. C'mon, c'mon. Relax, already, she begged him.

And then a movement at the corner of her peripheral vision caught her attention. Dorsal fin. Big one.

"Shark," she grunted, nodding in that fin's direction.

"*Shit.* Back in a sec." The guy let go and submerged, no doubt to warn the diver below. Redoubling her kicks, she managed to keep her patient afloat. Barely. That SEAL had a lot of confidence in her strength to dump his buddy on her like this. To distract herself from the agony building in her cramping calf muscles, she peered through the murky water below. She made out a harpoon in the submerged diver's hand. He had the sharks handled, then. *She hoped.*

The diver returned and grabbed the patient again, just as the seizure began to ease, leaving behind an ominous stillness.

"His heart's failing on me." She reached for the carotid artery. Yup. Pulse uneven and fading fast. "Here's the thing. His sternum may be fractured. If we do CPR, we run a real risk of puncturing his heart. If we don't do CPR, we risk brain damage and possibly not getting his heart going again once I get access to a defibrillator."

"You're the doc. You make the call," the SEAL replied.

She wasn't a top-notch emergency physician for nothing. She faced these life-and-death decisions all the time. And she had complete faith in her skills. "I'll do the CPR myself. My malpractice insurance is paid up."

The guy grinned briefly.

Using her left hand to support the patient, she kept her right hand plastered on his pulse. She'd seen dozens of cases like this—car accidents in vehicles without air bags where the driver wasn't wearing a seat belt and slammed into the steering column with his chest. She could only pray her current patient didn't have a lacerated aorta or something equally untreatable in the field.

"Incoming," the other diver murmured.

She glanced over her shoulder. And gulped. The dorsal fin was maybe fifty yards away, headed straight at them and, indeed, coming in fast. It dipped below the surface about thirty yards out. The shark would come up from below, striking his victim in the soft underbelly.

"You got Smitty." The SEAL ducked below.

Smitty. Her patient must be Chief Petty Officer Patrick Smith. She'd heard of him. He'd been a SEAL for nearly ten years and was a total pro. And still an accident like this could happen. Something in her rebelled at the thought of wasting a human life in a lousy exercise. It wasn't worth it. No matter that the SEALs—the entire Special Forces community, actually—insisted that realistic training was the key to their success.

A metallic, hissing noise from below startled her and then a mighty thrashing erupted in the water about twenty yards away. The gray, sinuous body of a shark breached the surface, writhing violently. She caught a flash of steel embedded in his belly. It seemed like only seconds until a second dorsal fin appeared, slamming into the wounded shark. The water around the twisting beasts frothed red and angry. Oh, Lord. She got to do meatball medicine on a gravely injured man mere yards from a full-blown shark feeding frenzy? Uncle Sam wasn't paying her enough for this day's work.

On cue, the pulse under her finger skipped a beat. And another. Lovely. The other two divers were below fighting off maddened sharks while she performed solo CPR on a guy who, if she made the slightest mistake in her technique, she'd kill. He'd be a tough patient lying in a fully equipped emergency room, let alone floating out here in the ocean.

Well, she'd signed on with the Medusas because she craved adventure. Bully for Uncle Sam for delivering, because this was one *hell* of a challenge! Practicing trauma medicine in an actual hospital was starting to look downright tame by comparison. And maybe that was the answer to the question that had been bugging her recently, of why she'd stay with a team whose primary mission was to kill: she was an adrenaline junkie. Why this came as a surprise, she had no idea. Lord knew, she'd been taking risks her entire life. She'd jumped off the roof of the house, the first time, before she'd turned six, for goodness' sake. It was a lousy reason to be out here doing this job, and it was going to bite her in the bonn-bonn someday.

But right now she was going to save this patient no matter what monkey wrenches he threw at her. Summoning all her skill, she commenced ever-so-delicate CPR as his heart stopped beating completely.

How long she carefully compressed Smitty's chest, stopping every so often to breathe into his mouth, she had no idea. But she was light-headed from the exertion of forcing air into his dying lungs, she was cramping from her hips to her toes from keeping both him and herself afloat, and in another minute or so she was going to puke from all the sea water she'd swallowed.

Finally a new noise intruded upon the thrashing and splashing behind her. An engine. Running at high RPMs and coming fast. As she moved from Smitty's mouth back to his chest, she spared a glance in the direction of the noise and saw a Zodiac holding six black-clad men flying across the water. *Hallelujah.*

In a matter of seconds, many strong hands reached down, lifting Smitty gently into the vessel and hoisting her into the boat. Without ado, she leaned over the side of the Zodiac and barfed up the entire seawater contents of her stomach. No time to feel sorry for herself, though. She had a patient to take care of.

The SEAL team already had the med kit open and a mobile defibrillator powered up. She snatched a scalpel from the kit and sliced open Smitty's wet suit. A dark purple, basketball-size bruise covered the collapsed center of his bare chest, and now that she could look at the damage, an unnatural dent in the long vertical breast bone announced that his sternum was, indeed, broken. She grabbed the paddles of the defibrillator and slapped them into position.

"Clear," she called tersely. She pressed the buttons on the handles, and Smitty jerked. "Get a breathing bag on him." She grabbed a stethoscope, yanked it over her ears and placed the listening end on Smitty's chest. *Dat a boy.* A nice, steady heartbeat. He was a fighter, all right.

"I need you guys to lift him straight up. Keep him flat so we don't dislodge that sternum, but I've got to get at the lacerated artery." The SEALs complied carefully. She reached in the med kit for a nifty pressure balloon invented by military medics for just this sort of situation. She lay down on her back and slid beneath her patient. Working at a distance of about three inches, she used a scalpel to widen the wound around Smitty's torn artery a tiny bit. Blood sprayed in her face—please, God, let this guy not be HIV positive—but there was no helping it. She inserted the balloon next to the torn artery and inflated it quickly, using pressure from the balloon to squeeze the artery shut. She swabbed the area and waited a few seconds for leakage. Nada. Good seal. The internal pressure bandage had worked.

She wiggled out from beneath Smitty. The wind tore at her hair, and she registered vaguely that they were streaking over the water. She did a quick exam. As she'd anticipated, Smitty's right arm was broken. It would need to be pinned, but the clean break in the middle of a bone was a full recovery sort of injury. He had six ribs broken outright. X rays would probably show several more fractured. Those were gonna hurt like a big dog before they healed. Left lung collapsed. Right lung holding up nicely, however. Would need the chest cavity suctioned for blood and seawater. She'd need a picture of the sternum, to determine whether or not surgery would be required to mend it. MRI would be necessary to see how contused his heart was. Hopefully the sternum had done its job and, by taking the brunt of the impact, protected the heart from serious injury. No sign of shock, yet. This guy had a hell of a constitution to be holding up as well as he was. Even his blood pressure was surprisingly good.

She continued to monitor his vital signs on the ride back to shore. An ambulance met them at the dock, and she rode to the hospital with Smitty. Only when she'd assured herself that the waiting trauma team knew its stuff did she relinquish control of her patient.

And then it was over. Suddenly weary as the adrenaline drained from her system, she walked back into the emergency room to update the anxious SEAL team waiting there. She announced in her thickest brogue, "All fruit ripe, mon. Barring any further complications, Smitty should pull through."

Everyone sagged in relief. Bud Lipton, the team leader, spoke up. "You did good, Doc."

Praise? From a SEAL? Wow. Her insides warmed with the compliment. "Thanks."

"Let me give you a ride back to your quarters. I expect you're ready to clean up and get out of that suit."

Getting bloody and filthy was part and parcel of trauma medicine, but the gore probably was a little unnerving to other people. And she'd completely forgotten that she was still wearing her rather revealing wet suit. "Me tink you right, bruddar," she mumbled. Sometimes it was easier to hide behind her islander persona than to feel naked in front of these too hard, too perceptive men.

Lipton and a couple of the others rode across the Navy base with her. When they pulled up in front of the visiting officer's quarters, Lipton said casually, "Next training evolution begins at midnight tonight. We'll be swimming, so bring your dive gear."

Right. One of their men had just escaped death by a whisker, but training went on. How harsh was that? Special Ops was a callous world that had no time for the weak.

So what was she doing in it, then? She'd asked herself that question many times since she'd joined the Medusas. She was a doctor. A healer. She'd signed up to work in a nice, safe hospi-

tal. She'd never seriously expected to get near danger in her career, even though she was technically a military officer. That is,
until she'd accepted the irresistible challenge Vanessa Blake had
dangled in front of her—to become a Medusa.

Ever since her first mission in the field a few months back
where she'd been ordered to shoot people, and had, this dilemma
had been building. How in the hell was she supposed to work and
live among these operators who held life so cheaply, to become
one of them herself, when she'd dedicated her entire life to saving lives, not taking them?

Houston, we have a problem.

Chapter 2

Aleesha rolled over and groaned as her muscles protested. Wicked pain there, girl. Last night's midnight swim with the SEALs had turned into four grueling hours of cold-water diving, and she hadn't found any of the answers she sought. She'd swear the instructors were trying to break the Medusas if she didn't already know that SEALs actually enjoyed causing themselves pain. She looked at her watch. Noon. She had to get up in a half hour anyway. The Medusas were pulling a harbor security shift this afternoon and had to be in the water by two. A big, fat dose of that seventy-five percent bo-o-oring duty, but someone had to do it. The Miami Port Authority was undermanned today, and the SEALs had jumped all over volunteering the Medusas for the diving assignment. At least it would be good practice for her teammates, none of whom had the diving experience she did.

She rolled out of bed. Might as well spend the extra half hour in a hot shower pounding loose her sore muscles. She turned on the water full blast. While it heated up she made a quick phone call to the hospital. Smitty was in serious but stable condition. Heavily sedated for pain control, but expected to make a full recovery. Hot damn.

She stepped into the shower and let needles of scalding water massage her aching muscles. God, that felt good.

About two hours into last night's swim, she'd exceeded her anaerobic threshold, and oxygen had become insufficiently available to her muscles, meaning they couldn't break down excess pyruvate. That state had, in turn, triggered glycogen production, which broke down into lactate acid and hydrogen ions, making the muscle tissue environment so acidic that muscle function began to shut down. Force of will had kicked in at that point. She'd overridden the signals from her body that told her to stop, and she'd finished out the swim.

Sometimes being a doctor sucked. Normal people just thought they were sore from a hard workout, but she knew exactly how badly she had abused her body. Unfortunately, she couldn't turn off the mental monologue. She was a physician to the core of her being. Like her grandmother before her, she'd felt like a healer ever since she could remember. She'd always wanted to be a doctor, nothing else, and had pursued it with ferocious, single-minded intensity. When the Navy sent her a brochure inviting her to apply for a full medical scholarship in return for an eight-year stint, she'd jumped all over it. Now here she was, a world away from her roots. Of course, it didn't take her diplomas or her training in trauma and sports medicine to know that the only cure for what ailed her body today was time and getting moving. Even grandmama's crude Obeah voodoo healing could've told her that. She briefly considered writing herself a prescription for a mild painkiller, but opted against it. Diving on any kind of medication was a bad idea.

The hot shower helped some, and she stepped out of it, her normally café-au-lait-colored skin rosy pink. At least she was able to move without too bad a hitch in her git-along. Time to suit up for the dive.

The Port of Miami harbormaster gave them a quick overview of which ships were docked where and when they were departing. Four ships would go out in all, starting at 5:00 p.m. with the *Grand Adventure,* a new luxury cruise ship carrying 2800 passengers and a crew of a thousand.

Aleesha did a quick equipment check on her five team members. And today no intuitions had her fine-tooth combing her teammate's gear for intentional sabotage. Praise God. Everyone's gear was shipshape. The SEALs had taught them well. You couldn't get a more qualified diving instructor than one of those guys.

She announced to Major Vanessa Blake, the Medusa commander, "Everything looks good, Viper. We're ready to go."

"Mamba, this show is right up your alley. You lead the way."

All the Medusas had field nicknames, after dangerous snakes, and *hers* was Mamba. Aleesha blinked. She was in charge today? "Hey, I'm only here to patch up people. I don't need to run the show."

Viper—Vanessa—shrugged. "If something happens to me, you're the next highest ranking member of the team. You'd be expected to take charge. It's time to let you get your feet wet."

Aleesha frowned. Her specialty was fixing hurts, physical and otherwise. She was a caregiver by nature, and that did not make her command material. She had joined the Medusas— aside from the fact that she never could turn down a dare—to make everything better. It was what she did. There was a beautiful simplicity to the world of Special Forces. Find the bad guy, stop the bad guy, restore order. The Medusas worked as a team of equals, and on the rare occasion that a command decision was needed, the job fell to Vanessa, who was extremely competent at making those calls. Meanwhile, Aleesha was here to heal, not kill. Or give orders to kill.

If she was being honest with herself, she'd admit that her aversion to command came from not wanting to be responsible for what happened on her watch. It was okay for someone else to order her to kill people, but she didn't want to be the one making that call.

But before she could think much more about it, Vanessa said, "You're the only certified divemaster among us, 'Leesh. Today's your shot at glory."

Misty, the team's blond, impossibly gorgeous, Air Force pilot from California, piped up. "Hey. Does that mean I get to be in charge if we go combat shopping on Rodeo Drive?"

Aleesha looked over at her boss and friend. "I'll pass, Vanessa."

Vanessa shrugged unsympathetically. "It's not open to negotiation. You need the experience in making command decisions."

Put her in a hospital and she'd make command decisions all day long. In an E.R. the choice was always to fight for life. In the real world the choice wasn't always so clear-cut. Aleesha sighed. Problem was, she knew a brick wall when she saw it. No sense bloodying her forehead against it. "Okay, okay," she said, capitulating reluctantly. "Sorry I hassled you."

Vanessa shrugged easily, clearly not holding any grudge. "The only person who truly hassles me is Jack."

Aleesha grinned. Jack Scatalone was the Delta Force lieutenant colonel who'd trained the Medusas, and he was also Vanessa's significant other these days. "How's de boogeyman, anyway?"

Vanessa's expression melted into fondness. "He's training a new class of Delta recruits."

Aleesha groaned at the memory of what he'd put them through in their initial training. "In other words, he's having the time of his life torturing some poor kids."

"Exactly," Vanessa replied drolly.

Lord, she loved the camaraderie of these women. They were a family—every bit as tight as the big, rowdy Gautier clan back home. Funny how fast the Medusas had gelled. Six strong, smart, independent women, and they functioned as one with only the rarest of disagreements. She'd give her life to keep these women safe. But then, that was her job. As the team's medic, she was responsible for keeping them all up and running. Although she didn't need a job assignment to do that. She'd been rescuing hurt birds and adopting lost kittens her whole life, and embracing this bunch had come as naturally as breathing. The only twist was that she happened to be damned protective of her loved ones, and that was a bit of a trick in their line of work.

Aleesha felt the tug of Vanessa checking her gear one last time, got a thumb's-up from her boss, and nodded at the harbormaster. He led them out to his tugboat moored to the dock outside, and they trooped aboard, hauling their air tanks and fins. It was a hot, humid day, and her wet suit felt like a custom-fitted oven-roasting bag. They motored out into the harbor just north of downtown that made up the Port of Miami. The harbormaster slowed his vessel, and the team donned its heavy air tanks, stepped into fins and pulled on masks. Aleesha waited until the other five women had fallen backward off the edge of the boat into the water, and then, with a quick thumb's-up to the harbormaster, rolled overboard herself.

The shock of the cold water, even through her wet suit, took her breath away. Her body adjusted in a few seconds, and she looked around, getting her bearings. The water was murky, a sickly shade of green. A thin film of surface oil obscured the sunlight. Visibility was about eight feet. Not great, but they could work with it. They'd start with a sweep of the area, and then move in close to the docks to check for explosive devices on or near the ships. Once that was done, they'd loiter nearby to be sure no hostile divers showed up at the last minute.

All of the major cruise ships had their own divers to help with underwater maintenance and repairs and to provide security in port. But they'd go aboard a few minutes before their ships sailed. The Medusas would cover the ships during those last few minutes until they actually got underway.

It was a routine patrol. At 4:45, Aleesha traded a thumb's-up with one of the divers from the *Grand Adventure* and, using hand signals, directed her team to take positions around the giant ship.

They'd go out of visual range, but they'd been over the drill a dozen times. Stay with the ship until it was moving faster than they could swim beside it, staying far enough back not to get caught in the suction of its mighty propellers. She and Misty, the Medusas with the most experience in the water, would take up positions farthest aft on either side of the ship, closest to the propellers.

At 5:01 p.m., the steel hull began to move. It eased forward almost imperceptibly. She kicked easily alongside the behemoth. As a kid in Jamaica, she used to watch these ships come into port and disgorge hordes of spoiled, rich tourists. She'd resented those people for all they had and all her people lacked. As she got older, though, she recognized them for the cash cows they were. Tourism was Jamaica's number one source of revenue. Someday she really ought to go on a cruise herself. She'd heard they were great vacations. And after the last few months of grueling, nonstop training, she was ready for a break.

Gradually the *Grand Adventure* picked up momentum as it headed for the mouth of the harbor, until it pulled away from her best efforts to keep up with it. She fell back, heading for the surface. Aleesha was the last to pop above water. The team swam to her, and they headed for the next ship.

Aboard the *Grand Adventure* Viktor Dupont marshaled his wife and her seven-year-old twin boys—his stepsons, legally adopted when he married their mother—to the railing on the top deck, oohing and ahhing appropriately over the view as they headed out to sea. He noted when the harbor divers surfaced and when a phalanx of dolphins picked up escort duty, racing alongside the vessel as it cleared the port and hit the open ocean. It was only a matter of time now. Six years of planning was coming together like a finely constructed piece of clockwork.

His entire team had slipped past the preboarding scrutiny without incident. The cruise industry relied heavily on customer screening to identify potential terrorists before they came aboard. But if a man was patient—willing to keep his team in place for nearly a decade, to help his men establish normal lives as American residents, to recruit actual American citizens to join him, to keep his team mostly out of contact with one another except through him—then it was fully possible to slip through that screening process successfully. Oh yes, he was a patient man.

He strolled around the pool deck, enduring the twins' squeals of anticipation over the water slide and the unlimited free ice cream and pizza offered poolside. How was it that some children lived lives of such innocent excess while others suffered and starved and died in the streets of his Basque homeland? His jaw clenched.

He was a wolf among lambs. He anticipated the taste of the kill on his tongue, the blood-scented satisfaction of justice to come, all the sweeter for the years he'd waited for it. It fell to the wolves, the men of action, to set the world back in its proper order.

There. A discreet security camera. He counted paces to the next camera. Roughly two hundred feet. Good to see that nothing had changed since he'd cruised on this ship's maiden voyage six months ago—a casing mission for the operation. A thousand-foot-long ship, five cameras two hundred feet apart down each side, ten cameras to a deck. His team would have to disable three, maybe four, cameras to make tonight's transaction invisible. No problem. Six men from his two-dozen-person team were assigned to the task.

He rounded up the twins and took them downstairs to dress for dinner. Time to scope out the ship's restaurants. They, too, had their part in the plan. As he passed through the four-story atrium and walked down halls luxuriously decorated with plush Aubusson carpets and teak paneling, he savored the idea that this ship would soon be his. Now that Operation Defiance had been set in motion, there was no stopping the inevitable. The plan had a momentum all its own.

Aleesha peeled off her wet suit, surprised to see Bud Lipton, their primary SEAL instructor, waiting for them in the harbor-master's office when they came ashore. "What's cookin', bro?"

"Last-minute training opportunity for you ladies. You up for it?"

"That sounded suspiciously like a challenge, Bud."

He grinned at her.

"Go on. Spill it before you bust a seam," she snapped when he said nothing more.

"A destroyer that's being refitted has hit a snag in its work schedule. It'll be down for the next week, and I've got the okay to run you ladies through a few training scenarios aboard her. We'd have most of the ship to ourselves."

"Sweet!" Aleesha exclaimed. "What will our operational limits be?"

Lipton answered dryly, "You can't sink her or cause any serious damage that'll hold up the refit schedule."

Aleesha grinned. He'd heard about the Medusas' take-no-prisoners approach, had he? They'd caught some flack for actually blowing up a building during their initial training.

He scowled. "Part of my cadre's on standby to meet us at the ship and act as hostiles for you."

That wiped the grin off her face in a hurry. It would be the very devil to go up against SEALs in their native shipboard environment. She glanced at Vanessa for her decision, but her boss gestured back that Aleesha was still in charge. Well, okay, then.

She looked around at the eager faces of her teammates. "It looks like we have a consensus, Bud. Make the call to your posse."

Two hours later, as she sat in the belly of a cargo jet bound for Norfolk Naval Air Station in Virginia, she had to give Bud credit. He didn't mess around. She'd no sooner said yes to his offer than he'd whisked the team back to their barracks to pick up their gear and hustled them out to this bucket of bolts, which was ready and waiting for them on the ramp at Homestead Air Force Base just outside Miami.

Bud caught a rare nap, as did several of the Medusas. Aleesha was tired, but she kept a doctorly eye on Vanessa to make sure the airsickness pills she'd given her boss did the trick. Poor

Vanessa was plagued by the barfing willies any time she got near an airplane.

The flight was smooth, and Vanessa came through it only vaguely green about the gills. They stepped off the plane in Virginia a little after dark, and Aleesha took a long, fond breath of the familiar mix of salt air and diesel fuel. The smell of the Navy.

Bud was all business. "Let's go, ladies. You've got an orientation briefing in a half hour, and then we hit the decks."

She should've known the idea of letting them get a decent night's sleep wouldn't have even crossed the guy's mind. She also should've forced herself to sleep on the ride up here. Tonight was going to suck rocks, doubly so because she was already tired. Too late to do anything about it now, though. At least it wasn't as if she was any stranger to sleep deprivation. Her medical school residency had seen to that. She steeled herself to tough out a long night.

He hadn't seen another member of his team since he'd boarded the ship, but Viktor could *feel* them moving into place, positioning themselves for phase two of Operation Defiance. He checked his watch as the bartender regretfully informed him the piano lounge was shutting down for the night—2:00 a.m. on the nose. Give the bartender an A-plus for punctuality. He shoved a five-dollar bill into the guy's tip jar and strolled out of the joint. Eight men would be making their way by various routes toward the rear of the ship right now, none of them interacting with each other in any way.

Precisely at 2:15, six men reached up simultaneously from where they lounged under the aft security cameras on Deck 5 and slapped pieces of black construction paper over the camera lenses, blacking out the entire starboard aft portion of the promenade deck's surveillance system. The two extra men lounging in the now camera-free area straightened quickly. One of them opened his jacket and tossed a white nylon line overboard, while the second man quickly lashed the end of it unobtrusively to the white railing of the ship. When the rope was secured, anonymous among the hundreds of other lines tied all over the ship, they moved away, splitting up and heading in opposite directions.

Precisely thirty seconds after they'd held up their black papers, the six men yanked them down, restoring the camera views. Casually, over the next several minutes, they all faded away, disappearing in various directions.

From the deck above, Viktor leaned on the railing with both elbows, peering out to sea, apparently in deep thought. He glanced at his watch when a white-uniformed ship's officer passed below him, walking quickly, looking up at the security cameras as he went. Five minutes and fourteen seconds. About as long as it would take to get from the ship's security office just off the bridge to the opposite end of the ship at a brisk walk. Not bad. He grinned sardonically to himself. But not good enough.

Aleesha crouched in front of the ammunition storage locker, using a stethoscope to engage in a little old-time safecracking. Newer locks could be broken only with diamond-bit drills or high-tech electronic gadgets, but a dinosaur like this could be opened simply by listening for the sound of the tumblers falling into place, or, more precisely, listening for the silence of the tumblers not being out of place. She almost had it.

Bingo, baby. She nodded over her shoulder at Misty and tugged gently on the door. Aleesha slipped a mirror inside the crack in the safe door, and ran it around the edge of the opening. Sheesh! Not one, but two separate flash grenades were wired to blow when she opened the door all the way. She pulled out a set of dental tools, and, holding her flashlight in her mouth, maneuvered the long-handled instruments with both hands. It took her several minutes of delicate work performed in tight confines to disarm the traps, but it was no harder than surgically reconstructing a shoulder joint. She eased open the safe's heavy door to the sweet sound of silence. She taped a note to the back wall of the safe detailing how much of the hypothetical dynamite she'd have helped herself to, were this not an exercise.

She hand signaled to Vanessa, "How much time left?" They'd allotted themselves ninety minutes for her to crack the safe and snatch the explosives. Unlike in the movies, in reality it usually took safecrackers hours to open these old tumbler locks.

Vanessa signaled back, "Four minutes."

Aleesha grinned. Excellent. She turned back to the safe and quickly rewired the pair of flash grenades to explode, using different connection points. For good measure, she wired up a dummy pair of trip wires to the original connection points, too. When the SEALs EOD—explosive ordinance disarmament— guy came back here to disarm his toys and collect them, he'd head straight for his trip wires, which were now the dummies. If he wasn't on the ball, he'd miss her new wires and get himself a little surprise, Medusa-style. Grinning, she stepped away from the safe and signaled that she was ready to go.

Viktor made his way in stages to the back of the ship over the next hour. He wouldn't be able to hear the high-speed RIB—rigid inflatable boat—over the ship's gigantic diesel engines, but then, neither would anyone in the ship's crew. The civilian version of the U.S. Navy's fast stealth insertion boat was readily available for purchase by any sportsman willing to shell out a little extra cash, and it lost very little by way of performance over its military cousin.

He wasn't likely to see the boat as it raced in, black and low to the water, partially hidden in the troughs of the choppy seas. Of course, the ship's crew wasn't likely to see it, either, for three reasons. First, it was constructed of a radar absorptive material that made it nearly invisible to radar sweeps. Second, it would approach from a specifically calculated angle, running up a narrow strip of sea toward the ship's eight-o'clock position—right at the edge of the coverage between the ship's aft radar dish and side-looking radar systems. And third, both the boat and the men in it were covered in matte black materials, nearly impossible to distinguish from the dull blackness of the sea on this cloudy night. There was only a sliver of moon in the sky, anyway, and it was too weak to shine through the clouds that were an unexpected but appreciated bonus.

The RIB should be running alongside the aft starboard corner of the ship now, maneuvering to hold its position in the turbulent water next to the ship's hull and dangerously close to the ship's propellers. They didn't have to stay there long, though. Just long enough for a man to catch the end of the rope dangling near the waterline and tie on a carefully packed bag of equipment. Viktor glanced at his watch. They should be done by now, backing out along that narrow, partially radar-blind corridor of water to a safe distance. The RIB would come to a halt, letting the *Grand Adventure* pull away into the vast expanse of the open water.

Time to go. He walked inside, riding the elevator down to the promenade deck. He loitered in the stairwell, monitoring his watch as the team of six men got into position under the cameras again.

Three...two...one. Once more, they simultaneously blocked all of the security cameras in this portion of the ship.

Viktor slipped outside and headed straight for the line. He hauled it up fast, hand over hand on the slippery nylon, until a black scuba bag came into view. He dragged the heavy, bulky nylon bag over the rail and quickly untied the rope. He unzipped the bag enough to toss the rope into it and glimpsed several MP-5 semiautomatic machine guns wrapped in bubble plastic and heavily taped to keep them dry.

He hefted the bag over his shoulder and quickly headed up the stairs toward his stateroom. The team of six men would leave the cameras blocked for a full two minutes this time. Time enough to be certain the ship's security officer would leave his post and come have another look at the offending cameras. And while Viktor walked down the long corridor to his room, hauling a heavy, suspicious-looking bag that had appeared out of nowhere in the wee hours of the morning, the security officer would be long gone from the banks of cameras that saw it all.

Viktor stepped into his room and eased the door shut. He stuffed the weapons into the closet and slid the door closed. His wife rolled over in her sleep as he slipped into bed beside her, but she did not waken.

Exultation shot through him. Phase two was complete. Now that he had his men and weapons aboard, the rest of the plan was a piece of cake. The ship was completely vulnerable to anything he chose to do to it from here on out. For all intents and purposes, the *Grand Adventure* was his.

Chapter 3

At the debriefing, Aleesha lounged in her seat savoring the grim set of their SEAL trainers' jaws. Apparently, they were not amused with last night's little surprise in the ammo safe. No doubt these guys would get even with the Medusas the next training evolution.

She leaned forward, listening intently as they were briefed on their next simulated target. They were to storm the bridge of the destroyer and seize control from the SEALs who would pose as the ship's crew. *Bloody hell. Revenge, indeed.* It would be an impregnable fortress! This sort of brute force maneuver wasn't the Medusas' style at all. They relied on stealth and cunning to get the job done with a minimum of confrontation. This would have to be an all-out frontal assault. She didn't need intuition to feel the very bad mojo coming from the smirking SEALs as they filed out of the room.

Vanessa glanced up from the pistol she was loading with rubber training bullets. "So, what does your voodoo magic have to say about this mission, Aleesha?"

She grimaced. "It doesn't take voodoo to know we're going down in flames on this one." Grim looks all around met her remark. Crud. They needed to come up with something unexpected and brilliant. Something outside the box. Something so shocking it might stand a chance of working. *Okay, brain. Be creative.* Of course, at that command, her mind went completely and totally blank.

Misty commented, "Too bad we can't just lock 'em all on the bridge so they can't come out and kick our butts."

Yeah. Too bad. Except…what if…

She gave her team a slow smile. "What's Jack's cell phone number? I have an idea, but we'd need his help."

Surprised, her boss rattled off the number. Aleesha punched it into her cell phone and waited impatiently while it connected. Jack Scatalone might have been an asshole while training the Medusas, but he was *their* asshole. By the time they'd been to hell and back for him and saved his life, for kickers, the intense loyalty endemic to Special Forces teams had run both ways between him and the Medusas. He'd help.

The worst of it was keeping the twins out of the damn scuba bag. At seven years of age, they were pesky brats and prone to poking into absolutely everything. God, he'd be glad not to have to put up with them and their sniveling mother any longer. Two interminable years of playing the devoted husband and loving stepfather, all to establish his cover. There had been a certain symbolic satisfaction in fucking an American, but the bitch had started complaining about his vicious attitude in the sack recently. She had no idea just how vicious he could be. But she was about to.

He left the wife with a credit card in the ship's boutique and told her to have fun. She mistook his gesture for tender loving care and gushed all over him before he managed to extract himself from her presence without attracting attention to himself. The boys headed down to the kids' adventure area to stake out good seats for today's airing of some comic-book, cops-and-robbers motion picture. The film wasn't due in theaters for a couple more weeks, but the ship would air the sneak preview later this afternoon to a packed house of screaming brats. It was that very preview, with its guaranteed concentration of children in one place at one time, that doomed this ship to its fate. That and the fact that it coincided with the low light conditions needed for sneaking the weapons aboard last night.

He pulled on swim trunks and a T-shirt, shoved his feet into a pair of deck shoes, slapped a Panama hat on his head and covered his eyes with a pair of mirrored shades. He looked like the quintessential American tourist. A far cry from the zealous Basque separatist he actually was.

Time to go surprise the living hell out of his team, who still thought this voyage was a final rehearsal for the real thing. Some of them would squawk because they'd brought along wives, children and girlfriends who might come into harm's way. Too bad. What were a few innocent lives sacrificed in the name of freedom? It was noble. *Necessary,* for Christ's sake. History proved that true freedom was bought and paid for in blood. The sacrifice of their families was part and parcel of the plan—albeit a part he'd neglected to mention to anyone else for obvious reasons of human weakness.

He hefted the scuba bag over his shoulder and sauntered out of the room. He greeted the ever-present room steward and continued down the hall. He rode the elevator up two decks to the spacious suite from which their team would stage the operation.

He knocked on the door. It opened to reveal Michael Somerset, a former hit man for a Northern Irish splinter group and one of the smartest bastards he'd ever met. Not a guy to cross. A good man to have on their side, though, even if he wasn't a native son of the troubled Basque region. He'd fought for freedom for his own land and lost. He understood the nature of the Basque struggle and was bitter that his own leadership hadn't been willing to do what it took to win. He had the right attitude for this operation, and his greatest usefulness was as the liaison between the Basques and non-Basques on the team.

René and Franco, both childhood friends of Viktor's, were already in the room. The three of them had grown up together in a hamlet not far above the town of Laruns, high in the French Pyrenees near the Spanish border. Together they'd learned their letters and the larger life lesson of how to hate. They knew how to lay an ambush and kill in silence by the time they'd finished grade school. He trusted them with his life. Viktor greeted them easily in Basque, the nearly extinct tongue of his nearly extinct homeland.

The three Montfort brothers, from another small village outside Laruns, were traveling in a bachelor pack. They'd been undercover in the United States the longest, establishing decade-long histories as reasonably upstanding American citizens prior to being activated for this mission by the Alliance. They were also the meanest street brawlers he'd ever run across.

The Basque Spaniard, Antonio, arrived next, followed by François, Alberto and Paulo. Viktor didn't know the last three as well as the others, but they'd come to him last year, highly recommended by the very top levels of the separatist movement. He'd taken them on because they'd been in the U.S. for years already, had covers firmly in place and were as intensely committed to an independent Basque state as he was. And that was saying a lot.

Accomplishing their goal would take strong-arming not one, but two, national governments into ceding land in the Pyrenees Mountains to the Basque people, not to mention convincing the global community to recognize its status as an independent nation. The Basques had been alternately negotiating and pleading for a homeland for decades to no avail. Clearly, it would take a dramatic display of force to achieve their goal. That's exactly what Viktor had in mind.

The American team members weren't here yet. They were late. Again. It was their one glaring flaw. They did everything according to their schedule and no one else's. He clenched his jaw and suppressed his ire. Unfortunately, the Americans were as necessary as the Basques. He needed the additional warm bodies to control a ship this size, and as Americans, they slid under the profiling radar of the cruise line with ease. Furthermore, they were angry men, good with guns, and could take an order. He didn't give a damn about their plan to topple the American economy and drive the U.S. back into an agrarian system à la the nineteenth century, when the country's values had been purer. The men had been willing to follow his plan and let him lead, as long as they got their moment on the world stage, too. He could live with that. There'd be plenty of fame to go around before this was all said and done.

Viktor looked around the room, pleased to see how calm his men were. Eleven soldiers, professionals, one and all. A good team. They each knew their parts of the plan already. The Americans would be useful in pulling shifts so everyone could get some sleep, and in confusing the authorities who would react to this crisis. His plan required precise timing, and their lack of punctuality might prove a problem. Hopefully, when it came time, they'd get their act together.

Eleven of the twelve Americans—the twelfth would stay hidden among the passengers per his orders—straggled in over the next few minutes, unapologetic. *Cochons.* Pigs. He didn't deign to react to their tardiness and merely asked the now-crowded room full of men, "Has anyone discovered any glitches that need to be addressed?"

Negative head shakes all around. Excellent. He hated surprises. "Then there's going to be a slight change in plan."

That got everyone's attention. He knew he had a reputation as meticulous, the type who didn't change plans midstream. Of course, he hadn't done that this time, either. It was just that nobody else had known what the actual plan was.

He said without fanfare, "This voyage is not a dress rehearsal. This is, in fact, the actual ship we are going to take over. Today.

The weapons and ammunition in this bag are real. We're ready, and there's no reason to wait any longer."

As he'd anticipated, a buzz of consternation erupted while everyone reacted to his announcement. Also, as he'd expected, it was Michael who asked the pithy question that cut straight to the heart of the matter.

"Why the change in plans, Viktor?"

He looked his number two in the eye. "I needed all of you to be relaxed, natural, when you boarded the ship, and not draw attention to yourselves. I also didn't want to chance some sort of security leak before the mission."

He looked around the room. Everyone seemed to be buying his explanation. Except for Michael, which was no surprise. He was frowning as if he smelled a hidden truth. Smart lad.

Of course, the hidden truth was that Viktor had gotten a tip concerning a plant inside his team. A snitch among the Basques who intended to expose them all after this last practice voyage. By luring everyone aboard the *Grand Adventure* on the pretense of a dry run, the snitch would come along, hoping to see the entire plan before going to the authorities.

Viktor hefted the heavy scuba bag onto a table. "These weapons still need to be unpacked, safety checked and loaded. The movie starts in a half hour, so we should get to work."

By holding this meeting so soon before the actual attack, he'd trapped everyone in this room and made it impossible for the snitch to warn the crew or other authorities. Whoever the bastard was, his thoughts had to be going ninety miles per hour right now, trying to figure out a way to get out of here and warn someone. Viktor watched the team members keenly, but not one of them showed signs of inner turmoil or chagrin. Either the tip about the snitch was wrong or the bastard was one cool customer.

Viktor passed out the various weapons and tools that would be required for the first part of the job. Overlooking no detail, he'd even packed lengths of chain and four padlocks. Antonio would take care of deploying them. The Spaniard was already slipping into a yellow maintenance coverall, embroidered with the Adventure Cruise Line logo. It was an actual company suit, obtained during Antonio's job as a maintenance man aboard this ship, terminated only a few weeks ago.

The others unpacked MP-5s and clips of ammunition for the compact, submachine guns. There were blocks of C-4 and remote detonators, too, but he'd deploy those later, himself.

Everybody checked their weapons and loaded them efficiently. They donned their radios and earpieces and did a quick sound check. Nods all around. They were ready to go. Now it was just a matter of waiting. Somerset turned on the television and flipped through the channels, piped in by satellite for the viewing pleasure of the ship's passengers. He found a soccer match and turned up the volume. The men watched the game impassively, a South American match-up none of them gave a damn about. The minutes ticked past slowly.

Nobody made an effort to leave the room or to be alone for a few minutes. Viktor continued to watch for signs of undue stress, but nobody acted out of the ordinary. Sure, they were tense at the thought that this was the real deal, but nobody was panicking. He didn't know whether to be alarmed enough to call the whole thing off or profoundly relieved that his tip about an informant was wrong.

His upper lip began to perspire. God *damn* it! He despised displays of weakness. Especially in himself. He wiped the moisture off with a vicious swipe of his hand. This was his moment of glory. Nothing and no one would take it away from him! The attack would go ahead as planned. Fuck the informant.

The kiddie movie's start time passed. He gave it ten minutes for previews and another twenty minutes for the kids to get engrossed in the movie. And then he stood up. Everyone looked at him quickly. On edge, were they? Good. Now was the time to be sharp.

"Let's do it," he ordered. "For *la patrie Basque*. And for whatever the hell it is you Americans are so hot and bothered about."

* * *

Aleesha hung up from her brief call to Jack, grinning widely. The rest of the Medusas looked at her expectantly.

"He liked my idea," she announced. "He's going to call the bridge of the ship and masquerade as a Navy officer who's working on the refit of the destroyer. He's going to tell the SEALs a maintenance team needs to come aboard this afternoon. The team knows to stay well away from the conning tower and the bridge, and it'll be doing some welding in the bilge compartments at the bottom of the ship. They've been briefed to stay out of the way and will be no factor in the SEALs exercise."

"And?" Vanessa asked. "There's more to this plan, yes?"

"Oh, yes." Aleesha couldn't suppress her grin. "We're going to dress up as that welding team. We'll walk onboard the ship as pretty as you please and head belowdecks. Eventually we'll make our way to the bridge, and we'll weld the main door to the bridge shut with the SEALs still inside. Then it's a simple matter of taking out the guys on the bridge, say with a couple of grenades tossed in through an air vent, and powering up the alternate ship controls down in engineering. Voilà, we'll have control of the vessel."

The other five women gaped at her for a moment, and then, as one, broke into gales of laughter.

Finally Vanessa chortled, "If we pull this off, those SEALs are going to kick our butts when they get out, exercise or no exercise. They'll come looking for us in our rooms tonight and give every one of us a blanket party."

Aleesha smiled broadly. "Then I guess we're not sleeping in our rooms, tonight, are we?"

Misty chuckled, "Motel No-Tell, here I come."

Their first challenge was to procure welding suits and equipment from the shipyard. But it turned out to be as easy as telling a work crew inside one of the dock's giant maintenance buildings that they were going to play a little trick on a bunch of

SEALs. The maintenance guys were more than happy to let them borrow some gear.

Only four of the Medusas would go aboard, suited up as welders. The SEALs would be far too suspicious of a six-man welding team, and besides, Kat and Vanessa were needed onshore to provide a diversion when the time came. Karen, after a crash course, would handle the welding torch, while Isabella and Aleesha got the dubious honor of hauling the portable tanks of oxygen and acetylene aboard the ship.

The women strolled aboard, and, in keeping with their cover story, headed straight down to the bowels of the ship. It smelled strongly of diesel oil and was cramped and cold. Aleesha went first, turning on lights and powering up a couple of generators as she went. The guys on the bridge would no doubt be tracking their progress via such signals.

Misty stayed in a bilge compartment with a wrench to pound on a pipe and turn on generators occasionally as if the team was still down here working.

The other three women crept forward in the dark, using their flashlights to wind their way through the maze of self-sealing compartments that made up this portion of the ship. Reviewing the destroyer's blueprints in her head, Aleesha stopped under a ladder midship that should take them all the way up to the bridge. It was going to be a bitch to navigate the narrow, steep stairs in silence with the fuel tanks and welding torch, but, Lordy, it was going to be worth it. Time to go shock the hell out of a SEAL team.

On the *Grand Adventure,* the men left the room in pairs, their weapons concealed, over the course of several minutes—another precaution to keep a snitch from alerting the crew. Only Viktor would proceed alone. He flung the scuba bag over his shoulder, a loaded AK-47 inside it. He walked down the long hall and stepped into the first elevator that arrived. To his annoyance, it stopped at the next deck. The door opened, and two couples crowded inside. One of the men jostled him, bumping squarely into the bag. Damn! Did the guy realize what he'd just hit? Viktor watched for alarm in the guy's face. Nothing. The guy probably thought the weapon was just a piece of scuba gear. The elevator opened on Deck 5, and the couples got out. *Sacré Dieu.* Alone at last. He pressed the button for Deck 4.

He stepped into the stairwell and headed for the kids' adventure area. He walked past Antonio without making eye contact. The Spaniard was almost done chaining shut the unmarked double doors that were the emergency exits from the kids' area. François loitered nearby. Perfect timing. Excellent. Time to move on to the main objective.

Viktor rounded the corner and saw the three members of his team who would converge on the entrance to the kids' area. Without a single one of them breaking stride, they all arrived at the wide set of doors at the identical moment.

If the Americans were on time for once, several of them should be walking into the ship's business center right now, seizing all its computer and telephone lines with ship-to-shore capabilities. Another group was headed for engineering, and the remainder of his men were headed for the bridge, led by Michael.

Viktor nodded once at the men with him. Shoulder to shoulder they strode forward, pushing open the swinging doors. With the precision of a drill team, they swung their weapons out from under their shirts, out of bags and out of waistbands. A female attendant wearing a bright orange shirt looked up, startled by their entrance. But then she actually smiled! What the hell did she think was going on here?

Somehow managing to be perky while whispering, she said, "You guys are early. The movie's not over for another hour. Do you want to come back then or do you have another appearance scheduled somewhere else on the ship?"

Viktor's jaw went slack until it dawned on him that the bimbo thought they were some sort of entertainment provided by the ship in conjunction with the movie premiere. Mary, Mother of God, what a fool she was.

"I'd suggest you turn off the movie. Now. It is time for us to make our grand entrance *right this minute.*"

"You've got to be kidding," she whispered back, still clueless. "The kids would mutiny on the spot."

"Do it," he murmured savagely. "Or I'll kill you where you stand."

She blinked, taken aback by his tone of voice, but in chipper, cruise-line-employee fashion she smiled again. And smiled her last. He tapped his trigger twice, dropping her to the floor in a pool of her own blood. The gunshot was mostly masked by the blaring action on the movie screen, but the noise did attract the attention of two more attendants, a guy and a girl, also sporting obnoxious orange polo shirts.

The guy knelt quickly by his fallen co-worker's side and lurched as his hand came away covered with real, warm blood. He looked up in horror and opened his mouth, but Viktor raised his AK-47 and pointed it at him. The guy's gaze riveted on the bore of the weapon in utter disbelief.

"Let's try this again," Viktor snarled. "Turn off the goddamned movie now, or I'll kill you, too."

The guy backed away, nodding frantically, and stumbled toward the sound booth, bumping into a couple of kids seated on the tiered steps of the room in the process. The kids squawked, but the guy kept going. Smart boy. Might even live long enough to get off the ship alive.

The overhead lights came on abruptly, and the movie cut off. An angry outcry went up from four hundred childish throats. Another orange shirt bounced up in front of the room with cheerleader-like energy and said loudly, "Don't worry, kids, we'll get the movie back on in just a few seconds. How do you like it so far?"

Another collective shout, this time of approval. Viktor stepped farther into the room, in plain view of all present, staff and children alike. He was flanked on either side by his team.

He announced loudly enough for everyone to hear, "Boys and girls, there's been a slight change in the schedule."

* * *

Aleesha peered around the corner using a hand-held periscope at a height of approximately two inches above the floor. She saw movement on the bridge through the glass portholes in the upper portion of the double doors, which were hung so they would swing outward. The triple-reinforced steel they were made of would make it damned hard for the SEALs to shoot their way out once they realized they were trapped.

Isabella carried the steel bar they would slip through the double door handles, and which Karen would weld in place to hold the doors shut. Aleesha watched Isabella ease forward and silently deposit the fuel tanks for the torch beside the door and carefully slid the bar into place. Then, she slipped off to run another steel bar through the handle on the captain's private entrance to the bridge.

Aleesha waited for Isabella's return and her quick grin indicating mission accomplished before giving Karen the thumb's-up to work her way over to the door. It was an exercise in self-discipline to wait and watch during the long minutes it took Karen to slime over to the door and set up her welding rig in utter silence. A couple of times men glanced out the door windows, and each time Aleesha yanked back the periscope lest it be spotted. After yet another such incident, she eased the periscope around the corner again. Karen had pulled her welder's mask down over her face, the signal that she was ready to go. Aleesha signaled over her shoulder at Isabella, who headed for the ladder behind them. Once she was clear of the immediate area, Isabella would radio Vanessa and Kat telling them to create a diversion that would draw the attention of the SEALs to the windows facing outside. The noise of explosives would also mask those first few critical seconds of noise from the welding torch.

With her eye still plastered to the periscope to make sure no SEAL was looking out the window, Aleesha stuck a single finger past the wall at floor height, signaling Karen to stand by. Now all they had to do was wait for the fireworks to begin.

It didn't take long. In under a minute, explosions boomed. Karen immediately fired up her torch and got to work. It was hard to believe that nobody inside heard the hissing burn, but then, Vanessa and Kat had a veritable barrage of flash bangs going off outside. They were using training charges in the grenades, only a fraction of the strength of real grenades, but they still made an impressive amount of noise.

The first door was lightly soldered to the steel bar. Karen moved on to the second door. She'd been at it about fifteen seconds when the noise outside came to an abrupt halt. The girls downstairs had used up all their toys. But it had been enough. The doors would be too hot to touch for several minutes.

The SEALs raced over to the bridge entrance and jumped back in shock as the first guy hit the door and singed his shoulder. Aleesha watched in grand amusement as their heads instantly disappeared from view. No doubt they were crawling around in there, setting up an ambush for whoever was about to burst through the door to take over their bridge. She grinned at their mistake. These guys would learn that the Medusas never did anything by brute force if they could avoid it.

The few seconds the SEALs took to set up on the other side of the door were enough. Karen had finished the second weld. Aleesha stuck her hand around the corner and signaled her to bug out. Now.

Karen turned off the torch, dropped it, and sprinted for the stairwell in one fluid move. She dived around the corner as the SEALs first rubber bullets hit the portholes in the bridge doors. For the purposes of the exercise, that would count as a clean getaway or at worst a superficial injury.

Aleesha led the way down a side hall and ducked into an engineering closet that supplied air-conditioning to the bridge. She tossed a couple of training grenades into the appropriate vent and watched in satisfaction as the first one rolled to a stop against a metal grate leading into the bridge. She ducked just before it blew, but popped up as soon as the initial smoke cleared. Yup, just as she'd thought. Even a training charge was enough to blow the grate out. She tossed a couple more simulated grenades down the vent and watched them disappear into the bridge. She wouldn't actually detonate those grenades because of the amount of sensitive equipment that they could damage, not the least of which was the eardrums of the SEALs currently trapped on said bridge.

Of course, actual grenades going off in the enclosed space of the bridge would splatter a real bridge crew like fish in a barrel. The SEALs knew it and would have no choice but to roll over and play dead for the remainder of the exercise.

The Medusas had done it. The ship was theirs.

Except…

As Aleesha led her triumphant teammates downstairs to take possession of the auxiliary controls of the ship, the victory felt hollow in her gut. She kept picturing those grenades rolling down the air vent and dropping out of sight. Did she have it in her to do that for real? Could she kill helpless, trapped men in cold blood under combat conditions?

She was a doctor, for God's sake. Had held up her hand and taken the Hippocratic oath to cause no harm to her patients. And, face it, by natural inclination it wasn't her style to hurt any living thing.

Yeah, it was a hell of kick working with the Medusas. She loved the adrenaline rush, the sheer excitement of what they did. But so far everything they had done, with the lone exception of the rescue mission to save Jack—which had gone off like clockwork and had not required her to personally kill anyone—had been training. Sure, she'd shot some men at that oil rig in Bhoukar. But she was good enough that she'd been able to drop them with nonlife-threatening injuries. And maybe that should have been a red flag.

Whether she wanted to face it or not, all of this fancy training the Medusas were doing added up to one thing. They were being turned into highly effective killing machines. Could she do that? Could she *kill* other human beings on command? Her first love and her first career were being a doctor. And military doctors were pretty much never called upon to kill. They merely fixed the people who did the dirty work. How was this second career as a special operator supposed to mesh with healing? Was she in an impossible situation? She knew one thing for sure. She needed to answer that question once and for all. Soon. Before the Medusas went operational for real.

The children didn't catch on right away, not even the older ones. But the staff did. They went sickly shades of pale that clashed with their garish shirts, and in terse tones they ordered the children to stay seated.

Viktor growled at the panicked guy in the sound room. "Call the bridge and tell the captain that we have taken approximately four hundred children hostage in the kids' adventure area."

Some of the older children went quiet at that. But the little ones bounced with excitement at this live action adventure playing itself out around them. The twins were in here somewhere. He'd bet they'd caught on the moment they'd spotted him. Although he'd never been overtly cruel, they'd always been cautious of him, probably sensing the danger lying beneath his average facade. When their mother wasn't present to shield them, they'd always trod lightly around him. The very fact that he couldn't spot them in the crowd, that they were laying low, was proof of their fear of him. Clever little brats.

The staff guy talked urgently into a telephone.

It was only a matter of seconds until a Scandinavian-accented voice came over the PA system. "This is Captain Dageskold. Please do not harm the children. What is it you want?"

Viktor murmured into his microphone, "Now, Michael. And be quick about it." He probably didn't have to remind the Irishman that speed was of the essence in this next maneuver. The rest of the Basques, led by Michael Somerset, must take over the bridge before the ship's crew realized what was going on and got any bright ideas about mounting some sort of counterattack.

* * *

Michael Somerset opened his briefcase and pulled out the sawed-off MP-5 inside. He released the safety and hefted the weapon easily in the crook of his arm. It felt surreal to be striding down the plush hallway of a cruise ship armed like this, the sound of his passage absorbed by the thick carpet beneath his feet.

An urge to take off running and flee this nightmare nearly overcame him. The back of his neck felt hot, and he even had to choke back a brief need to vomit. He would spin around and shoot dead the six men behind him if he thought he could get them all before one of them shot him back. But he dared not try it. The other hijackers all had their weapons in hand and at the ready, and in the amount of time it would take him to rake a field of fire across six men, at least one of them would have time to return fire at him. If even one man walked away from his attack alive to report it, Viktor Dupont would take it out in blood upon the children downstairs. And in the meantime, Michael would die, too, and those kids' best ally—a good guy on the inside— would be lost.

God*damn* Viktor for springing the mission on him like this! He'd had no time to warn the authorities, no time to avert the hijacking he'd been working undercover for two long years to thwart. He'd planned to gather the final details, then report to London one last time. A sting operation would no doubt be launched on both sides of the Atlantic to arrest the entire ring of would-be hijackers and bust up the conspiracy.

But thanks to Viktor's unexpected move, now there were children staring at the business ends of machine guns, and Michael was on his way to take over the bridge of a ship—by deadly force if necessary. In moments he and/or the men behind him might very well splatter the brains of the bridge crew all over the walls. What in the hell was he supposed to do now? Blow his cover? Identify himself to the captain and tell the guy to radio for help?

If it weren't for all those kids, he'd do it in a second. But Viktor was below and was perfectly capable of blowing away a couple hundred kids without a shred of remorse. The bastard had successfully tied Michael's hands by sending him up here with a half-dozen armed hijackers at his back.

And that worried the hell out of him. Viktor was violent, but extremely methodical in his thinking. No way had he randomly decided to turn what was supposed to be a dress rehearsal into the real thing. So why had he done it this way?

Viktor's explanation, that the subterfuge had kept everyone relaxed when they boarded the ship, was a load of crap. And that could mean only one thing. *He must know there was an informer in their midst.* Michael didn't know whether to swear viciously or give in to the lingering urge to puke.

Unfortunately, he had time for neither. The double swinging doors leading to the bridge loomed just ahead. He gestured to his men to move to the side, out of the line of sight of anyone looking through the small, round—undoubtedly bulletproof—portholes at eye level. He tried the varnished teak door, although the door should be locked even under normal circumstances.

Yup, locked up tighter than a drum.

For lack of any other alternative that wouldn't get kids killed, he keyed his radio according to the plan and reported to Viktor, "As expected, the bridge is locked." Silently he begged the captain not to test Viktor, not to measure just how far the Basque expatriate was willing to go.

Good Lord. Michael's palms were actually sweating. He hadn't been this nervous since his first dead drop in his initial espionage training a decade ago. Somehow in the next few minutes, he had to find a way to take over the damned bridge and *not* kill the entire bridge crew. How he was going to pull that off, he had no earthly idea.

Viktor looked up at the control booth. "Tell your captain to let in my men, who are just outside the bridge. He's to turn over control of the ship to them. Any resistance from the ship's crew will result in the death of several dozen of these children."

That got the kids' attention. The room went silent for exactly two seconds, and then the brats pitched a collective fit. The din was deafening. Viktor barely heard his earpiece when Michael announced tersely that the bridge was still locked.

Viktor shouted over the caterwauling to the young man in the control booth, "Tell your captain we have multiple automatic weapons aimed at these children. He has ten seconds to surrender the bridge or I will begin shooting."

Viktor allowed a few seconds for the message to be relayed, and then started counting. He waited calmly. It made no difference to him one way or another whether the bastard opened the bridge doors or not. He had literally hundreds of children at his disposal. He'd start with the noisy ones. The captain wouldn't hold out for long.

He saw the staff guy talking frantically on the phone. Probably verifying to the captain that Viktor wasn't lying and that one of his co-workers was dead already.

Nine…ten. Viktor pointed at a kid in the front row who was screaming his head off. Too bad it wasn't one of the twins. He'd enjoy blowing them away after all the headaches they'd given him over the last two years. "I'm starting with you, there, in the yellow shirt. You're making too much noise so I'm going to kill you first."

That shut them all up. Like turning off a faucet. Oh, they sniffed and sniveled, but the noise level dropped precipitously. He raised his AK-47 into a firing position, sighting in on the loud kid. His finger tightened on the trigger.

Michael pictured Viktor down in the kids' area issuing some sort of ultimatum right about now—unlock the bridge or else somebody would get shot. Hopefully the bastard would have the decency to threaten one of the staff members and not traumatize some innocent kid.

The men behind him started to get fidgety, and he murmured over his shoulder, "Steady, gents. Viktor will get us in. Just be patient."

Amateurs. Experienced operators wouldn't have to be told to cool their jets. No matter how committed to their cause these guys were, a decent counterterrorism rescue team ought to be able to pick them off. Not so the American contingent, however. Those guys were highly disciplined. Highly trained. Damned closemouthed, too. They didn't talk to anybody outside their tight little cadre. He never had figured out exactly who they were or where they'd gotten their training. But they could very well be trouble when it came time for a rescue.

God, so many details to work out and find a way to report. So much to do in the next few days, and so *damned* many innocent lives riding on his getting it exactly right.

A movement on the other side of the door captured his attention. A white uniformed ship's officer was approaching what was probably a number pad set off to the side of the bridge entrance. A beep, and the door swung inward.

First things first. He had a bridge to take as peaceably as possible. Over his shoulder he murmured, "Let me do the talking, lads."

He took a deep breath and stepped inside.

Michael's voice came across Viktor's headset, stopping Viktor at the very last instant before he blew the little rugrat's head off. The Irishman reported quickly, "We're in."

Viktor eased up on the trigger and smiled coldly at the child, who was frozen in terror. He'd been no older than that boy the first time he'd looked death in the face in the form of a French soldier in a riot line. This experience would be good for the brat. Would build some character in him.

It took under a minute for Michael to announce, "We have secured the bridge. The *Grand Adventure* is ours."

Exultation shot through Viktor's gut. And a grand adventure it was turning out to be, too.

Aleesha leaned against the wall, trying hard not to smile, while one of the real welders knocked Karen's solders off the bridge doors. Even underneath his mask, she saw the guy bust out in a big grin every now and then. The SEALs were still inside, blustering themselves blue over the damage to the bridge doors and bitching about it not being safe to lock them in like this—*ohh, puhlease*. Like they never did anything in their careers that wasn't safe? Smitty was lying in a hospital, having come within an inch of losing his life in the name of realistic training. More likely, Lipton and his boys were just royally ripped that the entire naval base was laughing at them. Poor babies.

She started when a beeping noise erupted from Vanessa, who was standing beside her. Probably Jack wanting an update on their little stunt. But then her own beeper buzzed and then Karen's and all the other Medusas'. What was up with that? If she didn't know better, she'd say they were getting launched on a mission.

And then she heard more beepers going off. From inside the bridge of the ship. Bud's SEAL team was also getting a launch call. What was going on? Both teams were in a training cycle right now, not on call for actual missions.

The welder finished opening the door and turned off his torch. The SEALs stepped out, all business, any vendettas against the Medusas forgotten for the moment. "You guys get a call, too?" Bud Lipton asked.

Vanessa nodded in the affirmative. "Any idea what's up?"

"Nope, but the call came from JSOC headquarters."

Aleesha frowned. Why did anyone at the Joint Special Operations Command abruptly need to talk to so many operators? Her gut screamed that something very bad was going down.

Bud snapped, "I'll drive. Let's go." He jerked his head for them to follow. They all raced down the midship passageway, Lipton shouting, "Make a hole!" as he led the way down the ladder.

Both teams crammed into the SEALs' lone van, and Bud drove them across the base at the speed of heat. They crowded into a secure briefing room filled with nothing but a table and a speaker phone. They'd barely wedged into the room when a

Navy captain—the equivalent of an Army or Air Force colonel—stepped in. He squeezed to the end of the conference table where they could all see him.

Without preamble, he said, "We've received a maritime distress call from a cruise ship called the *Grand Adventure*. JSOC has terminated all training and put all available resources on standby for an immediate launch, pending confirmation of the information we've received."

"And what's that information?" Bud asked tersely, all business.

"We got a single radio transmission from the *Grand Adventure* indicating that it has been hijacked. She's carrying 2500 passengers and a crew of a thousand. The captain only had time to say that armed terrorists were holding several hundred children at gunpoint and he was about to hand over the bridge to the remaining terrorists."

Aleesha felt ill. How in the world were they supposed to rescue 3500 innocents in the tight confines of a ship? It was an impossible task. And it looked like the Medusas were about to get sent out to do it.

Chapter 4

Michael Somerset looked at the spotless bridge and its defiant officers dispassionately. *Son of a bitch*. Viktor had pulled it off. The *Alliance* controlled the nerve center of the whole damned ship. Now to subdue the crew and passengers. Michael moved to the microphone at the captain's console, pushed the button that activated an electronic bell over the PA system and flipped the switch that sent transmissions throughout the ship. Amazing how much information was available from the manufacturers of ship components—like how their radios worked.

"Ladies and gentlemen, a situation has arisen that will require utmost cooperation from every last one of you. A group of armed men has taken control of the *Grand Adventure* and is currently holding several hundred children hostage. Do not make any attempt to see the children or rescue them or there will be severe and regrettable consequences. Lest you question the truth of my words, the captain will now verify what I have said."

One of the other gunmen prodded Dageskold forward.

Michael looked the grim-faced captain in the eye and said soberly, "You know the drill. Don't do or say anything foolish. Don't try to give the crew any instructions or emergency codes. In particular, do not use the phrase 'golden anchor.'"

Captain Dageskold blinked at that one. He probably wasn't expecting the hijackers to know the ship's secret distress code. It was used to alert crew members to any urgent problem on the ship without panicking the passengers.

Michael continued, "I'm going to give you a short statement to read. Do not deviate from it in any way. Understood?"

Another nod from the captain. Michael held out the microphone and a piece of paper. He couldn't resist giving the guy one last warning, murmured under his breath so the other hijackers couldn't hear it. "For God's sake, don't test the bastard with the gun on the kids. He wrote this statement and he won't hesitate to pull the trigger."

Dageskold gave Michael a long, hard look. Eventually the guy nodded tersely.

The captain took the microphone and the typed statement. The Swede cleared his throat and began to read. "Ladies and gentlemen, this is Captain Dageskold. The *Grand Adventure* has been boarded and is in the control of an alliance of freedom fighters. They are holding several hundred children hostage to ensure your cooperation. Make no mistake. While the alliance does not wish to harm anyone onboard, they will do what is necessary to maintain control of the ship. I urge everyone to cooperate to the fullest extent.

"All passengers are ordered to bring their ship identification cards and report to the restaurants immediately. Those passengers who dine at the early seating are to proceed to the Safari Lounge, and those who dine at the late seating are to proceed to the Galaxy Room. You will be given further instructions there.

"*All* crew members—no exceptions—are to bring their crew identification badges and report immediately to the ship's theater. Attendance at these three gatherings will be checked against the ship's manifest. One hundred percent attendance is mandatory or there will be serious consequences to the children. You have five minutes to be in place, starting now."

Michael snatched the microphone out of the captain's startled hands without warning. No need to let the guy sneak in some other signal that they weren't aware of. At this point, full cooperation by everyone was the safest route through the minefield he now walked.

The phones started to ring in the ship's security office just off the bridge, but Michael ignored them. Idiots. Go to the theater like everyone else, he told the callers silently. Hadn't they heard the captain?

"You won't get away with this," Dageskold announced as angrily as a stolid Swedish man speaking in English could manage.

Michael shrugged. "Looks to me like we already have." He said to his team of men over his throat microphone, "You know what to do." He couldn't bring himself to say it aloud. To take responsibility for ordering what came next. *He was being weak, dammit, and he couldn't afford that right now.*

His fellow hijackers nodded crisply, gesturing with their weapons for the officers who comprised the senior crew to step into three groups. Michael scanned the group, looking at faces and black and gold epaulets denoting rank on crisp white shoulders. He stepped forward.

"Lieutenant Johannson, you'll stay here with me. Lieutenant Leider, I need you to step out of line, as well." Two young women stepped forward, fear evident on their faces. The ship's token female officers. Of course, the ship's hospitality director was also nominally an officer, but she was out and about on the ship. No matter. They'd find her and pull her out when the crew assembled in the theater.

Pushing six feet tall, blond and Norwegian, Inger Johannson was a bridge officer. With all the autopilots and navigation computers up here, she'd have no trouble managing the ship on her own. He'd read up on the ship's controls just in case, but he hoped she wouldn't take after her Viking ancestors and do anything crazy to get herself shot in the next few days. Hannah Leider, a German, was a junior ship's engineer. Another useful, albeit not completely necessary, person to have at her post.

Keeping them alive was more about using them to maintain nominal control over the crew as this scenario unfolded. It had been his idea to spare the women officers what came next, in fact. He'd never dreamed he'd actually see this nightmare unfold. He'd assumed all along that he'd bust the ring wide open long before it actually carried out its plan. But here he was, trapped in the jaws of hell and helpless to stop the carnage around him.

Michael nodded at the other hijackers, watching grimly as the rest of the officers were marched out the door. Thank God he'd been assigned to stay up here during the next part of the plan.

"Have a seat over there, ladies." He gestured to a navigation table far away from the ship's controls or radios. "Make yourselves comfortable. We could be here a while."

The plan was to give the victims twenty minutes so every last straggler on the ship could get into place. Michael watched the minutes tick off slowly on the bridge's big, red, electronic time display. Jesus, it was hard to sit here and do nothing. Every instinct in his body screamed at him to stop what was coming. To get up and make a radio call to the authorities. To beg for all the help they could muster to stop this insanity. But it wouldn't do any good now. A madman was pointing guns at children. Michael's only hope was to maintain his cover and watch for an opportunity to do something—what, he had no idea—to take back the ship without endangering the kids.

About ten minutes into his silent vigil, the bridge door opened. He spun and dropped into a firing position all in one reflexive movement. Alberto. With a woman in tow. He lifted the muzzle of his MP-5 up and out of firing position as the Spaniard gave the woman a shove, nodded at him, turned and left the bridge. Yup, Alberto had places to go and things to do all right. Michael's jaw tightened in helpless frustration.

A disheveled woman righted herself and tugged her uniform jacket into place. Lieutenant Commander Gwyndolyn Klammerstand-Kvordsen. The ship's hospitality officer. Most people just called her Gwyn. And with a mouthful of a name like that, he could understand why.

He gestured toward the map table with the muzzle of his weapon, and she moved over to it as directed. She started to speak to the other two women there—no doubt her outgoing, friendly nature asserting itself—but he cut her off with a sharp gesture of the gun.

"Sit."

She did as he ordered, subsiding into silence. That had to be hard for her. According to Antonio, who'd worked on board for months, she never shut up.

He didn't intervene when she reached over and squeezed the two young lieutenants' hands, however. Who was he to deny them a little comfort?

When exactly twenty minutes had passed, he stood up. The women cringed away from him, almost as if they intuitively knew violence was about to happen. He walked over to the communications panel and flipped on the speakers so he and the women could hear the goings-on from the ship's theater.

"Since you three can't be downstairs with the rest of the crew to hear the briefing, I'm going to pipe it up here for you." God, he didn't want to listen to this. But if the three women across from him were going to get through this mess alive, they *had* to understand the rules of engagement. And, in a weird way, it felt like a necessary penance for him. If he couldn't stop what was to come next, he should at least stand witness to it.

Viktor's French-accented voice came across the speaker on cue. The guy was nothing if not punctual.

"Ladies and gentleman, your ship has been taken over by *L'Alliance de la Liberté.*"

A pause to let the initial buzz of reaction subside. When it faded away, tomblike silence came across the speaker.

Viktor continued with cool precision, "We are now holding all of the children on this ship at gunpoint. If any of you attempt any sort of takeover, some of those children will be killed. Lest you make the mistake of thinking I am not serious, I have brought a portion of the ship's officers with me to demonstrate my seriousness."

Shuffling noises came across the speaker, and Michael envisioned the officers being herded forward onto the middle of the stage.

A gasp from the collected crew verified that he was right.

Michael braced himself, his heart pounding in adrenaline-induced stress. He gritted his teeth and locked his gaze on the women sitting across from him. Even though he was expecting it, the abrupt burst of gunfire made him jump. A grisly image of pristine, white uniforms soaked in blood leaped into his head.

The speaker squealed as screams ripped across it, filling the bridge with the sound of horror. A matching scream rose into his throat, but he inhaled it back into his lungs unspent. To their credit, the three officers with him made no sound, although they all went a ghastly shade of gray and their gripped hands convulsed until their knuckles were snow white. The engineer, Leider, swayed slightly in her seat, but remained upright, staring at the weapon in Michael's hands.

He took a deep breath and said carefully, "In case the three of you didn't catch that, the Alliance just shot all of the officers in the theater. The same thing has just happened or will happen to the remaining officers who are split between the ship's restaurants. You three are the only ship's officers left."

The briefing room was silent, each of its occupants lost in his or her own thoughts while they waited for more details. Aleesha tried to picture what was going on aboard the shiny, white behemoth the Medusas had escorted out of port just twenty-four hours ago. The only image that came to mind was utter terror. Guns pointed at children? It was the ultimate nightmare scenario. This crisis, at least, offered up a simple choice. The lines between good and bad, right and wrong, were clearly drawn. Save the kids, wax the hijackers. Anybody vicious enough to use innocent children as hostages was unquestionably in need of taking out. *Pointing guns at children*—her indignation mounted the longer she thought about it.

Thank goodness this mission was one she could wrap her brain and her moral dilemma around. The last thing the Medusas needed now, when they were still establishing themselves within the Special Forces community, was for one of their members to declare herself a conscientious objector.

So, how were the SEALs reacting to this impending mission, anyway? She glanced down the table. For all the world it looked like all six of them were sleeping. Their eyes were closed, chins buried on their chests. Was the thought of rescuing 2500 innocents from armed hijackers really that routine? But then Vanessa shifted in her chair, and six pairs of SEAL eyes flew open, wary and alert.

"I've been thinking…"

Aleesha leaned forward as her boss and the SEALs launched into a tactical discussion of possible ways to take back the *Grand Adventure*. Although the consensus seemed to be that it wasn't going to be easy, nowhere in the conversation did anybody express doubt that it *was* possible. The idea of failure simply didn't cross these warrior's minds.

Was she truly cut out to be one of these supremely confident operatives?

Johannson managed a "Why?"

Michael replied as gently as he could, "Consider it a show of force to impress our seriousness upon the crew and passengers." It also eliminated the most likely source of any impetus to retake the ship.

His earpiece crackled and Viktor directed calmly, "Report." Nobody'd ever guess the bastard had just murdered nine men in cold blood. This whole thing was a walk in the park for him.

Paulo answered first, and Michael heard cries and screams in the background. "All the officers in the Safari Lounge are dead. The passengers are hysterical but doing as ordered."

René piped up from the Galaxy Room. "Same here. Officers dead, passengers freaked out but cooperative."

"Michael?"

Michael started. Hastily, he pulled himself together. "All quiet up here. I believe the ladies understand the situation."

Vigorous nods from his hostages as they continued to eye his weapon.

"Very well, then," Viktor replied casually. "On to the next phase. Michael, if you please."

"Coming up." He moved over to the ship's PA system. "We will begin with the Safari Lounge. All male passengers from that location will now move in an orderly, single-file line to the life-boat stations on Deck 5. May I remind you that your children's lives depend on your cooperation."

The three women across the room sucked in their breath. "You're putting the passengers off the ship?" Gwyn asked hopefully.

"Just the men," he answered absently. He moved to the door-way of the ship's security office, which opened directly off the bridge. He angled himself so he could watch the women and keep an eye on the progress of the evacuation via the ship's security cameras. The rotating camera views blinked throughout the ship, painting a scene of deserted decks and corridors punctuated by rooms full of terrified people. An image flashed across the screen of a row of crumpled piles of fabric on a stage and he looked away quickly. But not quickly enough. The image of the dead bodies burned into his brain, damning him to certain hell. But what else could he have done? There were the children to think about.

An image of them huddled together with tear-stained faces and huge, terrified eyes flashed on one of the monitors. He cursed viciously and yanked his gaze away from the picture. He concentrated on the long line of men filing down the promenade deck toward the lifeboats. A burst of gunfire drew his attention, and he felt the women behind him flinch.

He spoke over his shoulder. "That was the radios and engines being knocked out on the first lifeboat before the passengers are loaded. Nobody was hurt."

Why he felt compelled to reassure the women, he had no idea. Maybe he was reassuring himself more than them.

The disembarkation of the male passengers took a while. Each one was required to show his shipboard identity pass and was matched to the digital picture printed on the card. The cruise line had even been thoughtful enough to come up with hand-held scanners to read the bar code on each passenger ID card as passengers got on and off the ship. Under normal circumstances, the system allowed the ship's crew to make sure they left no passenger or crew member behind in a port of call. But today, it would be used to verify exactly who was on and off the ship.

Another burst of gunfire, and another fifty-man lifeboat was loaded up and winched down to the water. The boats looked like oversize clamshells with hard, domed covers that completely enclosed the passengers against rough seas. There was emergency water aboard each boat, and they were being dropped off near a major shipping lane. Someone would find them drifting in the water soon enough. And, once the first lifeboat was found, a massive search would no doubt be undertaken to find the others. It would be interesting to see who responded to that initial emergency call. Odds were the crew had gotten off a quick distress call before he'd taken the bridge, but when word got out to the international media from the rescued passengers, all hell should break loose.

The nationality of the rescue team had been the only point of uncertainty in the planning of this mission. The ship was well into international waters, and there was no telling which navy would ultimately end up responsible for reacting to the hijacking. The majority of the passengers were American, Bahamian waters were nearest, the ship's registry was the British Virgin Islands and most of the crew was Scandinavian. Odds were the Brits or the Americans would end up in charge, because of their powerful navies flanking the two shores of the Atlantic. Not that it really mattered. As long as all those children remained hostages, no navy was going to do a damned thing to the *Grand Adventure.*

After the Safari Lounge was emptied of men, the Galaxy Room's male occupants were logged out of the ship's computer and herded onto disabled lifeboats in similar fashion. And then it was time to move the male crewmen. Most of the remaining gunmen converged on the crew lest they have second thoughts about cooperating with their forced evacuation. They were herded down to deck one, the lowest level of the ship. One of the forward hatches right at the water line was opened, and the entire male crew was disgorged onto life rafts after showing their ID cards and being checked off the crew complement list. The cruise line hadn't been smart enough to leave their security men and divers off the list, either. They were tracked with special emphasis to make sure every last one of them was off the ship.

The passengers might get fancy boats with spare supplies, but the crew got good old-fashioned forty-man rubber life rafts. The men put up an initial protest at being loaded eighty men to a raft, but the ominous swing of MP-5s in their direction squelched the complaints. Overloading the life rafts so badly had been Michael's idea, too. Hopefully, his controls in London would assume the ideas he'd forwarded to them had been used in this attack and would react accordingly. But, since he'd had no direct contact with his handlers since he went undercover, it was hard to know if they'd be that smart or not.

The rafts would stay afloat—barely—and would be a handful to manage. The crewmen would be so busy surviving in the overcrowded, difficult conditions, they'd have no time to compare notes on what had happened and mess around with thoughts of retaking the ship. When other ships picked them up, it would take that much longer to gather intelligent ideas on the subject and relay useful information to the commandos who would make an attempt to rescue the hostages.

And therein lay his greatest worry. That some admiral somewhere would try to be a hero by sending in an underarmed, undermanned Special Forces team. Whoever came aboard, they would need a small army and a large arsenal. Viktor was a bloodthirsty bastard who wouldn't hesitate to slaughter the remaining passengers and crew, regardless of their age or gender. Hopefully, the rescued men would relay that fact in forceful terms to whoever found them.

He scanned the horizon through the bridge's panoramic windows, although he doubted they'd ever make visual contact with whatever rescue force was sent after them. They'd never see more than a momentary blip on the ship's big radar screen to indicate the cavalry had arrived.

And now the waiting game began.

They were sent back to their rooms to rest while Navy Intelligence tried to verify the distress call. Aleesha lay in bed for a long time, her thoughts spinning. Maybe it would turn out to be a hoax. Please God, let it be a hoax! Dread filled her, not about doing the job—her training was too good for that—but about the number of deaths that could so easily occur aboard a hijacked passenger ship. Thirty-five hundred men, women and children. The thought of how many might die before this was all said and done made her nauseous. Her physician's need to save them all rumbled strong in her gut. She would do this mission alongside her colleagues, but she emphatically did not share their certainty of a positive outcome for this scenario. And whether that made her the lone sane person or the lone nutcase was anybody's guess.

Eventually her brain retreated from the potential horrors, and she managed to fall asleep. But her dreams were as troubled as her waking thoughts.

Chapter 5

Aleesha jerked to full consciousness as her beeper went off. Time to go back onto the ward already? Navy hospitals were chronically understaffed with so many of their people deployed overseas, particularly when it came to trauma surgeons. When her boss scheduled shift rotations, it didn't help that she was unmarried and had no social life. She always got stuck with the oddball hours.

Aleesha blinked and sat up in the faint pink glow from a halogen streetlamp outside. The low rattle of an air conditioner. Gray wool blankets tangled at the foot of a double bed. A painting of an aircraft carrier faintly visible over a television. Wait a minute. This wasn't the residents' break room. Where was she? Her brain felt like mush as she swam through it toward consciousness. She was in the visiting officer's quarters at Norfolk Naval Air Station in Virginia. For an exercise. Except it wasn't an exercise anymore. They were working with SEALs. Didn't those bastards ever sleep? What sleep? They didn't need no stinkin' sleep. What time was it, anyway?

She reached over for her beeper, which was still trilling insistently, and pushed the button that turned off the painful noise. A digital clock in the corner of the display read 1:00 a.m. She'd gotten about three hours of sleep. Just enough to make her whole body ache desperately for another six hours' rest. She staggered out of bed and into the bathroom. Her head felt full of rocks. She splashed cold water on her face and felt a little better, but it was still godawful to be alerted on so little sleep.

She stumbled into fatigues, zipped up her boots and took a second to run a brush through her thick, sable hair. Because of her mixed ancestry, it was the true, midnight black of her African heritage, but it had the generally silky texture of her European ancestors. She pulled it back into a totally nonregulation ponytail. One of the perks of Special Forces: nonmilitary hair was not only legal but encouraged. It helped operators blend in with civilian populations.

She brushed her teeth quickly and started to feel marginally alive. *Marginally* being the operative word. She stepped into the hallway and Misty Cordell was coming out of her room next door. They rolled their eyes at each other and headed for the lobby. The other four Medusas were already there.

"Now what?" Misty asked.

Aleesha frowned. Good question. They didn't have their own transportation, nor did they have any idea where they were supposed to go. The phone number that had set off her beeper was Bud Lipton's cell phone, but there was no sign of him. She looked around the deserted lobby and spied the one thing that could make her feel more human. Coffee. It was one of the redeeming qualities of life in the military. No matter where she was, day or night, there was always a pot simmering somewhere nearby.

She headed gratefully for the coffeemaker and poured herself a stiff slug of the brew. She took a sip and grimaced. It was a miracle this stuff hadn't melted her spoon when she'd stirred in a little creamer. She didn't even want to think about what it would do to her stomach lining.

She'd just finished it off when Bud Lipton spoke quietly from the doorway. "Get a refill on the java and grab lids for your cups. We need to go. Now."

Aleesha spun around and studied him closely. Crap. She could see it in his eyes. The radio call had been verified. She and the others followed him to a van parked out front. They piled in silently, Aleesha in the front seat.

"What's up?" she asked him.

He glanced over at her and she recoiled at the look in his eyes. Whoa. Definitely something ugly going down. During their training, she'd seen operators launched for real several times and their intensity levels went from zero to sixty in nothing flat, but it was always eagerness she saw gleaming in their eyes. Tonight, Bud looked like someone had just murdered a baby. His baby. That was death glinting in his eyes.

"A Japanese cargo vessel found a little surprise floating around in the eastern Bahamas at around midnight. It confirms this afternoon's distress call from the *Grand Adventure*."

Okay. So far nothing to explain his extreme attitude. What could it be? Foreboding filled her. "And it was—"

"Some of the passengers off the *Grand Adventure*. In a lifeboat."

Aleesha frowned. "Did the ship sink?"

"Nope. According to the folks who've been picked up, the hijackers tossed all the men off the ship."

Sweet Jesus. Her pulse jumped and her brain went into overdrive. She recognized her crisis response mechanism and let it take over. In full trauma-surgeon mode, she asked, "Casualties?"

"All the ship's officers are reported dead."

Dead? Her brain froze, trying unsuccessfully to wrap around that one. A ship that size would have—what? Twenty or thirty officers? And they were all dead? She'd seen emergency rooms filled with that many victims. She knew how many family members milled around outside praying for that many loved ones.

They had wives, children, parents and a host of others, all of whom would be devastated by this.

She tuned back in to what Bud was saying.

"—bunch of children are being held hostage. We don't know much more than that. General Wittenauer said to bring you down with my team for the full sitrep."

The Medusas got to hear the full situation report? General Hal Wittenauer himself wanted them involved? He was the commander of JSOC—the Joint Special Operations Command—and was responsible for coordinating the activities of all the Special Forces elements within the armed forces of the United States. He was also the Medusas' boss. They reported directly to him, and through Wittenauer, to the president of the United States. The two men had created the Medusas in an extremely secret executive order last winter.

Did the fact that Wittenauer was including them in the situation briefing mean they were definitely going to take part in the response to this hijacking? Her adrenaline level leaped by several more notches. Abruptly, she was wide awake. And the coffee had absolutely nothing to do with it.

She eyed the glow of the flightline looming ahead and frowned. "Where exactly is this briefing going to happen?"

"Homestead."

"As in Homestead Air Force Base, Miami?" she asked.

He nodded. "Interrogators have flown out to the ship that picked up the first people and are talking to them now. They'll try to piece together what happened for us by the time we get to Florida. There's a search on for more passengers. So far, three boatloads have been picked up."

Without any more warning than that, she and the rest of the Medusas hustled aboard a Navy P-3, strapped into the uncomfortable web seats lining its cargo compartment and, along with Bud's SEAL team, winged off into the night with the clothes on their backs, their bellies full of coffee and their heads ringing with questions.

Welcome to the big leagues, baby.

* * *

Michael rubbed his eyes and glanced at his watch: 4:00 a.m. He probably ought to let one of the other guys take the bridge for a while and get some rest. But, truth be told, he hesitated to turn over control of the three women officers to anyone else. He cursed under his breath. He knew better. He couldn't afford to reveal any weakness that might tip off Viktor. His survival, and potentially the survival of hundreds of innocents, rode on him maintaining his cover and waiting for an opportunity to stop this madness. Michael took a deep breath. Stay cool. Be sharp.

He took another swig of coffee and focused on the bank of monitors. The Americans were still clearing the ship. It was tedious but necessary. As they'd expected, the list of men who'd been put off the ship differed slightly from the passenger and crew manifests. Four crew members and two passengers had been unaccounted for.

Both passengers had been found quickly, hiding in their rooms—how dumb was that—and eliminated. One of the crewmen had been located and similarly dispatched, but three crewmen were still at large. The team responsible for clearing the ship was doing it right, taking its time and being thorough with a room-by-room, hall-by-hall, cranny-by-cranny search of the vessel. Based on the Americans' techniques they'd probably been trained by some ex-U.S. Army Special Forces types.

He rubbed his hands over the stubble on his cheeks. He'd been in this business too damned long if he could identify the country of origin of a Tango by the search methods the blighter used. He'd been on some wild ops in his day, but this one took the cake. Hands down.

One of the women in the next room cried out and he lurched to his feet, battle ready. He raced out low and fast, his MP-5 in front of him. A quick sweep around the bridge. Empty. The three women huddled on the floor in the corner, using their uniform jackets for pillows. Their feet were tied together so they slept in a starburst pattern. They looked like a bad parody of an Esther Williams movie. Johannson was restless but unconscious. She must have cried out in her sleep. No surprise that young Inger was having nightmares tonight.

Staring at the sleeping women, he let out his breath slowly. He was wired way too tight for his own good. Or for theirs.

The flight took several hours, and this time Aleesha didn't make the mistake of staying awake once they were airborne. Sleep was a precious commodity in this line of work.

The sky was steel-gray, heralding the imminent approach of dawn, when they stepped off the jet in Miami. The air was cool and damp and carried the decaying, briny odor of the ocean. Yup, back in Florida. A van whisked them across the base to the command post. As they were let into the secure facility, she spied General Wittenauer and a team of intelligence analysts, already hard at work on phones and computers in the operations center they'd more or less taken over. No doubt teasing all the information they could out of whatever mysterious intel sources they called upon in a crisis like this.

The SEALs and Medusas were ushered through the semi-twilight of the communications room to an attached briefing room that sported soundproof walls and a glass window looking out on the communications center and its teeming activity.

They didn't have to wait long. Wittenauer made one last pass around the outer room to collect a series of note cards. He was still thumbing through them as he stepped into the briefing room and shut the door. Nothing like information hot off the presses. She leaned forward in her seat and noticed that everyone else in the room had, too.

The general wasted no time in getting down to brass tacks. "In the last four hours, eight more lifeboats of passengers and three boatloads of crew members from the *Grand Adventure* have been recovered. That's about one-third of the passengers and crew. And every last one of them is male. Looks like our hijackers are hanging on to the women and children."

Her stomach sank. Not a good sign. It showed a fair bit of

foresight to get rid of the people most likely to mount resistance. She asked tersely, "Where's the *Grand Adventure* now?"

Wittenauer moved over to a map of the Caribbean tacked to one of the walls and pointed to a red push pin stuck north and slightly west of the Turks and Caicos islands. "Satellite imagery places the ship right here as of about ten minutes ago. Appears to be steaming south."

"Destination?" she asked.

"Your guess is as good as mine. South America maybe. Could be any one of the islands within a couple-thousand-mile radius of her current position. The ship was fully fueled yesterday. She can sail for a solid week."

Aleesha did some quick math. Say twenty-five miles per hour, twenty-four hours per day, for seven days—they were talking a range of four thousand miles or more. Ouch. The *Grand Adventure* could make it to Europe, and that was assuming she didn't stop and refuel. Many of the small islands in the Caribbean were fully capable of refueling a ship her size. And with a lot of hostages onboard, it wouldn't be hard for the hijackers to trade a few for a supply of fresh water, food and a load of diesel.

Aleesha listened in dismay as General Wittenauer continued. "As for what happened aboard her, it appears that roughly twenty terrorists, mostly Caucasian males, calling themselves *L'Alliance de la Liberté,* took control of the children at gunpoint yesterday afternoon and immediately parlayed that into control of the entire ship. They owned the bridge about five minutes after they first hit the kids."

Even Bud Lipton whistled between his teeth at that one. These terrorists had been nearly as efficient as a Special Forces team would have been in the same situation.

Wittenauer plowed on grimly. "The crew put up no fight, with over four hundred children's lives at risk. But, here's the kicker. It appears the ship's officers have been slaughtered to the last man. According to the Adventure Cruise Line, there were thirty-two officers aboard."

Nobody said anything, but she noticed a whole lot of tight jaws.

Wittenauer sat down at the head of the table. "We believe the hijackers control all major functions of the ship. They have been in contact with no one, and we have no idea what they want or what they plan to do."

She leaned back as Wittenauer fell silent. Wasn't that special? Gotta love a world where hijackers flew their own jets and piloted their own ships.

A few minutes later an analyst stepped into the room and passed Wittenauer a piece of paper. The general glanced at it and remarked, "Still no word on where the children are being held. We don't know if they're being kept in a central location or if they've been dispersed throughout the ship. Assuming we don't pick up any boatloads of women and children, it looks like around a thousand adult female passengers and a hundred female crew members are still aboard. So with the kids, we're looking at roughly fifteen hundred hostages."

Bud Lipton, who'd been doodling on a legal pad in front of him for the past minute or so looked up. "Weapons?"

Wittenauer shrugged. "Nobody so far has reported seeing anything beyond a few submachine guns, but that doesn't mean the bastards don't have more toys. Nobody's alive who can tell us what they used to take over the bridge. Thing is, if they managed to get guns aboard, they could have just about anything else onboard, too."

"Who's going to run the op?" Bud asked.

Aleesha watched with interest as frustration and disgust warred in Wittenauer's expression. "The political wrangling has already started. A little birdie told me the Brits want in on it, but we're holding out for full control. Who the hell knows who'll come out on top? We have no orders at this time. But we'll ramp up for the op just in case."

Bud nodded, his mouth curled down in disgust that mirrored the general's.

A fax was passed to Wittenauer. "They've picked up another

raft of crew members. This bunch is reporting that the ship's hospitality officer—a woman—may still be alive. She was seized and dragged out of the ship's theater before the other senior officers were shot."

Aleesha leaned back in her chair. And now that hospitality director was the senior ranking officer in charge of the whole damned ship. That had to be a hell of a jolt to the poor woman. She was supposed to be commander-in-chief of shuffleboard and Bingo night, and now she was in charge of an entire highjacked ship.

And if that wasn't a cosmic object lesson to her, she didn't know what was. Aleesha's blood ran cold as a single thought filled her mind. Thank God Vanessa was here to take charge of the Medusas. Aleesha *so* did not want to be the senior officer on her team if this thing went south. *Coward,* a little voice taunted in the back of her head. She ignored it. She was here, wasn't she? A ship full of women and children was floating around out there somewhere, at the mercy of terrorists, and if there was something she could do about it, she would.

"Any guesses at what the Tangos' demands will be?" she asked.

Wittenauer replied, "Nope. They've turned off all communications, incoming or outgoing. Until they want to talk, or until we figure out who this *Alliance de la Liberté* is and what they want, there's not a hell of a lot we can do."

Bud Lipton leaned forward. "How are we tracking the ship?"

"We've got long-range radar off a tender ship about forty miles away from her. They're trailing the *Grand Adventure* until other assets can be moved into position. The terrorists have turned off the IFF systems, but we've identified every other vessel in the neighborhood. It has to be them."

Aleesha'd learned on the bridge of the destroyer yesterday—it felt like a lifetime ago—that IFF stood for Identification Friend or Foe. It was an electronic system that allowed moving vehicles like tanks, ships or airplanes to identify which radar blips were allies and which were enemies. Every country's armed forces had them. Aloud she asked, "What has their track been?"

The general shrugged. "They turned from a southeasterly course to a heading of due south about an hour ago. Could be making a run for South America—could be a misdirection. They may just be sailing around in circles until whatever plan they have in mind plays itself out."

"Does anybody have any idea who these guys are?" she asked.

"None. Nobody in our intel community has ever heard of them."

By rights, she ought to be sitting here quietly and observing. This was the SEALs' show. They were the experts on seizing naval vessels, and the Medusas were merely the trainees tagging along. By rights Vanessa should act as their mouthpiece. But someday they'd be the group on the hot seat, and Aleesha had to operate as if that day had come. And when had she ever held her tongue on account of military protocol? She asked, "Do we have blueprints of the ship? Any satellite imagery of her? Hell, publicity brochures?"

The general replied, "Working on it. The ship's practically new and her owners haven't gotten around to filing a set of blueprints with JSOC yet. We've contacted them and asked to have them faxed to us. But that could take a couple of hours."

Sheesh. In a couple of hours everyone onboard could be dead. Although she doubted it. The hijackers wouldn't have made a point of specifically keeping the women and children if they only had murder in mind. The hostages were a human shield for whatever the hijackers were really up to.

What would she do with a cruise ship if she were a terrorist? Scaring tourists away from that industry wouldn't hurt anyone's economy in a big way. It would be a logistical nightmare to retain control of something the size of a cruise ship and would require a lot of conspirators and a lot of careful coordination. Why not just hijack an airplane or take over a day-care center if they wanted to kidnap kids? Why a ship? The one thing a ship had was its ability to carry gigantic payloads over long distances. So what were these terrorists planning to move? Her mind remained frustratingly empty of ideas.

Wittenauer interrupted her thoughts. "For the next few hours, we're stuck cooling our jets while the situation unfolds. Go get some sleep. The folks here will work up some preliminary ideas, and I'll call you when we get more information."

She didn't need to be told twice to sleep while she could. Rooms were already lined up and waiting for them in the Q— the visiting officer's quarters. She stepped into her chilly, dark room, stripped and crawled into bed, physically tired.

Except her brain was having no part of sleeping. A niggle of doubt wormed its way into her head and wouldn't go away. How nasty would this scenario get before it ended? Women and children dead? Terrorists obliterated? Thirty of the ship's officers had already died, and this thing was just starting. A chill chattered across her skin. Grandmama would call it a ghost walking over her heart. Grandmama would also say it was the harbinger of bad mojo. Were the Medusas to get the call, could Aleesha board that ship and kill twenty men?

The mission was a no-brainer. Kill the bad guys so the children would live. But now, alone in the dark, she couldn't dismiss the physician in her. She was trained not to judge, not to see beyond a human being in need of medical care. In her experience, even the most hardened criminal was a regular person beneath it all. They bled and hurt and were grateful for compassionate care like anyone else. So, who were these hijackers? Why had they done this? What cause had motivated them to such passion that they did something so clearly suicidal? With a sinking feeling in her stomach, she realized she needed to know the answers to those questions before she barged in and blew the guys' heads off.

But she couldn't just march up to them and ask. So where did that leave her?

With her finger on the trigger and a whole lot of doubts about pulling it.

Chapter 6

Viktor threw Michael off the bridge just after sunrise. "Go. Get some sleep. I need you to stay sharp. You are my secret weapon when it comes to handling the unexpected."

Michael made his way wearily toward his room. Viktor was right. He did need to stay sharp. The last twenty-four hours had been more than a little stressful. And the fun was just beginning. Some secret weapon he'd been so far. Twenty-nine officers, two crew members and two passengers dead. Why he was keeping that macabre running count in his head, God only knew. Surely, by now, the powers that be knew what had happened aboard the *Grand Adventure.* Surely, somebody would respond soon and help him stop this madness. He'd shoot Viktor right now if it weren't for the Americans. But that bunch was fully capable of continuing with the hijacking on their own.

The American team members still hadn't located the three missing crewmen. Had they slipped behind the Americans as they cleared the ship or was the ship's manifest wrong? Such mistakes did happen. Until they were caught or accounted for, Michael couldn't let down his guard.

He drew his weapon and spun into his suite, checking every possible spot where a man could hide. Fortunately, in the compact confines of a ship, there weren't many spots like that, even in a suite like his. All clear. He stretched out across the king-size bed and savored letting go of the tension in his muscles. This was the calm before the storm. He'd better enjoy it while it lasted, because when this thing blew up, it would go sky high. He tucked his MP-5 under his arm like a macabre teddy bear and let sleep claim him.

Lieutenant Colonel Jack Scatalone leaned across the conference table and stabbed off the speaker phone. He made eye contact with the man at the end of the table. Henry Stanforth, the President of the United States. "Permission to speak freely, sir?"

"By all means."

Jack looked around at the cabinet members and members of the joint chiefs of staff. What was he doing swimming with these big sharks? He was an operator, for Christ's sake. A little minnow compared to them. He didn't play politics. That was Wittenauer's job. Jack was just a field schmuck, a team leader who crawled around on his belly and shot stuff for a living. He never should've taken the job as Wittenauer's aide.

But it wasn't like the old man had given him a choice. He'd told Jack that if he was going to make general, he had to pull a staff tour and learn how to play the game in Washington. He didn't give a crap about being a general, but Wittenauer had threatened to retire him from the teams if Jack didn't play ball. So here he was, whether he liked it or not. In a White House cabinet meeting, for God's sake. He sighed. A mission was a mission, be it hiding in a jungle or a command performance at the White House. He had his orders for today.

He spoke carefully, weighing every word. "The Brits are competent. And it is technically their ship. But we have ten times the assets nearby, and we've got resources that can get aboard the *Grand Adventure* unseen and stay unseen." Jack shot a significant glance at Stanforth, who nodded his understanding. Jack was talking about the Medusas, and they both knew it.

The Assistant Secretary of State leaned forward. "If that was speaking freely, Colonel, you lost me. What resources are you talking about?"

Jack gave the guy a level look. No way was he blowing his girls' cover. Only a handful of people knew of their existence, and it was his job to keep it that way. "I'm not at liberty to go into detail, sir, but I assure you, the Brits have nothing of the kind."

The assistant secretary gave him the most diplomatic fuck-you glare he'd ever seen. Jack absorbed the look dispassionately and never let his own gaze waver. Within a few seconds the State Department weenie looked away. Not too many people won a game of chicken with one of the Delta Force's most experienced operators.

Jack glanced around the table, inviting others to challenge him. He ended his survey with the president, conveying a silent reminder of their solemn vow to keep the Medusas' existence secret.

Stanforth's mouth tipped up in a smile so fleeting Jack wasn't even sure he saw it. Then the president cleared his throat and said sternly, "Thank you for the display of security consciousness, Jack. You can stand down now. Your secret weapon is safe. I'm not going to order you to reveal it."

Jack nodded his understanding and deliberately released the tension lying across his shoulders. God, he hated roomfuls of politicians. It was at this level of government that most Special Forces missions got sent to hell, and good men—and women— got set up to die. Jack's job was to keep these people's noses out of the mission planning. If only they could be convinced to stand the hell back and let the experts figure out how to get the missions done, the world would be a safer place, and his teams' jobs would be a whole lot easier.

The conversation devolved into how to diplomatically break it to the British Foreign Office that the Unites States was taking over the rescue operation. Jack let it flow past him. Not his job. Let the politicians do what they did best, and he'd stick to what he did best.

He started when Stanforth asked him abruptly, "So what do you need from me?"

God bless Henry Stanforth. "Just a green light and a clear playing field for my teams, sir. We'll take care of the rest."

The chairman of the joint chiefs piped up. "That's what JSOC is for. Coordinating between the services to make sure all the assets needed are available and in place in a timely fashion."

"Then see to it the job gets done," Stanforth retorted. He spoke into the intercom beside him. "I need to speak to the British prime minister. Now."

At 9:00 a.m. Aleesha's beeper went off, dragging her yet again from a deep, hard sleep. She popped up this time, though, alert right away. That beeper meant there was some sort of development in the *Grand Adventure* situation. She headed for the lobby and was startled to see General Wittenauer himself waiting for the Medusas. Silent, she and her teammates exchanged curious glances and followed him out to a waiting van.

"What's the latest?" Vanessa asked as he pulled away from the curb.

"In the command post," Wittenauer replied sharply.

Yikes. Something big had happened. And the old man didn't like it one bit. They filed into the secure briefing room once more, and the SEALs were there, waiting for them. Wittenauer stalked to the head of the table as the Medusas took seats across from the SEALs. This time, there were also a half-dozen civilians in the room in addition to the uniformed men working the phones. Wittenauer introduced them briefly as some of JSOC's senior intelligence analysts.

Wittenauer turned to face the group. "The Navy has picked

up the last lifeboats and verified that every male over the age of thirteen is off the *Grand Adventure*. There are six men unaccounted for. We don't know if they hid aboard the ship or if the ship's manifest is wrong. But we are operating on the assumption that everyone who's getting off that ship is already off it.

"The Navy sent an observation vessel out toward the *Grand Adventure* an hour ago. The second it got within twenty-five nautical miles of the ship, the hijackers broke radio silence just long enough to tell our vessel to back off or they'd kill a couple of kids."

An observation vessel, huh? A nice euphemism for a spy ship rigged to look like a fishing trawler. "Any voice print analysis on the radio call?" Aleesha asked. A spy ship would surely be capable of such a thing.

"The bastard was *American*," Wittenauer snapped. "And not under appreciable stress."

American? She blinked in surprise. Wow. That threw a nasty wrinkle into things. The SEALs were going to kill Americans, were they? Great. Now all kinds of political maneuvering were likely. Would the president openly authorize the execution of Americans, even if they were terrorists? It would be a political hot potato either way.

Wittenauer's voice broke into her thoughts. "We've got precious little information on what the hell's going on aboard her. We can't mount a rescue until we know more. We need real-time intelligence on what's happening. Where are the kids? Who are these assholes and what are they up to?"

"Can you get a satellite on it?" Aleesha asked.

The general shrugged. "Not much will be visible from the air. Whatever drama's playing out on that ship is likely to be happening belowdecks."

"What about parabolic microphones deployed from a submarine?" Bud Lipton asked. "Or microphones attached to her hull under the waterline?"

One of the civilians fielded the questions. "The *Grand Ad-*

venture has the latest in collision avoidance technology. That includes underwater radar that can paint a foot-long fish in front of her. It's improbable that a diver or a submarine could get close enough from below, without detection, to install such a device."

Lipton retorted, "Then how are we supposed to get close enough to board her at all?"

The civilian replied patiently, "We wait until the seas are choppy and go in on the surface. A low-profile fast boat is extremely difficult to pick out on radar. Under the right conditions, it looks just like a wave top approaching the ship."

"No kidding? Maybe the SEALs should give those a try."

The civilian took Lipton's rebuke gracefully, with a shrug and an apologetic look at the SEAL leader. Everyone was on edge. If—no—*when* they got called to action, this was one of those worst-case scenarios everyone dreaded. She didn't know about the SEALs, but Aleesha could feel the worry mounting in her own teammates. It was time to move this meeting beyond passive collection of yet more bad news and into the realm of the proactive.

Aleesha looked over at Bud. "What do you guys need by way of intel before you go aboard?"

"Precise data on the location of the children, the number and deployment of the hijackers and what sort of heat they're packing."

That information was nearly impossible to collect from satellites and observation ships over twenty-five miles away. Jeez. What a mess.

Wittenauer tipped his chair back, leaning against the blackboard at his back. He laced his fingers across his belly, and his eyes blazed with the raw intelligence that had helped land him his job as commander of JSOC. "Thoughts?"

Lipton went first. "We've got to get someone aboard that ship to run surveillance for us."

One of the civilians—who for all the world looked ex-military with a short crew cut and bulging muscles—dived in. "Ships are not built with tons of places to hide. Maintaining secrecy for forward observers is going to be a bitch."

"Nonetheless," Lipton said, "I can't go in blind to an area that size and expect to shoot my way to the kids before they get slaughtered. These bastards have already killed the ship's officers. They'll kill the kids if it comes to a shoot-out."

Vanessa leaned forward. "You're talking about clearing what? A thousand state rooms and maybe a hundred public spaces? You'd have to send a battalion of operators to hit with enough force fast enough to get to the kids before they were shot. Do we even have that many trained counterterrorist operators?"

Wittenauer snorted. "Not sitting around with nothing to do, we don't."

Vanessa shrugged at the civilian. "Then Bud's right. We've got to get eyes aboard that ship before we take it back."

Aleesha watched with interest as Vanessa rounded on Wittenauer, her shoulders hunched with sudden tension. Whatever her team leader was about to say next was the real point. And an instant before Vanessa opened her mouth, Aleesha knew what was going to come out. Not that it should have been any surprise. It was perfectly obvious, in fact.

Vanessa stated with quiet certainty, "And that's why the Medusas need to be the ones to board the *Grand Adventure*."

Wittenauer didn't react with nearly as much surprise as Aleesha expected. So. He'd been toying with the idea, too, had he? That was a heck of a vote of confidence for a bunch of relatively new trainees like the Medusas. The other men in the room reacted differently, however. The SEALs reared back from the table, violently displeased by the idea. Clearly, they'd expected to run the entire op, including the surveillance. The civilians collectively gasped in shock. The intelligence analysts for JSOC must not be up to speed on the full capabilities of the Medusas.

One of the white shirts said with thinly veiled indignance, "The CIA has several highly competent female agents who could infiltrate the ship with practically no risk of discovery."

Well, that answered who he was the liaison for.

A second civilian chimed in. "Consular Ops also has several

excellent female agents who'd be able to get aboard the ship and blend in with the passengers."

Consular Ops, huh? They were the intelligence gathering arm of the State Department, a shadowy bunch who managed to stay out of the spotlight, unlike their brothers and sisters at the CIA. She probably shouldn't be surprised that JSOC worked closely with that outfit.

"There are two vital pieces to this part of the mission," Vanessa replied calmly. "One is getting aboard the ship and blending in with the passengers or hiding outright. The second part is doing the type of surveillance those guys—" she pointed with her pen across the table at the SEALs "—need to do their job. Do civilian spies know what to look for and how to report it for a counterterrorism strike force? Are they trained in hostage rescue, room clearing, target selection, and sniper tactics?"

The white shirts glared at her in silence.

That answered that.

"We may not have the same experience with infiltration as civilian spies, but we do have training to report exactly the information they'll need." Another stab at the SEALs with her pen. "My team is trained to do *their* job. *We* have to be the ones to go in."

Lipton and his team's expressions relaxed a bit. Despite the pranks and ribbing that had flown between the Medusas and their SEAL trainers for the past month, Aleesha's impression was that, overall, the SEALs were damned impressed with the Medusas' skills and attitude. If they couldn't do the surveillance, the guys liked the idea of using operators like themselves. Enough to take up the argument with the civilian contingent. The SEALs came out of their corner swinging in favor of sending in the Medusas with their limited infiltration training but extensive counterterrorism training, versus using civilian spies with loads of infiltration experience and not one bit of training in doing forward observation for Special Forces teams and missions.

A spirited argument ensued, mostly between the men. Vanessa threw in an occasional comment, but Viper knew the value of not overselling the Medusas' case. Aleesha kept a keen eye on Wittenauer. After all, he would ultimately make the decision. He was definitely weighing the pros and cons, and he hadn't made a decision by the time the next update was carried into the room.

Wittenauer read the single sheet of paper that an aide placed in front of him and lurched in his chair. "Jesus. The bastards have just thrown thirty-three bodies overboard." He looked up at the lieutenant who'd delivered the message. "Tell the observation ship to move in as soon as possible and do everything in its power to recover those bodies. We need positive IDs, causes of death and, for God's sake, decent burials for them."

The aide nodded but didn't leave the room. "There's another problem, sir. As of now, all the male passengers and crew members have been transferred from the Japanese cargo vessel that picked them up to the *U.S.S. Theodore Roosevelt* aircraft carrier. The Rosie's crew is asking for directions on where to put the victims ashore."

Aleesha blinked. That was fast. The *U.S.S. Theodore Roosevelt* was an aircraft carrier based out of Norfolk. It must have already been cruising off the Atlantic coast to have sailed into the area so quickly. It would have a SEAL contingent aboard, plus a sizable Marine Recon Force. The Special Forces assets available for this situation had just doubled.

Wittenauer leaned forward abruptly. "*All* of the male passengers and crew are in one place, you say?"

"Yes, sir."

"Tell Admiral Kelso to keep them all on the *Roosevelt* until further notice."

"I beg your pardon?" the aide asked, startled.

"Tell the *Roosevelt* do not, under any circumstances, put them ashore yet. I don't care if the ship has to sail around in circles. I need it to stay at sea. Tell Kelso not to let any of the passengers talk to anyone ashore, either. No phone calls, no e-mails. I want a total communications blackout. And while you're at it, get me a comm line through to the captain of the Japanese vessel that picked up the lifeboats, pronto."

The aide hustled out of the room. Aleesha frowned. What was the general up to?

Within a matter of minutes, a phone rang on the conference table in front of Wittenauer. He picked it up right away. "Captain Yakamoto?" he said loudly. "General Wittenauer here. I wanted to call you personally to say thank you for rescuing those folks last night."

A pause while the container ship captain replied.

"Nonetheless," Wittenauer responded warmly. "Those people owe you their lives. And speaking of lives saved, I have one more favor to ask of you. We need to keep the problem aboard the *Grand Adventure* quiet for a couple of days. I need you and your crew not to tell *anyone* about what has happened. Not your friends and family, and certainly not the press. There are still hostages aboard the *Grand Adventure,* and for their safety, your silence is vital."

Another pause while Wittenauer listened to the captain. His shoulders visibly relaxed. The guy must have agreed.

"If it would help," Wittenauer offered, "I can arrange to have a U.S. Navy tender ship rendezvous with you at sea to refuel you and resupply you. On Uncle Sam's dime, of course," he added delicately. "It's the least we can do for you in return for keeping your ship at sea and your crew out of port for a few extra days."

Another short pause, during which, Wittenauer gestured through the glass window to a Navy chief manning a phone position. The general pointed at the telephone at his own ear and mouthed, "Make it happen."

The Navy man nodded. He'd make the arrangements for the container ship's resupply cum bribe.

Wittenauer set down the phone gently. "Let the shit start rolling," he muttered.

Vanessa quirked an eyebrow. "How's that, sir?"

Wittenauer sighed. "I just detained over a thousand people

aboard a U.S. naval vessel without asking for permission from a damned soul. If word of this gets out, my ass is going to be in a major sling."

Aleesha couldn't help but toss in lightly, "And that's why we love you, sir."

Everybody at the table grinned. The general had just put his career on the line to buy them a window of noninterference. He also might have saved a ton of lives by sticking his neck out like that.

"How's jurisdiction on the op coming, sir?" Lipton asked.

"I've got my best man on it. No word yet, though."

Aleesha caught the faint blush that jumped into Vanessa's cheeks. Jack Scatalone must be working the Washington, D.C., end of things. A good man, Lieutenant Colonel Scatalone. He, too, had put his career on the line. His sacrifice had given the Medusas a chance to prove themselves and earn a place in the Special Ops community. Besides that, he made Vanessa happy. The two of them were good for each other. Too bad he couldn't be here to fight for the Medusas' right to board that ship. He was a take-no-prisoners kind of guy, and would fight like a tiger for his girls, as he was fond of calling them. But the very fact that the Medusas were here and briefed was a clear statement that Wittenauer was considering using the Medusas.

Aleesha sighed and leaned forward. Time to take a page out of Scat's playbook. "Look, gentlemen. We can argue all day and all night, and nothing's going to change. Let's cut to the chase. The Medusas are here. We're briefed in on the mission. We have enough skill to get aboard the ship. We know exactly what information to collect for Lieutenant Lipton and his men, and furthermore, we're women, just like the hostages. Lives are on the line, here. We don't have time to pull in more experienced female agents from wherever they happen to be, brief them, and teach them how to do forward combat observation. You're stuck with us. The Medusas are all you've got. So let's quit wasting time and get busy planning the damn op."

She looked Wittenauer dead in the eye, daring him to dispute her.

He replied slowly, "I need you ladies to be square with me. No repercussions to your answer, but I need the God's honest truth out of you. Understood?"

She nodded and caught the nods of her teammates out of the corner of her eye.

"One of the reasons I supported the formation of your team is that you're all women. Every now and then situations arise where females can accomplish a mission that men could not. This is one of them. It's why I briefed you on this in the first place. You've heard some of what you'd be up against, you've heard what the experts have to say about this op. My question for all of you is this—are you trained enough to pull it off? Are the Medusas ready for this job or not?"

Chapter 7

Aleesha stared at him in dismay. Wittenauer's question pierced her like an arrow to the heart. *Was* she capable of this mission? Could she potentially kill terrorists—Americans—in the name of rescuing children and/or stopping whatever else the hijackers had planned? In the medical field, every patient was treated the same, pauper or prince, criminal or victim. She never asked where the injury came from. Hers was only to do her best to save lives. Could she choose who was worthy to live and who was not?

Next to her, Vanessa snorted soundly, announcing in derision, "Of course we're ready. We've trained for months, and this is exactly the sort of mission the Medusas were created to do. We can get aboard that ship and blend in with the female passengers, whereas a male team would be shot on sight."

Wittenauer eyed Vanessa narrowly, clearly measuring the truth behind the bravado.

Of course Vanessa was right. Physically they were ready. They'd trained their butts off. While they had practically no operational experience at forward surveillance, their training had been as realistic as possible and they'd taken it seriously. They *could* handle this mission. After all, it wasn't as if they'd have to take the ship back. They would only be the eyes and ears for the SEAL rescue team.

Vanessa leaned forward aggressively, and Aleesha was startled by her boss's leashed intensity. "You need us, sir. Don't even *think* about keeping us out of this op. We are the *only ones* who can get onto that ship and provide you with continuous, real-time, eyes-on-target surveillance, and you know it."

Wittenauer nodded, then stabbed at a spot on the map in the eastern Caribbean. "Latest satellite pass puts the *Grand Adventure* here. Hails on all radio frequencies are still being met with silence. Whoever's got her doesn't want to talk yet."

Bud Lipton interjected from down the table, "Probably still busy securing the ship. That's a whole lot of real estate to clear."

Wittenauer nodded again. "We just got the passenger manifest from the company and we're looking at 875 adult female passengers and 515 children, plus 180 female crew members still aboard the ship."

Aleesha shuddered. Dang, that was a lot of hostages. The good news was that it wouldn't be hard to know who to shoot. If it was male, kill it.

One of the intelligence briefers sitting in the front corner of the room spoke up. "According to the passengers, one of the hijackers spoke over the PA with a British accent. Another one was reported to have a Spanish accent and a third perhaps a French accent. Since the passengers and crew were immediately separated into different groups, we're unable to nail down exactly how many terrorists there are. Best guess right now says between sixteen and twenty. They're mostly Caucasian, although at least three are described as olive-skinned or dark-complected, which could indicate Hispanic, Mediterranean or Middle-Eastern descent."

"Anything more on their weapons?" Lipton asked.

The intelligence analyst glanced down at his notes. "Semiautomatic machine guns. Mostly MP-5s based on the descriptions the passengers are giving. A couple people report seeing sidearms. Nothing heavier duty than that."

"And they took over a ship carrying more than three thousand people?" Lipton shook his head.

Wittenauer responded, "It's not what they had but what they did with it. They marched into a kids' area during a movie, pointed weapons at several hundred children and threatened to start shooting. The captain handed over the bridge without a fight."

Aleesha winced. She understood the captain's decision. He was responsible for the safety of every passenger. He couldn't be expected to sacrifice the lives of hundreds of kids to save his vessel. He'd done what he had to do, and he'd paid the ultimate price.

Wittenauer continued, "After they killed the crew, a British-sounding guy gave a pleasant speech to the effect that they had no interest in hurting anyone else. As long as everyone did exactly as directed, everything would be fine."

Aleesha frowned. Why would the hijackers display such utter disregard for life and then claim they didn't want to hurt anybody? Her gut feeling was that the hijackers hadn't revealed their true purpose yet. And until they did, it was impossible to guess how much danger the hostages were in.

Lipton leaned forward. "What do you need us to do?"

Aleesha didn't miss the underlying meaning to his question. He was asking for permission to board that ship and kill the bastards.

Wittenauer looked around the room grimly. "Right now we're still working on finalizing jurisdiction over this situation. However, I want you to start planning scenarios. Meanwhile, we sit tight and wait for orders and a green light."

"Who are the players involved so far?" Vanessa asked.

A sigh from Wittenauer. "The *Grand Adventure* is in international waters. The Dominican Republic is the nearest sovereign nation at the moment, although the hijacking itself took place near the Bahamas. The ship's registry is the British Virgin Islands, the crew comes from all over the damn place and the bulk of the passengers are American. Take your pick."

Aleesha rolled her eyes. What a mess. She didn't need years of experience in the Special Forces to know a political goat rope when she saw one.

Wittenauer ran a hand across his face, and Aleesha took a critical look at the bags under his eyes and the pasty quality of his skin. The guy probably had gotten no sleep at all last night. Not much help for it, though. Wittenauer's job was to fight for resources and elbow room so his teams could do their jobs. He could *have* all that political wrangling.

Viktor stood by the railing of the promenade deck, well forward of the spot where he'd picked up the first batch of weapons. He watched their supply boat pull alongside the *Grand Adventure* once more, this time to shuttle up several large bags of gear.

He refrained from looking up at the sky. There probably was a surveillance satellite up there already, looking down at the ship. No need to flash his face to the powers-that-be behind those high-resolution cameras. He was happy to hide behind the American contingent and their burning desire for fame. For now.

Two of the Montfort boys pulled up the heavy bags, and a few of the Americans hauled the weapons and equipment to their headquarters in Michael's suite.

With a quick wave to the men on the dinghy below, Viktor followed the last bag inside and upstairs to Deck 9 and the Irishman's suite. Michael was already inventorying the contents of the bags, checking everything against a typed list. An organized man, Michael. Methodical. Solid. The kind of man Viktor liked to have at his back. An excellent second in command.

Michael looked up from his clipboard and nodded tersely. "Everything's here. We're good to go."

Viktor nodded. "Good. Is the cell phone detector at hand?"

Michael reached into one of the bags and handed over a small box about six inches wide by twelve inches long and about three inches tall.

Viktor turned it on. An electronic display across the front lit up with bars of green and red lights that would flash whenever it picked up a cell phone signal nearby. The illegal gadgets had been invented by criminals intent on hijacking cell phone numbers. Viktor planned to use this one to check for any rogue cell phones that hadn't been turned in earlier. He expected there'd be a few.

Cluttered now with piles of weapons, ammunitions, explosives, suits of body armor and anything else they'd anticipated a need for, the suite felt claustrophobic. He stepped into the hall with the cell signal detector. All of a sudden a stroll around his ship sounded appealing. To survey the kingdom, as it were. And of course to nail anyone who'd disobeyed his orders and was trying to call for help.

To their credit the SEALs didn't seem the least bit bothered by brainstorming with a bunch of women operators. The discussion got heated as plans were hashed out, revised and occasionally discarded. But it was never about gender. The men were happy to consider the Medusas' contribution.

Gradually as the day progressed, a plan took shape. The Medusas would sneak aboard with radios, parabolic microphones, spy cameras, microtransmitters and, of course, weapons and ammunition. They'd hide until they could make contact with some of the crew. Once they knew how the hijackers were managing the bulk of the passengers, if possible, the Medusas would find a way to join the hostages and blend in.

The worst-case scenario would be if the hijackers were holding all the passengers in one location. Then the Medusas would have to rely on straight stealth to hide and observe. The best-case scenario would be for the children to be in one spot, which would make them much easier to rescue, while the other passengers and crew were free to move around the ship to, say, eat. The SEALs and Medusas planned for both, along with a dozen scenarios in between.

Late in the afternoon a schematic of the *Grand Adventure* was finally delivered by courier and rushed to the planning room. The decks were assigned letters, A for Deck 1, B for Deck 2, C for Deck 3, etc. from the bottom of the ship up. Then the ship was split into ten sections from front to back, one being the nose of the ship, and ten being the very back. Once the Medusas had made radio contact with the SEALs via a super-secure frequency, the SEALs would act as their plotters in the TOC, the Tactical Operations Center. The Medusas would report sightings of the terrorists and hostages by deck and section. For example, an armed hijacker patrolling the promenade deck at the back of the ship would be reported as "One Tango pulling guard duty at E10."

A three-dimensional model of the ship was already under construction, and by midnight tonight, the SEAL plotters would place tiny figurines of Tangos, along with adult females and children, in their exact locations around the ship as the Medusas reported them. A 3-D computer model of the data would also be plotted in real time. While the high-tech approach had more cool factor, at the end of the day, many counterterrorism teams preferred the old method of scale models and tiny human figures to help them mentally prepare for what the rescue mission would look like.

Priority number one for the Medusas was to locate the children. Priority number two was to scope out the number of hijackers, how well they were armed and where they were arrayed. Additionally, the Medusas would be responsible for learning the ship's routine, assessing how competent the hijackers were and finding any holes in the Tangos' procedures that could be exploited. And third, Wittenauer's bosses—as high up the food chain as the White House itself—were screaming about finding out who the hell these folks were. It would be the Medusas' job to answer that, as well.

If they got the green light for this mission, the Medusas were going to be busy campers aboard the ship.

* * *

Jack bit back a curse and thought better of flinging his pen across the table. The Brits were insisting on participating in any rescue operation aboard the *Grand Adventure*. It was an election year in England, and the prime minister wanted the publicity. The guy was being flat pigheaded. But the U.S. had the Medusas and the British didn't. Thankfully, Stanforth hadn't wavered in his promise to keep their existence secret, despite Britain's intransigence.

President Stanforth looked only slightly less exasperated than Jack felt, but he sounded perfectly calm over the speaker phone. "Edward, I understand your concern about a British ship being boarded by Americans. But we have to think about the children, here. The ship is right off my coast, I've got an aircraft carrier twenty-four hours away and numerous other Navy assets already in the area, and I've got CT teams in place and ready to go right now."

Jack kept his facial expression neutral at that whopper. No counterterrorism team would dream of moving on the *Grand Adventure* without a hell of a lot more information than was currently available. But what the British politician didn't know wouldn't hurt him. The existence of the Medusas was a closely guarded secret and it needed to stay that way. Only a handful of operators, JSOC's senior staff, and the president himself knew about the snake ladies. Stanforth couldn't reveal to the Brits why it was vital that the Americans run this op.

Of course, it wasn't a done deal that the Medusas would be used. General Wittenauer was worried that the women didn't have enough field experience. Jack scowled down at the glossy conference table. They could pull it off. He *knew* them. They had the heart for it. Once they decided to do something, everyone and everything had better get out of their way. They attacked problems as fiercely as any operators he'd ever met.

One step at a time. First, he had to get this roomful of politicians and the corresponding roomful of politicians in London to agree to hand the op over to JSOC.

Stanforth leaned forward and punched the button to disconnected the call. "Jesus H. Christ, those people can be stubborn," he snapped, in a rare display of frustration. "No wonder we declared independence from them."

"And why are *you* being so stubborn, Mr. President?" the Secretary of State asked dryly.

"Because I'm right. We've got the best chance of getting all those people off that ship alive."

"The Brits have highly competent Special Forces of their own," the Secretary responded.

Stanforth looked down the table at Jack. Was that look a request to tell about the Medusas or was the president just punting the question to him? God, he hated political maneuvering. It was like wrestling with water.

Jack spoke carefully. "The Brits are good. No doubt about it. But the simple fact is, we're the best suited for this situation. The Americans are in the best position to collect the intelligence that a raid on the ship will require. Also, the boarding force may need to be very large. If the hijackers disperse throughout the ship, we're looking at clearing over a thousand rooms with something like fifteen hundred hostages scattered among them. The coordination necessary on an op this size is mind-boggling. The last thing we need is confusion caused by trying to coordinate British and American forces who've never trained together for a scenario even remotely like this."

Truth be told, the Americans, even working alone, had never trained a rescue on this scale. But his point was valid. This op was going to be incredibly difficult to pull off. But he sure as hell wasn't about to tell this roomful of Nervous Nellies that. Wittenauer had made it crystal clear that Jack was to make sure control of the op got handed off to JSOC, and JSOC alone.

The Medusas and the SEALs boarded choppers at midnight. They would fly out to a U.S. Navy tender ship currently steaming west out of the U.S. Virgin Islands toward the last-known location of the *Grand Adventure*. Tenders were basically floating convenience stores, delivering fuel, water, food, mail and a host of other supplies to naval vessels. But more to the point, tenders also had helicopter pads and could launch a fast boat holding a half-dozen operators and their gear.

With their gear crammed in all around them and some turbulence, the flight was uncomfortable for the Medusas. Tropical Storm Evangeline had spun west off the Cape Verde coast of Africa a few days back, and the leading edge of it was tickling the eastern Caribbean. Forecasters gave it a fifty-fifty chance of turning into a hurricane in another four to five days as it hit the warm, shallow waters of the western Caribbean. Another reason to get aboard the *Grand Adventure* now and get this situation resolved.

Vanessa was miserably sick the whole flight, but Aleesha had laid in a huge supply of Dramamine and airsickness sacks, and Vanessa wasn't close to filling the sacks yet. The good news was the motion sickness pills she'd prescribed for her boss the minute it looked like they might actually end up boarding the ship were beginning to mitigate the worst of her reaction to the bumpy flight. The bad news was Vanessa had to jump out of the pan and into the fire by stepping onto the gently rolling deck of the tender ship.

Aleesha *tsk*ed her sympathy. If only she had access to grandmama's herb garden back home, she could whip up a remedy that would knock out Vanessa's upset stomach *toute suite*. As it was, all she could do was pat Viper's heaving shoulder and hold her hair out of her face as she emptied her already-empty stomach.

"Give it a few hours," Aleesha said in her soothing doctor voice. "Those pills will kick in and you'll feel right as rain."

Vanessa threw her a bleary glare. "I damned well hope so," she croaked before she yanked a fresh airsickness bag out of Aleesha's hands.

"Hey, look at it this way. Morning sickness is going to be a piece of cake after this." Aleesha grinned.

Vanessa straightened abruptly, equal parts horrified and indignant. "Perish the thought. Can you just imagine Jack as a father? Good Lord, he'd bark orders and bully his children to death."

Aleesha shrugged wisely. "You never know. He might turn out to be a big, cuddly, teddy-bear pushover."

That put a speculative look on Viper's face. Until Vanessa bent over double and let Aleesha shove yet another sack under her. It was a hell of a way to start a mission. She didn't envy her boss one bit. Aloud she commented, "With your luck, we'll get green lighted while you still have your pretty little head stuck in a toilet."

Sure enough, the call came a couple of hours later, just as their fearless leader heaved up the dry crackers she'd choked down at Aleesha's insistence. As Vanessa shoved resolutely to her feet, she glared at Aleesha. "You've got to cut out that voodoo prediction stuff, especially when it foretells this kind of misery for me."

Aleesha shrugged, grinning. "If it keeps you alive, I'm going to go right on listening to my intuitions. Take another two pills, and I promise, this will be the dose that makes you feel human again."

She handed her boss a pair of small tablets, significantly more concentrated than was available, even with a prescription, in retail pharmacies. These suckers would shut down an elephant's digestive tract. Vanessa's motion sickness didn't stand a chance. She hoped. Every single Medusa would have to be firing on all cylinders for them to get aboard the *Grand Adventure* safely and undetected.

Chapter 8

No doubt about it, Jack was impressed with Stanforth's negotiating acumen. The Brits, particularly the prime minister, were beyond cranky at the idea of backing off from this op. The PM could seriously use a military crisis and its successful resolution to help him in the polls. Stanforth was implacable, however, and stuck doggedly to his guns until the Brits finally gave in. What tipped the scales was the presence of the *Teddy Roosevelt* carrier just north of the Bahamas. The Brits knew when they were outgunned, and a full-blown carrier group—complete with frigates, destroyers and various support ships—already on scene was more than they could match any time in the next week. Nonetheless, some English noses were seriously out of joint, in spite of how deftly diplomatic Stanforth had been.

The conference call was disconnected. The president leaned back in his chair and looked at Jack from down the table. "Well, you've probably fouled up next month's G8 economic conference all to hell, but you got what you wanted. Full American control of this crisis. Satisfied?"

Jeez. When the guy put it that way, it felt like the weight of the world had just landed on his shoulders. But it wasn't as if he hadn't carried the responsibility for saving lives before. Although, five hundred kids and a thousand women was a hell of a lot of lives.

"Yes, Mr. President. I'm satisfied," he answered soberly. "Now all I need from you is the go-ahead to take back the *Grand Adventure.*"

"Not so fast, young man," the secretary of state said from the president's end of the table. "You can't just go charging in there without a clear statement of goals and operational parameters."

Jesus H. Christ. Here it came. The political interference that always screwed these things up completely. He ought to tell them to take their goals and parameters and stuff them, but he was only a lousy lieutenant colonel with no clout to back up his big words. Common sense said to suck it up and keep his mouth shut. Except he'd been the guy out in the field before, bent over and screwed hard by these very men. He couldn't stand by and let it happen to some other Special Forces team, not if he was sitting right here and could stop the clusterfuck.

Jack swung his gaze to the secretary of state and said politely, "What sort of parameters did you have in mind, *sir*?" He couldn't help the extra emphasis. It just came out.

The secretary puffed up importantly. "There's a lot of potential for foreign nationals to get hurt or killed. We have to be careful in how we accomplish this mission."

Ya think? "By all means, sir. Why don't you tell me exactly how you'd go about taking over that ship and rescuing all those people. I'll pass it right on to the operatives who actually put their asses on the line. I'm sure they'll be more than happy to do it your way."

The guy bristled and Stanforth intervened mildly. "There's no need to be sarcastic, Jack."

Jack sighed and turned to the president. "I'm sorry. It's just that a hell of a lot of innocent lives are riding on this discussion. With all due respect, sir, the more parameters and limits you folks put on the op, the more likely people are to die. This is what we train for every single day. We know how to do our job. I didn't interfere when you were dealing with the British prime minister—being a politician is *your* job, and you did it masterfully. Tell us you want the hostages rescued and the ship freed, and then stand back and let us do *our* job the best and safest way it can be done."

He bit off any further pleas. He wouldn't beg in front of these men. He shouldn't have to. Damn it all, Hal Wittenauer could have this job!

The tension level in the room eased a bit, and Stanforth nodded. "Well said, Jack. And, unless anyone has any further comments or objections, you've got your green light. Go save those women and children the best and safest way it can be done."

Jack nodded and replied crisply, "Yes, sir."

At the president's nod of dismissal, Jack closed his briefcase and stood up to leave the table. As a Secret Service agent showed him out of the room, it didn't escape him that the president had assiduously avoided the topic of minimizing the use of force. Lord knew, *he* wasn't about to bring up the subject. He wanted his spec ops teams to have the freedom to do whatever was necessary to save the innocents and take back the ship from the hijackers. Including blowing the terrorist bastards to kingdom come.

Stanforth's silence was all about plausible deniability. If the president never gave the order to kill the bad guys and never discussed the issue, then his hands would be clean if someone complained later about the hijackers getting waxed. For it was inevitable that Tangos would die before this was all said and done.

Viktor stepped into the kids' adventure area and had a quick look around. The children's staff looked harried, and the general tone in the room was one of whining. A few of the ship's crew were clearing away the remains of supper, and the older kids were in the midst of getting out mattresses and spreading them on the floor in preparation for the curfew he'd imposed. Everyone went into lockdown in their cabins at eight o'clock. Nobody was allowed out of her room after eight. The arrangement let his team get some rest, and it cut down on the potential for the hostages to put their heads together and come up with any stupid ideas.

It would've been easier to stuff all the hostages in a big room and put a few armed guards on them, but Michael had made it clear that such a plan would make a rescue by commandos that much easier. Better that any rescuers face the prospect of having to clear a thousand rooms, rather than having a single location to assault and liberate. He would've liked to have spread the kids all over the ship, too, but he just didn't have the manpower to pull that off. Besides, what were a bunch of terrified mothers going to try with guns pointed at their kids? They knew better by now than to mess with him.

One of the kids' staff members looked at him pointedly as though she wanted to ask him something, but as his cold gaze locked with hers, she looked down and moved away, clearly thinking better of it. Smart girl. The kids had decent food, clean water and working toilets. That was more than he'd had growing up.

Everything had been a struggle when he was a kid. His mother struggled to scrounge up the next meal for her family as his father drank away what little money she earned. God, Viktor had hated his mountainous home. It was too remote, too damned cold, too forbidding. He'd wanted out so bad he could taste it. Only after he'd been gone from his homeland for a decade or more had the itch to return finally caught up with him. But by then he'd been a wanted man living in semi-hiding in America. An outcast. A stranger in a strange land with no country to call his own. And that's when the rugged beauty of the Pyrenees and the indomitable spirit of the Basque people began to call to him, when the dream of freeing *Le Pays Basque* had really captured his soul.

These kids on the ship could just shut up and be happy with what they had, the spoiled brats.

Aleesha supervised one last inventory of the gear piled in the middle of the supply locker. Standard complement of weapons, ammunition and explosives. Spare batteries for the radios—of which there were several state-of-the-art models to circumvent detection by the hijackers. A full surveillance kit with its parabolic mikes, telescopic sights, bugs and various electronic surveillance doodads. And then there was the miscellaneous stuff they'd need—food for a week, med kits and tool kits. Incongruous in the high-tech military gear was a pile of brightly colored, cruise-wear clothing: tropical beach print shirts and shorts, halter tops, bikinis, sweatshirts and even a couple of cocktail dresses. The Medusas had been helicoptered to the nearest inhabited island for a grand total of fifteen minutes earlier that afternoon to stock up on the civilian clothes they'd need to mingle with the passengers and observe the hijackers. She'd never shopped so fast in her life. They'd just grabbed the first stuff in the right size, charged it and run.

Hard to believe that they were actually going to do this. Adrenaline trickled through her system in spite of her best efforts to stay calm, and she felt jittery and on edge. But, given the importance of this op, she was probably entitled to a case of nerves.

"How are we looking, Mamba?" Vanessa asked from behind her, all business.

"Good to go," she replied. "It should take about ten minutes to pack this stuff into the waterproof bags the SEALs gave us, and then we'll be ready."

"Let's get it all bagged up, then."

The six women went to work in silence. Aleesha glanced up from the med kit she'd just stowed in an oversize gear bag. Her teammates were moving a tad jerkily. Wired. But they also radiated quiet confidence. A hell of a group of brave women. She was proud to be one of them.

Vanessa glanced around at the team. "Anybody feel in need of a pep talk?"

Karen, the tall Marine, replied, "Nah, we know what we've got to do. It's just another day at the office. No biggie."

No biggie, indeed. Every one of these women had spent most of their lives working toward this moment. Their first official op as bona fide members of the Special Forces. Aleesha grinned and retorted, "Speak for yourself, girlfriend. I've never been on a cruise before, and I'm looking forward to working on my tan."

Karen laughed aloud. "Wouldn't that just toast Bud Lipton's muffins if we ended up lying around in the sun by the pool, sipping piña coladas while making position calls?"

Aleesha's grin widened. The guy would have a stroke. "Now what?" she asked as she zipped up the last bag.

Vanessa shrugged. "Now we suit up and wait for the final green light. Everybody get what rest you can."

Aleesha reached for another gift from the SEALs—a high-tech wet suit that was waterproof when exposed to moisture, but breathed like fabric when dry. It was a dull-gray color and felt like little more than a Spandex bodysuit against her skin. A *very* good toy indeed. She finished shimmying into her suit and sat down next to a gear bag to make herself comfortable.

She watched Vanessa keenly as her boss stretched out and leaned back against one of the gear bags. "How are you feeling, Viper? Any more queasiness?"

"Shockingly enough, I feel great. Those little pills of yours are magic."

They *were* a great invention—an experimental drug that Uncle Sam had invented recently. They took about twelve hours to work fully into a person's system, but once there, they defied anyone to get seasick. Aleesha had given them to the whole team, including herself, to take through the day in preparation for tonight's fun. They couldn't afford to have any of the team go down on this op. They'd be spread preciously thin as it was, trying to observe an entire ship with just the six of them.

The one drawback of her wet suit was that it had no insulation value when dry. The steel floor beneath her rear end was as cold as ice and she started shivering in a matter of minutes. At least the gear bag she leaned on kept her upper body a tiny bit warmer. Over the last month of training, she'd gained a rich understanding of the effects of hypothermia on the human body and how to manage those effects. Right now she might be cold, but she was far from dangerously chilled. Thanks to the SEALs, she knew exactly what *that* felt like.

She let the barely discernable roll of the deck soothe her into a semiconscious state. She used to lie on the deck of her father's boat like this while the tourists tried their hand at sport fishing. It had been a good life, even though they hadn't had much. Food had been tight, especially when the fishing was bad, and there was never extra money for luxuries like new clothes. She'd spent her childhood wearing haute Goodwill couture. But there had always been the grandeur of the ocean nearby, the beauty of blue skies and emerald forests beyond the squalor of the slums. Besides, the poverty of her youth had given her drive, an ambition to better her circumstances that she might not have otherwise had.

She started when Vanessa's cell phone rang a few feet away, the sound hurling Aleesha into full consciousness before the first ring even ended. She sat up and watched her boss take the call.

"Blake here."

A pause.

"Hi, Jack. Yup, we're ready to go. Dozing on our gear bags in our wet suits."

Another pause.

"Roger. Will do. You, too. Bye."

Aleesha looked at her boss expectantly.

Vanessa said, "We're green-lighted. Jack says to be careful and have fun."

Fun, indeed. Aleesha grinned along with the others. Count on the man who'd trained them to know they could use a moment of comic relief to break up the prelaunch tension.

A seaman walked toward them quickly, looking self-important. He stopped in front of Vanessa and announced, "Your orders just came in. Helicopter's cranking up on the deck right now. We're ready to go if you are."

The women jumped to their feet and hefted the gear bags onto their backs. Aleesha's bag weighed roughly ninety pounds. As she settled its straps on her shoulders, she was grateful for the grueling hikes Jack had put them through carrying sixty- and seventy-pound packs on a regular basis. The good news was they didn't have to go far with these babies. Just up one level to the flight deck.

When they got there, a helicopter was indeed waiting for them. They climbed into the guppy-fat Huey, wedging themselves in between their gear and the bulky bundle that was the inflatable Zodiac they'd use to approach the ship. A crewman on deck gave them a thumb's-up and slid the door shut. Seconds later, the helicopter lifted off, jumping into the air like a young hawk eager to test its wings. Sort of like the Medusas themselves, untried, but antsy to get on with it.

Here went nothing. Or everything.

The Huey climbed up several thousand feet in the air for the first part of the flight. The mission profile called for it to drop down to wavetop level as they got within radar range of the *Grand Adventure*. It wasn't likely that the cruise ship would have its radar set high enough to paint aircraft, but they weren't taking any chances and would come in completely under it. The helicopter would drop them off a ways away from the ship—well out of visual range—and then the Medusas would motor to the ship on the Zodiac.

The helicopter swooped low all of a sudden, plummeting toward the ocean like a rock. Aleesha's stomach floated up around her throat somewhere, and she cast a concerned glance at her boss.

Vanessa yelled back over the thwocking of the rotor blades, "It's okay. I love roller coasters."

Dang, those pills really were amazing if Vanessa wasn't barfing her guts out on this thrill ride. Aleesha nodded and tried to enjoy the ride as the helicopter dropped right down to the surface of the ocean and skimmed over the waves. She glanced out the tiny window set high in the door and looked away fast as she saw a wave practically level with her eyes. How they weren't catching a skid in the water and cartwheeling to their watery deaths, she had no idea.

She glanced over at Misty, the Medusa's token pilot. She had a beatific smile on her face as if this wild ride were nearly better than sex. Well, if the pilot among them wasn't worried, things must be okay, then. But the contents of Aleesha's stomach continued to hover uncomfortably near the back of her throat.

The sound of the rotors changed pitch, deepening and slowing to a more rhythmic *thwock-thwock-thwock* above their heads. One of the pilots leaned back and motioned for them to open the door. The helicopter had been too full with them and all their gear to allow for a crewman in the back, so they'd have to launch themselves into the water. Good thing the Army had trained them on that very maneuver. Funny how little things like that became a big deal in the field. Over the decades of its existence, the Delta Force had accumulated a detailed list of oddball training items that had come in handy on past missions. Although it took years to get properly trained in every skill, the Medusas had made a good start on the major skill sets already.

Karen slid open the side door and clipped the long line attached to their folded-up boat to the skid just outside. Isabella, Kat and Aleesha pushed the Zodiac out the door while Misty yanked the cord that detonated its compressed air tanks and inflated it. In seconds, a fully formed rubber dinghy, with a powerful outboard motor attached, bobbed in the rotor downwash outside.

Karen jumped into the water beside the boat, then climbed into it. She took the bags of gear as they were passed down to her on ropes. Then, one by one, the other women climbed out of the helicopter, balanced for a second on the skid, and jumped into the water. Finally it was Aleesha's turn. She balanced carefully on the slippery skid as the rotor wash pummeled her worse than any hurricane she'd ever experienced. She slid the door closed behind her and latched it shut. She thumped her fist twice on the copilot's window and then she jumped.

The ocean out here was viciously cold, unlike the warm coastal waters she was used to diving in. The helicopter above churned the waves into a seething cauldron, and it was hard to tell which way was up. How rich would that be if the Medusa's divemaster drowned herself on her first operational water jump? She peered at the frothing bubbles around her and figured out which direction the majority of them were traveling. Following their dubious trail, she saw light just as she burst onto the surface of the water. She turned her head aside as the Huey peeled away, spraying her with icy needles of water in a two-hundred-mile-per-hour downwash.

"Over here," she heard Karen call behind her.

She turned and swam to the boat in the now much calmer water. She flopped aboard the Zodiac and pulled off her face mask and fins. Well, that was fun. And the good times were just getting started. She sat up, coughed out the seawater she'd inhaled, and crawled on her knees to the motor. With a sharp tug on its starter line, the engine turned over, purring quietly and powerfully.

This Zodiac rode lower in the water than she was used to, a combination of their heavy gear and this being a new design with an even lower radar profile than the model they'd trained on. She pointed its prow to the west and squinted into the white-orange ball of fire shimmering on the horizon.

The last fiery remnants of the sunset faded into a mauve-tinted dusk. Darkness fell quickly once the sun slid behind the flat rim of the ocean, and night abruptly wrapped, thick and impenetrable, around them. They were running blacked out, and the world narrowed down to the next swell lifting them gently and setting them back down. They had about a thirty-mile gap to close before reaching the ship, which was running south across their current course. The plan was to take a couple of hours to catch the *Grand Adventure*. They didn't want to board her much before midnight, when the ship's passengers would be out of the way if the infiltration went badly. They'd had to make the helicopter drop before dark, though, because the only pilots at hand on the tender ship weren't trained in Special Operations and couldn't chance running at watertop level at night.

Navigating via a handheld global positioning unit, Aleesha more or less homed in on the *Grand Adventure's* position. They cruised along for about a half hour, and then she pulled the radio out of her wet suit and put the earpiece in her ear. She transmitted a single beep on the preset frequency and then waited.

And waited. What was taking Bud so long to clear the frequency? She needed to get an updated position fix on the *Grand Adventure*. As big as it was, a cruise ship was a tiny speck in comparison to the expanse of water out here. It would be a bear to find her without current location information. Especially if she happened to change course again. Throughout the day, the *Grand Adventure* had made several course changes, sailing more or less in a giant circle and keeping the Navy hopping to stay out of its way and out of its radar range. Finally, two beeps came back. The frequency was clear and usable. Thank God.

She replied, "Hey, Boudreaux. It's me. Wha' appun, dude?" They'd agreed to keep their transmissions completely nonmilitary in case the terrorists had sophisticated radio frequency scanners with them. Once the Medusas got aboard, they'd be able to scan for such receivers and eliminate the possibility of the hijackers possessing sophisticated radios like theirs. But until then, she and Bud were stuck talking jive.

"Chillin' out, hot stuff. What's happenin' wit' you?" came back Bud's drawled reply. "Hot stuff?" He must think he was really funny.

"Pinin' for ya, babycakes," she shot back. "Where you be, anyhow?"

"Guess. I'm about five minutes from you."

The *Grand Adventure* had adjusted its course by five degrees, then. "Gimme a hint," she cajoled.

"Down by de beach," he replied.

Beach was their code word for west. Five degrees west. Aleesha squealed in outrage. "If you shackin' up at Janelle's flop, I'll kill you, I swear!"

Bud laughed, although the poor guy sounded taken aback. "With a firecracker like you hanging around, I'm too worn out to mess with Janelle."

"You better be telling me the truth," she warned. "If I fin' out you cockin' up dat bumboclot basement gal, I'll Bobbittize you into a chi-chi boy."

Now Bud really sounded back on his heels. "Me not dat horny nor stupid, baby. Run along now. And don't you check up on me. Makes me look henpecked."

"Henpeck this," she retorted, and then she signed off. She adjusted her heading and pressed onward into the night.

Misty asked casually, "What's a chi-chi boy?"

Aleesha shrugged. "It's Jamaican slang for a gay man."

Her teammates grinned while the evening's silence settled around them, interrupted only by the low roar of the boat's engine.

The temperature dropped gradually, but after a couple of hours of drenching salt spray and the thirty-knot breeze of their passage, she was getting damned uncomfortable. More of that lovely seventy-five-percent-boring action.

Every thirty minutes or so, she made a radio call to the TOC aboard the *Roosevelt* and her fake boyfriend Bud, aka Babycakes. Lipton alternately called her Sugar Mama, Chocolate Heaven, and her personal favorite, Pussycat—said with just enough R-rated innuendo to set her teeth on edge. He must think it was hilarious to call a Harvard-educated physician and trained killer "Lovemuffin." She vowed to herself that the next time she saw him, she'd seriously make him pay.

The *Grand Adventure* turned due west a little before midnight, which slowed its forward speed by a couple of knots as it headed into a stiff breeze. Tropical Storm Evangeline was in the air. As a native islander, she felt it in the heavy humidity and rapid pressure drop and in the ominous gusts of wind kicking up the very swells that disguised their approach to the ship. In a few more days, nobody would want to be out on this stretch of ocean in any vessel smaller than a jumbo cruise ship.

A few minutes before 1:00 a.m., Kat spoke up from where she lay on the bulging rubber prow of the boat taking a turn at spotting. "I've got a light on the horizon."

Aleesha waited until the next swell lifted them high and looked where Kat pointed. Sure enough, a bright speck of light blinked at them. It could have been a star were it not sitting right on the horizon. She remarked, "Based on the last position report I got from Bud, that should be the *Grand Adventure*."

Everyone was abruptly alert.

Vanessa ordered quietly, "You know what to do, Aleesha."

The problem was how to approach a speeding cruise ship without using a noisy engine to catch it. As quiet as the Zodiac's muffled motor was, it could still attract the attention of someone standing on deck. Enter the grappling hook and rope coiled by her feet. Aleesha continued running toward the ship until it grew into a ship-shaped silhouette, several miles away from their current position. Then she turned to the left, paralleling the ship's course at a range of about three miles.

When the ship was behind them, in roughly their five o'clock position, Vanessa nodded. "Let's make the run, Mamba."

It was interesting how, whenever they went into danger, they all fell naturally into using their snake handles. It was almost as if Mamba was her work persona and Aleesha was some other person who scuba dived and liked to cook and led a normal life.

With a last look over her shoulder at the speeding ship, she cut the Zodiac hard right and opened up the throttle all the way. They started a high-speed run directly across the path of the oncoming ship. When they were in front of the ship, Vanessa flashed a hand signal at Karen, who was manning the pile of rope coiled on the floor of the boat. As they sped along, Karen dropped a specially made, plastic polymer grappling hook over the side of the dinghy. It floated on the surface of the water behind them.

Karen fed out the rope, which was securely tied to the hook. The lightweight, black nylon line lay on the surface of the ocean, nearly invisible. It made a hundred-foot long, inevitable slash across the *Grand Adventure's* path. When the ship hit the rope, the line would slide along its bow until the grappling hook snagged the sharp prow. Whatever was at the other end of the rope, namely their Zodiac, would be dragged beside the *Grand Adventure* like a piece of clinging seaweed.

Aleesha cut the throttle. The silence was deafening. They bobbed gently in the water, watching the mammoth ship grow bigger and bigger as it approached surprisingly quickly.

Karen checked the knots securing the floating line to four anchor points down the left side of the dinghy. The multiple knots would diffuse the tremendous strain on the Zodiac when the grappling hook caught and they went from floating still to twenty-five knots of forward speed in a single yank. Physics being what it was, the rope would swing them inward, toward the ship, in an arc at the end of the rope until the Zodiac was tucked close beside the ship's hull, moving at exactly the same speed as the ship.

Once they'd survived that maneuver and stabilized, they'd pull themselves forward or let themselves slide back along the rope until they were opposite the forward crew service hatch on the right side of the ship. They'd climb up to the hatch, about twelve feet above the water line and enter the ship from there. No sweat.

Except a dozen things could go wrong. The nylon rope could break. The grappling hook could fail to catch the ship's bow. The passage of the ship through the water could suck the Zodiac underneath the giant vessel and into its mighty diesel propellers. Or the hijackers could spot them or even their rope. And then, of course, there were the numerous perils of boarding the ship itself. But they'd cross that set of bridges when they got there.

The ship, rising a dozen stories above the water, bore down on them like a whale intent on swallowing Jonah. Aleesha fought the rudder to hold position barely five hundred feet from the path of the giant vessel as it sliced through the ocean toward them. It was moving as fast as a powerful speed boat might pull a water skier.

For all the world, it looked as if the prow of the ship was going to cut right through their flimsy dinghy. Concentrating fiercely on holding her ground and her nerve, she fixed her gaze on the vague outline of the rope, lying across the path of the oncoming behemoth. Just a couple hundred feet to go. A hundred.

"Hang on," she called to her teammates over the roar of the ship's grinding diesel engines.

The *Grand Adventure* ate up the last few feet of water. And hit the line dead-on. The rope went taut, and the Zodiac lurched forward as if it had been shot out of a cannon. She grunted as the back rim of the boat slammed into her rib cage, jerking her forward and snapping her head on her neck. And then the sideways swing began, as the rope trailed along the hull of the ship. That inward swing was surprisingly violent, and moments later she grunted again as the Zodiac hit the side of the ship and the rudder bar slammed into her right side.

The wild ride was over as quickly as it began. The Zodiac's course and speed stabilized quickly, and it rode along smoothly in the calm waters inside the big ship's wake.

"I'm stable back here," she reported quietly to Vanessa. "Clear to reposition."

Aleesha watched as the other five women grabbed the black rope tied to the dinghy and hauled on it with all their might. Hand over struggling hand, they pulled the craft forward against the current pulling at them. People always underestimated water, but she knew it to be one of the mightiest forces of nature.

Vanessa grunted at her. "Give me a position report relative to the hatch."

Aleesha shifted quickly to the right side of the rudder stick and leaned out over the right rim of the dinghy. The ship's black hull swelled outward in a graceful curve overhead, making it difficult to spot the thin outline of the hatch they sought.

The ship had two crew hatches through which the crew embarked and disembarked during ports of call. Both were on the second deck, only a dozen feet or so above the waterline, and more to the point, both had a small, surveillance camera–blind entryway directly inside each of them. It was through the starboard one of these hatches that they planned to gain entry to the ship. Because of the pervasive cameras throughout the *Grand Adventure,* they'd had to toss out easier methods of boarding like climbing over a railing onto a deck or dropping in by parasail from above.

Aleesha announced, "Got visual on it. Thirty feet or so forward of our current position."

She continued to give distance calls as the other women laboriously inched the Zodiac forward until it was about fifteen feet behind the hatch. They had to stop here because a security camera looked back along the forward portion of the ship's hull. But, the *Grand Adventure's* chief engineer had assured them this afternoon that this particular spot was camera blind. And she'd bet he'd be installing more cameras in his company's ships to fix that little oversight as soon as this fiasco was over.

Karen tied off the rope in preparation for the next step of this tricky operation.

Aleesha helped Kat, by far the smallest member of the team, don a set of rubber climbing cleats over her boots. Attached to each cleat was a dinner-plate-size suction cup positioned over the inside of her ankle. Then, Misty passed Kat a pair of fist-size handles with suction cups attached to each of them, as well. Aleesha didn't envy Kat the next part of the job. She got to free climb the outward sloping steel hull of the ship up to the hatch they'd use to board the *Grand Adventure.*

"Go get 'em, Spiderwoman," Aleesha encouraged her.

Kat smiled back jauntily. "I've always wanted to be a cat burglar. Tonight's my chance."

Aleesha held her breath as her teammate scaled the ship, hanging from the suction cups like a leech clinging tenaciously to the curving hull. Kat worked her way forward until she was well in front of the Zodiac's blunt prow. If Kat fell now, she'd hit the water just in time to be run over by her own teammates. A couple more pull-ups and foot plants later, Kat was parked beside the hatch. Aleesha breathed a sigh of relief.

Another tricky moment was upcoming. They had to open a one-foot square panel beside the main hatch to gain access to an electronic lock that opened the hatch from the outside—all without blowing up the locking mechanism itself. Aleesha leaned hard to the right in the dinghy, craning her neck to watch Kat plant a small shape charge. It was a fist-size cone of peppermint-pink putty, a low-order explosive that looked like a cheerful little unicorn horn stuck to the side of the hull. Perfect. Kat had put it exactly where Aleesha'd told her to, right over the latch that held the panel shut. She slapped a hand over her eyes as Kat jammed a detonator into the putty and mashed the button on the remote controller at her waist to set it off.

The pink cone blew up with a quiet thump, and when Aleesha uncovered her eyes to look up, the small access door hung open, still on its hinges. *Hah!* And Bud Lipton had been skeptical that they could blow the cover panel without damaging the keypad beneath. She hadn't been trained in explosive ordinance handling by Delta's best for nothing! Of course, the pad had yet to work.

She held her breath as Kat keyed in the override codes provided by the Adventure Cruise Line's chief engineer. A crack of light appeared around the edges of a man-size rectangle. Bingo. They were in! And now they had to move like lightning to get on the ship and away from that door before an alarm on the bridge called down an armed investigation to a suddenly and inexplicably open hatch.

While Aleesha manned the rudder to stabilize the dinghy, the others hauled the dinghy forward, positioning it directly under the hatch. Meanwhile, Kat muscled the hatch open and stepped inside, rapidly unfurling a rope ladder from her back. She hooked it over the raised lip of the hatch, and tossed it down. Vanessa caught the bottom of the ladder to steady it. Quickly the other women went up, straddling one of the rope supports between their thighs and inserting their feet on the rubber rungs from front and back as they climbed the side of the ladder. It was the only way to keep a rope ladder from swinging out from under a person if the bottom of the ladder wasn't tied down.

Aleesha would go last, cutting loose the Zodiac at the last possible moment. They wanted to leave themselves an escape route for as long as they could during this critical first stage. Vanessa stepped onto the ladder next to last, and it jerked with her quick movements as she disappeared into the darkness overhead.

Then it was Aleesha's turn. She shouldered her heavy pack and slung her MP-5 over that. The weapon was a light submachine gun that had become practically an extension of her arm in the last six months of training. Aleesha moved to the front of the Zodiac beside the rope ladder. The dinghy slid sideways ominously with nobody tending the tiller. She set her foot on the first rung, and the ladder swung away from her weight. Without anyone steadying the bottom, it was even more vital that she climb the side of it and not try to use it like a traditional wooden ladder. Clinging precariously, one foot on a slippery rung and her left hand grasping the wet rope, she leaned down. The heavy pack at her back nearly overset her balance, and she checked hard to keep herself from tumbling into the ocean.

Damn, that was close. A fall now could very well send her under the ship and kill her. Her field knife grasped tightly in her right hand, she leaned down again—carefully—and sawed at the rope attaching the Zodiac to the grappling hook.

Her scalpel-sharp blade bit through the wet nylon in just a few strokes, and the Zodiac leaped backward, abruptly free of the line dragging it forward. She ducked as the dinghy's nose skipped into the air and flipped over. She glanced over her shoulder in time to see it go under, caught in the pull of the ship's propellers. A shudder rippled down her spine at the sight. So much for any evidence of their boarding.

She looked up at the square of light above and climbed the slippery ladder as quickly as she could.

They were committed now. Their only escape route had just been shredded to ribbons. They were stranded on the *Grand Adventure* with a team of violent terrorists, fifteen hundred innocents, the equipment on their backs and the skills at their disposal.

Just another day in paradise.

Chapter 9

Hands reached down to help pull Aleesha up the last few feet, and, as she landed on her belly on the floor of the entranceway, Kat hauled in the rope ladder behind her and closed the hatch.

"Let's go," Vanessa signaled. Aleesha waited as her boss eased around the corner and sprinted to the first security camera. She reached up and covered the lens with her hand. As the rest of the team came up behind Vanessa, Karen leapfrogged ahead and blocked the next camera. They moved to the first crossing hallway and ducked into it, pausing for a moment in the camera's blind spot. They figured they had sixty seconds to move before anyone would spot them on the ship's cameras. Aleesha glanced at her watch. Twenty seconds left.

Vanessa poked a hand-held periscope around the corner and signaled that the coast was clear. They'd duck into the first available crew quarters and lay low for now. Vanessa pointed out the order of movement, and Aleesha fell into line last. Rear guard was a high-risk position, but somebody had to do it. Truth be told, there was no safe place for any of them right now.

The ship was warm after the sea spray and cold night air. She settled her MP-5 in the crook of her arm and prepared to cover their rear as they moved out fast, heading for their first and most crucial hide aboard the *Grand Adventure*.

When the forward hatch alarm went off, Inger Johannson reached over to turn it off and then told Michael it was nothing, merely a bell indicating a momentary drop in oil pressure in one of the engines. She pointed out one of the gauges and showed him how the oil pressure was already back to normal. He nodded as if he bought her explanation, hook, line and sinker.

Good girl. A plausible lie he could pass on to Viktor and the others if one of them had heard the alarm. The thing was, in preparation for this mission, he'd studied the workings of the *Grand Adventure's* bridge in excruciating detail, and he knew damn good and well that particular warning light and bell meant a hatch had opened. That could mean only one thing. *Someone had just boarded the ship.*

One of the American hijackers moved to the instrument panel beside Inger. "What was that noise?"

Michael shrugged. "You heard the woman. There was a momentary drop in oil pressure."

The guy swung around to glare at Inger. "What caused it?"

She gazed back at the American steadily while Michael held his breath. *C'mon, Inger. Keep your wits about you.*

The Norwegian woman answered, "An oil filter was probably momentarily blocked by something in the oil. It's not uncommon. The next time that engine is shut down, maintenance will need to check the filters."

Nicely done.

The American frowned. "That sounded like a hatch alarm to me."

Michael managed not to stare in dismay. Damn. The guy must have some naval training. Quickly, he feigned surprise at the

American's announcement. "Have you got a patrol out? By all means, send them to check all the hatches."

The American nodded and spoke tersely into his microphone.

Michael glanced down at the now silent alarm. Who had just come aboard? Damn, the reaction to the hijacking had been fast! Viktor wasn't expecting a response for at least another day. The Basque team leader had figured it would take at least a day of political wrangling to figure out who'd be in charge of the response, and another full day to get a team into position. Frankly, Michael had thought Viktor's assessment of the response time was on the fast side, but he'd lost that argument during one of their planning sessions.

How in the hell had anybody gotten a Special Forces team out here in a scant twenty-four hours? It was a truly impressive reaction time. He only hoped the team's skill was equally impressive.

Moving fast, but feigning casualness, he slipped into the security office to have a look at what was going on at that hatch. He sat down at the desk and punched the right buttons to call up the bank of cameras in that section of the ship. He scanned through the camera shots quickly, looking for the intruders. Nada. Whoever'd boarded the ship had moved too fast and gotten under cover before anyone could spot them. Thank God.

Where would he go if he were in their shoes? He'd probably duck into a crew cabin, make contact with the crew members and try to hide in the warren of back passages the crew used to service the ship.

For the next hour he hunched over the television screen intently, studying it urgently, praying for a glimpse of the rescuers, for some way to find them so he could make contact with them. But they were too good. They'd gone to ground.

"Hey, Mike! It's two o'clock. You can go catch some *zzz*'s now."

Michael jerked violently at the voice behind him. Paulo. One of the Basques. Quiet guy. Easy to overlook.

"Relax, man. No need to be so jumpy," Paulo said.

Michael forced the tension out of his body and a grin to his mouth. "Sorry. You startled me. Guess I'm a trifle on edge."

"Yeah, well, go get some rest. It'll help."

Crap. He couldn't go. Not yet. He turned away from the console and said with desperate calm, "There are a couple of things I want to check on before I leave. Why don't you go take a piss and get yourself a cup of coffee before you take over?"

Paulo grinned. "You sound like my mother, old man."

Michael winced. He was only thirty-eight. Too young to be acting like an old woman. He retorted, "Hey. I've lived to be an old man. Listen to the wisdom of your elders and never pass up a chance to piss."

Paulo laughed and backed out of the room. As soon as he disappeared, Michael turned back to the cameras. Dammit! As much as he wished it, there was no sign of whoever'd sneaked aboard. *He'd lost them.*

They'd made it. They'd lain low in an empty crew stateroom for the rest of the night, crammed into its tight confines and on high alert. Several patrols had rushed past for the first hour after they boarded the ship, but gradually the hijackers had calmed down. At 7:00 a.m. female crew members moved past their door. The Medusas changed into civilian clothes and packed the gear they'd be needing soon into canvas totes. They hid the rest of their equipment in the room's closets for now. They would come back for it later when the coast was clear.

Over the course of the next hour, they trickled out of their hiding place in ones and twos. Aleesha and Isabella made their way to another crew stateroom that had been carefully chosen for its proximity to certain electrical wiring they'd need to access for the next part of the op. That and the fact that both of its male occupants were currently aboard the *Teddy R.*

They'd dubbed this room Point Bravo. The other Medusas took up positions in rooms in each direction down the hall from it to act as lookouts.

Aleesha moved to the far wall of the room, tapping the metal plating gently with her knuckles, testing the thickness of the steel. She commented over her shoulder, "According to the blue-prints, the line we need should run right about here." She had a nifty little gadget that would cut a piece of the wall out nearly silently. She'd splice into the wire behind it and put the panel right back. Slick as a whistle. She pulled out the hand-held welding torch and touched her throat mike. "Standing by to proceed," she murmured.

Misty reported from her position in a room at the far end of the hallway, "All clear."

Vanessa came up on the headset and said, "All clear at this end. Go for it."

Aleesha warned Isabella, "Don't look at this torch once I fire it up. The light could damage your eyes."

Her teammate averted her eyes, and Aleesha slipped on a pair of welding goggles and fired up the torch. It was dicey to cut through the metal of the inner hull without slicing up the very wires she was trying to access. But it was no harder than cutting into human skin with a scalpel. She exhaled smoothly, settled into surgeon mode and went to work on her steel patient.

A couple of minutes later, she carefully lifted out a foot-long piece of hot steel and set it on the floor. She dug into her pack and pulled out the clips and wires she'd need to make the splice. It only took a few seconds to connect her duplicates and secure them with electrical tape. She unrolled the wire, routing it around the edge of the ceiling and caulking it in place with a miniature caulking gun. Then she ran the wires down the intersection of the walls and along the floorboards to a tiny desk beside the bed.

Isabella unwrapped a small TV monitor with a built-in VCR in its base. As Aleesha fed the wires to the desk, she remarked, "Hell of a way to get the ship's pay-per-view movies for free, eh?"

Isabella chuckled. "All I need are the feeds that go to the ship's safety office, thanks. Then I'll be able to watch every inch of the ship."

With a few notable exceptions, of course, like the interiors of cabins. But anytime the hijackers moved through one of the ship's public areas, whoever was watching the monitor could see them. The job of babysitting this camera would fall to Isabella and Karen. Isabella because of her expertise as a real-time photo intelligence analyst. She'd been trained in how to assess images from cameras mounted on unmanned aerial reconnaissance planes. Looking at images from still cameras would be a breeze.

Karen would help because of the potential difficulties of Karen blending in among the other female passengers. Nearly six feet tall and muscular, Karen was an Amazon warrior of a woman. She stood out in a crowd not only because of her physical stature, but also because of her sheer presence, honed over years as a female Marine officer. No way would the hijackers have not noticed her before, and if she suddenly showed up among the passengers, the terrorists would smell a rat. The two women would hide in this room for the duration or until all hell broke loose and their firepower was required elsewhere. Good Lord willing, that would *not* be a factor anytime soon.

Aleesha made the connections to the back of the TV monitor and turned it on. It flickered once, and then an image of an empty hallway leaped into view. Isabella pushed a button on the remote control that went with the TV, and an empty restaurant came onto the screen. Aleesha packed up her tools while Isabella flipped quickly through the channels, learning how to navigate the two-hundred-plus security cameras on the ship.

"Up and running," Isabella murmured into her throat mike.

"Any terrorist movement?" Vanessa's voice asked.

"Not yet. Could take me a while to get the hang of the system and start spotting Tangos."

They would sit tight in their current positions until Isabella had a good feel for the ship's routine. Whether that would take hours or days was anybody's guess.

Pleading insomnia, Michael wandered the ship aimlessly for most of the night and all of the next morning. He didn't seriously expect one of the commandos who'd come aboard last night to walk up and tap him on the shoulder. Nonetheless, his inability to find them was enormously frustrating. They were here somewhere. But his chances of finding any of them were nil.

Wherever they were hiding on the ship, they undoubtedly had some sort of escape route laid out. Assuming he could actually find their hidey-hole, as soon as they saw him coming—and he had no illusions that he'd approach them unseen—they'd hightail it out of there. If he was unlucky and surprised them, these men would take him out without a moment's hesitation. A hell of a conundrum, it was.

A little before noon, Viktor radioed him. "I understand you had trouble sleeping last night."

"It's nothing," he replied smoothly. "Just getting myself onto a night schedule so I can pull the night shifts."

"That's generous of you."

Michael frowned. Was that suspicion he heard in Viktor's voice? God, he hated living and breathing to keep this madman happy. He replied hastily, "It's not about generosity. It's about you getting some decent sleep if I'm on the job instead of you."

Viktor didn't respond to that. He'd take such a gesture as his due. Instead he said, "I called to tell you to arrange to have lunch brought up to the suite. In an hour for about twelve of us."

"Of course. I'll take care of it right away." Michael glanced down at his watch. "Anything else I can do for you?"

"No," Viktor replied. "That will be all."

Bastard. Michael hung up his phone gently. When the time came, he hoped the commandos blew Viktor's head off.

Chapter 10

Aleesha plucked at her pink polo shirt, which wasn't quite wide enough across the shoulders. She had that problem a lot these days. After six months of being a Medusa, she was in better physical condition than she'd ever believed possible—and she'd been a fair athlete before she'd ever heard of the Medusa Project. She had yet to find a brand of clothes cut for the female superathlete. At least the white shorts she'd snagged on that whirlwind shopping spree were a reasonable fit.

Isabella had a surprisingly good feel for the shipboard routine within several hours. The children were being held in the kids' adventure area on Deck 5. Bud and his SEALs would be glad to hear that. The female passengers weren't allowed the run of the ship, but they had a little freedom of movement. Meals were served buffet style at 8:00 a.m. and noon. Supper had started promptly at 6:00 p.m. Women appeared to be free to go down to the meal anytime during the hour it was served.

Although they would ideally have done another few days of

surveillance to conclusively establish the routine, they didn't have that luxury. Vanessa had made the decision to send Kat and Aleesha out to mingle with the passengers during lunch. They'd be tasked with spotting terrorists and making initial contacts with passengers or crew members who might be willing to help the Medusas. No sweat! Except Aleesha's gut was completely tied in knots. How did that Eleanor Roosevelt quote go? Courage wasn't the absence of fear. It was acting in spite of fear.

Here went some courage.

It was easy enough to ride an elevator up to Deck 9 into the heart of passenger land and blend in with the women filing quietly toward the Galaxy Restaurant. Suppressed panic choked the air. It was the same urgency of a parent in an emergency room with a gravely wounded child. Aleesha ached to reassure the women, to let them know that help was on the way, that their precious babies would be returned safely to their arms. But she dared not. The hijackers would surely pick up on an abrupt improvement in the passengers' morale.

The simple meal was served buffet-style, and was surprisingly tasty, enough to actually draw her attention to it as she used eating as a cover to observe the armed guards patrolling the margins of the room. The kitchens might be operating with ten percent of their usual staff, but that staff was still composed of highly trained chefs.

Unfortunately, the food did little to assuage the tension rippling across her shoulders. She was, for all intents and purposes, alone. Kat was here somewhere, but she was so small she'd be hard to spot in a crowd. Plus, as a sniper, she had a real talent for fading into the background, even when she was out in plain sight.

The armed guards patrolling the room didn't particularly unnerve Aleesha, and that was a surprise. She hadn't realized she'd become so accustomed to the sight of weapons, nor that she'd become so proficient at looking at an armed man, instantly identifying his weaknesses and knowing how to disarm him or take him out.

The big blond guy overbalanced too far forward on his toes. She could simply push him over and give him a good karate chop on the way down. The wiry, dark-haired guy by the kitchen entrance would be overaggressive if attacked. She'd fake a strike at him, then stand back and let the guy throw himself at her wildly. Once he'd tangled himself up in his own attack, it would be a breeze to step in and drop him.

The tall, handsome hijacker who'd just stepped into the restaurant arrested her attention, however. He stood at the top of the steps, surveying the room as if it were his personal fief. Dark hair, dark eyes, athletic build. The fourteenth hijacker she'd seen so far. This must be the one Isabella had nicknamed Gorgeous George. The photo analyst was nicknaming each of the hijackers she spotted to keep them separate as she tried to get a firm head count.

The terrorists had to have several men guarding the children, and they had to have a number more sleeping right now, plus Aleesha had eyed a solid dozen men strolling through here so far. Whoa. She was looking at over twenty hijackers all told if her guess was correct.

JSOC had estimated only sixteen men. That number was in danger of being way low. She snorted. And that was why the Medusa were here, now, doing this surveillance op and getting accurate, real-time intelligence for the SEALs.

Gorgeous George moved down onto the restaurant floor and had a quiet word with the big, blond guy, whose body language was distinctly deferential toward ol' George. Was he the *leader* of the hijackers? She couldn't imagine why the guy would show himself so freely if he was. Most times the man calling the shots in a scenario like this stayed out of the limelight. He might talk to a hostage negotiator on the phone, but he wasn't the one who came out to do press conferences.

Not only did Gorgeous George have a distinctly Cary Grant look about him as he moved, he didn't exhibit any of the obvious combat weaknesses of his partners. He moved gracefully, balanced and well within himself. Hmm. Not a guy she'd want to take on in a hand-to-hand fight. A good candidate for a well-placed sniper shot because he'd be damned hard to drop in a direct attack.

His gaze passed over her, stopped, and came back to her. *Crud.* He'd noticed her looking at him. She looked down hastily and tried to fade into the woodwork. Surely he was used to women ogling him. Darn it, she'd finished her meal and had no food on her plate to occupy herself with. Thankfully, a couple of the other women at the table stood up just then, gathering the dishes to carry them over to carts placed around the room. With the ship as short staffed as it was, the passengers were pitching in to help the remaining crew members keep everyone fed and the ship reasonably clean. She grabbed an armload of glasses and joined the other women in depositing the dirty dinnerware on a rolling cart.

She turned to head for the exit and the safety of the Medusas' room when a male voice spoke behind her. He wasn't loud, but the hijackers allowed no idle conversation. The dining room was fairly quiet with only a murmur of female voices for him to speak over.

"I need someone to take food up to my colleagues. Would anyone like to volunteer or shall I pick someone?"

What first arrested Aleesha's attention was the politeness of the British-accented inquiry. Who'd ever heard of a gentleman hijacker? The second thing that froze her in her tracks, her mind racing a mile a minute, was the opportunity his request presented. She could very possibly get a glimpse, not only of most of the remaining hijackers, but into the heart of the terrorist conspiracy itself.

It was risky, for sure. It would draw all kinds of extra attention to herself. But it could also shorten the information-gathering process by days. What would the men do in this situation? Jack Scatalone would tell her to weigh the risks against the rewards and then do the smart thing; Wittenauer would tell her not to blow the mission; Bud Lipton would tell her she was biting off more than she could chew. Then there was Vanessa. Vanessa would tell her she trusted her team members and to use her best judgment. Fat lot of good they all were. At the end of the day, it was her neck on the line and, therefore, her call.

And her instincts said she should go for it.

She turned around slowly. Slowly enough to make the point that she wasn't overeager to volunteer. Gorgeous George stood there in the flesh, all the sexier for the machine gun slung casually across his shoulder. Dang! He was even better looking up close than he was across a room, and from a distance he could stop traffic cold.

His eyes were almost black they were such a dark brown. His hair was dark brown, too, the color of strong coffee. A few strands of silver at his temples hinted at the distinguished years to come for him. Men like him always got better looking with age. It just wasn't fair.

"I'll do it," she said quietly.

He nodded once. "I need meals for twelve people loaded onto a rolling cart."

She nodded in return, as submissive a head bob as she could pull off, and reached for the empty serving cart someone had just brought out of the kitchen.

Fingers of steel wrapped gently around her upper arm.

"Quickly, please," he murmured. "These guys don't like to be kept waiting, and it's important that they stay happy."

Huh? An armed hijacker was asking for her cooperation? Why didn't he just stick his machine gun in her ribs and tell her to hop to it? In all her months of training, she'd never even *heard* of an op where a Tango approached the good guys and said *please,* let alone asked for help. Completely, totally out of character.

Should she try to back out of this little excursion? She frowned, weighing the options fast. If she walked out of here with this guy, she might score a big intel windfall. But if she refused to go with him, he might make a fuss and draw a lot of attention to her. She could end up in serious trouble. She was unarmed, had no radio and was only generally familiar with the layout of the ship and the placement of the hijackers and hostages. She did have her fake passenger ID in her pocket, but that was a minuscule counterbalance to all the negatives. She was *not* prepared to find herself one-on-one with any of these guys, given how oddly this one was acting.

She looked up at him and opened her mouth to tell him she'd changed her mind, and then their eyes met. There was something in those dark depths....

Oh, puhlease. She didn't buy that whole business of "I saw it in his eyes. I just knew he was okay by looking at him" crap. She was a scientist. She relied on cold, hard facts and made decisions based on logic, not gut feelings. Sure, she joked around about her voodoo intuitions, and the Medusas had even been trained to listen to their instincts if there was no factual evidence to contradict them. But she wasn't about to let this good-looking killer throw her one look of soulful entreaty and sweep her off her feet.

So why, then, was she letting him lead her and her cart of food toward the side exit just behind the next row of tables? Why was she walking calmly down the hall behind this guy as he motioned for her to follow him at a distance? Why was she giving an infinitesimal nod of reassurance up at the security camera as she passed underneath it? She was a soldier! A highly disciplined covert operator who knew how to assess risks and make cold, calm decisions under the worst of fire.

Apparently she had, in fact, lost her mind completely, because not for a second did she actually doubt that she was going to go with this guy and find out why a hijacker was looking her in the eye in candid entreaty and saying *please.*

Hal Wittenauer snatched up the phone receiver and interrupted Isabella's latest secure-frequency radio report. "What do you mean, she just walked out with him? Where the hell did they go?"

"They're on the move now, sir. Traversing Golf 10 toward Golf 9."

The general looked over at the SEAL who was posting position reports from the ship. "Map it," Wittenauer snapped.

"Got it," the SEAL replied with businesslike calm.

Wittenauer ran a distracted hand through his hair. What in the hell was Aleesha up to? She knew better than to go in solo to the lion's den! It was Spec Ops 101 not to do something this colossally risky. It was all well and good for the Medusas to be mavericks in training, but this was the real deal! He took a lap around the room to burn off the acid churning in his gut. And ran into Bud Lipton's silent glare. The SEAL lieutenant commander had supported sending in the Medusas, and now, scant hours after they'd boarded the ship, one of them pulled a damn fool stunt like this. Wittenauer shoved a hand through his hair. He was going to be really ripped if he had to send in a rescue team to save the rescue team.

"Don't say it, Lipton," he snapped. He didn't even want to think about the egg he'd have on his face if the Medusas went down in flames on their first op. C'mon, ladies. Don't do this to me.

He whirled to the tech sergeant manning the phones. "Get me Jack Scatalone. ASAP."

A receiver was duly handed to him, and his senior aide's voice came across the line. "Scatalone, here. What can I do for you, sir?"

"Get your ass down here to Florida and get control of your team, dammit."

Alarm vibrated in Scat's voice. "What's happened?"

"Just get down here," Wittenauer retorted.

"I'll be there in—" a short pause "—four hours."

"Get over to Andrews, pull rank and make it three hours."

"Uh, okay. Three hours it is, sir."

Wittenauer set the receiver down in the cradle. "God *damn* it," he growled. And resumed pacing.

Gorgeous George walked down a long passageway ahead of Aleesha toward the high-rent suites. She followed at a distance, in some disbelief that she was actually doing this. Not once did he check over his shoulder to see if she was following him. Either he was supremely confident or a trained pro. But what kind of pro? Ex-military? A professional terrorist? Had he come out of some secret camp that one of the big terror networks ran? Fastest way to find out was to keep walking down this hall.

He turned right, ducking into a room without warning. Her steps slowed and she approached with caution. It took every ounce of discipline she had, but she looked straight ahead as she drew level with the door. To stop or not to stop? Go. Stop. Curiosity warred with common sense.

She jumped as the door burst open beside her. "In here."

What in the world was he up to? She'd come this far—she might as well see it through. She swerved and stepped quickly through the portal. She'd probably just given Isabella heart failure. For, surely, her teammate had been watching her on the ship's cameras.

A pair of strong hands grabbed her by the shoulders, shoving her against the door at her back.

Multiple impressions assailed her at once. Hands as powerful and competent as she'd expected, but he was restraining her without hurting her. And his hard gaze swam with urgency.

She replied evenly, "What do you want from me?"

His answer made her blood run cold. "I need you to get word out to the other passengers not to try anything stupid. Help is on the way."

Help was on the way? Had he seen them board the ship?

Holy shit! Then why were the Medusas still alive? Why hadn't the Tangos attacked her team the minute they set foot on the ship? If the hijackers knew the Medusas were aboard the *Grand Adventure,* why wasn't an all-out search underway? What game were these guys playing? It was insane for hijackers to knowingly let a counterterrorism team infiltrate their hostage population. Surely she'd jumped to the wrong conclusion. The very fact that she was alive meant he couldn't be talking about the Medusas. What then? What did he mean?

"We don't have much time."

No kidding. He started to drag her away from the door, but she'd had enough. She reached inside his grip on her shoulders with both of her fists and gave his elbows a good pop. With a grunt, he let go, but lightning fast, his leg whipped out, knocking her feet out from under her. She went down hard, twisting to land on her left side. She rolled into his shins, trapping his feet beneath her. She kept rolling into him and returned the favor, planting him on his butt. Following him as he went down, she leaped on top of him. *Pure suicide.* This guy was big and strong, and if he had the kind of training she thought he did, she was going to have a hell of a time subduing him. Nonetheless, she straddled his chest, planting her knees on his upper arms, preparing to fight for her life.

He stared up at her in shock and began to shake beneath her.

She tensed, waiting for him to try to throw her off. Nothing happened. More shaking. She blinked, staring down at him in shock. He was *laughing* at her. Laughing!

"What's so damned funny?" she demanded.

A grin broke across his face. "Nice takedown," he commented. "And here I was thinking you passengers needed help. My mistake."

His mistake, indeed. Might as well capitalize on being on top. "Who are you?"

Her challenge wiped the grin off his face. "Let me up."

"You can talk right here," she replied coolly.

He shrugged beneath her thighs, and she was abruptly aware of the fact that she was sitting on this guy's chest in a rather suggestive pose. And all of a sudden the bastard seemed prepared to sit back and enjoy the view. Eyes narrowed, she glared at him.

She saw the moment when he yanked his mind back to business and his features settled into grim lines, more appropriate to the situation around them.

"I propose a trade," he answered back, as cool as she'd been a moment before.

"What sort of trade?"

"You tell me where you learned to fight like that, and I'll tell you who I am."

Her eyebrows shot up. This was too easy. So easy her gut rumbled in suspicion. "I had brothers. Lots of them. I learned to fight as a matter of survival." It was a lie, of course, but then, he wouldn't be telling her the truth, either.

"My name is Michael Somerset. I'm British SIS, and I've spent the last couple of years infiltrating the terrorist group that just took over this ship. I need the passengers to stay calm until I can figure out some way to regain control of the ship."

Aleesha stared. Oh. My. God.

Reactions to his announcement crowded into her brain almost too fast to process. Disbelief. Elation. Caution. This guy was undercover SIS? If that was true, they could blow this thing wide open. An insider who could report on the hijackers' plans and goals before they acted on them?

But what if he was lying? What if the hijackers saw the Medusas come aboard, but not soon enough to intercept them before they went to ground in the maze of crew cabins? Was this a ploy to get an operator they'd spotted to lead them to the rest? Was this guy trying to use her to set up the rest of the Medusas? How in the world had he figured out she was one of the infiltrators? Or did he know that? Was he guessing because she'd volunteered to bring the food to the terrorists? Or was he using her to spread word among the passengers of his identity in hopes that it would reach the ears of whoever'd boarded the ship last night?

Her head was beginning to ache with all the permutations and possibilities.

Aloud she asked, "Why me? Why are you telling me this?"

"Some of my...colleagues...are known racists. You're—" Another pause.

She filled in, "Not Caucasian."

He smiled briefly. "Right. Not Caucasian. And, therefore, necessarily not the female terrorist I happen to know is hiding among the passengers."

Son of a gun.

She rocked back on her heels, her fanny coming into solid contact with rippling abs of steel. Good Lord, she was still sitting on top of the guy. Startled, she jumped up, stepping away from him as she did so. He climbed smoothly to his feet, tall, powerful and disturbingly close. She looked up at him and was jolted a second time by the intensity in his dark gaze.

She opened her mouth to speak. "I—"

The door opened behind her, rattling as it hit the chain holding it shut.

"What the hell is this, Michael? Are you all right? Paulo radioed down from the bridge that you might be in trouble."

Her companion cursed viciously under his breath and grabbed her by the arm. Moving at the speed of light, he shoved her into the suite's bedroom and whipped the door shut behind her. Through the panel, she heard him snap, "Take it easy, Viktor. I'm coming."

She looked around the bedroom hastily for a place to hide. Nada. The closet was crammed with weapons and gear. The bed was platform-style with drawers beneath it. No sofa to hide behind—the furniture was built into the walls.

The same French-accented voice that had called through the hallway door spoke from inside the suite this time. "Why the hell did you lock the door? What are you up to, my old friend?"

She didn't like the sound of that. The silky menace in the guy's voice as he called Michael "old friend" made the hackles on the back of her neck stand straight up. Damn. The Frenchman was bound to search the suite. And she was a sitting duck in here, trapped with no place to hide.

"What's this?" the French voice asked. "Your bedroom door is closed. Are you perchance hiding something from me?"

Shit. She was out of time and out of options. She yanked her polo shirt and bra off over her head and tore back the covers, leaping between the sheets just as the door opened.

Chapter 11

Jack walked into the perpetual twilight of the TOC in Miami three hours and forty minutes after he'd hung up with General Wittenauer. He'd failed to meet the general's demand to be there in three hours, but all in all, it was remarkable that he'd managed to haul ass down here so fast. A C-21—a speedy Lear jet—on alert at Andrews had been scrambled to fly him to Homestead, and the crew had done yeoman's duty getting him here as quickly as humanly possible.

Wittenauer was visible through a glass wall, sitting in a conference room eating a sandwich. He gestured for Jack to join him as soon as they made eye contact with each other. Jack had spent the entire flight trying to figure out what in the hell his girls had done to make the old man so mad. Thing was, he wasn't entirely sure his boss was angry. He thought he might have detected a faint note of fear in Wittenauer's voice. And that made Jack's blood run cold. The woman he loved was out there on that ship, her neck on the line.

Definitely the downside of being involved with Vanessa Blake. Sometimes it was possible to know too much about your loved one's work. She'd confessed to sweating bullets whenever he was out on an op and in harm's way, too.

As he stepped into the room, Wittenauer told him quietly, "Close the door."

Crap. Not good. If Wittenauer was only irritated, he'd be bellowing like a bull moose. But when the general was well and truly ticked off, he got quiet. Like this.

Jack sat down at the table across from the general. "What did they do?" he asked heavily. No reason to pussyfoot around.

"They were in the ship's restaurant at dinner observing the hijackers. Out of the blue, Aleesha Gautier strolled out of the room—alone—with one of the terrorists, apparently completely of her own free will."

Jack's brows slammed together. "She damn well knows it's against standard procedure to make direct contact with Tangos on a surveillance op. If she did something like that, I guarantee she had a hell of a good reason for doing it. Has she reported in yet?"

Wittenauer glanced up at the bank of clocks on the wall. "Nope. They're reporting in every four hours. Last we heard, she'd just ducked into a suite on Deck 9 with one of the hijackers and was out of contact with her team. I couldn't tell you if she's alive right now or if she's blown this op completely out of the water. The Medusas are due to check in with us in under an hour. Assuming they haven't all been rounded up and shot."

He ran a hand over his face and set aside the panic threatening to erupt in his gut. His brain went into hyperdrive, listing possible scenarios and their likely outcomes.

"Walk me through your thoughts, Jack," the general ordered.

He complied, saying, "We've got to assume she had a good reason for going with this guy. If that's the case, there's a decent chance she'll come out of that suite alive. And believe me, if some terrorist tries to go one-on-one against Aleesha, she'll kick his ass. She's a hell of an unarmed combat specialist." All of the

Medusas were. He'd made sure of that during their training. Nobody would expect it of them, and it would give them a huge leg up on staying alive in a crisis like this.

He continued, "We have every reason to believe this will turn out okay. I suggest we not draw any conclusions until the next report comes in."

Aleesha *had* to have a good reason for doing something so risky. Not that he could begin to fathom what it might be. The doctor was usually the soul of common sense. It wasn't her style to flake out like this.

Wittenauer pushed a plate of sandwiches across the table, and, with a sigh, Jack picked up a club sandwich on soggy toast. He wasn't worth a damn at waiting while his teams were out in the field, Vanessa or not.

Aleesha gasped as a lean, dark man burst into the bedroom with Michael close on his heels. Viktor, Michael had called him. His eyes glowed with the feral intensity of a zealot, and menace radiated from him. Without a doubt, she was looking at the leader of the hijackers, its mastermind and driving force. She let fear shine in her eyes and clutched the sheet over her bosom.

"Who is this?" the Frenchman demanded—for surely that was a French accent if she'd ever heard one. Sexual interest flared in the guy's eyes as his gaze dropped to her barely covered chest. Bastard.

"A little extracurricular relaxation," Michael answered smoothly.

Why he was covering for her, she had no idea, but she nodded fearfully in agreement with Michael's words. Might as well play on the Frenchman's sense of colonial imperialism. He probably viewed island natives like her as little better than slave material. It rankled to play up to that sort of prejudice, but if it kept her alive, she was all for marginalizing herself.

"We don't have time for this," Viktor snapped. "We're supposed to be having a meeting in ten minutes. Get her out of here. Now."

She looked at Michael, and he jerked his head at the door. "Get out," he ordered roughly.

When neither man made a move to give her privacy to dress, she stood up, dragging the sheet with her. Holding the bedclothes against her chest, she bent over, picked up her clothing and headed for the door. She was forced to step between the two men, neither of whom bothered to make room for her. She turned sideways to pass between them, and Michael's hand cupped her rear end, squeezing painfully. Her gaze snapped to his. Nothing but hard disdain glittered in his black eyes.

With her back turned to the men, she stepped into the living room. And stopped cold. Eight! Count them—eight terrorists stood there, staring at her as if they'd never seen a woman before.

"Good evenin', gentlemen," she said evenly, falling into a heavy, lilting, Jamaican accent.

They nodded, apparently too stunned to speak after finding Somerset, or whatever his name was, in bed with a woman. Her head held high, she dragged her sheet to the bathroom as if it was a royal wedding gown. Once inside, she dropped the sheet and shrugged into her clothes quickly. Now what was she supposed to do? Wish them all a good night and walk out? She opened the door and marched into the room. At least she had the presence of mind to make mental images of all the faces and physical descriptions for Isabella.

"Nice piece of ass," Viktor commented behind her. "After this is all over we should take turns with her."

She froze in her tracks. No man was going to talk about her like that and get away with it! Her grandmama always said if you once tolerated bad behavior from a man, you gave up the right to complain the next time it happened. She pivoted slowly, just in time to see Michael shrug. "I don't fuck used goods," he remarked. "If you want her, you can have her. I'll get myself another one."

Letting her indignation flow freely, she drew herself up to her full height and planted her hands reprovingly on her hips. In her best brogue she exclaimed, "Gentlemen! What would your mothers say if dey heard you speak aboot a lady dat way?" She shook a finger at Michael and Viktor. "Shame on both of you. Now you two eat your supper and keep a civil tongue in your heads." With a head toss for good measure, she turned around and sailed out.

She stepped out into the hall and closed the door firmly. Then she blinked. And then she nearly threw up! Had she just told off a roomful of armed hijackers? How in the world had she gotten away with that? Her intent had only been to brazen her way out of there, not dare them to kill her!

She moved away from the suite quickly, lest they reconsider and drag her back in to "share" now. Vividly aware of the security cameras overhead, she dared not return to the Medusas' room right away. She moved through the ship and found herself on the promenade deck. She sat on a deck chair there for nearly an hour, shivering in delayed shock, until the evening curfew went into effect.

Who was Michael Somerset? Why had he made excuses for her presence to that Viktor guy? Was he really an SIS agent? Was it possible? He'd certainly been polite to her and hadn't hurt her in the fight when he certainly could have. He *seemed* sincere.

And she was a trained professional. She should be able to set aside her feelings and analyze the operational situation!

A good enough actor could *seem* saintly. How long would it take the TOC to confirm this guy's story? And in the meantime, did she dare continue having contact with him or should she break it off now? Was the potential inside information worth the risk? She could talk to her teammates about it, or even to Lipton and company at the Tactical Ops Center. But at the end of the day, she was the only person with firsthand exposure to Michael. It would boil down to her call until the SIS verified this guy's claim.

The wind was heavy with moisture this evening, gusting fiercely, a harbinger of things to come. The storm, which was now a hurricane, was getting closer by the minute. Last report before they came aboard the *Grand Adventure,* was that it would affect these waters in about seventy-two hours and hit for real in four to five days. The Medusas were supposed to finish their surveillance in time for the SEALs to make the rescue before the storm hit. The clock was ticking.

She fell into the dejected crowd of women headed to their cabins for the evening lockdown and made her own way down to the crew deck. Several other female crew members were headed down the hall to their rooms, and she followed them into the narrow corridor. She knocked quietly on the door to the Medusas' impromptu headquarters. It opened immediately and she stepped inside. The entire team was there. They were staring at her expectantly.

All Vanessa said was, "And?"

"And, I think I just made our job a whole lot easier," she replied. The tension in the room dropped instantly at the reassurance that she'd actually had a good reason for doing what she had.

"Start talking," Vanessa ordered quietly.

Quickly Aleesha relayed her exchange in the restaurant with Michael and her reasons for deciding to follow him. Her teammates didn't comment until she concluded with repeating Viktor's parting shot about sharing her among his men.

Vanessa leaned forward intently. "And you think this Viktor guy is the leader?"

"No doubt about it," Aleesha replied.

Isabella piped up. "Give me a detailed physical description of him."

Thanks to their training with a police sketch artist, Aleesha knew precisely how to describe Viktor's appearance. A sketch artist in the TOC would translate her words into a picture for the SEALs to memorize. Ideally, the Medusas would get a photograph of him with one of their digital cameras to send to the TOC, but there was no guarantee that the guy would show himself again.

"What do you make of this Michael guy?" Misty asked her.

Aleesha shrugged. "I don't know. He could be exactly who

he says he is, a plant from British SIS. He could also be playing me to see if you guys exist. Maybe the hijackers saw us come aboard but didn't get down here before we'd faded into hiding. Maybe this guy's using me to spread the word among the passengers to draw out whoever boarded the ship."

And if either of the latter scenarios was the case, they had a problem. Vanessa's gaze met hers. Her boss had come to the very same conclusion.

Aleesha frowned. "If they've figured out we're aboard, it's not safe for us to show ourselves among the passengers anymore. We'll have to do all our surveillance by stealth."

"Which will slow us down," Misty commented.

Isabella shrugged. "I can gather most of the data we need from the cameras. It's just going to be a matter of waiting for all the hijackers to show themselves. It'll make getting a head count on the kids tougher, too. I can only get a partial view of the kids' adventure area, so I can't get an exact figure for how many kids are in that room to know if they're all there. They could have some of the kids stowed in an area the cameras don't cover, like a large suite or a spa."

Aleesha said slowly, "I ought to be able to move around the ship openly for at least a little while. They think I'm a passenger."

Vanessa grinned. "Yeah, and they may kill you the next time they see you after you slapped their wrists."

Aleesha grinned. "My grandmama temporarily possessed me."

Vanessa laughed. "I like her style. Thing is, it puts you in the position of being the only Medusa exposed to these guys. All the risk lands on your shoulders."

Aleesha shrugged said shoulders. "Sometimes that's the way it goes. You and Isabella walked into that hospital in Bhoukar to rescue Jack because you spoke Arabic while the rest of us stayed behind."

Karen spoke up. 'Yeah, but that doesn't mean we have to like it."

"This may all be moot. He may truly have approached me

with no greater intent than to get me in the sack. The SIS line could've just been a lie to impress me and win my sympathy."

Vanessa looked at her keenly. "Is that really what you think?"

And there it was. The sixty-four-thousand-dollar question. What *did* she think of Michael and his cockamamie story about being a British undercover agent?

She took a deep breath and let her instincts guide her. "I think he's for real. And I think the contact with him is worth pursuing. Obviously, we don't go into it blind and we take every precaution in case he's actually working with the hijackers to catch the Medusas. As soon as we can, we ask the TOC to verify his identity. In the meantime, I keep contact with him. My decision, my risk."

"All for one, one for all," Vanessa replied lightly.

Well, there was that. The Medusas sank or swam as a team. If one of them took a risk, all of them felt like the risk was their own. They were more than a team. More than a family. They worked as one.

"I'm sure about this," Aleesha insisted. "I can do it." She glanced over at the TV monitor behind Isabella. It was trained on the children, settling down for bed. A faint sound of muffled sobs was audible over the feed. Oh, yeah. She could do this for sure.

Vanessa's shoulders relaxed. Hallelujah. Her boss had made a decision. And from the worried wrinkle to her brow, she was going to let Aleesha have a go at playing out Michael Somerset.

Misty commented into the silence, "Well, if it's a setup, they sure picked a hottie to approach you with."

The others grinned in agreement. Now that they'd reached a consensus about how to proceed, they would all work together to make it happen in the safest, most effective way.

Aleesha asked Vanessa, "How do you want me to play this? Do you want me to approach him or let him come to me? If he's legit, he'll have to make contact again."

Vanessa frowned. "Even if he's trying to use you to draw out the team, he'll have to make contact again."

"Then why did he throw me out of his room like that? Why

didn't Viktor go along with the ploy to get close to me or at least stay the hell out of the room until Michael was done talking to me?"

Isabella piped up. "Maybe this Michael guy is telling the truth. Or maybe Michael was on duty when we came aboard and he's frantically trying to cover his ass and catch us before Viktor finds out about his failure."

Aleesha thought back. "He didn't seem afraid of Viktor."

Vanessa snorted. "You show fear to a predator like this Viktor character, and he'll eat you alive. Which leads us back to the question of how you should play this."

Working through possibilities, Aleesha said, "If he's going to contact me again, he won't be able to do it in a public way like he did before. Viktor was clear that Michael shouldn't mess around with any of the passengers. He'll have to come to me in a private place, like a stateroom."

Misty nodded. "So, we find an empty room, wire the hell out of it, put a couple of us next door for backup, and we make it known to Mr. Hottie where you can be found."

It sounded simple enough. Except she had a sinking feeling this would turn out to be anything but simple before it was all said and done.

Isabella spoke up, interrupting Aleesha's thoughts as she planned her strategy for a next meeting with the mysterious Mr. Somerset. "We've got a check-in with the TOC in two minutes. I'd suggest you make the call, Aleesha. Wittenauer about popped a gasket when I made my last report that you'd disappeared with one of the hijackers."

She winced. Oh, boy. The old man was not going to be a happy camper after sitting on that information for the past four hours. She sighed and nodded at her teammate.

Isabella reached for the radio. "I'll make the patch."

Aleesha waited while Isabella dialed in the next secure frequency from a list on a one-time-use pad. The intelligence analyst checked the freq, and only when she was sure it was clean did she pass Aleesha a pair of clamshell earphones.

"Go ahead, girlfriend," Isabella murmured. "And good luck."

Yeah, right. Aleesha took a deep breath.

Bud Lipton's front chair legs slammed to the floor and he pointed up at the window where Jack stood beside the general. Jack glanced up at the big wall clock. Well, his girls were punctual, at any rate. Their call was on time to the second. A good sign. Teams under duress didn't have the luxury of operating with such exactitude. They'd call in whenever they could. Jack reached over to a wall switch and turned on the speakers, piping the radio call into the briefing room.

"Hey, Romeo, this is Juliet."

That was Aleesha's voice. Thank God. An unfamiliar weakness in his knees surprised him. Lord, he hated this behind-the-scenes command crap. Give him a gun and a team any day of the week over this nail biting. "That's Mamba herself," he murmured to Wittenauer.

"Where ya been?" Lipton asked casually. "Your old man was worried."

A light laugh from Aleesha. "The flock of mother hens wasn't too happy, either."

A green light went on in the console, indicating that the frequency was still clear, even after their test transmissions. "Line's clear. Report," Lipton snapped. "And this had better be good."

Aleesha answered briskly, "One of the hijackers approached me. Said his name is Michael Somerset and he's British SIS under deep cover with the hijackers. I need that verified ASAP, by the way. He says he wants to use me as a conduit to the passengers to relay a message that he's going to try to reclaim control of the ship and they should sit tight. This guy could be for real or he could be a plant by the Tangos to draw out whoever boarded the ship last night. I don't believe he has any idea who I am."

Wittenauer lurched and Jack gaped. SIS? Well, that would be a hell of a development. He gestured to one of the techs in the pit below, holding his hand to his ear, mimicking a phone call. The tech nodded and dialed what was undoubtedly British Intelligence.

Aleesha continued, "We're going to play out the contact for now. I'll do it alone with the team backing me up. If he's who he says he is, the inside information we could get would be invaluable."

No kidding. Reliable insiders were, bar none, the best source of real-time intelligence data a Special Ops team could hope for. It was risky though. Damned risky. The general shook his head in the negative, running a finger across his throat. Wittenauer wasn't going to let the women do it.

"Speaking of which, I met the leader of the whole shooting match. Calls himself Viktor and has a French accent." She then rattled off a perfect description of the guy. Even without a sketch artist translating her words to a picture, Jack could see what the guy looked like as clear as a bell. The SEALs who would infiltrate the ship would memorize her description and keep a special eye out for him.

Even Lipton couldn't help but give a positive response. "I copy. Good work."

Jack lifted the receiver off the telephone hanging on the wall beside him and transmitted over the frequency, "Stand by for a minute, Mamba."

"That you, Scat?" Aleesha retorted, clearly surprised.

"Yo. Hold on a sec."

The general glared at Jack. "Don't even think about it. They're on their first mission, dammit. They're no way, no how, ready to infiltrate some terrorist outfit. Not with the stakes this high."

"Then when, sir?" Jack asked with quiet intensity. "When is there ever going to be a mission where the stakes aren't high, where the Medusas can get field experience without exposing themselves and innocents to risk? You either trust the fact that I trained them properly to do their job or I didn't."

"This isn't about you, Jack. Every last one of them is untried. They're babes in the woods!"

Jack snapped back, "Go ahead and say it, sir. They're *women*."

"Don't give me that crap, Jack. I went to bat for them. If I hadn't backed them, there wouldn't be a Medusa team today."

"Then let them do their job. You didn't create them to sit on a shelf and look pretty while the real world passed them by. You sent them in to do this job. So let them do it—their way. You and I both know missions always go to hell when the desk jockeys try to run the op. If Mamba wants to play this guy, then let her. It's her neck on the line. Not yours."

Wittenauer scowled. "No, it's only my stars on the line."

Jack shrugged. "What's a little tin compared to all those women and kids on the *Grand Adventure*?"

Wittenauer swore under his breath. "All right, dammit."

Jack squeezed the bar on the underside of the phone receiver that activated transmission. "You're green-lighted to make the play, Mamba."

Lipton's head whipped around below, looking up in disbelief at him and the general through the window. Another closet chauvinist showing his stripes. Didn't think the girls could pull it off, huh?

"I wasn't asking for permission," Aleesha retorted dryly, her voice crackling a bit over the radio.

Jack grinned. "Go git 'em and give my best to Viper."

"Roger, lover boy."

Chapter 12

Aleesha fidgeted on the couch in the dark. Waves broke against the ship's hull, the only sound interrupting the deep silence of the ship. The rhythm of the sea was seductive, luring her toward sleep as minutes stretched into hours. The sleep-deprivation exercises Jack had put the Medusas through early in their training suddenly made sense as she sat there fighting off an urge to doze.

She had no way of knowing if Michael knew or cared where she was. She'd worn a brilliant red dress to supper that even a blind man could've seen. Michael didn't make an appearance at the meal, but hopefully he spotted her, either in person or on the ship's security cameras, as she strolled around the ship afterward. He'd better have spotted her, darn it. She'd hiked the whole ship in high heels in the name of being seen. She'd waited until the last minute to go into the empty stateroom the Medusas had wired for this meeting, and had made absolutely sure one of the hijackers saw her enter it. The TOC had checked the ship's manifest and found this room one deck down from Michael's suite and conveniently near the elevators. She'd used her master key to get in. If Michael didn't know where to find her now, it was because he didn't want to know.

Midnight came and went with no sign of him. Doubt began to creep into her thoughts. Had she been wrong? Was his story about being British SIS a ruse after all? As the night stretched on, her doubts intensified.

She jerked to full combat alert a little after 2:00 a.m. That was a noise outside the door! She moved fast off the couch, leaping into the open closet just inside the door. She eased out of her high-heeled shoes in the cramped space, balancing lightly on the bare balls of her feet. She wasn't about to break her neck trying to subdue an intruder in heels. It might work on television, but not in the real world.

The door eased open a few inches, then it flew open fully. A tall, male form slipped inside quickly and closed the door fast and silently behind himself.

Aleesha jumped him from behind, her arm around his neck in a crushing hold that should have cut off his wind. The man grunted in surprise, then dropped to the ground, dragging her with him. He rolled over on his back, slamming her into the wall in the narrow confines of the stateroom. She let go, jumping clear of his attempt to trap her beneath his body weight, then she pounced on him, her forearm planted on his throat. He grabbed her fist and twisted, forcing her chest down over his face. Dang, he was fast. Strong, too.

Rather than try to brute force him, she would have to subdue him with superior skill. As he continued to twist her arm, she went with the movement, burying his face in her chest while she rolled around to the top of his head. Enough of this crap! She grabbed his ear with her free hand and gave it a vicious twist. He sucked air sharply between his teeth and after a moment, let go of her fisted hand. She took advantage of his momentary weakness, tucked her shoulder, and executed a partial somersault to land squarely in the middle of his chest. With a whoomp of expelled breath he went still beneath her.

Her hands went around his throat, but as he continued to lie there quiescent, she refrained from choking him unconscious. Damn, that had been close. Another few seconds and he'd have had her. She kept her hands around his throat just in case. No sense underestimating his willingness to fight dirty. She panted hard, still catching her breath. *Now* what was she going to do with him?

Without warning, he began to shake beneath her hands and between her knees. The bastard was laughing again! She peered down closely at him, finally able to make out his features in the dark. Michael.

Between gasps of silent laughter he choked out, "Uncle."

She let go of his throat and sat upright in disgust, planting her buttocks on his stomach. She panted hard after their wrestling match. Jerk. He'd given her all the fight she could handle and now he was laughing at her. Was that his idea of a fun date or something? She doubted she'd catch him off guard like that again, and surely the next time he wouldn't underestimate her skill. She might have taken him this time, but she wouldn't want to bet her next paycheck on doing so again.

"Any chance you can get off me so we can talk, or are you the type of woman who likes to dominate her men?"

She scowled down at him. "A, you're not my man. And B, I have no interest in any man I can push around."

Damned if his eyes didn't glint up at her in amusement. "Thanks for the dating tip."

He wished. She pushed to her feet and offered a hand to him in silence. He took it, and as she tugged him to his feet she warned, "Don't make me regret seeing you again." He was a heavy man for the lean profile he cut. Densely muscled, then. Fit. But she already knew that from the fight he'd just given her.

He continued to grip her hand, pulling her disturbingly close to his big, warm body. He murmured, "You couldn't hide from me if you tried. I can find you anywhere on the ship, even without the red dress and the sexy sashay in front of the cameras."

She glared into the black caverns of his eye sockets. "Wanna bet?"

"Exercise class is over. It's time for you to uphold your end of the deal."

"What deal?" she retorted.

"The one where you tell me who you really are. I just spent all evening going through the ship's passenger database. Funny thing, but it includes the bitmap of the ID photo of every passenger ID card."

Her stomach sank. She knew what was coming. She prepared her muscles to attack again, to subdue this guy long enough so she could get away.

"And, lady, you're not a passenger or crew member of this ship."

She stared at him in silence. What could she say? If she claimed it was a mistake, he'd know she was lying. She tried to waylay him by saying, "Maybe I be a mermaid?" in her sexiest Jamaican accent.

He ignored the comment and continued, his voice low and urgent. "You came aboard last night, didn't you? How many of you are there? Are you SEALs? Delta Force? Please tell me you brought enough firepower to knock these bastards out."

This time she was silent because she was too shocked to speak. He'd hit the nail *exactly* on the head.

"You're not talking, so I assume verification of who I am hasn't come down to you yet."

Enough was enough. She blurted out, "I don't have the faintest idea what you're talking about."

He rolled over her denial, hardly bothering to acknowledge it. "Whatever. I'll answer all the questions tonight, then."

Eyes narrowed, she assessed his facial features. They were open, relaxed. He looked as if he was telling the truth. But that was an easy enough trick to master. No, this man would have to prove himself with actions, and real information, not empty words. "Why did you come to me tonight?"

"Because you have a whole lot of things you want to ask me. Or rather your superiors do."

Damn, he was direct. What questions would a regular passenger ask a guy like this? She thought fast.

But not fast enough because he swore quietly under his breath. "So, it's more cat and mouse games until you know you can trust me. Look, we don't have time to waste while the politicians piss in each other's Wheaties. Tell you what. I'll talk and you listen."

She strolled over to the sofa and sat down on it. Isabella had planted an audio mike under the cushion at her elbow. Might as well put the man the Medusas wanted to hear right beside it. She lounged casually, but her body thrummed with tension, revved up from the fight. Would Michael pan out as a contact or turn out to be a bust? Had he been worth the risk? "I'm listening," she announced.

He parked on the other end of the sofa, tense. "There are twenty-four terrorists, comprised of two groups of twelve. One is a group of Basque separatists led by Viktor Dupont. They call themselves the *Alliance de la Liberté*. This whole insanity is Viktor's brainchild. He recruited the second group of terrorists to give him the manpower he'd need to actually pull off the hijacking. I don't know a lot about the second bunch. They're American and say very little. They're highly competent, and look to be U.S. military-trained. They're the greater threat of the two groups when it comes to a shootout. The Basques have passion on their side, but the Americans are skilled warriors."

Aleesha interrupted, trying hard to sound like an appalled civilian. "You say they're trained by the military. Are the Americans ex-military themselves?"

He shrugged. "Don't know. They may have been trained by someone ex-military. Either way, they're damned good. Tell your people to be very cautious of them."

"And there are twelve of them you say? Does the group have a name?"

"No. They only refer to themselves by code names and they've never called their group by a name. Not once. And Viktor's been in contact with them for well over a year."

That did smack of excellent discipline. That was a long time not to slip up. Aloud she asked, "Where are the terrorists on the ship?"

"Two on the bridge at all times. One monitoring the security cameras, one keeping an eye on the ship's controls. Four on the kids at all times, four to six more doing roving patrols of the ship. We work twelve-hour shifts, so there are twelve of us on duty at any given time. If a man wakes up early or isn't tired yet, he may stay on duty for a couple extra hours. So there can be up to eighteen or so active gunmen."

"Are the children being moved around?"

Michael shook his head in the negative. "Not yet. Doesn't mean Viktor won't decide to, but so far he's had them sit tight. And to anticipate your next question, he's been keeping them together for ease of control. And that, too, could change at any time. If he felt an attack from outside was imminent, I wouldn't be surprised to see him split the kids up and make multiple targets of them."

If the Medusas could verify this information, or verify that Michael was who he said he was, he'd just saved the team a good twenty-four hours of surveillance.

"I want inside," she announced.

He sat bolt upright in alarm. "Inside what?"

"Inside the organization. I want a firsthand look."

"Impossible."

"Not impossible. Just difficult."

"Too dangerous," he snapped.

"Tough." She shrugged. "You want me to work with you, that's the condition. Get me inside. I'll even pretend to be your girlfriend."

His eyes blazed at that, but he made no comment. She sat back to let him think on it, which he did. Ferociously.

Finally he heaved an unhappy sigh. "All right. I'll get you in. Watch out for Viktor, though. He's a suspicious bastard. Not to mention a sociopath. Tell your people he won't hesitate to shoot children by the dozens. And don't push your luck with him like you did this afternoon." He grinned. "I never thought I'd see the day when someone dressed him down and lived to tell about it."

"I won't," she promised grimly, intentionally not acknowledging the reference to "her people."

They stared at each other in the dark in silence, the weight of the disaster they were trying to avert heavy between them. If this guy was faking, he was the best actor she'd ever seen.

She spoke quietly. "And the sixty-four-thousand-dollar question, Michael. What in the hell is Viktor planning to do with this ship now that he's got it?"

Michael nodded. "Yes, that would be the question of the hour, wouldn't it?"

He opened his mouth to say more, but an electronic ringing noise erupted in the quiet room. Aleesha jumped, violently startled, and Michael reacted no less strongly. Well, both of their reflexes were in fine shape.

Michael swore under his breath and reached into his jacket. He pulled out a cell phone, looked at the caller's ID and answered it quickly. "Yes, Viktor. What do you need?"

She couldn't make out the exact words from the terrorist leader, but from the noise emanating from the phone, it was clear the guy was agitated.

Michael spoke soothingly, "I'll be right there and we'll talk about it some more. We'll figure something out."

He disconnected the call and stowed the phone inside his jacket as he stood up. "Gotta go. The boss is calling."

Aleesha asked quickly, "Everything okay? What's he so worked up about?"

Michael grimaced. "It has been twenty-four hours since the last life boat was dumped in the ocean and there's no publicity on the news yet. Viktor's freaked out that he's not the lead story on CNN."

Aleesha pressed her lips together. And she knew why, too.

Wittenauer's decision to isolate and sequester the male passengers and crew on the *Teddy Roosevelt* had been a great move.

Michael walked swiftly to the door, pausing with his hand on the doorknob. "Bring me breakfast in the suite I took you to yesterday at ten o'clock tomorrow morning. And wear those sexy white shorts you had on this afternoon."

He stepped outside before she could reply, the door clicking softly shut behind him. She gaped at the panel in shock. He'd noticed her shorts, huh? Whod've thunk? Her mind snapped back to business. What in the hell was taking him breakfast all about? She wasn't his maid! And then it hit her. She was, indeed, about to be his serving girl. That would be the cover he used to get her inside the terrorist ring. Good plan. Brilliant, in fact.

Belatedly, she spoke to the hidden microphones in the sofa cushion. "I hope you caught all that, because it looks like I'm going to be busy during tomorrow morning's check-in with the TOC."

She slept in the wired stateroom just in case Michael decided to come back and pay her another visit in the wee hours. Vanessa and Kat were in the room next door, one the TOC had verified had been occupied by a couple of men and was now empty. Misty was acting as lookout for Karen and Isabella, the three of them down in the crew quarters with the TV monitor. They were keeping an eye on the cameras in the corridors leading up to this part of the ship. They'd radio Vanessa and Kat if there was a problem headed their way, and in turn, those two would knock on the wall to warn her to take cover. It was a clumsy system at best, but she couldn't afford to wear a wire. The consequences of a microphone discovered on her would be catastrophic, not only to her, but potentially to the hostages.

She slept lightly, one ear cocked for a noise through the wall, and she was mildly surprised when she opened her eyes to sunlight at nearly nine o'clock the next morning. Six hours of sleep, even light sleep, in a real bed in the middle of an op was a heck of a luxury, and she was grateful for it. She went into the bathroom and took a quick shower, then dressed in the required white shorts. They did hug her rear end rather nicely, if she did say so herself. She pulled on a pale blue T-shirt—nothing to draw undue attention to herself. She was about to be the hired help, after all.

She headed to the ship's restaurant and gulped down a quick breakfast of her own. Then she went through the buffet line again and heaped a fresh plate with a traditional English breakfast of steak, eggs, stewed tomatoes and a rasher of undercooked bacon. She liked hers American style—brown and crispy—but she'd bet Michael was a purist and preferred the limp, pale version. She topped off the plate with fresh pineapple and mangoes. She juggled a glass of fresh-squeezed orange juice and headed for the exit.

One of the hijackers, a giant, baby-faced man she'd heard another hijacker call Montfort, dropped the muzzle of his AK-47 in her path and growled, "Where do you think you're going?"

She smiled up at him. "Michael asked me to bring him breakfast."

The big man's gaze narrowed. "Michael who?"

"I think he said his name was Somerset or something like that. He's in Room 9137. He told me to bring him breakfast this morning. He'll be very grouchy if it gets cold, don't you think?"

The guy's gaze flickered at that. So. Michael intimidated this guy, huh? Interesting.

The AK-47 muzzle lifted out of the way. Gaze downcast, she hurried from the restaurant and made a beeline for Michael's suite. If she didn't miss her guess, he wouldn't be alone in there today.

Sure enough, when she knocked on the door, a dark-haired man she'd never seen before opened the door. A long scar deformed the left side of his mouth and ran under his chin. He looked down at the plate in her hands, and his mouth twisted into a sardonic grimace that might pass for a smile. He said over his shoulder, "Your Lordship, your breakfast has arrived."

Aleesha catalogued as many details about the guy as she could. Spanish accent. Five foot nine. A hundred and sixty pounds or so. Left-handed. And, of course, that scar.

"Go to hell, Paulo," she heard Michael respond mildly from the living room.

Thank you, Michael. She attached the name Paulo to the Spaniard in her memory for relay to the TOC. He moved back from the door and she stepped into the room. Oh my God. She did a quick head count. Sixteen of the terrorists were here! Were they having some sort of staff meeting or something? She schooled her facial expression to one of submissive disinterest as she spotted Michael sitting at the round table near the picture window. She set his meal down, unfolded the linen napkin wrapped around his silverware and quickly laid a place setting in front of him. He took the napkin from her without comment. Were it not for their conversation last night, she'd swear he thought she was little better than dust on the furniture.

"Stick around," he ordered her casually. "You can take my plate when I'm through."

She nodded and stepped back, trying to fade into the curtains.

Michael was about half his leisurely way through the steak when Viktor walked in. The tension level in the room shot from zero to sixty in an instant. The guy was wired so tight he was about to explode, his face was flushed and his eyes were snapping. Something had him good and worked up.

She was surprised when Viktor spoke in rapid French, giving a few desultory instructions about who was covering what duty this afternoon. According to Michael, there were only twelve Basques aboard. That meant something like six to eight of these men were American. And apparently, all of them spoke French. Fluently. Unusual American terrorists, indeed.

And then her attention was drawn back to Viktor as he stormed over to the television and turned it to an all-news channel. He whipped around to face the roomful of men. "We have no coverage. Nobody knows what we have done! This must change, immediately. They must grovel before us. Beg for mercy. But that cannot happen until the entire world knows of our feat."

Aleesha managed not to roll her eyes. He sounded as loony as Hitler giving one of his pulpit-pounding tirades.

Viktor's voice changed abruptly. It dropped in volume and shifted to a businesslike tone. Whoa. That sounded like an almost schizophrenic personality shift, there. Not that something like that surprised her about this guy.

"Michael and I have devised a plan. One sure to rectify the lack of publicity for our accomplishment. We are going to dock this afternoon in Port-au-Prince, Haiti. Ostensibly, we'll be there to take on fresh food, water and fuel."

One of the Americans, judging by the bad French accent, spoke up. "How's that going to get the word out?"

Viktor smiled, the insanity from before shining in his eyes. "We'll pay for the supplies with hostages. That'll make quite a fuss, don't you think? There are buckets of journalists in Haiti covering the political problems there. They'll catch the story and it'll go all over the world. By tonight we'll be the most famous men on the planet."

It made a certain sick sense. Would no doubt work, too.

Viktor spent the next few minutes talking about who would be stationed where on the ship when it came into port and how they would go about handing over the hostages. He'd already decided to kick off the elderly, the sick and all the children under the age of three.

As Aleesha listened to Viktor spell out the details of the maneuver, it was amazing how thorough the guy's planning had been, especially given that glimpse of madness. She started as Michael caught her gaze and pointed at his plate. He jerked his thumb at the door. Kicking her out, was he? Well, he'd done great. She'd gotten a thorough look at the hijackers and would be able to give complete descriptions to the TOC of several more of the men. At this rate they'd have the whole shipboard picture for the SEALs in no time.

She took Michael's plate back to the ship's galley and then headed for Isabella and the comm link to the TOC. Time for an unscheduled call-in to report everything she'd just seen and heard.

* * *

Jack was standing over a schematic of the *Grand Adventure*, running possible attack plans, when a tech sergeant across the room let out a shout. Jack jumped and looked up quickly. That was the guy manning the link to the Medusas. But they weren't scheduled to call in for another couple of hours.

"Mamba's on the horn," the sergeant called out.

Crap. Something big must've gone down for the team to break radio discipline. Jack hustled to the comm console and slapped on one of the extra headsets. He motioned the tech sergeant to get out of the hot seat. "Is the line clear?" he asked the guy.

The tech sergeant nodded as he vacated his post.

Jack sat down quickly. He verified that the tape recorder was turning and picked up a pencil. "Go ahead, Mamba."

"I just got out of the Tangos' morning staff meeting. Thought you might be interested in their itinerary for today."

Jack about swallowed his microphone. Holy shit. How had she pulled *that* off? "Lay it on me."

"Viktor's upset that they're not getting press coverage. He's going to dock in Port-au-Prince, Haiti, this afternoon to trade hostages for food, fuel and water. I also have descriptions of four more Tangos for you. I think that makes twenty we've identified, now. It is almost certain that the only men on this ship are terrorists."

Jack nodded. Assuming that Somerset guy's information was legit, they only had four more Tangos to identify. A rescue team would have no trouble IDing all the Tangos on the ship. If it was adult, male and not a rescue team member, it was a bad guy. His mind rolled back to the first piece of information Aleesha had relayed. "Did you get a time frame for when they plan to dock?"

"Three o'clock local to give news crews time to pull together a story for the evening news."

"Considerate bastard," Jack growled. "Any other information?"

"Yeah. The Americans all speak French."

"You're kidding." Americans were notorious for not speaking other languages, and it was one of the bugaboos of the Special Forces community that it needed to bring its soldiers up to speed on operating in multiple foreign languages. Yet, this cell of American terrorists spoke French? They were sounding more and more like a military unit. A spec-ops-trained military unit. Not good.

Aleesha replied, "The meeting was conducted entirely in French."

"Copy. Anything else?"

"Negative. I've got to notify the women Viktor's planning to kick off the ship. Gonna brief them on what to do so they don't blow this chance."

"Roger." Jack reached over to save the recording of the transmission. It would be played back several times to harvest all possible information.

Wittenauer stormed into the ops center just as Jack was cueing up the tape to run it again. "Good timing, sir. Mamba had some interesting news for us."

Wittenauer listened to the tape in silence, his focus intense. The SEALs trickled into the room over the next few minutes, and Jack played the tape for them, as well. When everyone was satisfied they'd gotten everything Aleesha said, Wittenauer stared at the map of the Caribbean for a long time. Finally he said over his shoulder, "Too bad we can't keep the lid on this any longer."

Jack frowned. "There might be a way...."

Wittenauer whirled around and barked, "Talk."

Jack glanced over at Bud Lipton. "Am I reading that chart correctly? Is that green pin in the map just north of Haiti one of our tender ships?"

The SEAL glanced up at the wall chart. "Yes, that's correct."

Jack looked back at his boss. "What if we close the port and send everyone home. Then we could bring ashore a good chunk of that tender ship's crew and have them replace the dock crew in Port-au-Prince. They'd know how to service the *Grand Adventure*. We could use other crew off the ship to pose as civilians, Haitian soldiers and random people moving around the dock."

Wittenauer's eyes lit up. "We only have about four hours to get everything in place. I don't think the Haitians can order lunch in four hours. Although, I know the prime minister. In fact, he's alive because I helped him out a while back, but even with his cooperation it'd still be tight."

Jack shrugged. "I know a few people in Haiti who owe me favors. They could get the police to close the port quickly. The question is, can we get the crew of that tender into place in time?"

Lipton leaned forward. "I used to work for the captain of that vessel. He and his crew will get the job done. Especially if we tell them how many kids' lives are at stake."

Jack cleared his throat. "Perhaps a call to the White House is in order?"

Wittenauer grinned unrepentantly. "No time for that. Operational necessity dictates that I make a command decision, don't you think?"

Jack grinned back, relieved. "Absolutely, sir." And then he added, "Your head is going to roll after this operation is over."

Wittenauer shrugged. "If I can save all those people, it'll be a good way to go out. And some ops are worth sacrificing a career for. After all, what's a little tin in the trash, eh?"

Jack snorted. Hell. From his end of the business, he was expected to be willing to sacrifice his *life* for most ops. Killing off his career was kid stuff by comparison.

Wittenauer turned to the comm specialist Jack had kicked out of his seat. "Sergeant Bell, patch me through to the prime minister of Haiti."

Chapter 13

Aleesha pushed the door open with her back while she pulled the heavily laden cart of food. The kitchen staff had been more than happy to let her take a stint at facing the armed gunmen guarding the children. It was time to get a solid head count on the children in the kids' adventure area. An eager cry went up behind her. Apparently, the arrival of lunch was a big event. One of the hijackers headed over to keep an eye on the distribution of the food. What? Like she was going to pass out butcher knives to five-year-olds? She recognized the guy as one of the Americans. She nodded pleasantly to him, and the guy looked taken aback. Hey. She was all about collaborating with the enemy if it threw the Tangos off balance.

As she handed out plates of macaroni and cheese, mixed vegetables and warm brownies, she assessed the children's health and general well-being while counting them. They looked pretty strung out. The younger ones, in particular, were showing signs of severe mental strain. The SEALs needed to get in here in the next day or two and end this nightmare. Lord knew, she was doing her best to bring it to a close sooner rather than later.

The big, blond American reached for his ear. She recognized the telltale gesture. He was receiving a transmission and was blocking out the ambient noise of the excited kids.

"Are you Aleesha?" he snarled at her abruptly.

She started. "Uh, yes. Why?"

"Michael says to bring him lunch on the bridge in an hour. And it better be hot."

"On the bridge," she repeated. "Right. Hot. Yes, sir."

The American didn't seem to catch her sarcasm. Must have spent a lot of time in a rigid, militaristic environment where people were expected to react with such exaggerated deference. Some sort of extremist group, then. Even in the Special Forces, where military discipline was practically a religion, people didn't suck up to their superiors like sycophants. There was mutual respect but a minimum of ass kissing.

"Get moving, woman!" the American barked at her.

Whoops. She'd just been standing there, thinking. A *terrible* transgression. Definitely a fanatic, this American. Michael was right. If all the Americans were this way, they'd be dangerous when it came to a shootout.

She finished passing out plates and waited the fifteen minutes or so it took the kids to start finishing their meals. She occupied herself by surreptitiously finding both of the room's security cameras. They were tucked unobtrusively in the corners, high in opposite ends of the room. The far camera was right beside the emergency exits, which were currently chained shut, compliments of the terrorists. The near camera covered the area directly in front of the main entrance. She began collecting empty plates. One of the kids' area staffers came over in her distinctive orange shirt to hand Aleesha her plate.

"How are the kids holding up?" Aleesha murmured.

"Ragged," the girl murmured back, looking furtively at the guard.

"Don't look at him. Stay here and help me," Aleesha directed.

The girl did as she was told. They collected plates in silence for a few minutes and Aleesha kept an eye on the guard. When he moved away from them to look out a porthole, she said quickly, "Do your best to keep the kids calm and give the guards no trouble. Help is on the way."

"Who are you?" the girl whispered back.

"Nobody important. Hang in there for just another day or two." She might as well do what Michael had asked her to and pass on that message. If he was trying to pull some sort of stunt, it might be interesting to see where it led.

The guard noticed them speaking and strode back quickly, looking angry.

Continuing in the same low murmur as before, Aleesha said smoothly, "Okay, I've got this load of dishes. I'll be back in a few minutes to collect the rest." She nodded again at the guard and pushed her cart toward the door as if she hadn't done a thing wrong. She caught the American's frown and chuckled mentally. He didn't know what to make of a woman who wasn't cowering in fear before him and his big gun.

She made two more trips to the kids' area to collect dishes. On the last trip, she was able to pass one more quick message to the kids' staff girl that the moms on the ship sent their love to their kids. Then Mr. Grouchy swooped in again and ended any conversation.

Then it was time to take lunch up to Michael on the bridge. What was up with that? Clearly, he had something in mind. On a hunch she prepared a dozen plates of food. Michael had said there were always two, and sometimes more, Tangos on the bridge, and rumors among the female crew said a couple of female bridge officers were still alive up there, too.

She wheeled the cart to an elevator and rode up to the tenth deck. As she stepped outside into a brisk breeze, she was startled to see the distant smudge of land on the horizon. She peered through the haze. Yup, that was definitely the black hump of an island sticking out of the flat expanse of ocean. Must be Haiti, where they were due to dock this afternoon. Had Viktor changed the schedule? It was only a little after 1:00 p.m. Crap. If the SEALs had something planned for the *Grand Adventure,* was it about to get screwed up?

She hurried to the bridge door and rang the bell for entrance. A slight, dark-haired guy let her in. She put a name to him from this morning. Franco. A Frenchman. And if she didn't miss her guess, an old friend of Viktor's. Franco nodded at her but did not speak.

"You're late," Michael snapped from the captain's seat.

She cast her gaze down and mumbled an apology. Jerk. He probably got a big kick out of ordering her around like this in public. "I brought food for everyone. I hope that's all right."

Michael nodded at her disdainfully, and she carried plates to the three women officers at a map table. She smiled reassuringly at them but said nothing. Franco took his plate into the security office in front of the bank of video monitors. And last, she carried Michael's plate to him. His eyes glinted in amusement. It hadn't escaped him that he got lunch last.

"What did you bring me to drink?"

"Hemlock," she muttered under her breath.

He choked on a bite of grilled salmon and coughed hard. So. He had sharp hearing, did he? Served him right.

"Come over here and toss my salad for me. And cut it up into smaller pieces."

She picked up his knife and fork and ran her finger down the edge of the knife blade, testing its sharpness. She looked down pointedly at his lap, and set off another fit of coughing in the poor guy. She duly tossed and diced his salad and then murmured, "Do you need me to feed it to you? You seem to be having trouble swallowing today."

He glanced over his shoulder at Franco, and she did the same. The guy was engrossed in whatever he was watching.

"Are we early to Haiti?" she asked Michael quietly.

"No. Viktor wants to loiter out here for a while and see if any Navy vessels try to jump us."

"Let me guess. He's hoping they will, so he can kill some hostages and toss their bodies out of Port-au-Prince in front of the cameras."

"Probably," Michael agreed.

Franco came out of the security office to get a drink, and Aleesha drifted over to the three women from the *Grand Adventure*. "Can I get any of you anything?"

Gratitude shone in all their gazes. Inger answered, "A machine gun would be nice right about now."

Aleesha grinned and took a look around the bridge. "I dunno. There might be special satisfaction in using, say, that crash ax to dismember a few of these assholes. Or I might enjoy koshing them over the head with that nice, heavy sextant. Particularly the Englishman."

Aleesha was startled when Gwyn, the hospitality director shook her head in the negative. "Not him. He's a decent guy. He takes good care of us and seems to be trying to keep the bloodshed down." She added in a half whisper, "He's the only one of them who's not crazy."

"Really? How interesting."

"Enough talking over there," Michael barked.

Aleesha turned quickly. Yikes. Viktor had just stepped onto the bridge along with several other Tangos. She did a quick face check. Hot damn! Three more faces they hadn't identified yet. She carefully memorized the features of the three men. Only one more Tango to ID if Michael's number of twenty-four was accurate, and then the Medusas would have spotted the entire badguy contingent. Not bad for less than two days' work.

One of the Tangos caught her looking at him, and she bowed her head immediately. Time to do her submissive act again. She took the three women officers' plates and carried them to her serving cart. While she was there, she picked up the pitcher of fresh-squeezed lemonade she'd brought and poured glasses for the half-dozen hijackers now standing on the bridge, staring expectantly at the coast of Haiti and the ocean around them.

Sorry, boys. The Navy isn't that dumb. They're not about to give you any excuse to kill anyone. If Viktor wanted to spill blood, he was going to have to take the heat and the responsibility for it all by himself. She glided around the room for the next hour, refilling glasses, passing around cookies and generally cleaning up the bridge. When nobody kicked her out after the first few minutes, she figured they'd accepted her presence up here. Amazing how the hired help was invisible to these men. Elitist bastards.

At about two-thirty, Viktor pointed at the communications console, and Michael stepped forward. He calmly requested permission from the Port-au-Prince harbormaster to make an unscheduled fuel stop.

A familiar voice replied, "Say reason for this stop, *Grand Adventure.*"

That was Jack Scatalone! She'd know him anywhere, even with the darned close-to-authentic Caribbean accent he was laying on. She'd been yelled at by that voice more times than she could count. What were he and the SEALs up to? She listened as Jack duly gave the ship permission to dock and assigned them a pier.

One of the hijackers went to the navigation table and bent underneath it. Aleesha frowned, confused, until she saw the guy pull out a key and unlock a chain from around the table's center post. Inger Johannson stood up and made her way to the bridge controls, dragging a chain on her right ankle. Michael stood right behind her, watching her every move.

Aleesha's gaze narrowed. Maybe he was British Navy before he went SIS. He acted like he knew precisely what was supposed to happen in the docking procedure.

Inger spoke up hesitantly. "Normally the captain would go outside and stand on that little porch over there. He calls out distances as we approach the dock. I'm likely to hit the pier without that guidance."

Michael looked around the room and his gaze lighted on Aleesha. "You. Go outside and make the calls."

She gaped at him in shock. She didn't know the first thing about docking a giant ship like this! She was a support weenie in the Navy, not a field officer, and certainly not a bridge officer.

"Go!" he snapped.

It made sense. The hijackers wouldn't put one of their men in such an exposed position where he could be shot. And they wouldn't risk one of the ship's officers revealing critical information to the dock workers below. She lurched into motion, stepping out onto a tiny balcony, barely a meter square. Oh, God. The floor was made of glass. A wave of vertigo slammed into her as she gazed straight down at the water ten stories below. She grabbed hold of the wooden railing, its sleekly varnished surface smooth under her hand. How hard could it be to guide the ship? All she had to do was yell out how far from the dock they were. She was standing directly over the starboard railing, about a hundred feet back from the prow. It couldn't be any trickier than brain surgery.

But it came damned close. She constantly had to check herself against other reference points as the ship crept into the dock. At least Inger was bringing in the ship nice and slow.

The Norwegian woman called through the open door. "Tell me when the prow draws even with the end of the pier. That's when I'll throw the engines into reverse."

Aleesha nodded her understanding. The flat, wooden structure drew near. A few people moved around like ants, little more than specks far below. There! The *Grand Adventure's* nose had pulled parallel to the dock. "Now!" Aleesha shouted.

The ship vibrated, and a dull, grinding noise rumbled through the vessel's hull. Ever so slowly, the prow of the ship slowed. The shore drew closer and closer. Crap! She hadn't called soon enough. The ship was going to ram right into the big warehouse on the dock. Sweat popped out on her brow, and she wished desperately for a brake pedal that would stop the mighty ship's ponderous progress.

And then it was over. The ship came to a halt smack dab in the middle of the dock. A longshoreman ran up beside the ship, picked up a thick rope dangling from the ship's prow, and tossed it over a giant hook on the dock. A metallic rattle erupted, and Aleesha jumped. Belatedly, she recognized the sound of an anchor lowering into the water. Some naval officer she was. Didn't even know an anchor when she heard one. And she'd bet real Navy officers didn't about pee their pants while docking a ship. Amazing that she and Inger had done it. They'd safely docked the *Grand Adventure.*

Aleesha's knees felt weak as she stepped back onto the bridge. That was even scarier than the first time she'd cut into a living patient. She glanced over at the Norwegian woman. Inger looked ready to throw up. Must have been her first solo docking, too.

Michael caught her gaze and gave the briefest of nods, then turned to Viktor. He said casually, "It's time to send out the hostages and demonstrate your magnanimity to the world."

Viktor laughed loudly, startling Aleesha. He bellowed between gusts of humor, "I'm a lot of things Michael, my boy, but magnanimous is not one of them! What the hell. Go ahead. Toss them off my ship."

Aleesha was startled when Michael turned to her. "Go with the Montfort boys. Collect every child under the age of three, every woman over the age of sixty and anyone who's sick. Assemble them at the forward hatch on deck two." He added warningly, "I'm going to stay here and monitor the cameras to make sure there's no shenanigans. Hurry along with you."

And here she'd been wondering how she was going to get off the bridge so she could keep an eye on the women and children waiting to leave the ship. Three brawny Frenchmen stepped forward. The Montforts. They all had cruel eyes and didn't look like the brightest bulbs in the bin. Lovely. "Shall we, gentlemen?" she said lightly.

She stepped off the bridge, and the magnitude of actually getting nearly 150 passengers off the ship hit her. She turned to face the Montfort brothers. "Tell you what. Rather than you gents running all over the ship trying to collect hostages, why don't you go down to the hatch and I'll send the hostages to you?"

One of the brutes looked skeptical, but the other two nodded readily enough. They turned to head for Deck 2 and she took off in the other direction before they could pool their collective brainpower enough to reconsider. She'd expected at least one of them to tag along with her. But, hey. She wouldn't look this gift horse in the mouth. She hastened to the kids' area and told the staff it was time to go. They started sorting out the little kids to bring them to the hatch.

To the guards in the kids' area, she explained, "Viktor wants the little kids off the ship. You're to stay here with weapons on the older kids to ensure everyone's cooperation. The orange shirts will walk the children down to the forward hatch on Deck 2 and then come back here. If they fail to do so, you have permission to start shooting. You can radio Michael or Viktor on the bridge to confirm this."

The guy who acted like the leader of the bunch frowned but made the radio call. In a moment he nodded to the others. "She's telling the truth."

God, Michael was brilliant. Step by step he was establishing her credibility with the hijackers and setting her up as a collaborator to be trusted. She didn't know what she'd do with that trust once she had it, but it couldn't be a bad thing.

Now, to collect the women. Viktor had elected not to make a general announcement over the loud speakers for fear of triggering a stampede. He'd opted to notify by word of mouth only as many hostages as could be rounded up in ten or fifteen minutes. Little did he know that Aleesha had spent several hours immediately after the hijackers' staff meeting spreading the word to the appropriate people—including the moms of all the toddlers and infants who would play sick and get off the ship with their children.

She hustled to the kitchens where she knew close to a hundred women toiled, making supper for the ship. She burst into the tight, stainless-steel area and called out, "Quickly. It's time for anyone over sixty, anyone sick and any mother with a child under the age of three to come with me. You're getting off the ship now. Head down to Deck 3 and meet me in the forward lobby. I need to get word throughout the ship immediately to both groups of women. Anyone got any ideas?"

One of the women wearing a chef's hat stepped forward. "Tell housekeeping. They move all over the ship and are tracking where everyone is."

Housekeeping, huh? Who'd have guessed the maids would have already organized themselves into a spy network? Good for them!

She hurried out into a hallway full of staterooms and snagged the first cleaning lady she saw. She relayed her message and then hurried onward, telling every maid she ran into to get the mothers of the youngsters and the oldest female passengers down to Deck 3 right away.

She raced through the ship for ten minutes—all the time she dared take. It was the best she could do, but it should be enough. They all knew to be standing by for the call. She made her way to the third deck, where a murmuring mob of women was milling around. She glanced up at the security camera, praying that Michael was still manning the screens.

"Quiet, everyone. I've only got time to say this once. Your lives and your children's lives may depend on it. All of you who are over sixty years old need to make a point of showing your faces to the bridge of the ship as you leave it, and if you have gray hair, be sure to leave it uncovered. Got it?

"For the mothers. You're not supposed to be getting off the ship. Only the old and sick adults are supposed to be leaving. You'll need to act sick. Pick eight or ten of you to do a lot of coughing as you walk away from the ship. And here's the most important part. *Do not in any way* acknowledge your own children."

"Our children?" several of them cried out.

"Silence," Aleesha hissed. "*Listen to me.* All the kids below the age of three are waiting at the Deck 2 hatch right now. As you leave the ship, I want each one of you to grab a child until there are no more kids to be carried out. There are more adults than kids so you won't all have a child to carry. Don't worry about sorting the kids out or finding yours. They're all there. Just take the children and walk away from the ship. Do you understand me?" she directed with terrible urgency.

She was taking a huge risk. If Viktor found out what she'd done, he'd kill her first and then kill a whole lot of hostages, as well.

"There's one last thing. Three of the hijackers are downstairs. If you're not old, act sick as you walk past them. If one of them stops you, pretend like you're about to throw up all over him. I'll do my best to keep them occupied. Got it?"

Murmurs of assent sounded. Here went nothing. She waded through the women to the stairwell leading to the forward passageway and freedom for over a hundred women and some fifty children. She walked down the stairs, gesturing the women to follow her.

"Ahh, there you are gentlemen," she said loudly. "This is all the women I could round up on such short notice. Turns out the stress of this whole situation has taken a real toll on the ladies. I imagine you'll want to scan everyone's passenger ID card as they step off the ship, and you can keep an eye on the orange shirts to make sure none of them sneak out."

She barged over to where the dumbest looking Montfort stood by the end of the gangplank. "Let's go, ladies," she called out. "We don't have all day, here."

A mass of women pressed forward, and the Montforts actually took a step back from the rush. Perfect. Michael had sent down the three least competent terrorists. As the women started streaming past, Aleesha fussed around the guy who was trying to scan the ID card of each woman. She tried to keep him just distracted enough that he wasn't really paying attention to the women pushing past or the fact that so many of their names matched those of the children getting off the ship.

How Michael was going to hide the fact that all the "sick" women who'd left were the mothers of the children who'd also left, she didn't know. He'd just have to figure out a way.

One of the Montforts grabbed a woman by the arm and snarled at her in French. Something about her not looking very sick to him.

Aleesha jumped to his side, placing a solicitous hand on the arm of the terrified looking young woman. "Good grief, you look terrible," Aleesha gushed. "Is it the flu that's going around the ship? I hear you puke your guts out for three or four days, have terrible diarrhea the whole time and run a nasty fever." She glanced up at the terrorist looming beside her. "Careful not to get too close to this one or you'll catch the same bug she's got."

The guy frowned but waved the woman onward. "They all got the flu?" he growled.

"These are just the sickest ones," Aleesha shrugged. Time to trade in some of that credibility. "I thought Viktor might appreciate it if the passengers didn't barf all over his ship. With that hurricane coming, everyone's going to get seasick enough. You don't need ill pukers on top of that."

For some reason the mention of a hurricane distracted the guy. Maybe he was afraid of the idea of sailing into one. He moved closer to the exit where his brother was still scanning IDs. Within another minute the women and children were all off the ship. She looked outside and saw a trail of women all but running down the dock away from the ship. She held her breath, waiting for the sound of gunfire from above. But none was forthcoming. Praise the Lord.

She looked up at the security camera and nodded her gratitude to the man at the other end. Then she lurched as one of the Montforts growled, "Michael says you's to go to his room. Pronto. And he sounds plenty mad."

Chapter 14

"What in the name of God did you think you were doing, sneaking those extra women off the ship?" It was obvious Michael wanted to shout at her but dared not for fear of being overheard. "You could've gotten hundreds of hostages killed, not to mention yourself."

Gee, he actually sounded genuinely worried by the prospect of her getting her head blown off. Normally she'd stop to examine how that made her feel, but now was not the time. Aloud, she retorted, "They're mothers. How much more panicked would they have been if they'd been left behind on the ship and were separated from their children by an even greater distance? I did Viktor a favor getting those women off the ship with their kids."

Michael ran an exasperated hand through his thick, dark hair. "Jesus, that was a huge risk to take."

"Yeah, but it worked. With your help, of course. Great idea sending down those dimwit Montforts."

He rolled his eyes at her. "No more foolish stunts, eh? I might not be able to cover your ass the next time. As it is I had to scramble like mad to cancel the exit records of half those women in the ship's database. And now we just have to pray that Viktor doesn't call for any more head counts or he'll figure out a whole lot more women got off this ship than were recorded."

She shrugged. It had been dangerous, but she didn't think it had been foolish. And whether or not he wanted to admit it, he'd consciously or unconsciously set up a situation where she could do exactly what she'd done. She and Michael would just have to agree to disagree over her taking advantage of the opportunity he'd handed her. Time to change the subject. "You've got another problem, Michael. A big one."

He sat down heavily on the sofa. "Now what?"

"Once we pull out of Haiti and the rest of the hostages figure out they're not getting cut loose, morale's going to nosedive."

Michael frowned. "Viktor doesn't care about the morale of the hostages, and, frankly, I don't see how it matters. As long as they don't do anything stupid, we'll all be fine."

"That's the thing. They're going to do something colossally stupid."

He leaped to his feet, striding toward her until she found herself backing up against the wall in the face of his advance. "What have you done?" he asked menacingly.

Aleesha stared up at him, his physical closeness overwhelming. His eyelashes were thick and dark, his eyes black with barely contained fury. This man might be one of the good guys, but he was still capable of violence if pushed too far, and he was lethally trained.

She answered quickly, "I haven't done anything. But I'm telling you, the mood on this ship's going to get ugly. There's this phenomenon among women prisoners. You see, women don't back down well. They have this nasty tendency, particularly once their protective, mothering instincts are triggered, to draw a line in the sand and tell their captors to bring it on. If you don't want to have a revolt on your hands, you've got to get Viktor to give them something."

"A bribe, you mean?"

"Something like that. Something that will calm them down. Placate them."

"And I suppose you have something in mind."

She nodded. "I do. Visits by all the mothers to their children. Say, ten moms and kids at a time for, I don't know, fifteen minutes per day. It would do a lot to calm the mothers and the kids to see each other."

Michael spun away from her. "Viktor would never go for it."

She stared at the back of his head. "Then brace yourself for violence from the passengers very soon. You and I both know that quantity usually beats quality in a fight, if the numbers are overwhelming enough. I'll have a thousand royally pissed-off women fighting for the lives of their *children* to throw against your twenty-four terrorists. Who's going to win at those kinds of odds, Michael?"

He spun to face her, his hands going to the wall on either side of her head. His gaze burned into her like a laser. "It would be a blood bath," he snarled.

She looked him dead in the eye. "Yes, it would. And the women would attack anyway. They've got nothing to lose at this point. If this ship sails out of port and they're still aboard, all bets may very well be off in their minds. Nobody likes to see a safe port in their rearview mirror."

He stared at her for a long time. How she didn't disintegrate beneath the intensity of his stare, she had no idea. Finally, with a quick, powerful bunching of muscles, he pushed away from the wall. "Get out of here and I'll see what I can do. I can't make any promises, though."

She spoke quietly to his back as he reached for the doorknob. "That's all I can ask of you."

He cursed violently and then stepped out of the room. She followed thoughtfully.

* * *

Jack waded through the mass of sobbing women and children filling the warehouse. Debriefers were already questioning them urgently, and he did his best to stay out of the way of that process. He spotted General Wittenauer, decked out in a harbormaster's uniform.

The *Grand Adventure* was still outside, refueling. Crates of food had just arrived beside her and were being loaded via the rear service hatch, and the ship's freshwater tanks were already topped off, with the exception of one that was down for maintenance. Lord, it was tempting to storm her now. But there weren't enough assets in place. If only they'd had another twelve hours' notice.

Four more spec ops teams were en route to assist with the takeover of the ship, ETAs all within the next twenty-four hours. And until the good guys could get someone between those kids and the machine guns, nobody dared make any threatening moves against the *Grand Adventure*.

Jack was just approaching Wittenauer when a runner reported to the general, "Refueling and resupply are complete, sir. The *Grand Adventure* appears to be powering up and should be backing out soon. Do you have any further instructions?"

"Yeah. Send out those guys we dressed up as reporters and have them mill around the dock like they're taking pictures of the ship."

The runner nodded and sprinted across the warehouse.

Wittenauer turned to Jack. "That was a master stroke to suggest we come up with some fake reporters, too."

Jack shrugged. "I wasn't sure we'd have the warm bodies to do it after we emptied out the tender ship." It had taken almost the entire crew, hastily shuttled ashore, to man the large docks of Port-au-Prince's main shipping facility. But they'd pulled it off. Barely. The port bustled with activity, and to all appearances a normal day at the docks was in progress. It had been vital to get people into place who could actually do the jobs of port

workers and look convincing. According to the Medusas, the terrorist leader was paranoid in the extreme and had a hair trigger
when it came to killing his hostages.

The *Grand Adventure* had given them all a scare when she
showed up more than an hour before she was due. Fortunately,
the ship had loitered offshore long enough for them to get the
last Haitian dockworkers out of the area and the tender ship's
crew in their places. The *Grand Adventure* would never know
about the substitution. The only thing its hijackers would realize—some hours from now—was that they hadn't managed to
get the press coverage they sought.

And in the meantime, Aleesha had somehow managed to get
more than 150 women and children off the ship unharmed. It was
a drop in the bucket, but it was a hell of a lot better than nothing. The bomb was still ticking for the other women and children aboard.

He stepped out onto the dock to watch the giant white silhouette of the *Grand Adventure* as it backed up slowly, turned pon-
derously and headed back out to sea. It was hard to fathom letting
it go like this, but it wasn't like they had any choice in the matter. As long as Viktor Dupont had machine guns pointed at kids,
there wasn't a damned thing anyone could do to stop the ship.

Aleesha was in her wired-for-sound stateroom, alone, in case
Michael came to visit, when she was startled by a knock on her
door. She glanced at the bedside clock. Midnight. Michael
wouldn't knock at this time of night. He would let himself in with
a master key. She threw a heavy, terry cloth man's robe—owned
by the former occupant of this room—over her shorts and T-shirt
and cautiously opened the door.

One of the Americans stood there, looking disgusted.
"Michael told me to bring you up to him."

No wonder the guy was disgusted. He didn't like fetching the
boss's mistress. Probably disapproved of her, too, since she
wasn't Caucasian. *Poor Nazi baby.* She stepped out into the hall,

barefoot, and followed the guy up one deck and down the hall to Michael's suite. Her escort looked at her as if she was a complete slut. Which was just as well. All part and parcel of establishing herself as someone who was on their side. Even if the thought of sleeping with *any* enemy for the purposes of defeating him turned her stomach.

She knocked on the door of the suite, and the American made no move to go in with her when Michael opened the door. She stepped inside. Michael had a glass of whiskey in one hand and was shirtless, wearing only a pair of camo fatigue pants and his boots.

She closed the door and followed him into the living room. "Having a tough night, are we?" she asked quietly in doctor-patient mode.

Michael whirled as fast as a snake, dispelling any impression of drunkenness whatsoever. "I got him to agree to it, but I don't know how much it cost me. I may have just revealed myself as the snitch."

Aleesha took a step closer to him. "What snitch? What are you talking about?"

"Viktor got a tip before this cruise from hell started that there's an informer inside his French team. That's why he turned this rehearsal into the real thing. I overheard the Americans talking about it. If he figures out who I am, I'm a dead man. And all those damned officers will have died in vain."

Aleesha frowned as Michael paced a lap around the room, agitated. The pressure got to everyone now and then. And this man had been undercover for two years nonstop, infiltrating Viktor's network. But right now was a *really* inconvenient time for him to snap. What officers was he talking about? The ship's officers? "Why will they have died in vain?" she asked.

He whirled and snarled at her, "Don't you get it? I sat on that bridge and did nothing while thirty good men were executed. I could've stopped it. I could've shot my own men on the way to the bridge and maybe stopped the hijacking from ever happening. But I had to choose. The kids or the officers. Christ, I let those men *die*."

The light dawned in her head. He'd known the ship's officers were going to be executed, but had chosen to do nothing to stop it because he thought it was more important to save the hundreds of children. She went over to him and put her hand on his shoulder. Lord, he was tense. "You made the right choice. Sacrificing thirty officers was worth it if you can save five hundred children and a thousand women."

"I don't know if I can save them or not. Viktor's a madman."

She stepped in front of him and got right in his face, forcing him to make eye contact with her. She said resolutely, "We can do it. Together. You've got to keep believing that."

He stared back at her bleakly. "I don't believe in a goddamned thing anymore."

Bull. His remorse was real; nobody was that good an actor.

"You believe in saving those kids' lives. Some part of you still believes in good and bad. Right and wrong."

"Don't be deceived because I'm helping you. Hell, I had to kill a couple guys to get inside this organization. I'm no saint."

That gave her pause. It was typically the policy of governments that their undercover agents were not allowed to commit crimes in order to infiltrate criminal organizations. Particularly when the required entrance crime was murder. "Tell me about it," she said more calmly than she felt.

Michael shook his head. "Not much to tell. They were punks and wanna-be terrorists and got into a turf war with Viktor. He told me to kill them and I did. They never had a chance. I shot them with a silenced sniper rifle at close range as they came out of a pub. They never knew what hit them, and I got into the *Alliance*."

Whoa. Was he that callous or did he feel that strongly about getting inside Viktor's organization? At least he hadn't made them suffer. There was still a shred of humanity in him, then. "What did your government have to say about it?" she asked cautiously.

He shrugged. "I have no idea. I've only made one-way dead

drops to my control officer since I approached this bunch. Viktor is too damned suspicious for me to break cover or use electronic methods to talk to anyone on the outside."

More to the point, what did Michael himself think about it? "So, you killed a couple of criminals who deserved to die in the name of putting yourself in a position to stop this hijacking. And now you've let more men die to save the innocents on this ship. How's that different? How does that make you bad?"

He pulled away from her, leaving her arms feeling empty. "Don't give me that crap about it all being for a good cause. That's not the point."

"Then what is the point?"

"I didn't care. I killed those punks and I didn't feel a damned bit of remorse."

"But you cared when the ship's officers were killed. You care that the children are safe. You still have a conscience. You're not the monster you're painting yourself to be."

He grabbed her by the shoulders, his fingers digging into her flesh painfully. "Ah, but I am. And so will you be in a few years. You kill enough people because someone else tells you to, without knowing the reason why, and eventually you stop caring. You just follow orders and don't ask any questions. Innocent, guilty, good, bad or simply inconvenient to some politician—it doesn't matter. You just kill them and move on to the next job. You become a machine."

His words were a knife straight to her gut. They slid right past all of her defenses and pierced the core of her secret doubts and fears. Would this job steal her soul? Would she become the monster he described?

Stricken, she stared at him. He might not have lost all his soul, but he'd certainly sacrificed a big chunk of it. Was she willing to do the same? Was this cause noble enough—*right* enough—to warrant a similar sacrifice from her? "Isn't there another way?" she whispered.

His gaze was implacable, as black as his soul in that moment.

"There is no other way. This job demands no less." He took a rest-less lap around the room. "People get all up in arms about fanat-ics like Viktor being willing to die for a cause. But are you and I any different? Are we any better? We chose this path. We vol-unteered to become shadow warriors. We knew the odds against dying of old age. *And we did it anyway.*"

Dear God, he was right.

But something in her rebelled at the inevitability of her self-destruction.

She demanded, "Then why are you helping me if you're such a damned machine?"

He opened his mouth and then jerked as a noise rattled at the hallway door. He shoved her into the bedroom and threw the door shut behind them. "Strip and get into bed," he hissed before he slipped back outside.

Not again. In frantic silence, she tore off her clothes and slid between the sheets. And swore under her breath as the voice that responded to Michael's grouchy murmur was Viktor's. That guy had a veritable radar for when she was with Michael!

In the other room Viktor demanded, "Is she in there?"

Michael growled, "It's none of your damned business. Go down the hall and fuck your wife if you're so horny."

Aleesha's eyebrows shot up. Viktor's *wife* was on board? Was she the twenty-fourth terrorist? Crap. Had she given herself away by running all over the ship and gathering the mothers of the babies and toddlers and organizing their departure from the ship? Had Viktor's wife ratted her out? Was that why Viktor was here looking for her? Her speculation was cut short when Michael threw open the bedroom door, stormed inside, slammed the door—and thankfully locked it—and climbed into bed with her. A television abruptly blared outside the door, as if Viktor was de-termined to make his point through the wall. Very loudly.

"Uhh, excuse me," she breathed. "I'm naked here."

A grin curved Michael's mouth in the dark. "That's how I gen-erally like my women."

"I am not your woman," she whispered. Although why she was whispering she had no idea. They could have a shouting match in here and Viktor wouldn't hear it over the news in the other room.

Michael moved so fast she barely had time to register it, let alone react. He rolled on top of her, pinning her beneath him. She dared not fight him—that noise actually might carry to Viktor. At least they had Michael's pants between them to protect a smidgen of her modesty. But it wasn't a hell of a lot to hang her modesty on. Her breasts pressed against his naked chest, and there was no way her thoughts could avoid turning to sex. Surely Michael's did the same. He was a healthy, heterosexual male as far as she could tell.

She glared up at him in mutinous silence.

"Wanna be my woman?" he murmured. "We're a brilliant match. A couple of crusty old operatives making impossible choices and losing our souls together."

She stared up at him. Did he see something in her that she hadn't? What was it? This mission was about saving innocent hostages. Period. Not a tricky moral situation in the least. She was here to collect surveillance data for the real rescuers, not kill anyone.

"Why do you think I'm losing my soul?" she murmured, her ire at being sprawled naked beneath him forgotten for the moment.

"You know the hijackers' names and faces—you know which ones are smart, which ones are arrogant, which ones have French accents or New York accents or like ketchup on their scrambled eggs. They're human beings to you now, not just targets. And you're going to have to kill them. Trust me. It's going to cost you a chunk of your soul to do it."

She stared up at him in silence. She'd never killed anyone. Had assiduously avoided taking lethal shots on her one and only previous field experience. Dammit. If only she had a few missions under her belt, then she'd be able to defend herself against these accusations. She *would* be able to take the shots when the time came!

But an ugly image of the dimmest of the three Montfort brothers centered in her rifle sight popped into her head. He was a giant lump of a man and clearly mentally deficient to some degree. He was just following along, doing what his marginally brighter brothers told him to do. Did he really need to die to save the children? He was barely more than a child himself, intellectually.

She glared up at Michael. "I can do my job. I *will* do my job. And don't you ever doubt it."

"So that means you can kill me, then? I'm one of the hijackers, after all."

"You're still one of the good guys. You're helping us save those kids."

He leaned up on one elbow and pushed her hair back from his face with his free hand. He whispered, "How can a woman as smart and highly trained as you be so damned naive?"

Naive? Her? What gave him that idea? "I'm just out here, doing my job."

He shook his head. "Too idealistic, you are. It's going to get you in trouble. You'll follow your heart when you should be following your head."

Ironic words coming from him. He was the source of her current heart-head conflict! She shrugged, at least as much as she could with two hundred pounds of man plastered on top of her. "I think I'll hang on to those ideals, thanks."

He nodded slowly. "You do that. You hang on tight to them. Maybe—" He paused as though he wasn't going to finish the thought, but then he continued. "Maybe you'll get lucky and come out okay in the end."

The Medusas' trainer, Jack Scatalone, had talked to the team once about this. He'd talked about what it was like to question why you were doing a mission when it was all going to hell around you. Said it got people killed. He said you had to know exactly why you were out there and not lose sight of it. And then you had to shut down the soft emotions and just do the damned job.

But how in the hell was she supposed to shut down her softer emotions with this man staring down at her so compassionately? His body sheltered and protected her. He looked out for her continually. He'd been covering her back literally since the moment she came aboard this ship. Her heart said to trust him. Her head shouted at her not to be a fool. "Why me?"

"Why you what?" he replied, frowning.

"Why did you single me out from all the other passengers? Why are you doing all of this?"

He stared at her for a long time and finally replied gruffly, "First of all, you picked yourself. You were the only one brave enough to step forward and take dinner to the terrorists. Secondly, I picked you because—I saw—I sensed—" He paused so long Aleesha thought he wasn't going to finish. "You're my last hope for salvation."

Surely he was talking about her being his last hope for help in rescuing the hostages from Viktor and company. But darned if it didn't sound like he was talking about something else entirely. "I don't understand."

"Don't you?" he breathed. "Two years. Two *years,* Aleesha. And you're the first glimmer of hope I've had in all that time."

And for a moment, all of it was there in his eyes. The grueling mental strain, the constant fear of discovery, the relentless pressure of knowing how much was on the line. The toll of it all etched on his features, and her fingers ached to smooth it away.

Their gazes met. Held.

"I'm so sorry," she murmured.

And the spell was broken. His eyes shuttered once more, he rolled away from her.

Aleesha blinked. He left a conspicuous arm and a leg across her. Thought she was going to bolt, did he? And where would she go with Viktor sitting in the next room?

As if he'd heard her thoughts, Michael murmured in her ear, "He's watching the news. Waiting for coverage of the *Grand Adventure* to hit the airwaves. You're stuck in here until he sees himself on the telly."

Crud. If she didn't miss her guess, old Viktor wasn't going to see his mug on the TV anytime soon. The JSOC crowd had clearly pulled some sort of whammy on Viktor back in Port-au-Prince. And given how hard General Wittenauer had been working to contain the news of the hijacking before the Medusas came aboard the ship, she'd lay odds he'd done something in Haiti to circumvent Viktor getting the press coverage he craved. She rolled onto her side with her back to her impromptu bed partner.

Michael shifted, spooning himself against her. Oh, Lord, that felt nice. And a girl couldn't help but be grateful that he hadn't instantly taken advantage of her nudity to make some sort of pass. He murmured, "You might as well get comfortable."

Comfortable was not how she'd describe the hot tickle of his breath against her ear, the heaviness in her breasts where his arm brushed against them. Provocative, maybe. Or even flat-out sexy. But definitely not comfortable.

Slowly she relaxed in his arms. They lay there in silence together, listening for any movements outside. Both of them were no doubt thinking about the same things, running possible scenarios through their heads and planning best- and worst-case responses to each situation. And the longer she lay there, the safer she felt. Between the two of them, plus the combined resources of the American Special Forces community, there was nothing they couldn't handle.

But then a bellow of fury from the other side of the bedroom door jolted her to full combat alert. A spate of vicious French curses erupted as Michael sat up, the look on his face grim. "The press hasn't broken the story yet."

She sat up beside him, yanking the sheet up over her chest when it fell down around her waist. "I wonder what happened," she replied mildly.

"Michael!" Viktor bellowed from the other room.

For a moment, the stress of the situation showed on Michael's face—worry, loathing and exhaustion skated across his features. But then he pulled himself together and slipped out of bed. Poor guy. She couldn't imagine tiptoeing around Viktor for two years. It had to have been positively grueling. She watched in compassion as Michael paused with his hand on the doorknob, took a deep breath, and then stepped out to face the wrath of a madman.

She took advantage of his absence to jump back into her shorts and T-shirt. They weren't much protection against the pull she felt toward Michael, but they were better than nothing. As she was getting dressed, she happened to notice a jumble of wires and a small battery pack on the nightstand beside the bed. She knew what that was! An earpiece and microphone set. Must be Michael's. She pocketed the whole wad quickly. The hijackers no doubt had spare radios. Michael could get another one. If he was on the level, he'd make up an excuse and cover her theft. If he was trying to use her to flush out the rest of the rescue party, he'd probably be unwilling to admit to Viktor that he'd been careless enough to let one of their radios fall into her hands.

Viktor ranted and raved in the other room for nearly a half hour. And one extremely interesting bit of information came out of it, compliments of Michael, of course.

Viktor was screaming about needing to publicize the cause of the Basque people when Michael interjected mildly, "Well, when we get to Guantánamo and pull every last terrorist out of the prison there, you're bound to get global headlines."

Holy shit. Was that what Viktor had planned for the *Grand Adventure?* It made sense. There were at least a thousand hard-core terrorists being held at the U.S. Navy facility in Cuba. They'd all fit nicely on a ship this size. And what, exactly, did Viktor want with a thousand terrorists, not one of whom was a Basque separatist? The men in Gitmo were almost exclusively from Muslim extremist organizations. They'd be well trained and well connected, but they wouldn't give a hoot about a little patch of mountains between France and Spain.

But maybe she'd just answered her own question. The prisoners in Cuba would be well connected. Maybe Viktor was planning to ransom them back to their various organizations or take payment for their freedom in weapons or favors. If a little splinter group like *L'Alliance de la Liberté* could tap into the resources of the big dogs of terrorism, old Viktor might just stand a chance of getting his own country.

She continued to listen as his tirade finally wound down. With a last bellow of fury, he demanded that Michael fix the publicity problem, and stormed out of the room. Yikes. She wouldn't want to be Viktor's wife right about now.

Speaking of her, why hadn't Michael said anything about her yet? Was she that insignificant to Viktor and his plans? Or was Michael protecting her identity for some reason? If so, what was that reason?

Michael came back into the bedroom wearily. He sat down on the side of the bed, his elbows propped on his knees and his head hanging between his shoulders. She ached to reach out to massage away the terrible tension in his back. But this wasn't the time or place to act on her personal attraction to this man. Instead she asked quietly, "Need any help figuring out what you're going to do to calm down the Grumpy-mon?"

"Grumpy-mon?" Michael grinned, imitating the heavy Jamaican accent she'd used to pronounce the word.

"Well, somet'ing's pulling on his short hairs fair hard, dontchya t'ink?"

Michael turned to face her, smiling widely. Much better. "Fair hard, indeed," he replied. "So what do you suggest I do?"

She dropped the accent. "Ask Viktor to draft a statement for you to read over the airwaves. That should keep him busy for a few hours. Then, make a radio call from the bridge. If you broadcast a big message about having taken over the ship and being willing to kill hostages if your demands aren't met, Viktor should calm down."

"And who would I be broadcasting to?"

She answered, "Maybe you could get in touch with the guys who've been keeping this whole mess out of the news in the first place."

Michael's mouth twitched in humor for a moment, but then he waxed serious again. "That buys me twelve, maybe twenty-four hours. What do I do when he blows up again because he's still not in the news?"

She shrugged. "You cross that bridge when you come to it. One crisis at a time, eh?"

Michael grimaced. "Spoken like a pro. Maybe your Spec Ops buddies will get off their butts and rescue the lot of us one of these days so I can quit stringing along that maniac."

She had no reply for that. No way was she going to talk specifics about her teammates or the rescue plan with him. No matter how much she personally might trust him, that was a professional risk she wasn't about to take.

The TV went off in the other room. Crap. Someone had come into the room and she'd been so engrossed in her conversation with Michael, she hadn't even noticed. A *huge* lapse of awareness. *Major* screw-up. She started as Michael's arm snaked around her neck, pulling her to him without warning. Their mouths were only inches apart, their gazes locked—hers in startlement and his in dawning awareness. *Whoa. Sex appeal alert.* She stared at him, transfixed by the magnetism abruptly tugging insistently between them. A door closed and the outer room went silent. Whoever'd come in had left again.

Michael murmured, "Have I gotten around to telling you how beautiful you are and how attracted to you I am?"

"Uh, no," she managed to mumble, thoroughly startled by his directness.

He smiled crookedly. "Well, you are. And I am."

Now what was he up to? Was he for real or was this just a tactic to throw her off balance? If so, it was working like a charm. Time for a countermove just in case. "So are you. And so am I."

The humor faded from his midnight gaze, leaving scorching heat in its place.

Yowza.

He asked quietly, "What do you suggest we do with all this mutual attraction?"

She had to give him full marks for being a professional and a gentleman. Most guys she knew would already have been kissing her and moving ahead with getting her clothes off. And damned if his restraint didn't make him even more attractive! "Are you asking my professional opinion on the subject or my personal opinion?"

"I'm asking whichever opinion you're planning to act upon."

She dropped her head and closed her eyes. "As desperately as I'd love to spend the rest of the night making love with you—"

Lips touched her forehead, silencing her. His kiss was gentle. Soothing. Absolved her of guilt. He followed up by saying, "One of the things I find most attractive about you is your strength. Don't change. The right time for us will come along."

She groaned and pulled away from him, flinging an arm over her face. "I am such an idiot," she mumbled into the crook of her elbow.

A quiet chuckle from beside her. "You're a lot of things, but an idiot is *not* one of them." He paused. "But it is nice to know I won't be the only one having trouble sleeping tonight."

His forecast turned out to be true. In the wee hours he walked her back to her room where she tossed and turned. And when she finally did sleep, her dreams were steamy and sexual, robbing her of any decent rest.

When she awoke in the morning, Aleesha headed for the unofficial Medusa command post and was relieved to find the whole team there and awake as she slipped into the crowded room.

Vanessa looked at her closely. "Sleeping with the enemy now, are we?"

Aleesha pursed her lips. "*Sleeping* being the operative word. Michael had me brought up to his room last night. We were talking and then Viktor walked in, so I ducked into Michael's bedroom for a couple of hours—" she added for emphasis, "fully clothed."

Vanessa nodded shortly, taking her at her word. *Thank God.* "Learn anything interesting?"

"Yeah. Viktor's taking this ship to Guantánamo and picking up all the terrorists being detained down there."

Vanessa jolted. "Where'd you hear that?"

"Straight from the horse's mouth. Michael and Viktor were talking about it."

Vanessa looked slightly shell-shocked. "I've got to hand it to you. Cultivating Michael was a great idea. Any other bombs to drop on me?"

"Well, Viktor's wife is aboard, she's not the twenty-fourth terrorist and Viktor most likely hates her guts."

Vanessa frowned. "We probably ought to find her. See if she can tell us anything useful about Viktor."

"She may still be loyal to him," Aleesha warned.

"True, but I still think it's worth the risk." Vanessa turned to Isabella. "Can you ask your network of maids to find her?"

Isabella nodded. Then the intelligence analyst turned a piercing look on Aleesha. "Are you okay? You're spending an awful lot of time with the hijackers."

"Of course I'm okay. Why wouldn't I be?"

Isabella replied, "You going to be all right with shooting them when the time comes? No sympathy pains?"

She frowned. Funny that her teammates were bringing that up so soon after Michael had talked to her about the very same thing. Were they seeing something that she wasn't? Was she getting too close emotionally to the terrorists? Sure, the hijackers had taken on personalities and distinct identities in her head. And no, they wouldn't be total strangers when it came time to kill them. But they were terrorists. Threatening to kill children. Hadn't she just argued with Michael last night that he'd done the right thing to think of the kids first, even if it meant letting the ship's officers be killed? Surely if he could do that, she could pull the trigger against the people who would actually kill the children if properly provoked.

Belatedly she answered Isabella. "Well, I'm sympathetic to Michael, of course. But I could kill the others." Probably. No. Make that definitely. She could absolutely kill the others if she had to. Man, she'd done it this time. She was in big trouble. She gave up a silent prayer that it would never fall to her to pull the trigger. Thankfully, that wasn't part of the plan.

Vanessa cleared her throat. "Speaking of Michael, we've got some news about him."

Aleesha asked eagerly, "Did the Brits confirm his identity?"

"Yes, they did."

Hallelujah. Now she could speak and plan openly with him as the rescue drew near. That would make her life *so* much easier.

"But there's a problem," Vanessa continued.

Aleesha watched her boss carefully. That was Vanessa's "your dog has died" face. Crud. She waited for her boss to continue with whatever bad news she was about to impart.

"Michael Somerset *was* British SIS. But he's not now. His employment with them was terminated."

She felt like Vanessa had just punched her in the stomach. "When?" she managed to choke out.

"Two years ago. The Brits didn't give us the details. Something about not following procedures. He was given the ax."

The punks he'd killed. It must be. And the timing was right. But then, something odd occurred to her. She asked slowly, "This may sound stupid, but does Michael know he's been terminated?"

Vanessa frowned. "I'm sure he must."

Aleesha disagreed. "I'm not so sure. He told me he's been in deep cover for two years. He hasn't had contact with anybody at SIS except through one-way dead drops."

Vanessa said slowly, "I think you should break off contact with him."

Aleesha jolted. No way! "That makes no sense! I've cultivated him thoroughly. You just said yourself how useful he's been. He's doing whatever I ask him to and nothing he's told us has proven inaccurate."

"You're not thinking objectively," Vanessa retorted.

Aleesha rolled her eyes. "It doesn't take objectivity to know this guy can still be helpful." An ugly sensation rolled through her gut and she took a moment to identify it. Desperation. Oh, dear. She sighed. "Okay, I admit that I'm too close to this guy to make a completely objective call. But dammit, he'll help us. I know it as sure as I'm standing here."

Vanessa stared at her for a long time and Aleesha stared back, miserable.

Finally her boss spoke. "I'm going to catch a ration of crap over this, but my gut says he'll help us, too. Don't tell him he has been terminated. Let him continue to think he's one of the good guys."

Aleesha replied quietly, "He *is* one of the good guys. He's doing his damnedest to keep those kids alive."

"Right," Vanessa shrugged. "Just watch your six. It's still possible he's setting you up."

No, it wasn't. They'd just spent half the night in each other's arms. Sharing comfort. Sharing trust. And it hadn't been about sex. It was about two human beings connecting in an elemental way. He was fine. She knew it, dammit! But the harder she tried to convince herself of that, the more uneasy her gut became.

Jack looked up from the schematic of the *Grand Adventure* as someone across the ops center called out his name. Now what? This place had been a complete zoo ever since Isabella had radioed in Aleesha's latest report that the hijackers were heading for Guantánamo and its prison with the intent to empty the joint. JSOC was frantically adjusting the timetable on the rescue plan. A thousand more terrorists could *not* be allowed to board that ship. They'd never rescue the remaining hostages alive if that happened!

"Colonel Scatalone, it's the Adventure Cruise Line calling. They need to speak to you."

He picked up the phone at his elbow and nodded at the duty controller to send the call over to him. The receiver clicked.

"Colonel Scatalone here," he said.

"Hello, this is Les Lewis. I just got a call from the harbormaster in St. Thomas. He wants to know why the *Grand Adventure* missed its port call there. Apparently, the local merchants get annoyed when a big ship doesn't show up."

"What did you tell the guy?" Jack asked tersely. General Wittenauer had specifically instructed the cruise company's executives not to reveal to anyone that the ship had been hijacked.

"I told him we rerouted the ship to avoid Hurricane Evangeline."

"Good thinking. Did he buy it?"

"He griped about the hurricane passing well north of the Virgin Islands and that the *Grand Adventure* was plenty clear of it. I told him the captain was trying to avoid rough seas and didn't want to sail into the eastern Caribbean."

"Well done. If somebody like that calls you again, tell him you'll forward the call to the right person in the company, and send them to me." The longer the *Grand Adventure* was missing in action, the more strident those phone calls were going to get. In three more days, when the *Grand Adventure* failed to return to its home port and let off its passengers, the jig would be up. But until then, silence was an enormous ally. The last thing he needed was a flotilla of paparazzi lurking around the *Grand Adventure* in floating bathtubs trying to get a scoop and giving away what his teams were doing to the hijackers.

All five SEAL teams should have arrived onboard the tack force of Navy ships that was trailing the *Grand Adventure*. They'd finalized the last details of the plan last night based on the intel from the Medusas. The Medusas would have twenty-four hours to put the last pieces of the support puzzle into place, and then the rescue would commence.

Chapter 15

Late that afternoon, Aleesha was escorting the last reluctant group of mothers out of the kids' area after their fifteen-minute visits when a maid sidled up to her in the hallway. "Viper needs you now."

The maid moved off, pushing a cleaning cart down the hall.

Viper, huh? What was enough of an emergency to make Vanessa send a message through the underground network of crew members? With Viktor's wife still unaccounted for, it was a huge risk. Aleesha nodded at the surly hijackers who'd overseen the mother-child visits. They'd scowled over the entire proceeding, obviously convinced it was a bad idea to let the moms and kids see each other. But, as she'd forecast, the visits had been hugely therapeutic to both groups of hostages.

One of the hijackers, an American, actually nodded back at her. Son of a gun. Even the nasty Americans were thawing toward her.

She strolled nonchalantly out of the kids' area and headed

downstairs toward the crew quarters, carefully refraining from breaking into a sprint to more quickly find out what was so blessed important. Thankfully, over the last day the hijackers had relaxed the restrictions on movement around the ship, and the hostages had settled into a cooperative, yet passive, routine. Studiously ignoring the security cameras overhead, she slipped into the Medusas' headquarters. All of the team's other members were there.

"What's up?" she asked. "I came as soon as I got your message."

"We just got off the horn with the TOC. The rescue timetable has been moved up. We've got to take the ship back before it gets to Cuba and picks up a thousand more terrorists."

No kidding.

Vanessa continued, "All the SEAL rescue teams are in place and they'll come aboard as soon we finish a few final preparations."

Aleesha added dryly, "And then, of course, there's the small matter of the hurricane that's bearing down on us." She knew she was on a hell of an op if the imminent arrival of a hurricane didn't even rank as one of the team's top concerns.

Vanessa was speaking again. "Tonight Jack needs us to find three or four good hiding spots for the children. The hidey-holes need to be spaced throughout the ship. Ideally, all the kids will fit into one reasonably defendable location. Right before the op goes down, the Medusas will take out the guards around the children and move the kids to get them out of the line of fire. As soon as the kids are safe, the SEALs will make their run and board the ship."

It made sense to move the children. But where in the world were they going to find hiding places for four hundred children? The hidey-holes would have to be the size of a large room and would need to be quickly accessible from the kids' adventure area. To be defendable, each spot would need to have only one or two entrances. Heck, even finding *one* hiding place that fit the bill would be a challenge.

Aleesha asked, "Anyone got any brilliant ideas on where to hide the kids?"

Vanessa smiled without appreciable humor. "Nope. We've picked out a few possibilities on the blueprints, but someone needs to take a look at them in person. That's why we need you to go out tonight and scout out some spots."

Aleesha frowned. Move around the ship at night? A dangerous proposition with the eight-o'clock curfew still in place. As far as she knew, the hijackers' instructions were still to shoot on sight anyone out of their rooms after eight. If she got caught, Viktor could very well kill her just to spite Michael. Cameras were everywhere. She'd *never* be able to move around undetected.

Isabella spoke up. "Michael's pulling watch duty on the bridge from midnight till 4:00 a.m. I heard a couple of the hijackers talking about a schedule change earlier today. Apparently Viktor's mad that Michael might be fooling around with you and put him on that shift to cool his jets."

Why did she suddenly feel like a teenager at summer camp caught in a boy's tent after lights-out?

Isabella continued, "The good news is you'll be able to move freely around the ship without worrying about the cameras. Unless, of course, you've outlived your usefulness to Michael and he's ready to turn you over to his boss."

"Gee, that's a cheery thought," Aleesha retorted.

Isabella grinned at her.

As far as Aleesha knew, she hadn't outlived her usefulness. Michael seemed convinced she was still his direct link to the rescue team. Aloud, Aleesha asked, "And what if I run into one of the roving foot patrols? I've made friends with some of the hijackers, but some of them would still shoot me without thinking twice about it."

Vanessa nodded. "That's why we'll put you on a radio with Isabella. She'll track your movements with her monitor, keep an eye out for Tangos approaching you, and will call you if anyone's coming."

All well and good until she got caught. If the hijackers found her wearing a high-tech military throat mike and radio setup, they'd know she was an infiltrator for sure. She'd be *so* dead. Not to mention the Medusas' existence aboard the ship would be revealed. No telling what Viktor would do.

But then, danger came with the territory. They were trained to do this sort of thing—in fact, they'd trained a very similar scenario just a couple months back with Jack roaming around a training building playing bad guy while they avoided him using surveillance cameras and radios. Tonight should be no sweat.

But when midnight came and Aleesha actually stepped into the hallway, she was definitely sweating. There was something about sneaking around alone in a hostile environment that made her tense. At least when she was on patrol with the whole team, she knew she had plenty of alert eyes around her and backup if something went wrong. Tonight she was on her own. Sure, Isabella had two hundred electronic eyes around the ship. But these hijackers were unpredictable. No telling what Viktor might pull out of his hat.

Aleesha adjusted her utility belt, slung low on her hips over a pair of navy linen capri pants and a matching navy polo shirt. It felt extremely strange to be wearing her gear over civilian clothes. But, the Medusas had decided that in a pinch she could ditch her gear and pretend to be going to Michael's room. That was, assuming she didn't get caught in, say, the engine room. In that case, she was hosed.

Isabella murmured in her ear, "You're clear to take the forward stairs up to Deck 7." Vanessa wanted Aleesha to check out one of the deserted discotheques.

She slipped into the empty, dark club. "Too many doors," she murmured into her throat mike. "Four big entrances."

After an all-clear from Isabella, she moved down the hall to a bar nestled in the prow of the ship. Now, this had possibilities. It would seat about fifty adults. Surely several hundred kids could cram in here. She spied a door behind the bar and moved quickly to check it. Locked.

Crouching among the glasses and bottles of liquor, Aleesha

murmured, "Where does the door behind the bar go? Is it just a storeroom?"

"Standby one. I'll check the blueprints," came Isabella's impassive response. Then, a minute later, "Yup. Small storeroom. No other exits."

"Then I think we have a winner. The Cabana Lounge on Deck 7 has two entrances, each one opening onto a hall that runs aft along either side of the ship. We'd need to barricade the doors, and they're both double doors that swing inward by the way, but it's doable."

"Roger," Isabella murmured. "Time for you to skedaddle. A patrol of two Americans just went to Deck 7. They're at the other end of the ship, but headed your way. Exit into the starboard hallway and head down the forward stairs."

Aleesha jumped into motion and did as Isabella directed. On a maneuver like this, it was all about trust. Isabella was the absolute best when it came to real-time image analysis.

Aleesha made her way down to Deck 2, not far from where Isabella was operating, in fact. After a brief pause for Isabella to check the area, Aleesha slipped down a short connecting hall to the crew staircase to Deck 1 and the bowels of the ship. Generally the hijackers didn't patrol down here. *Generally*.

"Proceed aft with caution. I don't have full coverage into some of the side nooks and crannies."

Great. It was dimly lit down here with only a few widely spaced bulbs in wire cages. Although everything was uniformly painted light gray, the thickly clustered pipes, wires, valves and bulky fittings made it look much more like a really clean factory than a cruise ship. The ceiling was very low—not much more than six feet high. It, in combination with the narrow, winding passageway, pressed in on her in a surprisingly claustrophobic fashion. The throbbing beat of the engines gave this space an almost womblike quality.

Given Isabella's inability to see behind every pipe, Aleesha shifted into room-clearing mode. She spun around corners fast and low, knife at the ready, her senses on high alert. Anyone down here was bound to be a bad guy, so she didn't have to make a threat assessment. If it moved, kill it. Or at least neutralize it quickly and silently.

She'd hadn't been down here long when a swift movement far ahead in the gloom froze her in place. Aleesha peered off into the distance, but saw nothing.

Very slowly she reached for her throat mike and breathed, "I've got company. You see anything?"

Isabella's voice came back hushed, although nobody would hear her if she shouted through the custom-made earpiece that fitted entirely inside Aleesha's ear. "Nada. Proceed with caution."

Aleesha snorted mentally. No kidding. She eased forward, doing her best to blend in with the contours of the walls. She slipped her pocket periscope out of its pouch and peered around every corner before she advanced. One more fat pipe to get past, and then she'd be at roughly the spot where she'd seen that quick movement.

She slid the end of the periscope around the curve of the pipe. There! A shadow on the wall ahead! She strained, listening hard. A bare whisper of sound carried to her, but it was hard to tell over the noise of the engines grinding on either side of this central passage. The shadow moved. Shifted. Separated into two distinct human outlines. Was it a patrol?

Not likely. Whoever these two were, they'd been standing stationary down here for nearly five minutes while she'd approached them. And they were definitely talking. Who in the world was it? Could there be some sort of conspiracy among the passengers to rescue themselves that the Medusas hadn't gotten wind of? If so, she desperately needed to know about it and stop it before it interfered with the SEALs' plans tomorrow.

She had to get closer to the pair in front of her. But how? She looked around. There was squat for cover if she tried to slide around the pipe that now hid her. She glanced up. But…

There was a gap between the rows of pipes overhead. If she

could wedge herself up there, she might be able to slide forward far enough to hear what the people were saying. She jumped up silently, catching a wrist-size pipe with both her hands. Here's hoping it could support 140 pounds of special operator. Slowly, she pulled her feet up over her head in a grinding abdominal crunch that hurt like hell. There. Her right foot hooked over a small pipe about two feet from the one she hung from. She looped her left foot over the same pipe. Carefully, she pulled herself up, twisting to come parallel to the pipes and stretching out along the steel spaghetti that lined the ceiling.

She reached over her head and pulled herself forward a few inches. Her shoulders began to ache as she held herself up without any support under her torso, using only her legs and arms to brace herself against the ceiling. Another few inches. And another few. Her shoulders felt like they were on fire. *Oh, man. Spider-man could have this job.*

One more careful pull forward, and the pair below came into sight. She nearly let go of the pipes and fell as she spied a man and a woman conversing urgently. The woman had her back turned to Aleesha, but there was no mistaking the shoulder-blade-length blond hair and curves of a female.

The blonde was speaking to one of the Frenchmen, François, in a language Aleesha didn't recognize. After hanging out around the terrorists for the past two days, she'd guess it was Basque, the ancient tongue of the Pyrenees that bore surprisingly little resemblance to French or Spanish.

Even though she couldn't understand what they were saying, the way in which they were saying it spoke volumes. They were having an argument. And more to the point, it wasn't a spat between lovers. This was an intense disagreement between two equals. The woman was an equal to François?

Had she done it? Had she found the twenty-fourth hijacker? Except the information they'd gotten from TOC indicated that Mrs. Dupont was a slightly overweight brunette named Susan. C'mon. Turn around, lady. Let me see your face. But the blonde continued to hiss at François, her back squarely to Aleesha. Dang it! The woman was right in front of her and Aleesha couldn't get a decent look at her. She had to find some major identifying feature the SEALs could use to find this woman when they cleared the ship tomorrow.

The woman's blond hair was straight. Dry. Like she washed it too often—or maybe swam a lot. She had a tan that corroborated the swimmer theory. What else? Average height and a lean build, her arms muscular. Not a hell of a lot to go on. The woman raised her hands, gesticulating in frustration. François wasn't going along with whatever his companion was saying.

Something metal glinted in the low light. The woman's watch. Aleesha started as she recognized the model—an expensive, stainless steel diving watch with a built-in depth gauge and dual faces, one for telling time and one for tracking the length of a dive.

Aleesha dared not move any closer or else she'd bring herself right into François's line of sight. She tried to push herself backward a few inches, and her shoulders knotted into useless masses of pain. Crap. She couldn't move. Now what?

Fortunately, François and the blonde only snarled at each other for a few more seconds and then moved off. Aleesha clung to the pipes for as long as she could, and then, with a grateful grunt, dropped to the floor, landing lightly on the balls of her feet. Her arms felt like overcooked noodles.

She reached for her throat mike. "Where are they?" she murmured to Isabella.

"They split up. He's heading away from you toward the forward staircase. Just passing point Alpha One now. She went up the midships staircase. Approaching Echo Six. Is walking down the hall."

"Can you get a good look at her face?" Aleesha asked urgently. "It's not Viktor's wife. The only other woman who'd be able to move freely during curfew is the last terrorist."

"The resolution's not all that hot on these cameras. If I was back at the office I could enhance the picture, but I don't have that kind of capability here."

Damn. The mystery terrorist's identity was threatening to remain secret. "Get a room number on her at any rate. Maybe we can track down her identity through the cruise company headquarters."

"Roger, wilco," Isabella replied.

Wilco was short for "will comply," and Echo was their shorthand for Deck 5. But all the terrorists had commandeered rooms on Deck 9. Definitely masquerading among the passengers, then. "I did make out a few details about her," Aleesha murmured. Quickly she relayed the sparse details she'd been able to gather on the blond woman.

"Copy," Isabella murmured moments later. "You'd better get on with your hunting."

Right. Hiding places for the kids. In the excitement of spotting François and the last terrorist, she'd completely forgotten for a minute why she was here. Sloppy. She knew better than to let her mind stray into tunnel vision where she focused on only one thing at a time.

She moved forward quickly now, assured that this area was deserted, or else François and the blonde wouldn't have chosen it for their secret meeting. The narrow passage opened into a much larger room filled with four cylindrical, steel structures that looked like miniature oil storage tanks. Except in this case it was water they held.

Something rustled, and she dived for cover behind one of the giant tanks, which was easily fifty feet across. She froze, listening to the silence, interrupted only by the rumbling of the ship's engines, which was more faint in here. Another distinctive rustle and some quick chewing noises. She released her breath in disgust and stood up straight. The *Grand Adventure* had a mouse.

As she moved, her elbow banged painfully against the wall of the water tank beside her. Aleesha frowned at the hollow metallic clang that echoed throughout the chamber. That was odd. A tank full of water should give off a dull thud. She knocked on the tank again with her knuckles. That hummer sounded empty.

She walked around the side of the tank and, tucked away in

the back, facing the hull of the ship was a small, round hatch at about knee height cracked slightly open. She knelt down and peered inside. Empty. She pulled out a flashlight and shone it inside. Its beam was swallowed up in the cavernous blackness. Intrigued, she crawled all the way into the tank. It was completely dry inside. Must be broken or down for maintenance or something.

Oh, yeah. It was perfect. It would be a tight squeeze for four hundred people, but they were children. They could all get in here. She shone her flashlight up toward the ceiling and was relieved to see another larger hatch in the center of the dome above, and better yet, it stood wide open. The kids would have plenty of fresh air.

She backed out of the tank, taking careful note. The second tank on the left. She pushed the low maintenance hatch completely shut, but for good measure, pulled out a piece of chalk and drew an inconspicuous line down the side of it.

She had the lounge and the water tank—two hiding spaces down and one to go. She mentally reviewed the ship's blueprints with a sinking feeling in her stomach. The only other place the Medusas had found that was remotely suitable was a large conference room on Deck 9, right in the heart of the rooms the hijackers had commandeered for themselves when they took over the ship.

"Adder, you up for a challenge?" she asked Isabella.

"What've you got in mind?" came the wry reply.

"Guide me up to that conference room on Deck 9."

"Mamba, are you nuts?" Isabella squeaked. "That's about fifty feet from Viktor's suite."

"Like I said, a challenge. But he won't be in his room tomorrow. Especially if he thinks something is up. He'll go to the bridge. I bet none of the hijackers will be anywhere near their rooms once the shit hits the fan."

"Good point," Isabella replied. "But right now I place half of them in suites all around that conference room."

Aleesha shrugged at the security camera she happened to be

passing right under. "So, you'll be careful and I'll be quick. It's all good. Let's do it."

"Okay," Isabella replied, back to her usual emotionless, professional self. "Head up the midship staircase…"

Aleesha had to duck into a linen closet once and use her master key to dive into staterooms twice before she made it up to Deck 9. The second time, she startled the hell out of a sleeping woman and barely managed to identify herself and quiet the woman. There was, indeed, a fair bit of terrorist activity on Deck 9 as 4:00 a.m. and a shift change neared. She only had a few more minutes with Michael at the cameras, and then she'd have to disappear.

"Into a room, Mamba! Patrol heading aft straight at you, distance three hundred feet and closing fast."

Aleesha dived into a stateroom yet again. Empty! She leaned against the door, breathing hard as two pairs of footsteps moved past. Man, that had been close.

"Coast is clear," Isabella murmured a few minutes later. "Proceed to primary target."

Aleesha slipped back into the hall. She glided past Viktor's room, holding her breath in spite of herself. Then, a silent sprint on the balls of her feet and she was there. She turned the door handle carefully and eased into the conference room. It wasn't as large as she remembered on the blueprints. Then, squinting in the dark, she made out what looked like a closed, folding room divider. She dared not pull out her flashlight to take a better look, but she did move over to the wall and pull it back a tiny bit to peer into the space next door. That was more like it. With this wall folded back, there'd be plenty of room for the kids. Each section of the room had a single door leading out into the hall. No problem. There'd be at least two Medusas with the kids and available to cover the exits. Assuming it wasn't bolted down, the conference table dominating one end of the space could be used to block one of the doors. If that didn't work, there were plenty of big, leather armchairs.

Okay. She had her three hiding places. Time to get out of here.

"Problem, Mamba. I just spotted Michael leaving the bridge."

Crap. Now why had he gone and done that? He'd surely been tracking her movements all night on his banks of cameras and knew she was still out here. He'd have known that if he left his post he'd trap her in here. Whoever'd taken over must have put him in an awkward situation where he couldn't stick around for a few extra minutes without raising suspicions. Nonetheless, that didn't change her predicament. She was stuck in here until daylight and the lifting of the night curfew.

Damn! She might as well settle in and get comfortable. She was going to be here a while. She crawled under the conference table, pulling the chairs in behind her to disguise her presence.

It sure as hell wasn't comfortable lying on her side in between chair legs and the hard pedestal of the table, but it beat the hell out of cold, sticky mud in the pouring rain. And, compliments of Jack Scatalone, she knew exactly how that felt.

She started violently a few minutes later when an abrupt flood of light into the room announced someone's entrance. Please God, let it be Michael, or at worst a patrol that would poke their heads around for a moment and then leave. Her heart lodged in the back of her throat and she clutched the knife hidden in the pocket of her pants.

The door closed, plunging the room into darkness once more. She held her breath, assessing the silence enveloping her. Was she alone or not?

"It's me," said a quiet male voice. "You can come out now."

Praise the Lord. *Michael.* She crawled out on her hands and knees and took the hand he held down to her. He yanked her sharply to her feet and pulled her roughly against his chest. His eyes were glowing twin embers, glaring furiously at her in the near total dark.

He growled, "What in the bloody hell do you think you're doing, roaming around the ship like this? Is the rescue going down now? Why didn't you tell me? Don't you trust me? *What aren't you telling me, Aleesha?*"

Chapter 16

Oh, God. Busted. She wasn't supposed to tell him anything sensitive, now that his status as a good guy was in serious doubt. Crap. He was way too smart for her to bullshit. He'd sense his change in status in a heartbeat. What the hell was she supposed to say?

While she frantically tried to think up something to draw his attention away from the subject at hand, Michael shoved her backward without releasing her. Her thighs slammed into the conference table and she fell across its glossy surface, only narrowly missing cracking the back of her skull on its hard surface. Michael followed her down, pinning her in place with his body weight and his hands on either side of her head.

"Start talking."

"Do you think this is really the place for that?" she asked lightly. Anything to distract him. To buy her time.

His eyes narrowed. "What's going on? Have the SEALs boarded the ship?"

"You just got off the cameras. You tell me," she replied assertively. Maybe in this case the best defense would be a good offense.

Michael stared down at her speculatively for a moment. "They're not aboard yet, but they're coming soon. You're making final preparations."

Damn, he was good.

"So, what's the plan?" he demanded.

She stared up at him doubtfully. If he'd been playing her this whole time, that would be exactly the question he'd ask now. Was he a plant by Viktor? Were Viktor's suspicions about her and Michael all an act to lend credibility to his second-in-command's claims of being an undercover good guy? After watching Viktor operate for a few days, the bastard was fully capable of running a devious game like that. Hell, he had a female terrorist posing as a passenger, didn't he?

"Look, Michael. I don't know exactly what the plan is, nor do I know when or even *if* it's going to happen."

He loomed close to her, hesitated for an instant, and then his mouth mashed against hers, their teeth clicking together. His tongue invaded forcefully, startling her into fighting. This wasn't about sex. It was all about power. And probably about keeping her from shouting out in frustration at being physically subdued. Fury erupted in her head.

But Michael was big and strong, and he had her arched backward over this damned table and pinned down like a bug on a board. She wrestled against him to no avail. His hands shifted, gripping her upper arms painfully, his thumbs digging into the groove between her biceps and the bone. After a few seconds she realized her arms were more or less useless, compliments of the highly effective nerve pinch he'd just used on her.

She heaved upward in desperation, but all that earned her was the crushing weight of his body smashed against hers, holding her down by main force. She'd known this guy would be tough in another fight, and she hadn't been wrong. She'd let her guard down and not seen a move like this coming. It was her own damned fault. She'd trusted him. Trusted their relationship. She'd forgotten that he was the enemy, and he'd taken ruthless advantage of it. Resigned to her physical defeat, she stopped fighting.

Michael's mouth eased up, his tongue sliding smoothly across hers. Oh my, that felt good to her, all dark and wet and intimate, the kiss throbbing between them and taking on a life of its own. His tongue plunged deep and then retreated. He did it again. And again. Man, that felt like great sex. Her body responded accordingly, her breasts suddenly aching and her private places going swollen and hot.

Was this a ploy? Was he playing her to get her to talk? Except, with his tongue coaxing hers to come dance and his lips moving across hers like a rapacious conqueror, there was no way she could talk. He wanted her. And he was man enough to let her know. Ah, Michael. Dark, angry, noble Michael. He was going to be devastated when he found out the Brits had fired him.

Two years of his life he'd spent in hell with Viktor—*two years*. And for what? Termination without a pension for doing a deadly dangerous and soul-sucking job? It just wasn't fair. She realized her arms had come up around him, offering him solace he didn't even know he needed. And something inside him changed. Tension released and he relaxed against her, opening up, both physically and emotionally. The hot, wild tangle of tongues and limbs unfolded into something smooth and sophisticated, a silky slide of skin on skin, lips on lips. His hand caressed her hair the way she'd wanted him to for a while now. She returned the favor and trailed her fingers down his neck, savoring the corded muscles that betrayed his power. He was a killer. But in the name of good and right. A man who could meet her on her own terms, on her turf, and stand as her equal. She might not have been in this game for long, but she'd bet there weren't a whole lot of men who could do that. The emotional strength he must have, to do what he'd done, took her breath away. And here he was, letting her inside that cast-iron fortress. Inviting her in. Beseeching her in. How could a girl say no?

She tensed her stomach muscles and lifted her head off the table to kiss him. And unleashed a firestorm between them. It struck with a vengeance. His hand went around the back of her head, pulling her near, sucking her into the kiss. His mouth slanted across hers, raw and wild, murmuring words of lust and need, gluttony and greed. A vortex of heat inhaled her, scorching her. Her very core exploded in response, driving her half out of her mind with need. And he met her step for step, breath for ragged breath.

Whoa. Reality check here, girlfriend. She was letting a potential terrorist kiss her brains out! Startled, she broke the kiss. It jolted him, too, and he stared down at her in disbelief. He was as rattled as she was. Well, that was comforting, at any rate.

"Uh, well then," she mumbled.

"Yeah. Right," he mumbled back.

She did notice, however, that he was in no hurry to get off her. He continued to sprawl across her on the table. Not that she was making any big point of shoving him off, of course.

Reaching for a jocular tone, she commented dryly, "You're a hell of a kisser, English."

But his voice came back, sexy and low, "You're not too bad yourself, island girl."

Oh my. He could kick her butt in hand-to-hand combat *and* he was a closet romantic. She was a goner, for sure.

He flicked at the earpiece still lodged in her ear. "Who's at the other end of that thing?"

Aleesha's defenses flew up instantly. "A friend. Helping me dodge your buddies patrolling the ship."

Michael snorted. "They're not my buddies."

Damn, he sounded sincere. Was he really that good a liar?

"So, what's up, Aleesha? Your primary operators have to come in soon. We'll reach Cuba tomorrow night, and Hurricane Evangeline will be here by the following day."

"Maybe there's not going to be a rescue. Maybe the logistics of securing a ship this size with the number of hostages and Tangos aboard was too big a job," she retorted.

He snorted, ignoring her remark. "I'd recommend late morning for the assault. The night shift hijackers will still be asleep, and there's a lot of movement on the ship. Viktor and friends won't be expecting an attack at that time of day, and the kids will be alert and follow directions well. You dare not wait until the last minute before we hit Cuba. You could run into problems getting your people into Cuban waters without a diplomatic incident, and you sure as hell don't want the Cuban Navy coming out to help Viktor."

She stared up at him in silence. She wouldn't be at all surprised if that wasn't exactly the logic Jack Scatalone and Bud Lipton had used in picking the time of the attack.

"Go on," she said.

"I'd secure the kids first, then head straight for the bridge. Viktor analyzed dozens of plans for taking the ship by force, and it always came down to exactly that. The kids and then the bridge. It worked for him, and it'll work for your people."

Aleesha shrugged beneath him. "I wouldn't know."

He grinned down at her. "Yeah, right. You're just the surveillance schmuck. And that's why you've nearly handed me my butt in a sling several times now. You're just some chick with binoculars and I'm the Tooth Fairy."

She grinned up at him. It was damned hard to deny being a highly trained soldier when she was lying here wearing the latest in high-tech military gear and had demonstrated deadly combat skills. Not too many housewives from Poughkeepsie—or Kingston, Jamaica, for that matter—were Krav Maga masters.

His eyes narrowed as he gazed down at her. Uh-oh. That meant he was thinking again. Probably not a good thing just now. She asked hastily, "What else do you recommend in this rescue op of yours?"

"You tell me," he asked lightly, pushing away from her without warning. He didn't step back, however, and his thigh between hers effectively trapped her where she was. She'd have to throw one leg high up in the air and clamber awkwardly across the wood surface to get off the damned table. She sat up at any rate, her inner thighs gripping his leg in a blatantly sexual fashion.

He crossed his arms and looked down at her steadily. Assessingly. Crud. Not going to back down, huh? She should've guessed he wouldn't. He'd realized she was holding out on him. And he was pissed. She would be, too, if she were in his shoes.

He said flatly, "I'm not letting you out of here until you tell me what in the hell's going on."

The very lack of threat in his voice made it that much more menacing. He meant what he'd said. Damn it. Jack always said to tell the truth whenever possible. Smart people could smell a lie. And Lord knew, Michael was nothing if not brilliant. Fine. So he wanted the truth, did he? She'd give him truth. And then she'd pray like crazy that it was enough of a shock to distract him.

"I heard back from the British intelligence service. They deny having any employee named Michael Somerset on their roster."

He looked startled for a moment and then relaxed. "Of course they'd deny it. I'm an undercover agent. They don't run around spewing their agents' names."

She sighed heavily. Choosing her words carefully, she said, "I didn't ask through public channels. It went through the highest levels of my government to yours, and the answer was the same—you're no longer on their books."

"What?" He stared blankly at her. "What are you saying?"

"I'm saying the British government terminated you. Did they catch wind of those punks you killed, maybe?" Lord, she hated sucker punching him like this. But her revelation did the job. It effectively drew his attention away from prodding her for information about the imminent rescue.

"What else did they say?"

"They said you haven't been in their employ for nearly two years."

He stalked a lap of the large room. "Were they even getting my messages? Did they have any idea that Viktor was planning this whole fiasco?"

Aleesha shrugged. "I don't know. I doubt it. Viktor sure as heck wasn't popping up on American radar as a threat, and according to you he's been in the States for years planning this little excursion."

Michael whirled and advanced on her. "What do you mean, 'according to me'? Don't you believe me?"

"Of course I believe you. I'm here talking to you, aren't I? Would I do that if I thought you were a turncoat or unreliable?"

That seemed to placate him. And that caused her heart to contract in pain. Ah, Michael. Don't underestimate me because I'm a girl. I'd take the risk. If I thought you were Satan incarnate, I'd still be here talking to you. Heck, I'd still be kissing you if I thought it would help save those kids.

But Michael bought the explanation. Ultimately he hadn't been trained around women operators, and he just didn't know their true capacity. Of course, it was this very thing that would make the Medusas so effective in the long term. Everyone would underestimate them. But still, it hurt to have a man she respected—hell, a man she *cared* about, underestimate her.

Okay, did she just admit to herself that she cared for Michael? Personally? A string of highly unladylike expletives streaked through her mind. Now, what did her heart have to go and do that for? She didn't need to have these kinds of feelings for anyone, and certainly not for a man she wasn't entirely sure wasn't a terrorist. Darned if she couldn't hear grandmama cackling somewhere in the back of her head. Grandmama had always said the heart went where it willed and only a fool tried to steer it.

"What do you need me to do?" Michael asked tersely, interrupting her self-castigation.

Kiss her senseless? Make love to her until she was too weak to stand up? "Uh, come again?" she mumbled.

"What can I do to help the rescue op?" he asked impatiently.

Oh. Well. That was different. "I honestly have no idea if there's even going to be a rescue attempt, let alone what the plan would be. So I can't really answer that question. I suppose you could always unlock the door to the bridge," she added, her tongue firmly in her cheek.

He grinned briefly. "Good idea. I'll keep that in mind."

"I'm really sorry, Michael…." she started tentatively.

"Sorry about what?"

"You know. The whole thing with the Brits. You got a raw deal. Maybe after you come in from this op you can talk to them. Work it out. I mean, it wasn't as if you were in any position to defend yourself, undercover like—"

He stepped near and pressed two fingers against her lips. "Enough. It's over. Don't worry about it."

"But I do worry about you," she protested.

His answering grin was lopsided. "Thanks."

They stared at each other in silence for several endless seconds. This was one hell of a mess. The last thing either of them needed right now was to get tangled up in a relationship that might distract them from their jobs. Especially with his status in doubt. And the last thing either of them had the power to do right now was change a blessed thing between them. There was a fire here, like it or not.

Finally, reluctantly, she broke the silence. "Any idea how I'm supposed to get out of here? Or do I get to spend the rest of the night on this extremely comfortable table? Or perhaps more accurately, under it?"

He grinned. "Think you can pretend we had a tryst set up in here?"

Her mind shot back to that incendiary kiss they'd shared. "I don't think that'll be too hard to do."

"Then we should be able to just walk out of here and down the hall to my room, as pretty as you please."

"Who's working the cameras?" she asked.

"Franco. And he's a bit of a voyeur. He'll get a cheap thrill out of imagining what we've been up to in here once he figures out we've both been here all this time."

It was a big risk to take. But, by the same token, gaining access to Michael's room tonight would position her perfectly to carry out her next task before the SEALs came aboard the *Grand Adventure*. God, she hated taking advantage of Michael like this. But a job was a job, and a whole lot of children were counting on her. She nodded up at him. "Let's do it."

Michael opened the door and stepped out into the hall as if he hadn't a care in the world. Aleesha took a deep breath and followed him. Immediately he wrapped his arm around her shoulders, pulling her close against his side. Right. Franco.

Michael paused, pressing her back against the wall, and started kissing her neck in a way that sent lust zinging all the way down to her toes. She didn't know if Franco was getting into this, but she sure as heck was. Michael's tongue swirled into her ear, wet and hot and her knees nearly buckled. Dang, he was good at this seduction stuff!

He straightened, dragging her down the hall again. She wondered idly as she stumbled along beside him whether he'd had any formal training at doing that. Given the iconic popularity of James Bond, she wouldn't put it past SIS to teach their operatives how to kiss like gods.

She twined her arm around Michael's waist and leaned into him, not having to work hard to feign wanting in his pants. Franco might be eating this up, but she expected Isabella would just about swallow her tongue in dismay. Aleesha could only pray her teammate wasn't sending blow-by-blow descriptions of all this back to the TOC. But, hey. It wasn't like Bud Lipton could get away with hanging all over Michael like this. Being female had gotten her inside information a traditional male team would never have managed to collect in so short a time.

Michael opened the door to his suite and pulled her inside after one last, lingering caress of her derriere for Franco's benefit. Good thing she wasn't usually inclined to make a lot of noise during sex, because she was going to start moaning aloud soon if Michael kept touching her like that.

Sheesh, she was a mess! But when Michael kissed her all the

way into his bedroom, she couldn't summon up the gumption to care. Life was short. They both might die tomorrow. Why not seize the day—or the night, as it were?

He speared his hands into her hair, backing her against the closed bedroom door, kissing her with his entire body. She managed to mumble, "This is insane."

"Completely unprofessional," he agreed, lifting her shirt over her head.

"Stupid." She tugged his belt from around his waist.

"Colossally dumb." Her bra gave a soft pop and fell away.

She arched into the impossibly erotic caress of his long, lean fingers against her skin. When she finally managed to tip her head forward and draw a breath, she reached out to unbutton his shirt and push it off his delicious shoulders.

Leaning forward to kiss his neck, she said against his warm, raw satin skin, "We're going to regret this in the morning."

He replied huskily as he kissed his way down her neck, "Mmm-hmm. Deep regret. Passionate, pounding regret."

"We've got to stop."

"Absolutely." He lowered her to the bed and followed her down into a steamy, dark abyss of tangled sheets, a hot, slick slide of flesh on flesh and, eventually, the oblivion of sated exhaustion.

She woke up in the morning, drowsy and relaxed as she swam lazily toward consciousness. Michael's leg was tangled between hers, and her arm lay across his powerful chest. Responding to the nearly psychic link they seemed to have forged between them somewhere in the sexual tempest they'd created last night, he opened his eyes and gazed warmly at her, his expression untroubled and trusting. And that was what broke the spell.

If only she could believe it. If only she could be sure it wasn't all an act. Did he harbor the same doubts about her? Was he uncertain as to her motives? Surely he must be. Both of them were playing a dangerous game, engaging in this deadly dance, both needing to trust, wanting to trust, but both knowing better than to give in to the impulse.

And for better or for worse, she had work to do this morning. In her pouch were two dozen state-of-the-art microburrs, tiny transmitters barely the size of a pin head, designed to stick to the clothes of a target and transmit a signal that could be used to track their position for up to six hours once activated. The burrs were too small to have much more battery life than that, and their range was limited to a few hundred yards, but they were perfect for today's purposes. With each of the hijackers marked by one of the burrs, the SEALs who made up the rescue team could monitor the exact position of all the terrorists aboard the ship in real time. Her job was to stick the burrs to as many of the terrorists as she could locate between now and 11:30 a.m.

She frowned and peered over the edge of the bed. The first order of business was probably to remember where Michael had ditched her utility belt. Somewhere between the front door and the bed. It wouldn't do for Viktor to stroll into the suite and spot it in the living room.

Michael spoke lazily from behind her. "I moved your stuff in here so nobody'd see it if they got here early for this morning's briefing."

"Briefing?" she asked lightly, hope bursting in her chest. If the whole terrorist crew assembled at once, it would make her job a piece of cake!

"Viktor wants to go over the procedures for anchoring in Guantánamo and ferrying the prisoners out to the ship. We'll get there at about four o'clock this afternoon, I think."

Better not act too interested in the briefing or clever Michael would smell a rat. Instead she asked, "How about I go get us some breakfast and bring it up?"

He rolled onto his back and glanced over at the clock on the bedside table. "Ugh. I've got to take a shower and get dressed. The others should start arriving in about fifteen minutes."

Reluctantly she got out of bed. Time to start the biggest day of her life. "Go take your shower. Would you like your usual English breakfast? Steak, eggs and kippers?"

"How about a couple of muffins and some coffee?"

She smiled warmly. "What? I didn't work up any sort of appetite in you last night? I'm devastated."

He rolled over fast. Trapping her beneath him and smiling down at her. "Don't tempt me. We don't have time."

She looped her arms around his neck. "Later?"

He nodded in the affirmative. "That's a promise."

God, if only it truly was. In unison, they rolled out of bed. The interlude was over. Time to get back to reality and their respective responsibilities. Ugh.

For lack of anywhere to hide her utility belt, she grabbed a towel off the pile of dirty ones by the door of the suite. Hauling the wrapped bundle, she left Michael's suite and raced down to her room on Deck 8. She jumped in the shower for about thirty seconds, flew into clean clothes and hurried down to the restaurant. She loaded up a serving cart with pastries, fresh juices, pots of coffee and an assortment of fruit. It would give her an excuse to move around the room while Viktor's briefing proceeded and tag everyone with a burr. Last, she loaded the cart with the business-card-size pieces of paper that held the microburrs. She covered them with a linen napkin, close at hand. Here went nothing.

She headed over to the two guards stationed in the corners of the restaurant today. Americans. Good. Native English speakers. She could strike up a conversation with them without giving away the fact that she spoke fluent French. She picked up a burr on her left index finger and approached the first hijacker from an oblique angle.

"Excuse me," she said pleasantly, reaching out to place her left hand on his sleeve. "Can I get you something to drink?"

Startled, the guy whipped around to face her. "No. Uh, thanks."

Thanks, huh? He'd sure thawed toward her since the first day she'd run into him and he'd nearly shot her. She smiled. "Let me know if you need anything."

The guy nodded at her. One down, twenty-three to go.

She caught some of the dirty looks other passengers threw at her as she headed for the other side of the restaurant. Good for them. From their perspective she was collaborating with the enemy and should be shunned. Hopefully, the Americans or whoever was manning the security cameras caught some of those venomous glances being tossed at her. The looks lent credibility to her act that she'd fallen for Michael and sympathized with the hijackers.

After she finished marking the other Tango in the room, she headed for the bridge. Franco let her in. Must be getting near the end of his shift. He'd been up here for nearly six hours. No doubt he'd want coffee. She picked up another burr and the stainless steel pot of brew and headed for the desk in the security office. Three down.

It was an easy matter to brush past the terrorist sitting in the captain's chair in the center of the bridge and mark him with a transmitter. Four.

And now, on to the briefing.

It was simpler than she ever dreamed it could be. She moved around the room pouring drinks and passing out snacks, and marked every last one of them in under ten minutes. No sign of the woman, though. And damned if Aleesha had the slightest idea how to find the blonde from last night. Kat was supposed to pose as a maid this morning and enter the room they'd seen her disappear into. Kat would try to mark the mysterious twenty-fourth terrorist with a burr.

Aleesha yanked her attention back to the task at hand.

And then it was Michael's turn. By rights, she ought to mark him, simply because he would likely stay near other hijackers, and in particular Viktor, when the rescue went down. Michael's location might end up being important at some point. She fussed with the fruit plate while she debated the issue in her head. Problem was, the burrs only showed up as dots on the handheld tracking monitor. There'd be no way for the SEALs to differentiate between Michael and any of the other Tangos. And she had no doubt the SEALs would come aboard with orders to kill every Tango they came across.

Was she willing to take complete responsibility for Michael? If she didn't mark him, and he turned out to be one of the bad guys, the entire rescue could be blown. Her feelings for the man she'd just spent most of the night making love with warred with her professional judgment. It would be insane not to mark him. It was breaking her heart to have to.

In the absence of a compelling argument one way or another, she followed her instinct. She slipped the last two cards and their remaining burrs into her pocket. She glanced at her watch, startled to see that it was nearly 11:30 a.m. already. She had places to go and things to do.

The rescue plan was gathering momentum and speed. Of course, there was still time to call a halt to the op if something terribly unexpected happened in the next few minutes. She could always put new burrs on the Tangos' clothes another day. But the Medusas were fast approaching the point of no return. Once the next phase of the op was complete, there'd be no turning back. And it was time to go do it.

Chapter 17

Viktor took one last stroll around the bridge. The *pièce de résistance* was in place. He smiled to himself. They all believed he planned to rescue the detainees at Guantánamo. What did he care about a bunch of religious fanatics looking to die for their god? He had a bigger goal in mind. A strike at the heart of the very system preventing his homeland from having its independence. The United States itself.

But he couldn't very well tell that to the American half of his team. They might claim to want to topple the current American regime, but they thought of themselves as patriots. No telling how they'd react to the idea of killing American sailors. Especially when so many of the American team members had been soldiers themselves.

No, no. It was best that he keep the end game entirely to himself. And when he'd gotten word of the snitch in his midst, he was doubly glad he'd played it that way.

He walked over to the radar console. The young Norwegian

woman stood there, tense as he approached her. "Show me the American Navy," he barked at her.

She nodded and increased the range on the radar to paint the American naval task force trailing behind the *Grand Adventure*. Just as he'd anticipated. There'd been some question about which country would manage the hijacking, but he'd had faith in U.S. persuasion and stubbornness. "Are they still holding position in our five o'clock at twenty-five miles?"

The Norwegian nodded. He could see very well that the U.S. Navy was holding its position, but it was good to test the hostages now and again. Keep them honest.

On the other side of the radar screen, the coastline of a small chain of islands came into view. Insignificant specks of rock, except that they marked the exact spot where he'd have his revenge on the United States.

"You see that island right there? The crescent-shaped one? Sail this ship exactly three miles off the tip of it at a heading of 270 degrees. When you get to this point here," he stabbed at the radar screen, "you will turn due north and cut forward speed to five knots. Understood?"

The girl looked perplexed but nodded.

She didn't need to understand. Nobody did but him. Only he, of all his men aboard this ship, knew that there was a deadly string of mines planted under the surface of the ocean a half-dozen miles off the tip of that crescent island. The divers who'd planted the mines were another terrorist cell he ran—they had no connection to the teams aboard the *Grand Adventure*. The Americans would have to make their strike tonight. The hurricane was due tomorrow.

The course he'd just described to the Norwegian girl would put that line of submerged mines squarely between the *Grand Adventure* and the carrier task force tailing him so steadily and predictably.

He had utter confidence that the predictable Americans would send a team of commandos in small boats to board the

Grand Adventure. And when they hit his underwater gauntlet of death, the last laugh would be his.

When Aleesha walked into the Medusas' staging room, controlled chaos was the order of the day. The other women were just finishing gathering into bags the same gear they'd come aboard the ship wearing—Kevlar utility vests, radios, knives and MP-5s. They already wore their gray all-terrain body suits under their clothes. For a moment she saw her team as an outsider might see them and had to admit they were an imposing bunch. She sure as heck wouldn't want to mess with them in a dark alley. Once the rescue got underway, they'd wear their full military gear so the SEALs who came aboard could identify them quickly among all the other women on the ship. That way if one of the Medusas called out an instruction or gave a signal to one of the SEALs, he'd know it for a legitimate military communication.

Aleesha leaned over Isabella's shoulder, peering at a readout on a laptop sitting beside the intel analyst. She noticed her teammate was wearing the radio Aleesha had stolen from Michael, its pink earpiece in her left ear.

"They saying anything interesting?"

"Not yet. Give it a few minutes, eh?" Isabella fiddled with the laptop computer.

Aleesha glanced down at what the intel analyst was working on. A program to overlay the radio signals from the twenty-two microburrs on top of a schematic of the ship. It wasn't three dimensional, but it was a darn sight better than nothing. Fortunately, the hand-held units each of the Medusas had in their utility vests would give a 3-D image up to a range of a hundred feet or so.

Isabella asked, "Who did you miss?"

"The woman…" She hesitated and then answered candidly, "And Michael. I was worried the SEALs would kill him out of hand if he were marked."

Isabella threw a penetrating look over her shoulder. Finally the intel analyst murmured, "Your call."

Aleesha sagged in relief. They might not understand why she felt so strongly about Michael's allegiances, but her teammates trusted her judgment. God bless them.

"Better suit up," Isabella said.

Right. It was almost time for the big show. Aleesha stripped to her skivvies and donned her sea-land suit. She doubted she'd need its wet suit function today, but it was comfortable, durable and gave her an unrestricted range of movement. The suits even helped control bleeding if one of them got shot or otherwise injured. Over the top of the suit, she pulled on a pair of pants and a long-sleeved T-shirt. She tucked the suit's hood inside her shirt for now. They needed to hide their distinctive outfits until they reached the kids' adventure area so whoever was manning the security cameras wouldn't spot them and send up an alarm too quickly.

The mood in the room was calm and focused. They knew what they had to do, and it was well within their capabilities. All in all, she had a good gut feel about today. And it was always nice not to be going against grandmama's voodoo intuitions.

Vanessa came over to Aleesha. "Sync your watch to mine. I got a time hack off the SEALs about an hour ago."

Aleesha nodded and set her watch forward to the next new minute with the second hand at twelve o'clock.

Vanessa counted quietly, "Thirty-two past eleven in five…four…three…two…one…hack."

Aleesha mashed the start button on her watch exactly as Vanessa called the hack. In this business, a second or two either way could mean the difference between life and death.

"Ammo check," Vanessa ordered everyone.

Aleesha checked the clip in her MP-5. Full. Two spare clips—both full—in the left-front pocket of her utility vest, ready at hand. Four more clips in her utility belt. And she sincerely hoped she didn't need any of them. In addition, as the team's demolitions specialist, she carried det cord, detonators and C-4 in two-pound miniblocks around her waist. And then, of course, she carried the usual contingent of grenades, wire cutters, mirrors and other doodads that might come in useful in a pinch.

"Everyone ready?" Vanessa asked. "All clear on the plan?"

The plan was pretty simple. A group of maids was going to stage a major argument with some of the kitchen staff. It would involve a lot of screaming in several languages and should momentarily draw the attention of whoever was manning the security cameras. Meanwhile, the Medusas were going to burst in on the kids' adventure area, take down the guards fast and hard, then move the children out. Isabella would stay here with the camera monitors and guide them to whichever one of the hidey-holes had no terrorists along the route. And if there were terrorists between the kids and all the hidey-holes, she'd send them on the route with the fewest Tangos and they'd clear it as they went.

The Medusas left the room over the next several minutes singly and in pairs. They made their way through the ship by different routes, all arriving in the middle of Deck 4, where the kids' area was located, at roughly the same time. Vanessa and Misty would take the front door. Aleesha, Karen and Kat would take the fire exits.

One last time check. Forty seconds until 11:40. The ruckus in the Safari Lounge should have just broken out. She slowed down slightly and reached the doors just as her second hand swept up to the top of her watch. Time to rock and roll.

Jack pulled the yellow rubber rain slicker more tightly about him as the launch bay door opened and salt spray battered him. The seas were kicking up fifteen-foot waves in front of a freshening breeze compliments of Hurricane Evangeline. Not ideal conditions to make a twenty-five-mile run in fast boats, but then, SEALs weren't paid to operate under perfect conditions. They earned their stripes on days like this.

He heard the team leaders behind him barking out the final equipment checks and lining their guys up to board the boats. Five sleek, black speedboats rested in their sliding launch ramps, quiet now, but ready to devour the waves before them.

Static sounded in his ear, and he pressed his hand against the earpiece to hear better over the noise of the ship's diesel engines. Isabella Torres's voice announced crisply, "Medusas in motion. Proceeding to Task Alpha."

"Roger," he transmitted back. "We are a go."

He looked up at the men behind him and stuck his right fore-finger up in the air. He twirled it several times over his head and then pointed at the open launch bay. Forty SEALs moved as one, leaping into place on the boats as crewmen converged from both sides to release the vessels and shove them into the frothing surf.

The men straddled the oversize saddle horns rising up out of the centers of their seats, gripping the padded posts with their thighs. Particularly in seas like these, the horns would help keep the men from getting tossed overboard as they pounded across the ocean. The good news was the run would only take a little more than half an hour. The fast boats could do twenty-five miles in less time than that, but not with the high seas today. No matter. The plan had been adjusted to account for the extra running time.

The fast boat engines roared to life. Crewmen attached to the SEAL teams and those brought aboard the tender ship to support this mission traded hand signals with the SEALs, and the launching locks were released. The boats slipped down the ramps and into the ocean, peeling into wide arcs as their propellers dug into the water and shot them forward.

All the teams reported in tersely on the operational frequency, the same one the Medusas were transmitting on today.

Jack made a single brief transmission to them all. "Good hunting."

And then the long wait began.

An infinitesimal nod from Karen, and Aleesha and Kat stepped in front of their Marine teammate, who pulled bolt cut-ters from inside her pants and quickly chopped through the chains holding one of the doors shut. There were two hundred security cameras onboard, and the odds of this camera being up on the screen in the security office were slim with the cat fight upstairs in full swing. Not zero chance, of course, but slim. Hence the body shield by Kat and Aleesha. But the risk that they'd be seen was acceptably low.

"I'm through."

There was no need for Aleesha or Kat to say anything in response. They all knew what to do next. Had practiced it a hundred times. They'd spent months in the schoolhouse, bursting into rooms full of simulated innocents and Tangos and neutralizing the threats without harming the hostages. They'd done it over and over until they never missed, never misidentified a friend or foe.

Aleesha followed Kat through the door, pulling out the MP-5 from under her shirt as they went. Kat stepped to the right and Aleesha took the center field of fire. A thunk behind her indicated that Karen had dropped the bolt cutters just inside the door and would now be peeling off to her left and brandishing an MP-5, as well. The three of them stood at ninety-degree angles to Vanessa and Misty, assuring that they wouldn't hit each other in the cross fire. A maneuver like this was all about controlling the fields of fire—where the bullets flew.

The two guards on this side of the room turned in surprise, their weapons coming up to the ready. It was odd how slowly they seemed to move. Or maybe it was just that Aleesha was operating in overdrive. Based on the hijackers' angles of approach, it was Karen and Kat who double tapped the triggers of their weapons and dropped both men with neat shots to the forehead and heart.

Aleesha couldn't help it. She took a moment to check and see who they'd killed. Two of the Americans she didn't know personally. Dammit all if relief didn't flood her gut. *Uh-oh.* But she had no more time to think, for Vanessa was calling out, "Report!"

She called to her boss across the room, "All clear. Two down and confirmed neutralized." Given that neither guy had the top third of their head anymore, it was a pretty good bet they were both out of the fight for good.

Vanessa responded, "All clear here."

Aleesha leaped for the corner and the nearest of the two security cameras, reaching into her right vest pocket as she went. She pulled out a small can of black spray paint and shot it at the camera lens, blacking it out completely. She turned to check on her teammates, and across the room Karen was done spray painting the second camera. The hijackers were now blind in this room.

No doubt it would get reported to Viktor as soon as it was discovered, and he'd send someone to check on the cameras—and the kids—immediately. And that meant the Medusas had to have all the children out of here before those terrorists arrived.

One of the orange shirts recognized her in the chaos of screaming children that was just now registering in her ears. "What's going on, Aleesha?"

"We're rescuing you. We need you guys to get the kids quiet and standing in three lines. Immediately."

Her eyes like saucers, the girl nodded and ran over to her colleagues. While they corralled the kids, the Medusas grabbed the bodies of the guards and dragged them over to a storeroom and stuffed them inside. Aleesha snatched the AK-47s the men had been carrying and grabbed two of the radios, as well. It took her precious seconds to unthread the wires through the dead men's clothes, but being able to eavesdrop on the terrorists' chatter was worth it. There. The second radio was free. She hauled the gear outside with her.

The kids had figured out this was a rescue and were doing their level best to cooperate. They were already standing in lines, albeit practically jumping up and down in their nervousness, frantic to go.

Aleesha passed one of the radios to Vanessa and stuffed the other one in her pouch. No time to put it on just yet. In a few minutes. She spoke into the charged silence, "Any of you staffers have any experience handling guns?"

Two of the young women raised their hands. She passed each of them an AK-47. "The safeties are off. Just aim them and pull the trigger. Use short, half-second bursts. Ta-da-da. Ta-da-da. You'll get about thirty shots that way. Got it?"

Both young women nodded. Aleesha popped the clips out of the other two weapons and pocketed the ammunition, discarding the weapons themselves. No sense leaving extra firepower lying around for the bad guys.

Vanessa gave a hand signal to Aleesha to move out. Vanessa and Kat would stay in the kids' area to respond to the Tangos who would be heading down here soon. Karen would take the rear and guard the kids' retreat while Aleesha led the way, blacking out cameras as she went. And Misty would head the other direction, spray painting random security cameras all over the ship to act as a false trail away from where Aleesha was leading the children. Isabella would be plenty busy tracking all their movements over the next few minutes. The good news was the microburrs on the terrorists' clothes actually made that kind of multitasking possible.

"Talk to me, Adder," Aleesha said to Isabella.

"Head forward on Deck 4. Deck 9's active but not alarmed. I've picked up a couple radio checks as guys have just come up on the Tangos' frequency. They've undoubtedly gotten word that some cameras are down, but they haven't panicked yet."

Aleesha turned to the kids, who looked at her expectantly. "I need all of you to stay together, move fast and be absolutely quiet. Your lives depend on it. Okay?"

Nods from all of them. God, they looked scared. Good Lord willing, this would all be over in the next hour.

She moved out, jogging down the hall. She moved well ahead of the kids and spray painted the security cameras as she went. Hopefully the trail of cameras Misty was painting out was confusing whoever was working the security station on the bridge—or at least slowing down the response to the cascading camera failures.

She neared the forward stairwell and muttered, "Up or down, Adder?"

"Just a sec. Crap. Movement on Deck 7. *Down, Mamba. Fast.*"

Down it was. Although fast might be another story. She had

a hundred-foot-long living snake of children trailing along behind her, and they could only move so quickly. There were small children aplenty, and it was a minor miracle they were still in somewhat orderly lines, let alone not stringing out along half the length of the ship.

The good news was that the unused water tank was her favorite of the three hiding places. Once the children were hidden inside it, the Tangos would really have to look hard to find them. A quick pass through the ship wouldn't do the trick. The SEALs could proceed with taking back the ship without any fear of children getting caught in the cross fire. There were still a thousand adult women aboard, but they should have the common sense to get out of the way of a firefight. Ideally, the SEALs would strike so hard and fast that the terrorists wouldn't have time to snag women to use as human shields.

She hustled down the forward staircase and glanced back over her shoulder at the kids who were just starting down it. They were staying fairly well clustered together and didn't look in imminent danger of stampeding down the stairs and hurting each other. Outstanding.

She raced ahead, knocking out cameras as she went. Once she'd blacked out everything between the kids and their hiding place, she circled back to urge them forward as quickly as possible. The children crowded into the narrow gray hallway, which was barely wide enough to accommodate three lines, as she led them aft to the ship's water plant.

She heard whispers behind her and called over her shoulder, "Quiet!" Sound would echo like crazy in here with all the metal surfaces. Even if the cameras were knocked out, someone patrolling on Deck 2 might hear the kids through the floor. The sound of tennis shoes shuffling and squeaking became the only noise once more.

They arrived at the water tank, and she opened the crawl hatch. She reached into a pouch on her belt, pulled out a half-dozen cyalume glow sticks, and bent them until she heard the internal glass ampoules break. She shook the six-inch plastic tubes to mix the chemicals and passed the now brightly glowing sticks to the first kids to crawl inside the tank.

"Quickly," she said every dozen children or so. To the oldest ones, she occasionally mentioned, "Keep everyone moving away from the door. You all have to fit inside."

After the first few orange shirts crawled inside, she didn't have to tell the kids that anymore, and she heard the adults inside directing the kids.

"The Tangos have figured out something's up," Isabella announced a few minutes later. "I wouldn't call it a full alarm yet, but two more men just headed for the bridge, and Viktor just left his room and is headed that way."

Crap! Not all the kids were inside the tank yet. It was taking a long time for them to crawl, one by one through the tiny door.

"Status, Mamba," Vanessa said.

Aleesha looked down the hallway. "A hundred to go. Five to six more minutes."

Isabella cut in. "Two guys appear to be heading for the kids' adventure area. Repeat. Two Tangos."

Vanessa and Kat should have no trouble taking them out. And when the Tangos failed to report in, Viktor would send down more men. But in the meantime she should have the extra few minutes she'd need to get the kids tucked away safely.

While she continued to herd kids into the water tank, Aleesha pulled out the radio she'd taken from the dead American. She put it on, sticking the earpiece into her left ear as best she could. It was too big and wanted to fall out, but she would be able to hear what the Tangos were saying to each other—at least until they realized they were missing radios and changed to a backup frequency.

There wasn't much chatter yet. Viktor must have called for his patrols to check in, though, because they were reporting in one after another. No surprise that he'd directed two of the Montfort boys to go look in on the children. With a pang, she hoped the slowest Montfort wasn't one of the two that Vanessa and Kat were about to take out.

The end of the line of children came into sight. Maybe twenty more kids to go. "Hurry, hurry," she urged them. Two orange shirts brought up the rear, and then they were all inside.

She squatted down to have a look. It was a tight fit. Misty tapped her on the shoulder—she'd circled back and joined the party—and Aleesha moved aside to let Misty and Karen climb inside. They'd guard the kids until the SEALs finished the op.

"Take care of them," she murmured off microphone to her teammates. They flashed her thumb's-ups and she gently closed the door without latching it.

"All tucked in," she announced over her radio frequency.

"Copy," Isabella said. Aleesha's acknowledgment was the signal for Isabella to move to the next step of the plan and clear the SEALs to board the ship. They should be only a few minutes away by now, coming in on fast boats.

The first thing Viktor would likely do once he suspected something was amiss was confirm that the children—his most valuable hostages—were still secure. Once he got word that the kids were missing, the SEALs predicted he'd send his men throughout the ship in search of the children. Just like hornets under attack, they'd pour out of their rooms looking for someone to sting. It was during this first all-out search that the SEALs would board the *Grand Adventure*. And it was during this time that the Medusas would be at the highest risk. Their job was to lay low, stay out of the way and help the SEALs as needed. Aleesha would loiter in the general vicinity of the water tank where the kids were hidden and would draw off any terrorists who got too close to the children.

Once the SEALs snuck aboard with as much stealth as forty heavily armed commandos could manage, they'd move fast through the ship. They'd make heavy use of the microburrs to avoid the hijackers while boarding and to locate and take out as many terrorists as they could find once all the SEALs were in place. The SEALs would neutralize terrorists singly or in pairs until Viktor figured out what was up and circled the wagons, drawing his men all together, presumably surrounded by a bunch of the women hostages.

Now a quiet knock sounded from the other side of the hatch, signaling everything was okay inside. It was time for Aleesha to move on to her next task—hiding from the hornets so she wouldn't get stung.

Jack monitored the SEALs' progress from the *Roosevelt's* bridge. They reported in every five minutes or so, their voices taut and the boats' engines straining in the background. It sounded as if they were getting the hell pounded out of them in the rough seas.

He checked his watch constantly. The Medusas should've assaulted the kids' adventure area by now. A few minutes later, the kids should be clearing out of the adventure area. Now, the kids should be getting into their hidey-hole. The SEALs should be about halfway to the *Grand Adventure*. The terrorists were probably checking out the inoperative cameras, and the kids should be safely tucked out of the line of fire. Very soon Isabella should be calling the SEALs and clearing them to board.

Sure enough, about a minute later and right on time, Isabella, who was coordinating the movements of the Medusas, radioed for the SEALs to complete their run and board the ship. So far, so good.

But about two minutes later—twenty minutes into the mission—all hell broke loose. The radar operator across the bridge of the tender ship called out that he'd just seen something big pop up at exactly the spot where the SEALs should be right now.

"How big?" Jack called out.

"Ship-size. But it's gone now, sir."

He frowned. What in the hell was that about?

And then the radio in his ear erupted with shouting SEALs. "We're hit! Man down! Get a head count! Medic!"

The chaos was complete. Gripping the edge of the map table before him, Jack strained to make sense out of it. Any sense at all. As best he could tell, four boats had been sunk and the fifth one severely damaged but afloat.

They'd been attacked. Hit hard. But by *what?* He raced over to the radar con. "Show me where you saw whatever you saw," he ordered the seaman.

The kid pointed out a spot on the plotted course of the SEALs, at a distance from the *Grand Adventure* of about three miles. Well within the range of a shoulder-launched surface-to-surface missile like a Stinger II. God *damn* it!

"What did you see?" Jack ordered tersely.

"I'm not sure," the radar operator answered.

"Guess."

"It looked like an explosion. Threw up a big plume of water or debris. I painted it for only a couple sweeps of the radar, and then it died down and I'm painting nothing."

Jack swore under his breath. How in the Sam Hill had the fast boats been blown up? Missiles from the *Grand Adventure?* Aleesha's contact inside the terrorist group hadn't said anything about missiles being aboard. Had the guy withheld information? Was that Michael character a terrorist plant after all? Had he only been trying to infiltrate the rescue operation? Were the Medusas, and maybe this whole mission, compromised?

What about underwater mines? Were they a possibility? Except how in the hell could Viktor position the *Grand Adventure* next to a minefield in the middle of the flipping Caribbean at exactly the time the SEALs made their rescue attempt? How unlikely was that? Unless…had Aleesha had let something slip to Michael and *he'd set up the SEALs?*

"Status!" Jack barked into the radio. "How many men down?"

"Stand by," Bud Lipton ground out, the sounds of men yelling coming through behind his voice.

Damn. That sounded like a complete clusterfuck out there. "Do you need a rescue helicopter?"

"Damn straight, I need one," Lipton yelled. "I've got thirty men in the water. Six of them are seriously injured and need airlift ASAP. Twenty more have moderate injuries. I've got one boat afloat with the casualties and it's sinking fast. It's got maybe ten minutes, and then we're all swimming. There's a crapload of blood out here."

Holy shit. This was the time of year sharks migrated through these waters.

Jack spun and ordered the immediate launch of a rescue copter. The rescue mission was blown. Somehow, some way, the terrorists had figured out the Navy was coming and had set a trap for the SEALs. The Medusas—oh, shit! The Medusas! They were already rolling with the op. They had the kids hidden and were in the middle of running around the ship knocking out security cameras right now!

He jumped onto the radio. "Adder, abort! I say again, abort!"

Isabella's voice came back, scratchy, but clear. "Unable, repeat, unable. We're committed."

Jack closed his eyes. Holy Mary, Mother of God. All those hostages. *And nobody was coming to rescue them.* He spoke fast to Isabella. "The boats were blown out of the water. The teams are down. You're on your own. Can you halt operations?"

"I'll try, but I doubt it. Stand by."

Aleesha moved toward the middle of the ship, tucking herself into one of the very crannies she'd worried about someone hiding in last night when she was down here scouting out the place. Her right earpiece—the Medusa headset—crackled.

She moved out from behind the pipes, and her earpieces—both of them—erupted in chaos. Something godawful was happening to the SEALs. They were completely jamming the frequency with their shouts and calls. Stunned, she looked at her watch. They weren't supposed to be here for another eight minutes. Surely they hadn't arrived at the *Grand Adventure* so wildly off schedule. But they'd sure as shootin' sounded as if they were under attack.

She frowned as she caught bits and pieces of a transmission from Isabella above the din from the SEALs. "…destroyed… multiple injuries…can't abort. On…own…" What the heck was going on?

The heavy silence that settled in Isabella's transmission spoke volumes. Something very bad was going down. Crap. What had she missed? Aleesha darted out from her nook and sprinted down the hallway, clear of the worst of the pipes and vents.

"Adder," she whispered, "say again."

The answer was immediate and cut right to the chase. "The SEALs aren't coming. We're on our own. We're changing to the back-up frequency in sixty seconds."

"Copy," she mumbled. *Oh my God.* There was no way to halt this op, no way to put the kids back in the adventure area, no way to unkill the terrorists who'd already been taken out. They were committed. And they were flying between two trapezes without a safety net. Nowhere to go but forward or down. *Hosed* didn't quite capture the severity of the situation. Neither did *screwed.* Or *completely nuked.*

Innocents were going to die. Hundreds of them. And their blood would be on the hands of the Medusas.

"Suggestions?" Vanessa's voice cut across Aleesha's near panic—sharp, determined.

It snapped Aleesha back into the moment, back into combat reaction. They were far from done. The six Medusas were heavily armed and fully trained to fight in an urban hostage scenario. With a little bit of ingenuity, and maybe a little bit of help, they just might be able to pull this thing off. They knew the layout of the ship like the backs of their hands, they knew the habit patterns of the hijackers, what their likely responses would be to combat decisions. They could do this. She was *not* going to let innocents die on her watch.

She spoke up. "How about we spread a little chaos? Viktor surely knows by now that the kids are gone and some of his men are dead. What if we really up the confusion level on the ship?"

"Like what?" Vanessa asked.

Aleesha recognized the tone of voice. Her boss wasn't mad—just intensely focused on finding a way to succeed. None of the Medusas were good losers. It was part of why she herself was a hell of a trauma surgeon. She refused to yield gracefully to death.

"How about I blow up the electrical generators while I'm down here? It'll knock out all the communication and navigation capabilities of the ship. Heck, if we're lucky, it'll knock out the engines, too."

Karen piped up. "Not likely. The engines probably have their own internal generators for the fuel injectors and the like. Not important, however."

Aleesha continued. "We can set off the fire alarms. Anyone know if there are automatic sprinklers on this baby?"

She could almost hear the grin on Vanessa's face as her teammate replied, "Go on. Then what?"

"Then we do what the SEALs were going to do. Under the confusion of it all, we move around the ship using the microburrs to track the Tangos and pick off as many as we can before they get scared and cluster together."

"And after they clump up?" Vanessa challenged.

An image of Bud Lipton's SEAL team clustered on the bridge of the destroyer in Norfolk a lifetime ago popped into her head. They'd known then that the Medusas were ill suited to a brute force takeover. They were still ill suited for it. But unfortunately teams like theirs didn't get to pick the scenarios that were handed to them in the field. They might have dodged the test in Norfolk, but they were going to have to look the real thing square in the eye here and stare it down.

She answered Vanessa slowly, "Then we duke it out with the bad guys. I'd bet on Cobra against the best shooters in the business, and the rest of us aren't too far behind. We'll hold our own."

"We can't just hold our own. We've got to win this one. A hell of a lot of lives ride on it. This is an all or nothing deal."

Aleesha knew what Vanessa was saying. This was a succeed-at-all-costs mission. *All costs.* If every last one of them had to die, then that's what they'd have to do. "Let's do it," Aleesha answered quietly.

Apparently, she spoke for the whole team because nobody else offered any other suggestions or disagreed with the parameters Vanessa had just laid down for them.

"How quickly can you blow the generators?" Vanessa asked.

"Give me three minutes to get there and two to slap down some C-4."

"You've got it. Adder, we need your firepower out here, and you're about to lose electricity anyway for your monitor. Python, Sidewinder, I need you up out of that tank. Can the staffers down there handle the children without you?"

Karen answered dryly, "I think we're scaring the kids. They'll be calmer without commandos and semiautomatic submachine guns in their midst."

"Then come up here. We're in the disco on the port side of Deck 7 forward. We'll work on setting a fire up here. All three of you, split up and take different routes. Set off the fire alarms as you go."

"I'll be there in under five minutes," Isabella replied.

"Give me one last look at Deck 1, Adder," Aleesha grunted as she took off running for the rear of the ship and the ship's power plant. She dropped her weapon into a hip-firing position, ready to blow away on the run anyone who happened to get in front of her.

"Deck 1 is clear all the way to the engine room," Isabella said. "There's a Tango moving down the aft stairwell, passing Deck 6. He could be a problem. And I'm outta here."

Aleesha made it almost to the aft staircase without incident. The electric power plant lay just beyond it. But then, as she ducked around a big, square ventilation shaft, a human shape stepped out of a doorway almost directly in front of her. Her finger flinched on the trigger as her brain did light-speed assessment. *Civilian! Shit!* She yanked the MP-5 up and away from the maid, who was just stepping out of what must be a laundry, based on the tall stack of towels in her arms and the steam heat emanating from behind her. The woman stared at Aleesha in frozen disbelief.

"We're the good guys," Aleesha panted. "Tell all the women to arm themselves with whatever they can find and to hide!" And then she was off and running again. Who knew if the terrified woman had understood a word of Aleesha's instructions.

She spared a glance at her watch. Three minutes left to get those generators blown up. She skidded to a halt in front of the electrical plant. With a quick look in both directions—all clear—she ducked into the cramped room. Four large generators were bolted to concrete platforms. Perfect. If she planted charges underneath the generators, the concrete would reflect the concussion of an explosion into the steel equipment standing upon it. Tearing supplies out of her belt, she slapped blocks of C-4 under the generators and poked remote-controlled detonators into them all. If she didn't set it off from afar she'd surely be turned into spaghetti when the explosives blew, and she didn't have time to run a bunch of wires into the hall.

She backed into the hallway. And froze. She heard something. Someone. She strained to make out another sound over the throbbing beat of the ship's nearby engines. Nothing. But that had definitely been someone moving. Was it another maid heading for the laundry? A passenger looking to hide? Or maybe it was the Tango Isabella had seen in the stairwell, searching for the missing children.

She plastered herself against the wall in a shadow. There it was again. A scraping of leather on concrete. A shoe had made that sound. Probably a male shoe. She tensed and jumped into the hallway, crouching low. A man, probably twelve feet in front of her. His weapon swung up fast, but it was his undoing that the weapon wasn't already in a firing position. She squeezed her trigger before he could get off the shot. And the Frenchman, René, dropped to the floor, a blossom of red in place of his nose. Her bullet would have entered his skull, bouncing around inside at nearly supersonic speeds, until the mush that had been his brain finally halted the flight of lead. The guy was definitely dead.

Oh. My. God. She'd just killed a man. It had been a kill-or-be-killed situation, and she hadn't hesitated. *There you have it, Michael. Satisfied?* She reached for her mike button, faintly ill.

"Number five down. One of the Frenchmen." It was a macabre necessity in a scenario like this to keep careful count of how many Tangos had been eliminated. "I'm ready to blow the generators," she added.

"Do it," Vanessa muttered.

Must be terrorists nearby for her to be speaking so quietly. Aleesha backed some fifty feet down the hall. Any farther away, and she was afraid the remote control's signal wouldn't reach her detonators through the steel walls. But too much closer and she'd still risk being caught in the blast zone. She mashed the button in her fist. The floor jumped beneath her feet and a muffled boom shuddered through the ship. And then it went pitch-black.

Excellent. The Medusas liked the dark. They embraced the invisibility that came with it. And she'd lay odds the terrorists weren't nearly as prepared as her team was to handle it. She yanked out a pair of night-vision goggles and slapped them on. They weren't a particularly high-resolution set, but the hallway jumped into sight, a study in lime green. She jogged down it, toward the midship stairs. The aft stairs should be filled with smoke and cement dust right about now, and she anticipated that whoever came down here to find out what had happened would come from farther forward. Of course, it was possible that Viktor would surmise that a saboteur had blown up the electrical room without feeling a need to verify it. Either way, she needed to get out of here and make her way up into the parts of the ship where the terrorists would be roaming.

Time for the hornets to become the prey.

Chapter 18

Aleesha waited at the foot of the midship stairs for several minutes, but no one came. Eventually it occurred to her that her radios had been silent for way too long. She must be in another dead zone. She stepped a few paces to one side, and her left earpiece erupted with Viktor's voice, barking out orders like crazy. He was sending men down to the generators and more men to the kids' adventure area to find out where in the hell those dimwit Montfort boys were. A third group of men was dispatched to guard the bridge, and most ominous of all, the rest of the terrorists—the entire American contingent, in fact—were sent out into the ship to round up as many hostages as they could find fast. They were to bring the women to the Safari Lounge.

Aleesha activated her throat mike but was cut off by Vanessa, transmitting in exasperation, "Dammit, Mamba, report!"

She transmitted again, "I'm here. What's up?"

"I gather by the utter darkness around me that you have successfully blown up the generators?"

"That's an affirmative," she replied. "Thought I'd head for the Safari Lounge."

"Roger, we're converging there," Vanessa confirmed. "My gut says those bastards are going to start shooting hostages soon. We need to get inside the restaurant and stop a bloodbath."

Ten Americans remained. The six Medusas would normally have no trouble knocking out a group like that, but there would likely be hundreds of women crammed in the room with the terrorists. It would be a hell of a tricky shooting gallery. She sprinted up the midship stairs; the elevators would be out, thanks to her handiwork, and besides, exiting an elevator left a person with no option but to go forward. The sprinklers made the steps slippery, and she ducked through the shower of cold water, squinting to see.

She ran on the balls of her feet as silently as she could. That was why she heard the huffing ahead of her. Someone else was moving quickly and quietly up the stairs, trying to be stealthy. But they obviously hadn't been taught the same methods of breath control the Medusas had. Creeping upward in a half crouch, she plastered herself to the outside wall so the Tango couldn't see her if he glanced down the center of the stairwell.

Another audible exhalation on the next flight up. She exhaled slowly herself, drew in one last slow, careful lungful of air and jumped around the corner. Aim high, she told herself. It was a common shooter's mistake to aim too low when shooting up stairs and to hit the target around the knees, if at all. *Male target. Hostile.* She squeezed her trigger twice in quick succession. And then leaped nimbly to the side as a large, muscular body toppled straight at her. His shoulder knocked into her hard, nearly taking her down. She staggered, grabbed the handrail and managed by the skin of her teeth to keep herself from falling backward down the stairs with him. God, she was turning into quite the killer.

"One American down in the midship stairwell," she broadcasted to her teammates. "Nine Yankees to go."

"Roger," came Vanessa's terse reply.

Aleesha continued her wet upward journey to the eighth floor and its large restaurant. She exited the stairwell, crouching behind a giant, potted asparagus fern beside the stairs. It looked like a damned rainforest in here. The sprinklers definitely were adding to the general chaos. Her hiding spot was across the main atrium from the double doors leading into the Safari Lounge.

Noise erupted from her left—a man's angry shouting accompanied by screams and cries from several women. A Tango was herding a half-dozen panicky women at gunpoint toward the restaurant. She lifted her weapon, took careful aim and pulled the trigger once. It was a head shot, high. Only way to hit him without coming dangerously close to the moving women. Of course, in the Medusas' training, it had been commonplace, when she'd played hostage, to actually feel the air moving against her skin as bullets whizzed past, mere fractions of an inch away.

The guy dropped, and the women passengers froze, too horrified to scream anymore and too terrified to run.

Aleesha stood up. "Run," she ordered them. "Hide. And tell every woman you see to hide."

The women gaped at her. "Hey, aren't you that Jamaican women who's been helping them?" one of them asked.

"I'm here to help you." As the women continued to stare stupidly she added sharply, "Go. Now!"

They finally obeyed and took off running, back to where they'd just come from. There must not have been any more Tangos down that hallway, or they'd have bolted in another direction. Aleesha jumped behind her fern again, this time putting her back to that hallway to cover the other side of the ship.

That was why she saw the barrel of the AK-47 poke out at knee height from behind the corner of the far wall an instant before the Tango wielding it rolled into view to pop off some shots at her. It was definitely why she pulled the trigger almost before the guy made his move. He rolled right into her bullet. With his throat. His aorta spouted blood like a fountain, and she heard the horrible rasping of his breath failing to get past his crushed larynx to his lungs. The guy would bleed out in a few more seconds. Another American down.

A barrage of gunfire erupted from the hallway behind her. Crap. Those were MP-5s. The Medusas were shooting at someone. Aleesha darted to the corner and poked her periscope around it. Two Tangos backed toward her with about a dozen females huddled in a terrified mob on the other side of the terrorists, acting as shields against Vanessa and Kat. Aleesha jumped out, tapped off two half-second bursts into the terrorists's backs, and they dropped like sacks of sand. She paused long enough to identify them. One more American and the Spaniard, Antonio. She *had* to stop doing that! She had to just shoot and move on, dammit! But she couldn't help it. Couldn't help the lurch of her heart into her throat every time a Tango went down. *Please God, let Michael get out of this mess alive and unharmed.*

The women passengers turned to face the new threat—her—screaming. More screaming broke out as they caught sight of the bloody, mangled corpses of their captors.

"Quiet!" Aleesha barked in her most authoritative emergency-room voice. The women subsided, startled by the crisp order. They looked like half-drowned rats in the cascade of water.

Vanessa chimed in, "I need all of you to go to the kitchen behind the Galaxy Room. Arm yourselves. Grab knives, meat cleavers, brooms, mops, whatever you can find. Take as much stuff as you can and pass it out to your fellow passengers. Tell every woman you see to arm herself. We're rescuing this ship. Now. Anyone who wants to help can meet us at the Deck 10 pool. The rest of you hide."

The women stared in complete and utter disbelief.

Aleesha stepped forward. "We've already taken out several of the bad guys, and the kids are hidden someplace safe on the ship."

That news seemed to perk up the women considerably.

A movement out of the corner of her eye made Aleesha whirl around, her weapon at the ready and her finger already on the trigger.

Crap! Isabella. She released the trigger instantly.

She nodded at her teammate, who nodded back. Then Isabella jerked her head toward the restaurant and held up four fingers. Four Tangos inside. Aleesha turned fast and relayed the hand signals to Vanessa, who immediately flashed hand signals telling Aleesha to collect Isabella. The two of them should rush the main entrance to the restaurant while Kat and Vanessa took the side doors. Hopefully, the cries, screams and general hysteria coming from inside the restaurant had masked the sound of the gunshots out here.

Aleesha spun and sprinted across the atrium, bent low as she passed in front of the restaurant doors. *Ping. Ping.* Instinctively, she zigzagged randomly, diving for cover behind her erstwhile fern as her conscious thoughts finally caught up with her ingrained training. That was gunfire. From a rifle. Probably a sniper rig up on Deck 10 shooting down over the railing at her.

"Do you see him?" she gasped off microphone to Isabella.

Her teammate murmured back from just behind her, "I got a muzzle flash. Assuming he doesn't relocate before his next shot, I'll nail him when he sticks his head up again."

"How many women in the restaurant?" Aleesha asked quickly.

"Lots. I'd estimate four hundred. And I couldn't see the terrorists when I last looked in the doors. Probably in the corners. And it's not raining in there."

Isabella had already looked in the doors? Wow. She'd been busy for having just arrived up here. Aleesha quickly repeated the information to Vanessa while Isabella kept her eye plastered to the sight of her MP-5, waiting for the sniper to show himself again. It would be a split-second shot.

Vanessa asked, "Any thoughts on how to get in there without these guys opening fire on the hostages?"

Lord, it sucked having to freestyle a rescue like this. It went against everything in their training. They were supposed to outtrain, outplan and outthink their enemies. But this was a freaking Wild, Wild West show. They had to do something outrageous, and fast, or they were going to get pinned down in this atrium, which didn't have anywhere near enough cover to make it a good site for a shootout.

A shot rang out beside her. And a man slumped against the railing above, blood pouring from his mouth. She jumped, startled.

Isabella announced calmly, "Another Frenchman bites the dust. Looks like Paulo."

Aleesha winced. He'd been decent to her for the most part. And now he was a bloody corpse. What in the world had these men been thinking to hijack a ship like this? Didn't they know how impossible it would be to succeed? The Medusas had to end this. Quickly. Before any innocent blood was shed.

On cue, a truly outrageous idea popped into her head. Aleesha took a deep breath and spoke it aloud. "How about I just walk into the restaurant? I'll stroll in and say hello to the Tangos and ask if there's anything I can do to help. That ought to pull their attention in my direction long enough for the rest of you to get in the side doors and take them out."

"Too risky," Vanessa replied.

Arguing in the middle of an op was always a bad idea. But Vanessa was wrong. "I spent all that time cultivating these guys so I could pull off something like this. Let me do it."

Silence.

"I'll make it easy on you, Viper. I'm going in. Now. So the rest of you better get into position at the side doors to cover me and take your shots." And with that, she stood up, tucking her MP-5 underneath the canvas beach bag that held her utility vest and belt. She pulled her hair forward over her ears and yanked the collar of her mock turtleneck up over her throat mike. When she reached the etched-glass doors of the restaurant, the madness of what she was doing hit her. Well, at least she knew she hadn't gone nuts. Her brain had registered that this was an incredibly stupid, suicidal stunt.

And somewhere in the back of her head she could hear Grandmama chuckling in disbelief. She'd always said Aleesha was a little bit crazy. *The pot calling the kettle black....*

* * *

Jack listened in an agony of suspense as the first rescue helicopter reached the scene. The pararescue jumpers were swearing freely as they surveyed the water below. Not a good sign. They'd seen it all in their day, and to react like that, it must be an unholy mess.

For the next several minutes, he alternately listened to the SEALs coordinating with the PJs to get the most critical guys into the copters first, and in his other ear, he listened to the Medusas formulating an impromptu plan to take back the *Grand Adventure* on their own. *Keep talking, ladies.* They'd need every ounce of teamwork and cooperation they could muster to pull this one off. If only they weren't so damned inexperienced! If that had been his own Delta 3 team, which had been together for years and had years of combined experience in Spec Ops before they'd come to the Delta Force, he'd feel much more confident about their ability to isolate and kill the terrorists. But the Medusas were six untried women, not even officially out of training, who didn't have a lick of Special Operations experience prior to this assignment.

As their plan unfolded, he continued to listen. He'd have interjected his own thoughts if he had any better ideas, but he didn't. And, frankly, the Medusas had been on the scene for three days. They had a better feel for what would work against Viktor and his team than anyone else. Despite his fears and doubts, the Medusas were the most qualified to do the job.

A phone rang in his breast pocket. He yanked it out and looked at the number on its face. Wittenauer. The general was listening to this fiasco unfold in the TOC, which had been moved to the *Teddy Roosevelt* that morning.

"Go ahead," Jack barked into the receiver.

"I've ordered the *Roosevelt* task force to head for the *Grand Adventure* at top speed. It'll be there in a little over an hour. The *Teddy R*'s Marines are suiting up to board the *Grand Adventure* and take her by force."

Jack frowned. It was a last-ditch maneuver, bound to get hundreds of innocents killed. It was better than letting Viktor go scot-free, but it wasn't a hell of a lot better option. He asked, "What about the Rangers on standby in Puerto Rico? Can we launch them instead?"

The Army had a hundred Rangers sitting on the ramp at Roosevelt Roads in eastern Puerto Rico, prepped to jump out of C-130s and make an air assault on the *Grand Adventure*. He'd feel better if they boarded the ship. They were more highly trained to handle an urban hostage scenario than a bunch of regular Marines who, although perfectly competent, were trained mainly at beach landings and taking over patches of dirt in combat and defending them.

Wittenauer replied, "The winds are too high for airborne troops to jump. Thirty-five knots and gusting occasionally to sixty." Jack winced. It would be suicidal for troops to jump into such severe conditions, not to mention they'd stand a great chance of getting blown off course and not landing on the ship anyway.

The *Roosevelt* wouldn't arrive for an hour. And it would take more time after that for the Marines to board the *Grand Adventure*. Two hours before the Medusas would have real help.

In two hours this thing would be long over. One way or another.

No way around it. The Medusas were on their own.

Aleesha paused casually inside the Safari Lounge, on the top step of the five shallow stairs that led down onto the floor of the restaurant. Quickly she glanced at the four terrorists standing in each of the four corners of the room. She was looking for someone she recognized and had struck a rapport with. Over there. To her right. One of the shortest, dark-haired Americans. He'd always been polite to her, if not particularly warm.

"Hey. What's up?" she asked him boldly. "The lights in my room went out. Why are all these women in here?"

"Christ, Aleesha," the guy snapped. "Get out of here. Go back to your room and lock the door."

"Why?" she demanded, striding toward him. Okay, Vanessa. Anytime now. If she didn't have the full attention of the terrorists now, she wasn't going to get it.

Then she heard the sound she'd been waiting for. Quick bursts of MP-5s behind her. The guy she'd been talking to and his buddy swung their weapons up and appeared to commence firing in superslow motion. She dived for the floor. She shot up at the friendly American from underneath her sack of gear. He dropped, his chest exploding toward her in a mass of lung tissue, bone and blood.

Whether it was her shot that killed him or a shot from one of her teammates, she had no idea. Either way, remorse speared through her. The accumulation of blood on her hands was starting to get inside her head. What was she doing? She was running around like some killing machine, knocking out everyone she saw. She was a healer, for God's sake. Wasn't there some other way? Could she drop these guys with nonlethal shots? Maybe just take them out of action and not kill them?

But she knew they were soldiers. They'd go down fighting, just as she and the other Medusas would. All of them understood the rules of engagement here. This was a fight to the death. And if she needed a reason for why she was doing it, all she had to do was look around the room. Literally hundreds of women sobbed in relief or stared in shock. These were innocents. They hadn't asked to be here.

Vaguely she heard Vanessa giving her speech about the women hiding or arming themselves and joining the Medusas in the Deck 10 pool area if they wanted to help take back the ship. In a strangely detached frame of mind, Aleesha considered Vanessa's choice of a rendezvous spot. It made sense. The terrorists would scatter throughout the passenger and crew areas of the ship, looking for the children, and the pool deck was nothing but a large open area with glass railings and deck chairs by the hundreds. Nowhere for anyone to hide. The hijackers would ignore it. And by now, all the Tangos who were planning to hunker down on the bridge would already be there. Best of all, the bridge took up the entire forward section of Deck 10. It was only a short walk from the pool area.

The women in the restaurant surged one way and then back the other in riotous panic. Aleesha shouted at the women nearest to her, "Those two guys over there are still alive. We've got work to do elsewhere, so you'll have to finish them off. Can you do that?"

Aleesha reeled back from the bloodlust that lit up in the women's eyes. Yikes! No wonder folks said what they did about not tangling with an angry woman. She backed away from the two badly wounded hijackers as a horde of at least two dozen women jumped on each of them, kicking and punching, swinging chairs and anything else heavy they could lay their hands on. It was a brutal sight. She wouldn't wish that kind of death on anyone, not even these men. A few days ago she'd seen them as monsters in need of killing. But now she knew their names. Knew how they took their coffee. Fortunately, both men had already been nearly dead and hadn't suffered much. But it wasn't a sight she'd soon forget.

The head count of eliminated stood at eleven Yankees and five Frenchmen. That left eight Tangos, assuming the woman had shown herself and joined her companions. But Michael was included in that number, so it was really seven against the Medusas' six. She hoped. *No, she prayed.* Michael *had* to be one of the good guys. She knew it in her heart. Now she just needed him to confirm it in her head.

"I think I just heard Viktor order all his remaining men to fall back to the bridge," Vanessa said over the radio.

Just great. They could barricade themselves in there for a good long time. It was practically a fortress. And the Medusas would have to go in and take it by brute force, the way they'd dreaded doing. This time they didn't get to cheat like they had in the Norfolk scenario. Seven on six. Not bad odds at all. They'd trained against much worse. Hopefully, Viktor hadn't crammed too many hostages on the bridge with him. Depending on how crowded the room was, they could have a hard time getting clear shots at anyone.

And Michael…saints preserve him! He would surely be on the bridge. How was he going to get out of this alive? There wasn't a damned thing she could do to stop her teammates from taking him out along with all the other terrorists when the shit hit the fan. The SEALs had been set up. Attacked. And Michael had said nothing that could've saved them. If he'd known about it, then he'd broken faith with the Medusas. And now they probably thought of him as just another terrorist. They'd kill him like one, too.

Chapter 19

Getting to Deck 10 proved to be very easy. The remaining terrorists had apparently already made their way to the bridge, and the coast was clear for the Medusas as they headed up to the swimming pool. They still used a threat formation and leapfrogged positions as they moved forward, though.

Aleesha was on point, just peering out of the aft stairwell onto Deck 9 when two people came into sight. She swung her MP-5 at them, but jerked it up and away as she realized it was a pair of middle-aged women.

"Over here," Aleesha called out quietly.

The two women jumped, frightened out of their skins. They turned toward her, and she saw they were both brandishing butcher knives. "Are you those girl soldiers who are going to save us?" one of them asked.

Aleesha replied, "Yes. Come over here. We're headed up to the pool now. You can come with us."

The women's shoulders sagged in relief. She had to give them credit. They were scared spitless, but they were out here anyway, obviously willing to help take back the ship. Aleesha directed the two civilians into the middle of their formation beside Isabella and Kat. With a quick hand signal to her teammates, Aleesha moved out once more. One more flight of stairs. She raced up the steps and paused inside the Deck 10 stairwell. The rest of the Medusas and the two civilians joined her. Vanessa twirled a finger beside her head and pointed out the door. The signal to go.

Aleesha burst outside low and fast, spinning to the right side. Misty spun out to the left, and Karen and Vanessa moved straight ahead. There was a collective gasp from in front of them, and Aleesha gaped in surprise. There had to be close to a thousand women up here! The entire pool deck was crammed with women holding all manner of improvised weapons, from fire axes to mops and everything in between. The Medusas straightened, looking at each other in disbelief. Practically every woman on the ship had shown up to help them!

A murmur from the women swelled around them. Crap. They had to keep the women quiet! Aleesha jumped up on the nearest chaise longue and raised her hands, palms down, signaling urgently for silence. Thankfully, the noise subsided rapidly.

She announced clearly enough so her voice would carry, but not in a shout that would ring throughout the ship, "Give us a minute, ladies. We weren't expecting this kind of turnout. And please, keep as quiet as you can."

She stepped down and huddled with the other Medusas. Vanessa was just saying, "What are we going to do with all of them? They'll get in the way if we take this many."

Aleesha shrugged. "Yeah, but you have to give them all a role to play. They're jonesing to get revenge on the SOBs who've terrorized them for the last several days."

"Ideas?" Vanessa asked.

Aleesha remarked, "You know, I've been thinking about that take-the-bridge scenario back at Norfolk ever since we did it. It always bothered me that we went around the real test. And I was wondering. What if we take a couple of fire hoses with us when we break onto the bridge? If we shoot a full-pressure stream of water at the terrorists, I think it might knock them off their feet, maybe disarm them. It would also obscure their vision. And I expect it would change the trajectory of any bullets passing through it enough to throw off the their aim a little."

Vanessa nodded slowly. "We could use a couple dozen of the strongest women to hold the hoses for us. That would leave us free to fire our own weapons around the wall of water. But what about the other thousand women up here? We've got to get them away from the firefight."

Aleesha shrugged. "Tell half of them to go guard the lifeboats and keep the terrorists from getting off the ship in case they make a run for it. Send the other half—preferably the mothers—down to act as human shields for the children."

The others nodded along with Vanessa. "They know you, Mamba. You tell them what to do and where to go."

She nodded, then jumped back up onto her chaise longue and announced, "I need about two dozen of the strongest of you to help us take over the bridge of the ship. It will be dangerous and you'll potentially get caught in the middle of a gunfight. In a minute, I'll need the rest of you to split into two groups. I want all the mothers to go to where we've hidden the children and guard them. The rest of you will need to go to Deck 5 and guard the lifeboats. It'll be your job to keep the terrorists from getting off the ship if they make a run for it. Understood?"

Nods all around.

"Okay. Volunteers to help storm the bridge, step up here to my teammates. Moms to my left, everyone else to my right. Let's move, ladies."

About forty women stepped forward to help them take the bridge. Vanessa quickly picked out the ones among them who looked the strongest and told them to go talk to Misty. The other sixteen or so women were sent down to take charge of the mothers guarding the children. Karen took them aside to give them some extra directions while Aleesha walked over to a group of some two hundred women and told the mothers exactly where the children where hiding.

"What are we supposed to do?" one of them asked her. Many others nodded at the question.

There wasn't much she could teach the women in two or three hurried minutes, but she supposed anything was better than nothing. She told the women to post lookouts, to set up something to trip or slow down anyone who approached, to find positions where they could take cover if someone shot at them and, if they attacked a terrorist, to overwhelm him with a lot of women at once, striking him hard and fast en masse.

Then it was time to go.

Except a woman stepped forward, out of the crowd of mothers, and placed a restraining hand on her arm. The soft-looking woman grasped her with a surprising strength that would not be ignored.

"We've got to go, ma'am," Aleesha said as she unsuccessfully tried to disengage her arm.

"There's something you have to do for me."

Aleesha stared, arrested by the woman's urgency. "What's that?"

"Kill my husband."

"Are you Susan Dupont?"

The brunette nodded. "Promise me you'll kill him. He's a monster. My little boys will never feel safe until he's dead."

Aleesha answered grimly, "I expect most of the people on this ship feel the same way. We'll stop him for good. I promise."

The woman nodded and her hand fell away. "Godspeed."

Her jaw set, Aleesha gave the signal to move out.

As they moved toward the bridge, she split the impromptu hose company into two groups of twelve women. "Ladies," she told them, "you get to be two fire-hose crews. In a few minutes I'm going to unlock the door of the bridge, and you're going to open fire with full pressure streams of water from both hoses. Have any of you ever had the opportunity to man a fire hose?"

Negative head shakes all around.

"Well, they're like trying to hang on to a really mad python. They're going to throw you all over the place if you don't hang on to them really tight. You'll need to work together. Follow the lead of the woman in front. She'll aim the nozzle and the rest of you are there to provide muscle for her."

She looked around, picking out two muscular women who didn't look completely terrified yet. "How would the two of you like to be the leaders?"

Both women nodded resolutely. For a bunch of civilians, these ladies were stepping up to the plate big-time. She couldn't help but be impressed. She peeled off her bulletproof vest and Isabella followed suit. They passed the garments to the two hose crew leaders.

"What I need you two to do is point the water at everyone on the bridge. Don't worry about hitting any hostages they might have up there. The water won't kill them. It will probably knock everyone down, however. And that's the idea. We need you to knock weapons out of bad guy hands, blind the terrorists and distract them so we can shoot them. Got it?"

"Got it," the two women replied in unison.

She declined to tell them that they'd undoubtedly get shot at and maybe hit during the assault. Just as undoubtedly, they already knew it. It was funny how extraordinary courage showed up in the oddest places. Here were two women who'd expected nothing more than a nice vacation, and they'd just volunteered to risk their lives for the good of everyone else aboard this ship.

"Who are you guys, anyway?" one of the women asked her.

Aleesha shrugged. "Just a bunch of soldiers trying to help out."

They both looked skeptical, and one said aloud, "Yeah, right. I didn't fall off the turnip truck yesterday."

Vanessa spoke from behind her. "We need to roll before the hijackers get any more time to organize. Are you ready, Mamba?"

Aleesha nodded and gestured her teams to follow her. They reached the first fire-hose station just beyond the stairwell. Kat pulled out a glass cutter and sliced open the glass window covering the coiled hose. While Karen fed it out to them, the first team of women hauled it forward, getting a foretaste of what was to come in manhandling the hose. The good news was they'd only have to drag it a few yards once it was full of water, and then they'd only have to point it side to side.

The second hose station came into view. It was mounted in a curving section of wall, barely out of sight of the bridge doors. Kat crept forward, cutting the glass again. She fed the hose back carefully, keeping it close to the wall. The second team of women got into position. The Medusas fanned out in a fighting formation in front of the two teams of women. Crouching low, they sidled forward along the wall.

Aleesha took point, since she was the team's lock-picking expert. Her surgeon's fingers had a magical touch for opening just about any lock. The curve of the wall was so gradual that a periscope wouldn't do any good. She just had to press forward and hope for the best. The outer edge of the porthole in the right-hand bridge door came into view. She took one last look over her shoulder at Karen and got a quick nod. Everyone behind her was ready to go.

She dived forward, aiming for the floor just under the door. She rolled to a silent halt inches from the panel. According to the engineers from the Adventure Cruise Line, the bridge doors were bulletproof, ironically to keep the ship from being hijacked. So, down here, she ought to be safe from gunfire. She looked up at the lock above her. Oh, boy. It was a complicated double-action dead bolt augmented by an electronic keypad. This was going to be a bitch to get through. And the longer it took her, the more time the Tangos had to put a plan together.

And then something tickled at the edges of her memory. She wondered…was it possible? She reached up, and very carefully gave a tug on the door. *It cracked open,* maybe a millimeter. Sonofagun. *He'd remembered.* Michael said he'd leave the door unlocked and he actually had. God bless him.

She flashed a hand signal over her shoulder, and the Medusas slid into place behind her, the fire hoses in their midst. The signal was passed back to turn on the water. A hissing sounded behind her. They waited just until the hoses were engorged and rock hard. The civilians got a solid hold on them and nodded grimly. The women who'd turned on the valves joined their teams, and they were ready to go. It typically took several strong firemen to manage a hose. These dozen women had their hands full, but they could manage the beasts.

Vanessa gave the go signal.

One of the radio techs called out from behind Jack, "We're coming into range for the parabolic microphones."

The *Roosevelt* had deployed giant listening devices in an attempt to hear what was going on aboard the *Grand Adventure*.

"What's our range from the target?" he called out.

A guy at the radar station answered, "Eighteen miles."

Close enough for the cruise ship to see them coming, and too far away to do a damned thing to help the Medusas. Especially since they'd had to slow down and employ anti-mine tactics. Frustration churned in his gut. Jack whirled and headed to the radio panel. He picked up one of the extra headsets and slapped one clamshell over his left ear. He was still monitoring the operating frequency the Medusas were using with his right ear, but they'd gone radio silent in the last several minutes. They should be setting up their run at the bridge right about now.

A chatter of French voices erupted in his left ear. Someone was calling out the range of the vessels closing in on the cruise ship. That would be the *Roosevelt* task force the hijackers were seeing on radar. Someone else was shouting about none of the Americans answering the radios. A furious voice shouted over the din, barking out commands in French. Viktor.

He was ordering men to shoot every woman on the ship. He was ranting and raving about it not mattering if the Americans were dead. They were pigs, anyway. He was demanding that Michael organize a team to kill every woman they could find. In one particularly manic moment, it sounded like he must be holding a gun to the head of one of the female ship's officers, for he screamed about blowing her brains out this minute.

A second, much calmer, male voice interjected in British-accented French, suggesting that they might still need the services of the junior ship's engineer and perhaps they should wait a little longer before they killed her.

That must be the infamous Michael Somerset. Jack frowned, perplexed by the guy. He'd been fired by the Brits for killing a couple of guys, yet he still seemed bent on stopping Viktor Dupont. Was it a personal vendetta? Or did the guy just have some sort of hero complex? Why stick his neck out like this for the good guys? What did he have to gain? And why in the hell hadn't Somerset said anything about that minefield in the ocean?

Most important of all, could he be counted on when it came to a shooting match, which, if Jack didn't miss his guess would happen any second now?

God, he hated being helpless on the sidelines like this!

An abrupt burst of noise exploded in his left ear at the same moment that Vanessa shouted into his right ear, "Go, go, go!"

He did the only thing he could as the assault began. He closed his eyes and prayed.

Isabella yanked open the bridge door, and the other five Medusas spun in low and fast in a fan formation. They split and raced down the side walls, shooting as they went. The hose crews burst onto the bridge with the hose valves opened, sending a violent blast of water into the room.

The terrorists, who'd been in the midst of shooting back at the Medusas gaped as the jets of water slammed into them. As forecast, the fire hoses caused instant and complete chaos. Gunmen were tossed about like twigs on a raging river. Aleesha squinted. She couldn't see a blessed thing. Weapons fired wildly in the direction of the hoses, but nobody was hitting the broad side of a barn at the moment.

There. She made out a hijacker in front of her. In one fast movement, she took aim and fired. The guy dropped. Bursts of gunfire started to rat-a-tat around her as her teammates spotted Tangos and the terrorists collected themselves after the onslaught of water. The hose crews advanced farther into the room, arcing their jets of water back and forth. The terrorists were dodging the water now, jumping from cover to cover in an effort to get an angle on both the Medusas and the hose crews. But the Medusas had the other women's flanks.

Then everything seemed to happen in slow motion. The remaining terrorists started dropping fast as the Medusas got a bead on their targets. Aleesha spotted Michael by the map table, crouching under it, no doubt trying to free the three women chained there. Abruptly, the officers jumped up, diving for cover behind a radio console. Two of the four remaining terrorists dropped, and the last two terrorists simultaneously realized they were the only ones left standing. In an instant of horrified clarity, Aleesha identified the last two hijackers. Viktor and Michael.

She saw the muzzles of her teammates' weapons swinging toward the two threats. A bullet slammed into Viktor's right shoulder, and red blossomed on his shirt. He staggered from the blow, but righted himself.

And then she saw something that made her blood run cold. Viktor was turning toward Michael, his AK-47 swinging up from his side. *He was going to shoot Michael.* He'd figured out that Michael was the plant inside his team, and in a last act of defiance, Viktor was going to take Michael out before he died himself.

Viktor staggered again, and a spurt of blood gushed from his left forearm this time. Kat. Only the team's sniper was that accurate. She was trying to avoid killing the guy; he'd be worth a lot of intel alive. But he wasn't going down like he ought to. His fanaticism was holding him upright. Awkwardly he hefted the heavy Russian machine gun onto his hip with his nearly useless right arm, still determined to kill Michael. His lips curled back in a sneer of fury. She had to do something! She had to save Michael. *And she had no shot at Viktor.* Kat was behind Viktor, in the same field of fire.

Michael's gaze swept the room, looking for her. She recognized the look in his eyes. He knew he was about to die. His gaze met hers. A smile, and a look of infinite peace, passed over his face.

Her worst nightmare had come true. Death was raining down all around her. A man she cared about deeply was going to die. The violence of this profession had finally caught up with him— with them both. Her head and heart were screaming in denial; Michael was going to die before her very eyes at the hands of a madman.

She didn't stop to think about it. She acted on instinct. Her own weapon swung up in front of her face, and she pointed her MP-5 directly at Michael. Shock filled his features. And then she pulled the trigger.

He slumped to the floor, a look of enormous surprise on his face. *She'd just shot the man she loved.*

Viktor lurched, surprise painted on his face, as well. Determination stiffened his jaw, and hatred glinted in his eyes. He pulled the AK-47 up with his marginally good arm. The other Medusas fired on him simultaneously. He dropped like a rock.

He ought to have been dead before he hit the floor. But Aleesha, who was only ten feet or so away from him, saw his eyelashes move. A single blink, so slow she almost didn't believe she was seeing it. His arm twitched, his hand sliding a few inches toward his waist. And then, too late, she saw what was he was reaching for.

"Nooo!" she screamed as she dived for him. That little black gadget at his waist was a remote detonator.

But it was too late. She watched in utter dismay as his finger depressed the little red button. A tremendous explosion rocked the ship. The deck shuddered hard beneath her cheek and the entire ship lurched as if it had been punched in the side.

She blinked, shocked to still be alive. She'd been sure in that nanosecond before he touched the button that Viktor was going to blow up the bridge. So, what had he wired? That had been a series of eight to ten simultaneous explosions, or she'd turn in her EOD badge.

"Jesus H. Christ, what was that?" The sound of an explosion hurt Jack's left eardrum.

"High-order explosives, sir. Numerous simultaneous blasts," someone answered.

"Thank you so much," he snapped. "I'd never have figured that out on my own. *What* just blew up?"

Silence greeted his question.

"Satellite imagery?" he demanded. "What's it showing?"

"Stand by one, sir. The feed just wobbled. Should stabilize in a few seconds. Ah, got an image. Zooming in now…holy shit!"

"Talk to me," Jack ordered tersely.

"Eight holes in the side of the *Grand Adventure,* down low at the waterline. Hull's bent outward, so the blasts came from inside her. Taking on water. Fast."

Son of a bitch. The bastard was scuttling the ship. Jack whirled to face the admiral personally manning the wheel of the *Teddy Roosevelt.* "Can this thing go any faster?" he asked desperately.

"Mines be damned, we're running at full steam, son," the admiral answered grimly. "I'm pushing thirty knots and, in seas this rough, that's about the best any ship this size can do."

"Can you send the rest of the task force ahead?"

"Sorry. Even for an emergency of this magnitude, I can't leave an aircraft carrier undefended." He added as Jack opened his mouth to beg, "I can send out the frigate ahead of us. It can make another ten knots or so of forward speed. But I don't know how much good it'll do."

Jack replied urgently, "If the *Grand Adventure* is sinking, there are going to be a whole lot of women and children in the water. They're going to need help sooner rather than later."

The admiral nodded to one of his junior bridge officers, who radioed the two frigates escorting the *Roosevelt* to make full speed ahead to the *Grand Adventure* and prepare to pick up civilians in the water.

Jack breathed a tiny sigh of relief. It might not be much help to the Medusas, but it was better than sitting around doing nothing.

"Confirm kills," Vanessa ordered sharply.

Aleesha, who was all but lying on top of Viktor now, felt for a pulse in his ruined neck. His face was destroyed, his chest cavity pulp from the shots they'd poured into him. No pulse. The bastard was finally and irrevocably dead. Number 23 down. So where was the woman? She'd never shown herself and they'd never ID'd her. She'd opted not to go down with her comrades, eh? Harsh. Cold.

Frantically she crawled over to Michael. He was lying facedown on his stomach a few feet away. Oh, God. No! *Please* let him not have been killed by her shot. She'd aimed at a nonlethal part of his body, but accidents and nicked arteries happened.

"Medic!" Vanessa called out tersely behind her.

Reflexively, she turned to the distress call. Was one of her teammates hit?

"Civilian down." Vanessa knelt next to a white-clothed form. *Oh, no.* One of the ship's female officers. She raced over to where Vanessa and Kat were working urgently on the victim. They moved aside as Aleesha dropped to her knees.

Vanessa said, "She's shot in the back of the head. The bastards murdered her."

Aleesha bent down to look behind the young woman. Maybe if she found the piece of missing skull…she had a field kit with her…she could cauterize some of that bleeding…defibrillate her heart…

She reached for her med kit frantically, and a hand clamped around her wrist, stopping her. She looked up at Vanessa.

"You can't save them all," her boss, her friend, murmured to her.

The words pierced her soul like arrows. But she was a doctor! She was out here to save innocents. All of them! She tried to shake off Vanessa's hand, to reach for her med gear.

"Let it go," Vanessa said soberly.

Aleesha closed her eyes for an anguished moment as sanity returned. The back of the girl's head was completely gone. Inger Johannson was dead, and no medicine was going to save her.

She'd failed. Inger was depending on her, and she'd failed her.

Aleesha thought back quickly to where Inger, Hannah Leider, and Gwyn had moved after Michael unchained them. All three of them had run, crouching, toward the Medusas—their backs to the hijackers. She'd seen them dive behind one of the big radio consoles that housed the ship's navigation computers.

Aleesha looked down at Inger's head injury again. Based on the direction and angle of entry, the bullet that killed her must have come from behind her. Indeed, one of the terrorists had shot her. The sheer spite of it took Aleesha's breath away and stripped away any remorse she might have had over killing every last one of the hijackers.

"She's gone," Aleesha muttered. "I let her die."

A wail startled her. Gwyn, the hospitality officer, rocked back and forth on her knees, hugging herself and sobbing.

Aleesha looked around the room, searching for any more civilian victims in need of life-saving medical attention. The order of triage in a scenario like this was civilians first, Medusas second and Tangos last. Karen was field bandaging the arm of one of the hose crew members, and several more of the civilian volunteers were nursing cuts and contusions. Then her gaze lighted on a prostrate male figure.

"Michael." She again raced to his side and dropped to her knees. She rolled him gently onto his back. Blood seeped from just below his left shoulder.

He groaned and then cracked one eye open. "Is he dead?" he murmured between closed lips.

She replied, "Viktor? Oh, yeah." And then nearly fainted with relief as Michael sat up gingerly. He'd been playing possum! She was going to *kill* him for scaring her like that.

"You shot me!" he accused indignantly.

She couldn't help but grin. Clearly the man was not on the verge of dying. But she noticed her legs felt like rubber. She retorted, "Viktor was raising his AK-47 to you. I figured if I beat him to the punch and shot you first, it might convince him you weren't the traitor, and he might not bother to shoot you again. Oh, and I figured I could shoot you without killing you, whereas Viktor had every intention of blowing your head off."

Michael stared narrowly at her. "So you shot me to save my life?"

"Well, yeah. Basically," she answered.

"It was a big risk to take," he muttered, apparently only partially mollified.

"Better than certain death." Then she added quietly, "I didn't want to lose you."

They leaned toward each other. Lord, she needed a hug right now. But then the detonator at her waist poked her, jolting her back to the situation at hand. "What did Viktor just blow up?" she asked tensely.

Michael blinked. "Blow up?"

"He mashed a detonator as he went down."

"So that wasn't your Navy firing on us?"

"No. They wouldn't try to sink a cruise ship full of innocent passengers—" She broke off, horrified. *Sink it.* Viktor had tried to sink the ship! It made perfect sense, knowing him. If he couldn't get off the ship alive, by God, he wasn't going to let anyone else get off it alive, either. Sometime during the last several days, he'd wired the *Grand Adventure* to blow.

"Viper!" she yelled. "I think Viktor tried to sink the ship. We need to do a damage assessment, ASAP!" She leaped to her feet in dread as a rush of certainty overcame her. The kind of intuitive certainty deep in her gut that she'd learned to trust implicitly. "Those explosions happened near the waterline. He planted charges all down the side of the ship so the antiflooding bulkheads would be useless."

Then another thought hit her. It nearly made her throw up. "The children. They're on the first deck."

She took off running without waiting for anyone else to join her. She heard footsteps pounding behind her but didn't look to see who it was. Panic like she'd never experienced before spurred her forward. Oh, God. All those children!

If possible her panic deepened as she noticed a very slight tilt to the deck under her feet. The ship was taking on water. Fast. She took the midship stairwell in great knee-jarring leaps, jumping down flight after flight of stairs as fast as her body could possibly go. Whether or not she remembered to breathe, she had no idea. She just knew she had to get down to those kids and get them out before their hiding place became their deathtrap.

She turned the last corner and looked down at the first deck. Oh. My. God. It sloshed maybe knee deep in water. She charged into the water, running in an awkward high-kneed gait, splashing her way against the dragging weight. High-pitched screams became audible as she approached the tank. The hall was clogged with panicked women fighting against one another as they all tried to reach the water tank holding their babies.

"Make a hole," she bellowed as loud as she could.

But the mothers' terror was too deep for that. She used her superior strength to elbow her way past them all. As she careened into the water plant, she heard the sound of hands pounding on the metal walls of the tank *from the inside* over the noisy sloshing of the sea water and the cries of the mothers. The water had risen to nearly midthigh, now.

Thirty or forty children milled around outside the tank, clearly unsure of what to do. They must've swum out through the maintenance hatch. They turned huge, frightened gazes on her as she splashed into sight.

"Ladies, listen to me!" she shouted. "I need all of you to head down that hall and upstairs to Deck 5," she ordered. "You're not doing me a damned bit of good down here, and you're getting in the way of any rescue attempt. Clear the halls now! I'll take care of your children."

It was too much to ask of them. They didn't leave.

She tried again. "Fine. Then form a chain of women down the hallway one person wide. As the kids come out of here, I need adults to guide the children up to Deck 5 and onto the lifeboats. Set it up like a bucket brigade of kids. Will you do that much for me?"

The women acted on that order. They'd leave, as long as they still felt like they were taking part in rescuing their children. She couldn't blame them.

Most of the women and all of the kids who'd already gotten out of the tank took off, half swimming, half wading toward the stairwell.

She moved over to the water tank and shouted against its surface, "I'm here! I'll get you out. Don't worry!"

The lower maintenance hatch the kids had used to get into the tank was flapping in the swirling waters, patently unsafe for anyone trying to pass through. She took a deep breath and ducked under the water. She pulled the door fully open, but a rush of water nearly slammed it shut on her legs as she swam through it into the tank. She stood up inside the dimly lit space. Jeez, what a mess. The chaos in here was complete. Panic reigned with children screaming and clawing at the walls.

She passed out the rest of her cyalume sticks and shouted into her throat mike, without any idea of whether or not a transmission would make it out of this metal-enshrouded space, "I need help down here!"

Off mike, she bellowed at the top of her lungs, "Quiet!" The sound was impressive, banging around against the metal walls. It quieted everyone down for a moment in stunned surprise.

"Everyone is going to get out of here alive. Nobody's going to die. But you all have to be quiet and follow directions or I will leave you in here and let you drown. Is that understood?" she said in her fiercest possible voice. Hopefully, if she was scarier than the prospect of drowning, the children would focus all their attention on her.

"Okay. Everyone who can swim underwater, come over to this door right now and form a single-file line. You—" she grabbed the nearest orange shirt "—swim through the hatch and hold it open from the other side. A line of mothers are waiting to take everyone up to the lifeboats on Deck 5."

She leaned close to the staffer and said more quietly, "Try to get word to the soldiers that I need all the help I can get down here ASAP."

The girl nodded, and Aleesha gave her a little push toward the hatch. "Go. Hurry."

As the swimmers started exiting, she looked around the tank. How in the hell was she going to get what looked like close to a hundred children who couldn't swim out of here? *The top hatch.* It was wide-open, creating a good eight-foot gap in the ceiling. The ceiling of the water plant was only a few feet higher than the tank.

She felt the pouches hanging off her belt. Oh, yeah. She still had a block of C-4 left. And she had an idea.

But how in the hell was she going to get up there to do it? The insides of this tank were perfectly smooth, and she hadn't seen any ladder rungs on the outside of the tank when she'd reconned it last night.

She jumped as a male voice said behind her, "Need a boost?" *Michael.* Praise the Lord. "Yes, I do."

"Climb on my shoulders."

She nodded and wasted no time in moving behind him, putting her right foot on the top of his thigh where he bent it for her, and then putting her left foot onto his left shoulder. He made a funny sucking sound between his teeth—hey, she wasn't that heavy!—oh wait. She'd shot him in the shoulder. He held his hands up over his head to steady her. Carefully, he took a step and stood upright. She teetered, straightening up carefully.

"A little to your left and a couple steps forward," she directed him.

He moved as she indicated, and she extended her arms over her head. The lip of the opening was tantalizingly out of reach, maybe a foot over her head. "I can't quite reach it. I'm going to jump for it."

A grunt of assent from Michael, and she felt him brace himself beneath her feet. She bent her knees and gave a mighty push as she jumped. Her fingers grabbed the edge of the opening. And slipped! She lurched, regripped with her right hand and stabilized, hanging from the metal rim. Now to get out the damn hole.

She put her weight on her left hand and quickly reversed the grip of her right hand. Then she released her left hand and rotated her entire body, turning 180 degrees. She caught the rim again with her left hand, now grasping it behind her head. She swung her feet out and up, taking several swings to build up momentum. Then, one last big swing and she kicked her feet up and over her head into a somersault that landed her belly first on the roof, looking down into the water tank.

A cheer went up from below.

Michael was bent over, gasping in what appeared to be pain. No time to worry about that now. She had to get those kids out.

She rolled over onto her back and pulled out the C-4, rolling it into a cone between her hands. She needed a directional charge to blow all the force of the explosion through the steel deck above her and not back down into the water tank. She hollowed out the bottom of the cone and pressed the whole thing against the ceiling a little to the side of the water tank. She reached for a detonator in her utility belt, but had to grab the handle of the hatch beside her as the ship dipped abruptly and listed about ten degrees to the side. *Oh, Lord.* The ship was already starting to roll. Not good. The *Grand Adventure* was going down soon.

"Hurry," Michael called up to her.

No kidding. Her fingers found a detonator and yanked it out. She shoved it into the plastic explosive. Ready. She pulled out a length of nylon rope and quickly lashed it to a metal piece of the top hatch. Then, straining, she pulled the hatch mostly closed, leaving only a thin gap for her to slip through.

"Look out below!" she called as she slid down the rope in a controlled fall. She splashed into water that was now waist deep.

About half of the kids who could swim had already exited via the maintenance hatch, and that operation looked to be progressing in an orderly fashion. But the nonswimmers inside the tank were a different matter. Lots of the kids were barely keeping their heads above water, the staffers and taller kids supporting the smallest children. Crap. They were running out of time.

She stopped the next kid in the line to swim out, a boy who looked to be about thirteen, and directed him, "Tell the moms outside to cover their ears. I'm about to blow a hole in the ceiling. And tell some of them to get up to Deck 2 directly over this spot to help the kids we pass up there to get to Deck 5. Got all that?"

The boy nodded, took a deep breath and ducked under the water.

"Hands over your ears, everyone!" she yelled. She gave them a few seconds to comply, and then she blew the C-4. The sound was tremendous, ringing through her head until her eyeballs hurt. Some of the children started to cry. She hoped she hadn't blown any eardrums. Although that was a lesser evil than dying.

She shimmied back up the rope, slipping through the gap in the top hatch to sit on the edge of the tank. A ragged hole gaped in the ceiling. Outstanding. Now to get the kids through it.

Jack jumped as a female voice transmitted over the Medusa's operational frequency, "*Roosevelt* TOC, we have twenty-two Tangos accounted for and neutralized. Michael's helping us, and there's no sign of the supposed twenty-fourth, probably a woman among the passengers."

"Hot damn, they've done it," Jack yelled in triumph. "They've taken back the ship!"

"Yeah, but it's about to be sitting at the bottom of the Caribbean," the admiral retorted.

Jack transmitted back to Vanessa, "The *Big RV* is en route, estimated time of arrival thirty minutes. Frigates will be in the area in twenty minutes. Evacuate the *Grand Adventure,* over."

"Negative, TOC," Vanessa replied. "We've got several hundred kids trapped on Deck 1. Will proceed with rescuing and evacuating them."

Jack's elation evaporated in an instant. The children were trapped at the very lowest levels of the ship? "Say water depth inside ship."

"Waist deep and rising fast on Deck 1," came Vanessa's ominous answer. "The ship's listing about fifteen degrees."

"Hurry, then," he urged her. "The frigates will put rescue boats in the water as soon as they get into the area."

"Launch rescue copters, TOC. This is going to be close. Out."

Jack sagged against the counter in front of him. To have gotten this far, only to face losing all the children? He could barely wrap his mind around the prospect. C'mon, snake ladies. Pull another miracle out of your hats.

Chapter 20

Aleesha called down into the tank, "Michael, can you and the orange shirts build some sort of human pyramid that the little kids can climb? I'll reach down and haul them up here."

"Yeah," he grunted.

"Send up one of the tallest, oldest kids first. I'll need help up here."

In a matter of moments, children started clambering up Michael and onto the other staffers, who'd wasted no time making like cheerleaders and forming a pyramid with Michael as its anchor in the center. In the dim glow from below, she saw him grimace with pain every time someone stepped on his left shoulder. He must be hurt worse from her bullet than he'd let on. Damn.

But then the first child was in front of her, a boy. She grabbed his hands and bodily dragged him up the last several feet. He crawled out onto the gentle curve of the tank's roof beside her.

"Go over to that hole in the floor and help the little kids climb through it."

The boy nodded gamely.

"You're being a real hero," Aleesha added warmly.

He smiled tentatively at her.

Another child came up. A girl this time. And another. They started coming up fast, one right after another. The staffers below had clearly worked out some system for getting the kids up efficiently. She reached down again and again, hauling children until she thought her arms were going to fall off. But it wasn't as if she could take a break. And she'd be damned if she'd let any of these kids die on her watch. The water was nearly up to Michael's chest now, and all the remaining children were clinging to adults to stay afloat.

Someone was going to drown in that mess down there. A kid would get tired and let go and nobody would notice. It was such a bloody quiet way to die. She hauled up yet another child, and then jumped when a voice beside her murmured, "Need some help?"

Thank God. Vanessa.

Her boss took one look at the situation and said, "I'll take over hoisting the kids. My arms are fresh. You jump into the tank and help keep kids afloat. The rest of the team will be here in a few seconds and I'll send them down to you."

Aleesha nodded and wasted no energy replying. She merely rolled off the edge of the hole and into the water. Her arms felt like mush. And almost instantly, little arms wrapped around her neck, all but strangling her. She reached out, supporting the smallest children as she took a quick head count. Four kids hanging on to her.

"If any of you feel like you're going to let go, you tell me, okay?" she told them.

She felt nods and heard a few frightened okays.

Man, the water was up to her armpits, now. She took a quick look around. They had maybe forty kids left to lift out. They weren't going to make it. The water was going to get too deep in here.

She jumped as a head popped up out of the water beside her. Karen. And another head. Misty. And then Isabella and Kat.

Misty said jauntily, "I hear you guys are having a party in here. Can I play, too?"

The remaining orange staffers all but wept in relief. Over the next few minutes, a good half of the remaining kids were passed over to Aleesha and her four teammates to wear like precious little angels around their necks. The water was lapping over Aleesha's shoulders now, and she was starting to get cold. Heck, she had on a full wet suit. The kids must be freezing. She felt the small bodies of the children shivering against her.

"Not much longer now, guys," she said encouragingly, "and then it'll be your turn to go. We got rid of all the bad guys, you know. Your moms are upstairs waiting for you. As soon as you get out of here, you get to go on a really cool lifeboat. And then you get to go on a big ship. I think your daddies are there, waiting to see you. How awesome is that?"

The kids nodded at her, blue-lipped but game. Gutsy, they were.

She stretched up on her tiptoes for as long as she could, but the water continued its inexorable rise. Hell, at this rate, the water would just float the kids to the top of the tank and they could all step out like getting out of a swimming pool.

"Hey, kids," she said calmly. "I'm going to have to start kicking my legs to keep us afloat. I need all of your to pull your knees to your chests and curl up in little balls so I don't kick you. But keep your arms around my neck, okay?"

The children nodded. Besides, the fetal positions would help the kids retain a little more body heat while they waited their turns to be rescued.

The water level was definitely rising more quickly now. The holes Viktor had blown in the ship must be getting bigger as the rush of water flooding into the ship tore them wider. And the water tank was showing a definite tilt. She'd estimate it was up to nearly twenty degrees. At some point, a ship this size would reach the angle where it would topple over of its own weight, and capsize. And pretty much anyone left on the ship when that happened was hosed.

The other issue was whether or not the lifeboats would launch properly once the ship was leaning over too far. The downslope boats could still launch, but the upslope life boats would be trapped on the sides of the ship. Big passenger liners were designed for the lifeboats to handle a fairly impressive list—the tilt of the ship—but ship designers weren't miracle workers.

One problem at a time. All the remaining orange staffers had offloaded their burdens of kids and were helping pass children up the human pyramid to the roof. Michael's chin was in the water, now. He wasn't going to be able to anchor the human ladder for more than a few more seconds before he'd be underwater.

"Quickly," Aleesha urged the staffers who were still passing up kids.

Michael started to cough and choke.

"That's it!" Aleesha shouted. "Everyone get down off Michael!"

The others jumped down into the water and he surfaced, still coughing and gasping for air.

"Now what?" one of the orange shirts asked, looking up longingly at the ceiling.

"Viper!" Aleesha called out. "Can you tie a bunch of knots in some rope and throw it down here?"

"Affirmative," came the response from above. "Stand by."

The line that Aleesha had used to climb back down into the tank earlier disappeared above. Vanessa was undoubtedly combining that line with hers to increase the thickness of the rope to make it easier to climb. Indeed, in under a minute, Vanessa tossed down the end of the doubled-up rope, now with knots placed every foot or so along it.

"Okay," Aleesha called out. "Which of you kids know how to climb a rope?"

Thankfully, a good dozen kids responded with yesses. Swimming around with their heavy loads of kids, the Medusas took turns maneuvering over to the rope to transfer children onto it. Michael treaded water below, steadying the rope as the kids climbed. It was much slower going than the human ladder before, but every child they got out of here was one more life saved.

Aleesha's legs were starting to cramp up. She'd passed tired a while ago and was well into the realm of forcibly ignoring the piercing pain of overextended muscles, because she had no other choice.

The Medusas talked the remaining orange shirts into climbing the rope, as well. And that left only the five Medusas, Michael and fifteen children in the tank. The ceiling of the tank was only about five feet over their heads, now.

Vanessa called down, "Karen, if you'll come up here and sit on my legs, I think I can lean down far enough to grab some kids."

"Roger that," Karen called back. She passed off the three children she was supporting to Michael, and headed for the rope. The glow sticks floating on the surface of the water cast an eerie yellow light. Aleesha noticed how, even taking the funky lighting into account, Michael was starting to look pretty out of it—dazed, and maybe even in shock. She frowned, but there wasn't a damned thing she could do about it at the moment.

Karen hauled herself up the rope and flopped onto the roof of the tank. In short order, Vanessa dangled upside down, hanging from her hips. She instructed the kids, "I'm going to reach down and grab you, and then you'll have to climb me like a ladder. Put your feet in the armholes of my vest and on my belt. Okay?"

The first children nodded. The procedure worked for the oldest remaining children. But the last half-dozen little kids couldn't pull it off. They were simply too cold and exhausted.

Now what?

A sailor on the birdwalk, the narrow balcony running around the carrier's bridge, called out, "I have visual on the *Grand Adventure*."

Jack bolted out the door and all but ripped the large set of binoculars from the guy's hands. He looked through them, and his stomach dropped to his feet. A half-dozen lifeboats were already in the water, their white shapes bobbing like corks on the angry sea beside the bulk of the giant cruise ship. Gaping holes were visible in the side of the ship, and it was listing a good twenty degrees.

Merciful God in Heaven.

"Say status," he barked into his radio at the Medusas.

There was a short pause and then Karen snapped, "We're busy right now."

He replied evenly, not offended in the least, "Then just listen. I've got rescue boats in the water and a rescue helicopter is orbiting the *Grand Adventure.* Four more helicopters are ready on the *Roosevelt's* deck for immediate launch. The topside evacuation of the *Grand Adventure* looks to be going fairly smoothly. The crew was alert enough to launch the upside lifeboats first. They got eight off the ship before the list got too bad. There are fourteen more lifeboats hanging on the downhill side of the ship, and we estimate that only twelve will be necessary to complete the evacuation. What appear to be crew members from the *Grand Adventure* are directing the loading and launching of the boats. We will be in position to start recovering life boats from the water in five to seven more minutes."

"Copy," Karen grunted, obviously in the middle of some significant physical exertion.

He shut up. He knew a busy team when he heard one. And whatever they were doing to rescue the children right now, they clearly had their hands full.

Aleesha called up to Vanessa, "It's only going to be a few more minutes until we float up to the roof. How about we just ride it out until then and hand the kids up to you when we're close to the rim?"

Vanessa looked down at the tank doubtfully. "It won't leave us much time to get out of there. A couple minutes at most."

"We've only got six kids to go."

Vanessa nodded. "Okay. That's probably safer than trying to climb the ropes and asking the kids to hang on to your backs."

It grew quiet in the tank. The Medusas and Michael treaded water in silence, each lost in a private hell of pushing through the pain and keeping moving. Every few seconds Aleesha did a mental check of the grips of the three children hanging on to her, making sure that none of them were weakening.

She'd had enough of death for one day. She'd faced her worst fear—having to pull a trigger against another human being—and she'd prevailed. She'd done the right thing and killed when she had to. Now was the time for saving lives. Odd how, in the course of one mission, she'd been called upon to both take lives and save lives. But, she was learning, such was the duality of her work.

And such was the pain of her work. Her body was screaming for relief. But it was just like her days in the Medusas' initial training. There came a point when the mind—the will—simply overcame whatever limits the human body believed it had. No matter how bad it got in this tank, she was *not* quitting. These three kids would survive at all costs.

In the darkness and the cold, something dawned on her. She might not be able to save them all, like Vanessa had said on the bridge. But in this job, she got a fighting chance to try. On her very first day of medical school, a professor had warned her entire class that they were not miracle workers. They were only human beings who would be trained to do their best. That would have to be enough for them and their patients. And out here she wouldn't stop every bad guy or save every innocent. But the two weren't mutually exclusive. It was possible to kill and still be committed to saving lives.

It was enough for her. She'd be the best Special Forces soldier she could be, killing and all, and she'd save as many innocents as she humanly could. But she wasn't a god, and she wasn't a miracle worker. She was only one human being standing in the gap and doing her best. Peace came over her.

Or hell, maybe she was just too damned cold to feel the pain anymore.

One of the kids clinging to her started to let go. Aleesha

wrapped her right arm around the little girl quickly and pulled her close. Oh, no. Not a single child was going to drown on her watch after all she'd gone through down here to save them. A burst of joy filled her as she felt the little girl revive a bit, that tiny body nestled trustingly against hers.

Come to think of it, she loved this job. Where else did a person get a chance to literally hold the life of a child in her hands like this? She'd been blessed with not one, but two careers that gave her that very opportunity. Medicine and the Medusas weren't so different after all.

"Can you hang on a little longer?" she asked the child gently.

A nod against her neck. She cradled the tiny body against hers for a moment longer and then guided the girl's hands back around her neck.

How long she treaded water in the dark and cold, Aleesha had no idea. And it didn't matter anymore. *However long it took.*

Vanessa finally called down an eternity later, "I think I can pull them up now."

The Medusas passed up children as quickly as they could, but everyone was exhausted and clumsy. Then finally, blessedly, the last child was handed up. The water level was within a foot of the ceiling of the tank.

"Everyone out," Aleesha called. She waited in the water as her teammates climbed out one after another. And then it was her turn. She crawled out of the water and lay gasping on the cold, tilting steel.

She heard Vanessa say behind her, "C'mon, Michael."

God, it felt good just to lie here for a moment.

Vanessa said more sharply, "What are you waiting for? Let's go!"

And damned if Grandmama's voodoo intuition didn't kick in again. Something was terribly wrong with Michael.

Vanessa shouted, "Michael!"

Aleesha swung around, peering into the tank. And saw Michael's dark head slip beneath the surface of the water.

Oh God, oh God, oh God.

The ship groaned and lurched a good five degrees, sloshing water all around them. The down-slope edge of her hole through to the second deck was almost touching the water line now. The water was rising so fast she could see it creeping up as she looked at it.

"We've got to get out of here," Vanessa shouted over the splashing and roaring of water.

Aleesha shouted back, "I'm not leaving without Michael. We don't leave another Medusa behind. Ever! And without him, we couldn't have done this mission. He's as much a part of this team as I am. I'm going in after him!"

Vanessa opened her mouth, clearly to order her not to jump back into that black abyss. But instead, her boss merely passed her the end of the knotted rope and shouted, "Let's do it."

The two of them jumped into the water together. Each keeping a hand on the rope to guide them back to the hatch, they took deep breaths and submerged. It was surreal, swimming around in the cold and utter dark. Her eyes were useless, and she felt her way forward, trying to envision where she'd seen his head disappear. The night-vision goggles she had on her belt weren't the underwater variety. Damn! She thought fast. He wouldn't necessarily sink straight to the bottom of the tank. If he still had a little air in his lungs, it might give him enough buoyancy to float, suspended in the water.

Her own lungs burned. And then screamed. And then absolutely demanded that if she didn't surface, she was going to pass out. Frustrated, she kicked hard for the top of the tank.

She came up for air and was startled that there was barely enough room between the water and the tank for her head to clear. She took a couple of deep breaths and went under again. *Grandmama, if you've ever helped me before, help me now. Help me find Michael.*

She swam forward, her hands outstretched. Time slowed to a crawl as she searched, the water roiling around her and her entire life condensing down into this single instant.

Then her hands hit cloth. She lurched, feeling that direction again. And bumped into something solid. She'd found him! She grabbed onto the cloth and tugged, kicking for all she was worth toward the top of the tank. Partway up, she readjusted her hold, hooking her hands under his armpits. It was amazing how heavy a human being was with little air in his lungs to help him float.

She ought to be near the surface now. She kicked again, and her head bumped into metal! Oh, God. The tank had filled up. There was no more air pocket! Silently blessing her SEAL swimming instructors who'd drilled all the panic out of her in situations like this, she tugged on the rope she still held. That way. The hatch was to her right.

She followed the nylon lifeline and glimpsed a faint light ahead. Her lungs about to explode, she swam toward it and broke the surface of the water just as she was sure she couldn't hold her breath one more millisecond.

She drew in a great gasping breath of air. Water poured down all around her now, rushing through the hole in the second floor. Vanessa was there, in the gap, drawing several hard breaths, as if she planned to go back down into the tank.

Her boss didn't speak—neither of them had the breath for it—but she helped pull Michael's limp body over to the hole in the floor. The two of them started to hoist him through it when hands reached down from above without warning and lifted his weight away from them. Karen and Misty. Together she and Vanessa climbed carefully through the ragged hole in the floor.

Lord, it was already knee-deep in here, and the walls tilted at a crazy angle. Karen was already pounding on Michael's back, clearing water from his lungs. As the Marine rolled him over onto his back, Aleesha crawled over to him.

She plastered her mouth on his and, plugging his nose, breathed hard into his body. She felt Karen starting chest compressions beside her. Aleesha counted the requisite number of compressions and blew into his mouth again.

She felt the moment when he tried to draw a breath. She

rolled him onto his side and held his head while he emptied his stomach and lungs of the water clogging them. She plastered her hand to his carotid artery, a pulse throbbed again. They'd done it. He was alive. The cold water had slowed down his bodily functions, including blood loss, enough that they'd had time to save him. Thank God for small favors.

Vanessa spoke over her shoulder, "We've got to get out of here. Can he be moved?"

Aleesha realized she was kneeling in a good three feet of water, and on the downhill side of the hallway, it was more like four feet deep. "I don't think we've got any choice. Looks like this ship's trying real hard to sink."

The women nodded and stood up.

"I'll take him," Aleesha grunted.

Thankfully, her teammates didn't argue with her. They understood her need to save this man. Karen hoisted Michael into a vertical position, and Misty arranged his arms around Aleesha's neck from behind in a fireman's carry.

She staggered forward under his weight, found her balance and took off down the hall, slogging through the water as fast as she could. Vanessa sent Kat and Isabella ahead to scope out how they were going to get off the ship.

They reached the forward stairwell, and Aleesha started up it. Each step was an exercise in agony. Her legs felt like noodles, her feet as heavy as lead. But no way was she stopping. Step by agonizing step she climbed, up and out of the bowels of hell.

She heard footsteps rushing at them from above. Kat called down to them.

"The lifeboats have launched, and everyone else is off the ship. We need to get up to Deck 10 and there'll be a rescue helicopter for us."

Aleesha groaned. It figured. Vanessa and Karen, on either side of her, reached out and put their hands under her armpits to help her.

"Just like the old days back in training, eh?" Vanessa grunted.

Aleesha grunted back. She wasn't too proud to accept the help at this point. And Lord knew, they'd all dragged each other up enough mountains back in the days when Jack Scatalone was still doing his best to make them all quit Special Ops training.

A flood of light spilled into the stairwell ahead and a silhouette stood in the door. "This way," Kat called out.

One more flight of steps. Aleesha counted in her head. Twelve steps. And then they were there. Light burst all around them as they stepped outside. Squinting, she saw Isabella waving them over toward the high side of the deck to an open area where all the lounge chairs had slid away. A U.S. Navy helicopter hovered overhead, a pair of PJs—pararescue jumpers—hanging in the door already, a cot-size basket on its way down to Isabella below.

Aleesha staggered over to the basket and let her teammates lift Michael off her shoulders and lay him in the basket. She watched him as the PJs winched him up in the copter. It seemed like hours until the basket lowered again. But finally Kat, Isabella and Karen climbed into it and rode up to safety.

The basket lowered one more time. Misty climbed in first, and then Vanessa shouted over the rotor noise, "Your turn, Mamba."

They'd done it. They were getting off the *Grand Adventure*. Mission accomplished. Almost in a state of shock, she climbed into the metal basket, ducking under the support chains. She helped Vanessa climb in, and then Misty gave the signal to the PJs to go.

The cargo bay of the helicopter was not large enough to accommodate Michael and the PJs working on him plus all six Medusas, so Misty, Vanessa and Aleesha got a thrilling ride in the mesh basket to the looming flat top in the distance.

"That looks like the *Roosevelt*," Vanessa shouted.

Aleesha nodded back. Good. The aircraft carrier had excellent medical facilities and a fine trauma doc on board. She'd met him at a couple of medical conferences.

She kept looking up anxiously at the helicopter above until Vanessa finally shouted, "The PJs know what they're doing. And Karen will kick their butts if they don't keep him alive."

That might be so, but she wasn't going to relax until she saw Michael—alive, conscious and on the mend—with her own two eyes.

"*Roosevelt* ops, we have the last seven passengers from the *Grand Adventure*. Request emergency medical response meet us on the flight deck."

Jack's heart skipped a beat. *The Medusas and Michael.* Who was hurt? And how badly?

The helicopter pilot must've heard his unspoken questions, for he continued, "We have one casualty. Male. Gunshot wound to the upper chest, suffering from blood loss and shock."

Praise God. His ladies were okay.

"You heard the man," the admiral barked from behind him. "Let's get a trauma team up to the flight deck on the double. That bird'll be here in three minutes."

"Do you need me up here, sir?" Jack asked.

The admiral answered dryly, "I know how to direct the recovery operation to get those lifeboats out of the water. Get out of here. Go say hello to your girls."

"Yes, sir," Jack replied smartly. And then he turned and sprinted out the door.

Their helicopter drew near the *Roosevelt*. The pilot lowered their basket onto the flight deck and hovered until the three of them had jumped out of it. Then, as they ran off to one side, it descended, setting down gently. Karen, Kat and Isabella hopped out while the two PJs from inside the bird and four more corpsmen rushed Michael onto a gurney and into the ship. Aleesha ran beside him, listening as the PJs briefed the trauma doctor on duty.

"Gunshot wound to upper left quadrant of the chest… shock…hypothermia…blood loss…"

Nothing life-threatening to a good medical team. Michael wasn't out of the woods by a long shot—his wound would need a thorough cleaning, he needed a transfusion and to get warmed up, and they'd have to monitor his shock carefully. But odds were he'd live. Abject relief almost made her ill.

The group careened into the ship's hospital, and she was shoved out of the way unceremoniously as the trauma team went to work. Her legs wobbled. A medic moved beside her and put a supporting hand under her arm. "Why don't you have a seat, ma'am?"

He wrapped a heavy wool blanket around her, and she huddled in its scratchy warmth as the doctors worked on Michael. It seemed to take forever, but in reality it took only an hour or so to stabilize and patch up the patient. A reasonably quick job as trauma medicine went.

Finally the doctor stepped back from the gurney, stripping off a pair of bloody surgical gloves. The floor was littered with bloody towels, blood-soaked gauze pads and sterile wrappings. Thankfully, not too much actual blood pooled on the floor beneath Michael. They'd given him two pints so far, and that had helped stabilize his blood pressure. A third pint of whole blood and a saline drip were hooked up to his arm, as well.

The doctor came over to her. "Doctor Gautier?" he asked in surprise. "What in the world are you doing here? The last time I saw you at that conference in Denver, you were stationed at Great Lakes."

She smiled up at him humorlessly. "It's a long story. Really long. Is he going to be okay?"

The doc glanced over his shoulder. "The bullet didn't hit anything vital. Cracked his collarbone. I'll set that later when he's a little more stable. We'll have to monitor him for further shock, of course. Keep a close eye on his vitals for a while. But he's strong. In good shape. Yeah. He'll live."

She sagged in her chair. "Is he awake?"

"He's groggy. I'm running some heavy-duty painkillers into that IV drip. He may not be lucid."

"Can I talk to him?" And how many times had she heard these very same questions from the loved ones of *her* patients?

It felt weird being on the giving end. She could almost recite the doctor's answer as he gave it to her.

"Only for a minute or two. Don't overtax him. He needs his rest."

She nodded and stood up. Dragging her blanket with her, she moved over to Michael's side and took his hand in hers. It was cold. Pale. So lifeless. "Hey, English," she said softly. "Some hero you turned out to be. You know, you could've told me you were about to pass out down there in that tank. We'd have relieved you."

His eyes opened partway and he smiled up at her weakly. "Thought you'd go for the hero type. Wanted to impress you."

She reached up to smooth the damp hair off his forehead. "Oh, I'm impressed all right. Right down to my toes."

One corner of his mouth tilted up faintly. "Glad to hear it. I'm pretty impressed by you, too. Who'd have guessed? Women commandos..." His voice trailed off.

"Sleep now," she urged him quietly. "You and I are going to have all the time in the world to compare résumés once you're feeling better."

His eyelids cracked open a fraction, sluggishly, as if it was a tremendous effort to do so. "Promise?" he mumbled.

"Yeah. I promise."

His fingers tightened on hers ever so faintly. And then they went slack and fell away from hers. Her heart jumped for a second in panic, and her gaze snapped to the monitors beeping softly beside the bed. Vitals were stable. She released the breath she hadn't realized she was holding.

The doctor touched her shoulder. "I'll take good care of him."

She nodded, her eyes burning. Oh, yes, Michael Somerset. She promised, all right.

"Ma'am?"

Her eyes lurched open.

A seaman stood there, diffidently. "They need you on the flight deck."

They who? Her teammates? Was one of them hurt? Her protective impulses were already on overload. She dropped her blanket immediately and nodded to the seaman to lead the way.

She stepped outside and was buffeted hard by a gust of wind. Mother Nature had held back about as long as she was going to. Hurricane Evangeline was almost on them. She had no doubt the *Roosevelt* carrier group was already turning northwest, away from the storm.

Ducking her head low, she caught sight of her teammates standing in a tight cluster by the helicopter that had brought them in. She trotted over to them. "What's up?"

Vanessa shrugged. "I don't know. The admiral told us to come out here."

Weird.

"By the way," Vanessa commented, "I'll be glad to write a letter to the British government telling them what Michael did for us and how he helped save all those people if you think it'll help."

Aleesha smiled her gratitude at her boss. "If the Brits won't reinstate him after this, I may have to sic Jack on the queen."

Misty laughed. "How about all the Medusas? The Brits won't stand a chance."

Aleesha nodded. "That's a deal. Speak of the devil…"

The Medusas turned around as Jack hurried over to them. Apparently, he and Vanessa had already had a private reunion while Aleesha was still downstairs with Michael, for they only traded brief smiles.

Jack announced, "We've got the interrogators briefed up to explain to everyone from the *Grand Adventure* that you're all CIA agents. It's not great, but it's better than nothing. Oh, and the initial pass through the female passengers doesn't show anyone who meets your description of the twenty-fourth terrorist. She's either still on the *Grand Adventure* sitting on the bottom of the ocean or she found her way off the ship by some other means."

The Medusas absorbed that one in silence.

But then Aleesha shrugged. "Hey, we served the innocents—

except the officers and Inger, of course." She added quietly, "Somehow I don't think she minded dying to save those kids. She was a brave girl."

They were all silent, reflecting upon the noble sacrifice of courageous people who'd died at their posts.

And into that sober void a seaman stepped around the nose of the helicopter and gestured for them to follow him. "This way, ladies."

The six women walked tiredly around the copter and stopped cold. Standing in front of them was a crowd of men, women and children stretching all the way across the deck. The passengers and crew of the *Grand Adventure*.

They were all cheering.

Aleesha blinked, stunned. Damned if those weren't tears welling up in her eyes! She felt Vanessa's arm go around her shoulder, and she did the same to Misty on her right. They didn't usually go for group hugs or big displays of affection, but today the Medusas walked arm in arm toward the waiting crowd.

"Not a bad day's work," Vanessa murmured.

Misty added jauntily, "I'd hate to be the security officers who have to make all these people swear never to mention our existence, though."

The Medusas laughed. And the grateful crowd closed in around them, congratulating and hugging them. It was a mad scene that took them a good half hour to wend their way through. But finally they were ushered away from the crowd and into a relatively quiet passageway. They all took deep breaths and grinned at each other.

A good day's work, indeed.

* * * * *

*Every month Silhouette Bombshell has
four new books to rock your reading world.
Turn the page for an exclusive sneak peek
at one of next month's thrilling adventures!*

STRONG MEDICINE
by Olivia Gates

October 2005
Available at your favorite retail outlet.

"Hello?"

The deep, cultured voice poured through my ear, penetrated my brain. Landed in an electrified rock in my stomach.

Paralyzing anticipation drained away, disappointment flooding in its wake, liquefying my legs. I staggered down onto the bench and slumped, my whirling head clunking on the wrought-iron back.

Not Dad.

Then who?

Another pulsing hope hit me. One I'd never thought I harbored. Not in eight long years. *Jake?*

Lord! Where did *that* crazy idea come from, anyway? Jake was long lost. Long *dead*.

Still, that voice badgered my memory only to flit out of its grasp. The need to hear more of it got my paralyzed vocal chords to function. I croaked a wavering, "Yes?"

A moment's silence almost had me bellowing with frustration.

Then the man's voice broke over me, a breaker of cool, maddening decorum. "Have I reached the number of Dr. Calista St. James?"

My name. My full, real name with doctor attached to it.

I hadn't heard it in five years. I'd never thought I'd hear it again. Never thought it would hit me that hard to hear it.

I couldn't breathe.

I had to.

I did, hyperventilated. The crushing disappointment was enough on its own.

But hearing someone asking so rhetorically for Calista St. James on—who was I today?—Hannah Simmon's cell phone, *that* justified freaking out.

My cover was blown!

No, your cover isn't blown.

The exasperated, staid voice of reason sighed. I hated that voice. Made me feel so stupid. Then it amended, *Actually it is, but it doesn't matter, since it's* him!

No wonder his voice had reminded me of Jake's. Modulated, cerebral, elegant. British. And once it had the benefit of a full sentence, instantly recognized.

Sir Howard Ashton. The man who'd changed my life, then had stood by and let my enemies tear it apart.

Tangled emotions skewered through me, egging me on to coo a syrupy *wrong number,* jam my thumb through the disconnect button, tear out the SIM card and gnaw it to pieces.

"Calista, are you there?"

I debated my plan for one more second then cooed that syrupy answer. The content turned out way different from *wrong number.* "Why, Sir Howard, I can honestly say I'm definitely not there and mean it. Calista St. James no longer exists. Thanks to you and your allies of pen-pushing, cigar-smoking, sanctimonious jerks."

Silence expanded, tautened. Then an alien sound filled the extraclear connection. Laughter! Peal after peal of it!

My temperature shot up. "I beg your pardon. If you're laughing, you can't be who I thought you were—a Midas-rich, backstabbing bastard who plays philanthropist on weekdays and God on weekends. His face would crumble if he as much as smiled."

Choking sounds carried to me. Good. May he choke for real!

He didn't, brought himself under wheezing control. Shame. "Dear Lord, Calista! It has been unendurably dull without you."

"What can I say? I'm the light of life. Too bad you haven't died of boredom, Sir Howard."

A surprised bark escaped him. "Ah—it's so good to talk to you again. Although I note a marked sharpening to your temper."

The indulgence in his voice—how dared he? After what he'd done? Outrage numbed my lips and fingers. "Listen, *Sir* Howard. Only my father comments on my temper. If you've gone senile and forgotten our last *chat,* let me refresh your memory—you're *nothing* like that to me!"

The microwaves transmitted his dimming mood. It wasn't enough. I needed it extinguished. I needed *this* terminated.

"I apologize, Calista." Boy, did he have haughty penitence down to an art. "However delighted I was with being exposed to your panache again, I shouldn't have laughed. You have every right to your acrimony, in the past and now."

Oh, no. He wasn't strumming my gullible strings. Not again. That he even tried made me even angrier. "How generous of you to grant me that! So—to what do I owe the aggravation of this call?"

Another silence-soaked moment, then he sighed. "I knew my personal overtures would have been met by your deserved rancor. That has been why I haven't directly contacted you all these years. But I've kept my eyes on you, followed your new…career…"

The hesitation before he said *career* spoke volumes. It also zapped me with resentment. "Delighted to discover you've been spying on me." I'd find out how he'd managed *that* later. "Would you mind skipping this sickening, pseudo-sentimental prologue?"

"I haven't been spying on you." His voice rose a notch. Hallelujah. He *did* have sore spots to scrape. "I followed your actions to ascertain your safety, to offer whatever help I can…"

That was a sucker punch. I groped for air again. "You've been helping…me?"

"This is not an opportune time to go into particulars."

"I beg your pardon…" *Dammit. Breathe.* "But this is the *most* opportune time."

"I thought you wanted me to get to the purpose of this call."

"As far as I'm concerned, you've reached it."

"That has no bearing on why I'm contacting you today."

The man was effective, I'd give him that. Convoluted and slippery and a hell of an exhausting negotiator. He wasn't exhausting me. I had too much at stake here. I had to know what I'd been oblivious of. If he could keep such close tabs on me, who else had? Was? "Here's an ultimatum of my own, Sir Howard. If you don't enlighten me about the extent of your involvement in my life and work those past years, then *I* will end this call, and you can resume your voyeuristic activities." And maybe I should end this anyway before I begin to sound more like him.

His exhalation was long and resigned. "Very well. I've been following your every step since you walked out of Global Crisis Alliance headquarters…"

"Since you threw me out, you mean?"

"I didn't throw you out, Calista."

"Oh, no?" I tried to stop. I was taking his bait, steering us away from the details I needed to hear. I couldn't. His patient, long-suffering lies smeared my vision red. Who knew my wounds were still open? Open? Seemed they were festering! "You stood by as they threw me out. Same thing."

A new heat entered his composed tones. "Not at all. It was beyond me to stop it after you confessed to the crimes."

"I confessed to the ones I *committed*." *And I am living to live them down,* I wanted to scream. "And those weren't *crimes*."

"This could be debated ad infinitum, Calista."

"And I don't want to rehash this. There is no truth here, just point of view. I did what I had to do and was ready to take the consequences, death included. I understood everyone's need to resolve the incident by getting rid of its perpetrator. I accepted being indicted by PATS and getting kicked out of GCA. What I'll *never* forgive was having my medical license revoked."

A full minute passed, reverberating with the raggedness of my last sentence. Then he exhaled. "I though you didn't want to re-hash this." That maddening indulgence emerged again. If only he'd been in front of me. I bet he hadn't lost one hair of his im-maculate, iron-gray mane. One good smack to mess it up…

The image of him with mussed hair and indignant crimson cheeks worked wonders. I calmed down. "I don't. And I don't need a license to be a doctor. It's what I am whether the system sanctions it or not."

"So I hear. You've been involved in increasingly risky busi-ness, Calista. Rules are not all made to be broken."

"Remember that memo about not being my father?"

His exhalation was filled with the reprimands he barely curbed. For now. That was all I needed. That he postpone any ar-ticulate objections to my methods till later. A later I'd make sure would never come. Now I wanted this conversation over. Dad might still call. "There was a point to all this?"

"Yes, there was, and here it is. Even though I am no longer head of GCA, I am calling you on their behalf."

Incredulity erased my simulated calm. "That sense of humor you had grafted is something. As if I care what you or GCA want! A fat, final *no* to whatever you're asking. Can't say it was nice hearing from you since it sure wasn't. Goodbye, Sir Howard."

He brushed aside my tirade. "A number of your fellow GCA operatives long believed dead have been discovered alive and are being held hostage. We need you and your team to retrieve them."

Dammit. Two sentences and he had me ready to sign on to anything again. But I was damned if I'd give him instant grati-fication. Let him sweat it.

Yeah, sure. As if he had sweat glands like mere mortals. And he'd probably have *me* asking how high when he said jump. Just like when he initiated Combat Doctors program for GCA volunteers and had me pledging my soul for a chance to enlist.

Sure enough, after a pause calculated to mess up my wiring, he drawled, placid, nonchalant, "Before you declare an irrevocable no, you should know that among the now located operatives is Dr. Jacob Constantine. Your long-lost lover."